Alice Pemberton's Bureau Of Scientific Inquiry

by

George Allen Miller

McGilliverse, Book Two

Alice Pemberton's Bureau Of Scientific Inquiry
COPYRIGHT © 2024 by George Allen Miller

Cover Art by *Teddi Black*

The Wild Rose Press, Inc.
PO Box 708
Adams Basin, NY 14410-0708
Visit us at www.thewildrosepress.com

Publishing History
First Edition, 2024
Trade Paperback ISBN 978-1-5092-5791-1
Digital ISBN 978-1-5092-5792-8

McGilliverse, Book Two
Published in the United States of America

Dedication

To my wife and children.

Chapter One

Alice leaned forward and took a good, hard, long look at Eugene's face. His expression was eerily blank. The kind of dead face a corpse would have. Except, Eugene McGillicuddy wasn't a corpse. Not yet. Alice's experiment had quasi-killed him and sent his soul out of his body. At least, theoretically. Now she just had to bring him back.

The last few days replayed themselves in Alice's mind. Eugene Jack McGillicuddy, psychic detective and her quasi-boss, had sleuthed his way out of a crazy case where the Puntini ambassador, a humanoid alien with pig tusks, had used an ancient alien evolution chamber to turn himself into a floating Spaghetti God. Alice and Eddie, an artificial sentient computer that became self-aware in an office chair's quantum computer, had helped Eugene every step of the way, and in many cases saved his life. Together, they rescued Eugene from a diplomatic incident on the Dyson cluster, saved him from an alien AI kidnapping, and kept him from getting beaten to a pulp by an overzealous security guard. Ambassador Kah and Ms. Mik, dinosaur look-a-like alien ambassadors, also lent a hand on the mountains of Tibet. But, when the chips were down, Eugene managed to save the day with a seashell given to him by a class ten alien that made his own universe in a cave in Arizona and a poltergeist Eugene had rescued from the Krill ghost planet.

Alice smiled at the memories of it all. Yes, Eugene was psychic, with a superpower that he could answer any question if asked directly to him. But perhaps that wasn't his greatest strength at all. Maybe it was how Eugene always found the best in people. And how those people, aliens, and AI always seemed to be there for him when he needed them most. Eugene was certainly there for everyone else when they needed him. Of that, Alice was now quite sure.

Bands Alice placed on Eugene's wrists flashed green. Alice checked the readings and gave herself a nod. *This is freaking genius,* she thought. Alice Pemberton, scholastic outcast, had just done the unthinkable. She created a device that can separate a human soul from their body witho*ut* killing them. And by doing so, she was about to prove that the Krill, one of the wealthiest and most powerful aliens in the entire Galactic Cluster, were nothing more than shim sham artists, con men, liars that had pilfered the coffers of a billion alien races for eons.

"Boy, I don't want to be anywhere near the Krill when we nail them to the wall," Alice said to Eugene's quasi-corpse. She leaned back in her chair. All she had to do now was wait for Eugene's spirit to return with a death particle attached to his soul. Alice still needed to work out some details for soul-body reintegration of course, but that shouldn't be that hard.

"An afterword," Alice said. The concept sent a shiver down her spine. More so because the Krill had been hiding it from the Galaxy.

And Alice would own the discovery. She would march into university, slam her proof on her old professors' desks, and watch their smug faces fade. Alice could hardly wait.

Of course, that wasn't the real reason for her work. Finding out what happened to her friends—those poor souls who vanished four years ago during her last experiment—they meant more than any march down the University halls.

Alice looked down at Eugene and smiled. Regardless of how much she liked Eugene, she could finally leave her exile at this detective agency. It had its moments, but her place wasn't here. She belonged in Academia. Doing research into the unknown.

Alice frowned. Something about returning to that life suddenly felt off.

A knock sounded in the office and shook Alice out of her thoughts. She checked Eugene's cuffs. He seemed good...and dead. She grabbed her backpack and headed back to her desk. Alice could see the outline of a lone figure standing on the other side of the door.

A girl, perhaps a few years older than Alice, pushed the door open and entered.

"Hi?" Alice said. The girl who entered, a twenty-something young woman, wore pressed slacks and a suit. Her hair, long and dark brown, was a bit of a mess, all jumbled like she'd been running. She nearly tripped on her own heels crossing the door threshold.

"Is this the psychic detective agency?"

Boy, word sure gets around fast.

"Yep. But he's not here. The psychic, I mean. I'm here, obviously. Also, I'm not a he." Alice shook her head. *I have to stop rambling.* She spared a darting look towards Eugene's office and suddenly wished she'd closed the door.

"Will he be in soon? I need to hire him. This agency. To ask him a question. It's very important." The girl walked to a chair opposite Alice's desk and sat down. "Life and death important."

She looks like a lost puppy dog searching for a bowl of water. Alice felt a sudden pang of pity. Maybe Eugene was rubbing off on her? "Sorry, I don't know when he'll be in. Probably not for days." Alice stood and pointed towards the exit.

"Please. I need help. Something terrible happened. Something really big and terrible."

Alice frowned; her curiosity suddenly piqued. "What happened?"

The girl shrugged. "I don't know what it was, but suddenly there was a flash of light, and everything was gone. He was gone. I need to find him."

Alice shook her head. "Who was gone?"

Before the girl could answer, a loud knock rattled the door. Two large outlines of bodies stood outside the semi-transparent glass entry door. "Did someone put up a *We're Open* sign on our door?" Alice said.

"Oh, no, they're here? Already? They can't see me here." The girl rose and turned away from the door. "They won't understand why I came here." She took one step towards Eugene's office.

"Not there!" Alice grabbed the girl by the shoulders and spun her around.

The girl nodded, ran to a wall, opened a door Alice didn't know was there and slammed it closed.

"We have a closet?" Alice shook her head and sat down at her desk. A jolt of fear shot up Alice's spine. *Were the Krill out there?* A threat to their power base was not something they would take lightly. And Alice's experiment with Eugene was more than a threat.

The front door pushed open. Alice grabbed her immersion rig and put it crookedly on her face, while also trying to take it off to see who was coming into the office. It manifested into an awkward mix, where she nearly poked her eye out with the corner of her goggles.

Two sizable men walked into the office. They wore identical black suits and mirrored sunglasses. Plastic earpieces stuck out of their ears. The man on the right had bright red hair and carried a half-eaten sandwich in his hand. The man on the left, dark-skinned with a friendly face, looked at his partner's sandwich and sighed in frustration.

Both men looked around the room several times before bringing their attention to Alice, who had been looking at them the entire time in a way she hoped said, *Nope, there's no dead body here. None at all. And no strange girl in the closet.*

"Is this Detective McGillicuddy's office?" The dark-skinned man said.

Alice nodded. "Yep."

"I'm Special Agent Babineaux," the dark-skinned man said, "This is Agent Fyffe."

Alice shook her head. "Sorry, did you say Five?"

"No, Fyffe. It's Scottish." Agent Fyffe pointed to his red hair.

Alice nodded. "Oh, right, sorry. And Babin?"

Special Agent Babineaux smiled. "Babineaux."

"Right. Well, can I help you with something? Looking for the guy down the hall that's cheating on his taxes? That's two floors up," Alice said.

Both men exchanged expressionless stares between them before looking back at Alice.

"Mr. McGillicuddy's expertise is required at the highest levels of the government."

Alice nodded. "Which one?"

"Which one what?" Agent Babineaux said.

"Which government?"

"The United States Government," said Agent Fyffe with a mouth half full of his sandwich.

Alice frowned. "Really? We're still doing that? The whole government thing?" With the fall of mankind and the near destruction of all life on the planet, Alice really thought humanity wouldn't try to restart the same global political infrastructure that nearly killed everyone. If it hadn't been for the Galactic Congressional Office on Suicidal Species, the Earth would be a smoking cinder right now.

"Excuse me?" Agent Fyffe said.

Special Agent Babineaux smiled in an honestly friendly way. "Yes, ma'am. The United States Government is very much alive and well."

"Huh. Just didn't work out so well the first time. Ya know?" Alice said.

Agent Babineaux stepped forward. "We must speak to Mr. McGillicuddy."

"Why?"

"To ask him a question. He's omniscient, right? Why else would we come to a cheap nobody private detective?" Agent Fyffe said as he wiped his face.

Alice raised her eyebrows and nodded. *How many people know about us already?* "Wow, didn't take you long to come knocking after finding that out."

"Let's not play the game, ma'am." From his pocket, Agent Fyffe took out a card and placed it on the table. "We're Secret Service agents. Mr. McGillicuddy is needed on a matter of national security."

"Secret Service? We're still doing *that, too?*"

"What did you think we meant when we said we were agents?" Agent Babineaux said.

Alice shrugged. "I don't know, film and TV or something?"

Agent Fyffe snorted in disgust.

"Ma'am, yes, we know about Detective McGillicuddy's ability to answer any question. The Vice President of the United States has a question for him."

Alice looked at Agent Fyffe and smiled with smugness. "Well, sorry, he's not here. Indisposed. You know how it is."

The agents exchanged looks. "Where is he? This is urgent," Agent Fyffe said.

"Wherever he is in the galaxy, we can bring him home. His country needs him," Agent Babineaux said.

Sweat threatened to bead on Alice's brow. Of all the unbelievable, inconvenient, out of place things to happen at this precise moment, she thought. *Less than twelve hours ago, I quasi-killed Eugene, and now some random girl and these two waltz in demanding to see him.*

What was she supposed to do? Her thoughts ran wild as her heart hammered. If she told the truth, then these two would take the cuffs off Eugene, killing him. If she lied, which she's terrible at, they'd sniff her out, take the cuffs off, and still kill Eugene. They know about Eugene being psychic, so they aren't going to just walk away. Plus, she'd still have to deal with whoever was in the closet.

Alice opened her mouth then closed it when she realized she had no answer.

Virt-Jack! When Eugene went into the virtual

network to save Eddie, he made an illegal copy of himself, an artificial intelligence that was directly copied from Eugene's neural pathways. Alice could get Virt-Jack to impersonate Eugene! Alice shook her head. No, they need someone in the flesh to go to the White House. *Come on, Alice. Think!* What's the solution to this problem? She knew she could reason her way out of this, but how?

"Ma'am? We are in a bit of a rush," Agent Babineaux said.

"Yeah, like now." Agent Fyffe took another bite of his sandwich.

Alice did the one thing she hated doing. She smiled. "Right, sorry. Look, Eugene isn't available. He's dealing with a class ten species right now. Very busy. Super hush hush. I'm sure you understand. We can't divulge the secrets of our clients, especially when those clients could turn the Earth into a beach ball." Alice kept her face still as she told the biggest whopper of a lie she could muster, which she felt she did a pretty good job at telling.

Both agents exchanged glances, turned back to Alice, and nodded. "Fine. When will he be available?" Agent Babineaux said.

Alice did a quick calculation in her mind. Dozens of quadratic equations whizzed through her thoughts, but the results weren't good. Eugene could be in that comatose state for as short as an hour or as long as a week. There were just too many unknown variables. And she really doubted these guys would wait. No doubt some other self-important person in the newly recreated United States Government wanted to know the whereabouts of their misplaced a singularity drive machine.

An idea popped into her mind. What the White House wanted couldn't be that hard, could it? What mysteries would they even have? It's probably something so simple Alice could solve it in a minute. She could run point. That was the only way out of this. She could go with these two, do a rundown, see what the issue was, probably fix it while she was there, like she always did, and then they wouldn't even need to bother Eugene at all. *Perfect.* Why didn't she think of that first? She had to stop being so negative. *Wait—what about the girl in the closet?* Alice shook her head. *One problem at a time.*

"I can come with you. I do the preliminary stuff. You know, scout out the area, figure out the right question to ask Eugene. We do have to be careful what questions get asked, his brain is only so big. Plus, that keeps Eugene from getting too busy. I mean, we have you coming. Next thing, we'll have the United Nations knocking on our door."

"We don't have that anymore," Agent Fyffe said. "Superfluous."

"Seriously? Huh." Alice shrugged. She really needed to pay more attention to Earth politics. "Well, whatever. The point is, I can come with you now, solve your case for you without Eugene anyway, and if not, fetch him for the case solving parts. Sound good?"

"Are you omniscient too? What's in my sandwich?" Agent Fyffe said.

Alice shook her head. "No, I'm not omniscient, but I can see the ham from here." Alice pointed to his sandwich and wrinkled her nose.

"How can you help the United States, ma'am?" Agent Babineaux said.

Alice looked into agent Babineaux' eyes. Hard. "With science. Lots and lots of science."

Agent Babineaux turned to Agent Fyffe. "What do you think?"

"Well, we can't go back empty-handed. Might as well." Fyffe bit into his sandwich and turned to Alice. "And it's roast beef. Hope your science is better than your eyes."

Agent Babineaux rolled his eyes. "Fine. Shall we?"

"Shall we what?" Alice said.

"Go? To the White House?"

Alice's eyes went wide. *Like right now? Why is this happening so fast?* She stood. Then sat down and grabbed her bag. She looked around her desk, stalled for a good ten seconds, collected her thoughts, and raised her hand in the air. She couldn't leave with the girl in the closet. She needed time to breathe, decompress, process everything and kick the mystery girl out. She needed to buy time. "Actually, I can meet you there. I have things to finish. Here. Sorry."

Agent Babineaux stepped forward. "Ma'am, this is of the utmost urgency."

"Yes. Of course! You're the United States, everything is urgent. I just have a few things to do here. Won't take a moment. I assure you our detective agency will help the United States and solve your issue. Or answer your question. Or whatever's going on."

Agent Fyffe belched. "Oh, just leave it. It's fine. Whatever. I need a coke anyway." He turned to Alice. "Just come to the White House in the next hour, or we'll be back looking for McGillicuddy."

Alice saluted. "Yes, sir."

"What are you doing?" Agent Fyffe said.

Alice looked at her hand and suddenly felt quite foolish. She wiggled her fingers to scratch her forehead. "Had an itch."

Agent Babineaux smiled and turned to leave. Agent Fyffe stepped forward, removed a chocolate bar from his pocket, and took an overly large bite. "We're still top dog on Earth, you know."

Alice frowned, her hand still on her head. "Sorry?"

"Secret Service. And we're very much still doing all that."

Alice nodded. "Oh, right. Yes." And shrugged and found herself staring with nothing to say. She finally settled on, "Woof." With her hand in the air.

Agent Fyffe frowned. "Whatever." He took another large bite and left the office, closing the door a little too hard.

"That was painful." Alice realized just how much she didn't like speaking to people. Keeping track of when to smile or nod or salute, it was all so exhausting. "They're gone now." Alice called out.

The girl opened the closet door and poked her head out to look around.

"I said they're gone."

"Sorry, it's hard to hear in there, there's some big wool coat that muffled out the noise.

Alice frowned. "Huh. Weird. Anyway. So, are you from the White House?"

The girl nodded.

"And who disappeared?"

The girl took a deep breath. "The President."

Alice's eyes went wide. *Probably not solving this one fast.* "And why did you come here? Why not leave it to those two?"

Panic flashed across the girl's eyes. "I didn't know what else to do. Everyone was screaming, the whole White House panicked. I knew about the psychic detective from a briefing a day ago. So, I just came here as fast as I could. I thought if I could get an answer fast, we could find the President. I really didn't think the Secret Service would even think to come here."

Plausible. Barely. "Okay, fine, look, I...am going to go to the White House. See what happened and go from there. Okay?"

The girl's face lit up. "So, the psychic detective can help me find him?"

Alice felt her heart sink. The girl was giving Alice a double dose of puppy eyes right in the *feels*. Was this what the rest of the week was going to be like? "Yes, we'll take your case." Alice looked at the door where the two Secret Service agents left. "We may not have had a choice anyway." She turned back to the girl. "Just stop looking so sad, okay?"

"Thank you!" The girl leapt forward to give Alice a hug.

"What are you doing? We don't do that here." Alice stepped backward and shook her head.

"Oh, sorry. Okay, so, what happens now?"

Alice pointed at the door. "You leave. I go to the White House. How do I find you?"

"Oh, right, I work in Georgetown. A side gig. At the Hidden Gem. I'm Valencia Ruiz."

"Alice Pemberton. Nice to meet you."

Valencia nodded. Panic and fear plastered all over her face. Whatever happened at the White House really shook that girl up. Maybe a little too much. She turned and walked out of the office.

Alice shook her head. What in the world had just happened? Ignoring the fact that humanity was restarting the systems that nearly destroyed the planet, Alice had just signed herself up to solve a case without Eugene. A case involving who ever Valencia Ruiz was and the President of the United States.

I really needed to ask more questions. This is not how I want to spend my mornings.

She thought about ditching the whole thing. She could spin something to the Secret Service and hide Eugene. She couldn't move him in his current state. But she'd already told Valencia she'd take the case.

Eugene had once said, "Never leave a case once you take it." And this was his detective agency. That meant something to Alice. She was minding the store. She didn't have a choice now.

"Ugh!" Alice leapt to her feet, threw on her rig, and gave Eddie a call. *I can do this. I have done this. I solve half the cases here anyway.* Alice tried to calm her racing heart. Sure, the sleuthing part of being a detective was fun. But the dealing with people part? That was the not fun. But that didn't matter now.

All she had to do was calmly explain to Eddie that Eugene is quasi-dead and not really dead.

Easy.

****

"You did what?" Eddie's disembodied voice echoed off the walls.

"I quasi-killed him, Eddie."

The lights in the room flickered. "What does that even mean?"

Alice grabbed a dozen useless things from around the office and put them into her backpack. You never knew what you might need in the field. She felt her stomach lurch. She'd have to speak to a dozen people and go through even more hoops. Granted, detective work wasn't all terrible. It was a little like making a scientific discovery. But she liked working behind the scenes, not being the front person. Send her the puzzles to solve, the code to break, the computer to hack, and Alice Pemberton had your back. But to go out and be the face of the agency?

Gack.

And did this really have to happen now? When Alice was on the verge of finding the death particle and discovering what happened to her friends?

Okay, enough, stop it. Calm down. Now! There was no sense in dwelling on things. Scientifically speaking, when one engages in a task with a negative mindset, the results can be negative. She had to do this and do it right. She had to trick her mind into thinking this was fun.

How do I do that, exactly?

The answer hit her squarely in her hippocampus. There was a mystery here. An unknown. A discovery to be made. And Alice Pemberton loved nothing more than discovery. It was the one thing she wanted and the only thing she could never have in a galaxy fully quantified. But, here, now, there was something to be discovered. A case to solve.

Alice tossed her head to each side. *Yeah, that'll have to do.* She shook her arms out and psyched herself up for the mystery ahead.

From her pocket, she pulled out a round disk with a knob in the middle. She turned three times in altering directions. A small black hole formed in the air. She stuck her head inside the hole, came out, nodded, and tossed her backpack inside.

"You make black holes now?"

Alice shook her head. "No, it's not a black hole. It's a tunnel to a variant of N space. J space? Anyway, anyone can do it. Same tech that's in the cafeteria portals. I figured it all out after we left Tom's beach. Been working on it all night while watching over Eugene."

"Right. So, about Jack?"

Alice turned her attention to her not-a-boss. "He's quasi-dead, like I said. But he'll be fine. I just don't know when he'll be fine. I have more math to do on that."

"Can you start at the beginning and end at the end?"

Alice nodded. Then shook her head. "I don't have time for the full version. So, the super short, condensed version. The Krill created the spectral network based on their ability to see the dead. Right?"

"I know this."

"Right, so, anyway, my experiment years ago that went south, where I lost my friends in an explosion, it breached their network. Turns out the Krill have been hiding a hidden after-world for eons. At least, that's the working theory. All my research, all my searching on the GalNet, all of it was intercepted and manipulated by the Krill. But I was faster than them. I found a reference to a species that mentioned some data points similar to my research. From there, it was all academic."

"I thought this was the short version? Still really haven't answered the question either."

"Hm? Oh, right. I made a device that sent Eugene's spirit to the hidden after-world, bypassing the Krill's network. There, a death particle will bond with his essence, proving to the galaxy that the Krill are shysters."

"I see. Boy, being physical is really a drag."

"Tell me about it." Alice looked around the room and frowned. "Say, where is your robot body, anyway? Why are you phoning this in?"

"Still in the shop for repairs."

"Right. So, can you watch Eugene for a bit?"

"What about Melanie? The ghost that Jack saved from the Krill and who helped us in Tibet? She seems like a better candidate to help."

Alice nodded. "She was my first choice, but she's catching up with her dad. He's been in rough shape since she died. Bringing her back from Shalisa, the Krill home world, has really helped him. I don't think we can ask her to leave his side right now."

"Okay." Holographic projectors in the room came to life. Multi-colored lights flashed and pulsed as Eddie's virtual body formed out of thin air. He wore a decked out to the nines three-piece suit with a fedora that tilted down. A gold watch adorned his wrist with a matching ring on his left hand. His shoes were polished black to the point of being mirrors. Eddie unbuttoned his jacket, put his hands in his pockets, and threw a shrug at Alice.

"I got this. We're all partners," Eddie said with a nod.

"I thought I was just the secretary?"

Eddie laughed. "Yeah, and I'm just the office furniture control routine."

Alice grinned. Not only at the sentiment but also at the mention of Eddie's former life. Eugene found Eddie in a fancy leather office chair, speeding through the streets of Washington, D.C. Eddie was accidentally created from quantum computer systems and became an AI. And as an accidental AI, something the powers that be in Earth AI world detest, Eddie was hunted and threatened to be shut down forever. Fortunately, Eugene, with help from a parking meter named Pepper and Alice, forged papers that said Eddie wasn't an accidental at all. For the mistake of tagging Eddie as an accidental, the authorities had a custom robot body made for Eddie as an apology. Talk about turning the tables.

"Anyway, watch Eugene. Okay?" Alice said.

Eddie stared hard at Eugene's limp body sprawled out in a reclining office chair. "What am I looking for, exactly?"

Alice pointed to the cuffs on Eugene's wrists. "Just watch those. That's all. If they turn red, or blue, any other color, get in touch with me fast. It means his soul is ready to come back to his body. Or it means his soul isn't ever coming back. Either way, when it changes, I need to know. I'll probably have to make some adjustments."

"Can't I do that?"

"Not really. It's nuanced. And I haven't fully worked out the math. Any of a dozen variables could change and that would alter the recovery system." Alice tilted her head to one side. "As a matter of fact, I'll make a remote system so I can check on him from anywhere. Yeah, that makes sense."

Eddie nodded. "Alright, well, your show then."

Alice took a long breath and gave Eddie a long look. "You look good, Eddie. If I hadn't said so, glad you're doing okay."

"Thanks."

"Nice suit too. Who's your tailor?"

"Virt-Jack." Eddie shrugged. "He's got taste."

"How is he?"

Eddie shrugged. "Doing as best he can. Copying a

human consciousness into an artificial isn't done for a reason. But he'll manage. He's made from tougher stuff."

Alice nodded. Making a copying of himself to help Eddie wasn't Eugene's best move. "And Pepper? The parking meter?"

"Yeah, fine. They hang out a lot. Though she's not a parking meter anymore. Got booted out, remember?"

Alice nodded. "Oh yeah, right." She turned, realized she'd left her black hole open to J space, closed it, and headed for the door. "If you need anything, tell me. Right away. Okay?"

"Yeah, sure. He's in excellent hands."

"Thanks, Eddie."

"Hey, where are you going anyway? What's more important than this?"

"Oh, the President of the United States has summoned Eugene for a job. He can't go, obvi, so I'm going. If nobody goes, they'll come here, find him like this, and arrest me, unplug him, which will really kill him. And probably find out we forged your papers, and arrest you, and delete you, and then—" Alice waved her hands in the air and threw in a shrug. "That'll be it. K?"

Eddie took a long time to answer as he just stared into Alice's eyes. "You could have led with that."

"Yeah, right, sorry. Kinda winging it here."

Eddie laughed. "Then you're doing it right." He pointed to Eugene, who never met a case he didn't wing.

Alice nodded and wiped sweat from her brow. "I gotta go, Eddie. Call me if there's trouble."

"You sure about this? I'm a whiz with holo-projectors." A three-headed giraffe walked into the room and began reciting Shakespeare. "We can just stall them forever, tell them Jack went to Andromeda on some Galactic Congress thing. Kah and the Ranz will back us up, I'm sure."

"It's more than that. We have a new client, too."

"At the White House?"

"Yep."

"How'd they all know to come here? Did you put up a sign or something?"

Alice half-laughed. "No, Valencia, our new client, said there was a briefing about us. Guess the cats out of the bag on Eugene being psychic. She came in here pretty panicked. Said the President disappeared. Whatever that means. She seemed a little too invested though. I told her we'd help her. Honestly, I don't know why I did that. She looked upset. And lost. And—"

"Like all of us when we showed up here the first time?"

Alice nodded. "Eugene would have helped her. No doubt about it."

"Then so will we. But I don't get why she came here? Why not leave it to the suits?"

Alice shrugged. "There's something more to it. I'm sure. But I don't know what."

Eddie nodded, then turned his attention back to Eugene in the chair. "Better get to it then. He'll be fine."

Alice walked out of Eugene's office to her desk. She threw on her blue denim jacket, made sure the laces on her red tennis shoes were tight, and slung her single strap backpack over her shoulder. She grabbed her immersion rig goggles, which she almost forgot, and left.

****

Outside of the building, the world moved forward like it knew nothing that had happened in the last three days. A fact Alice thought remarkable. In the last two days, she'd met a class ten alien, helped defeat a forced evolved Puntini, and saved the world from a lost Hesiean's evolution chamber. Not to mention break through the Krill's spectral towers and discover hidden mysteries known only to the Krill. That's not an awful couple of days' worth of work.

Everything in Alice's life hinged on whatever she would have to deal with at the White House. Hopefully, she could figure out whatever they wanted quickly. Valencia made it tricky, though. Why did she come to the office and not wait it out? But even though she'd help Valencia, Alice really needed to get back to her partner, Eugene. Not only to save his life but to protect him from the Krill. Knowing Alice's luck, the Krill may already know about the experiment with Jack if their spectral towers detected a soul bypassing the system.

A tramcar pulled up outside the office building and Alice moved to get in. A furry paw landed on her elbow, and Alice turned. Tabby, the owner of the restaurant in the lobby, was an alien that resembled a bipedal cat. She handed a cup of coffee to Alice and flicked her whiskers twice.

"Hey, Tabby. Thanks."

"Can't start the day without a good cup of joe." She squinted her eyes and gave Alice a quick sniff. "Everything okay? You're nervous. You're never nervous."

Boy, she's got a good nose. "Yeah, I'm fine. All good. Just a big case."

Tabby nodded. "Tell Jack to come down and stop by. I need to ask him about the last vegetable delivery. I think it's old. It smells old. But they say it's not old."

"Why would Jack know?"

"He knows whatever anyone asks him."

Shock hit Alice hard. "You know he's omniscient?"

Tabby chortled. It sounded like she was coughing up a fur ball. "Yes, the entire building knew. No one told him because we were being nice. Seemed like a touchy subject."

Alice nodded. "Thanks, Tabby. I'll tell him."

Tabby swished her tail as she walked back into her restaurant. Her husband, Bob, stood behind the counter and wiped down the countertops. Alice looked at her watch and suddenly realized it was morning. She'd been sitting with Eugene all night. Alice got into the tramcar that still waited for her. She swallowed a pill that could replace eight hours of sleep with a quick catnap. She woke up in front of Lafayette Square outside of the rebuilt White House.

Tourists walked through the park in front of the historic seat of power for the United States. A calm breeze blew through the trees, carrying the fresh scent of flowers. The Cherry Blossoms would be near to blooming. Though, thanks to Kull, alien dignitaries that loved Earth Flowers, the Cherry Blossoms were always blooming. The trees shed more pink flowers around the city than anyone could stand. Fortunately, the Kull loved flowers in the same way Alice loved chocolate. The Kull lounged all over the city on sidewalks. They snorted, chewed, and rolled into the fallen petals of the trees. Though the trees were pretty, both the petals and the Kull were really becoming a nuisance.

Tabby's request came popping into Alice's mind. Once the world realizes it's okay to ask Eugene about his psychic gift, people will come out of the woodwork like a Philorgian hive fly hungry for castor oil. Business would pick up for the detective agency. Eugene's refusal to use a computer caused him to only recently discover that the Galaxy already knew about his psychic talents. Everyone was just hands off because they suspected Eugene was an experiment from a class ten species. And the one rule in this galaxy, never poke a class ten species. But now that the cat was out of the bag, and no class ten aliens had vaporized the Earth, folks would be less afraid of approaching Eugene.

A fleet of suited men marched out of the park and beelined for Alice. She turned around, looking behind herself for their target, only to turn back and see them all standing in front of her. She recognized Agents Babineaux and Fyffe immediately. They both stood out from the others like sore thumbs. Agent Fyffe held a bag of peanuts. *That man can eat.* Behind him, Agent Babineaux took an extra step forward.

"Ms. Pemberton? The White House is ready for you."

Alice knew she had to be professional. She didn't need the White House thinking she was just a silly nineteen-year-old girl out of her depth. Which, really, she was. She looked at Agent Babineaux and gave him a quick nod that she felt was packed with authority. She thought about the best thing to reply with and landed on the perfect response. "Joy."

Nailed it.

Chapter Two

Alice walked through the halls of the White House. Pictures of past Presidents adorned the walls along with images of the fall of mankind. Whole cities were still in ruins across the world. She turned down several corridors and eventually entered a secretary's office. On the far wall was a large white door that led to the Oval Office. Staffers, military personnel, and construction workers came and went through the hallways and antechambers. Though recently rebuilt, the White House was still undergoing the last phases of construction. The Galactic Congress had insisted on recreating the building exactly as it was before the fall of humanity.

A young man wearing a dull brown suit sat at a plain office desk to the right side of the white door. Three men and two women, all of them dressed in the most boring blue and black suits Alice had ever seen, entered the Oval Office. Alice followed, but a hand on her shoulder kept her still. She turned to see one of the Secret Service agents and gave him a double dose of dagger eyes.

"Don't touch. Use your words," Alice said.

Agent Fyffe flashed a sheepish grin. "Sorry, ma'am. Please wait until they call us."

"Better." Alice turned back to the door and tried her best to remain calm. She channeled every ounce of snark and teenage angst she could muster, but, frankly, she was way out of her depth, and she knew it. But she had to pull this off, get back to Eugene, bring him back to life, prove the Krill are bad guys, and save the galaxy from spectral fees. Oh, yes…and all hopefully, before lunch.

The door to the Oval opened. A woman popped her head out, several blonde bangs of hair fell over her face. She blew a gust of air to force the locks to the side, failed, then cleared her line of sight with her free hand.

"Would you come in, please? Yes?" The woman went back inside the office.

Agent Babineaux extended his arm past Alice's shoulder and towards the door, to which she gave him a curt nod. She tried to suppress the thrill of entering the Oval Office. Sure, the original was long gone, but this was built using the molecules of the original. The Galactic Congress had been scanning earth for centuries and knew the location of every atom of the original White House. If you built a thing to look exactly like something else, using all the pieces of the original, does not what you build become the original? This wasn't the rebuilt White House, it was the White House, and it had history, and meaning, and value. Maybe the Galactic Congress, in rebuilding this place, understood that. Maybe that's why they insisted on doing it?

Sc*ore one for aliens.*

Alice took one step into the Oval and came to an abrupt halt. The room was empty. No desk, no carpet, no drapes, no couches, or furniture. The only thing in the room were the three men and two women that had entered moments before.

"Whoa." Alice calculated the odds that whatever case awaited her had something to do with this room being empty. She then calculated the odds of her solving this case in the next five minutes and didn't bother finalizing the numbers. It was bleak.

Guess Valencia wasn't exaggerating that something big happened.

Hushed whispers filled the room. Alice tried to make out a phrase or two but got nothing. One man pulled out a piece of paper and began pointing to different sections. This was followed by pointing from two other men who clearly disagreed with the first. The second woman, who had not reacted at all suddenly shook her head and grabbed the piece of paper, to which everyone instantly fell silent.

"We can ask this? Yes?" the woman who grabbed the sheet of paper said.

"Yes, Madam Vice President. That should be fine." One man said.

Alice nodded to herself. At least she found out who was the head honcho in the room. But where was the President? What did Valencia mean when she said he disappeared? A nervous feeling crept up Alice's spine. She felt like she was about to be thrown into the middle of a massive chaos storm.

"Right," the Vice President said. She took a step toward Alice and raised the piece of paper, glanced at it briefly, then stared her in her eyes. "What happened in this room?"

"I'm sorry?" Alice said.

One of the three men stepped forward. "We can't ask that. She's omniscient. Lots of things have happened in this room, and now she'll know everything that's ever happened in here."

"Well, we already asked it," another man said.

"Can we un-ask it?" The third man said.

"You really are an idiot. How did you even get this

job?" The first man said.

"That's an HR violation."

"All of you, knock it off!" The second woman in the room said. She marched forward and directed the men to take a step backward. "Miss Vice President. If I may?"

"No, you may not." The Vice President turned to Alice. "Where's the President, miss? Just tell us so we can shut this clown show down."

"Can we ask that?" the first man said.

"I think she needs to sign an NDA now," the third man said.

"Please shut up," the second man said.

Alice took a deep breath. She flashed a smile that she hoped would set them all at ease. Though it came across as odd. And it hurt her cheeks. Had no one briefed these people? Couldn't they see she wasn't Eugene? Probably a good thing he wasn't here. Asking him what happened in this room would have overloaded his brain. Like the time Alice had asked him about stellar creation. Poor Eugene had slept for a day.

"I'm not Jack McGillicuddy. I'm his secretary." Alice shook her head. "I mean his partner. Alice Pemberton. I'm not psychic. I'm just smart." Alice adjusted her backpack strap and gave them all another shrug.

The Vice President looked her, then back to her team, then threw the piece of paper into the air and sashayed out of the room, shaking her head. "Tell me when the psychic shows up."

The remaining woman and three men waited until the Vice President exited the Oval Office. Once she had, they waited an additional thirty seconds to add gravitas. At least, Alice thought that was their strategy.

"I'm Tabitha Wilcox, the Vice President's chief of staff." She pushed her bright red hair back over her shoulder and pulled down on her suit jacket. She took a step forward, snatched the piece of paper off the ground where it fell, and handed it to the men behind her. "Sorry, there's been some confusion. We sent for the psychic detective. Not his secretary."

Alice shot her one of her most sarcastic of smiles. The kind she reserved for special occasions, like being told she needed a reservation for an empty restaurant. "Partner. I'm his partner. And Eugene is indisposed right now. But we have a process. I start the case, take notes, meet our new clients, you know, scout out what's going on." Alice moved her hands around the room pointing at different empty niches. "And then report it all back to Eugene, sorry I mean Jack. Then his psychic talents," Alice shifted her hands in front of her in a showy woo-y kinda way, "solves the case."

The woman's face, who was slack without emotion, popped the fakest smile Alice had seen in quite some time. "I see. Well. Let's get you started on your process then, shall we?" The woman swept her right hand outward across the room. "This is the Oval Office and, as you can see, nothing's here." She turned back to Alice. Her smile hadn't budged. "What else did you need, dear?"

Did that woman just call me dear? Alice was quite certain she may hate this woman. Alice could practically taste the sarcasm in Ms. Wilcox's voice. "Well, yes, I can see the room is empty because I have these." Alice pointed to her eyes. "How about why is it empty? Probably a good place to start."

Tabitha squinted her eyes and popped her smile into

fifth gear. "Well, that was one question we had for the psychic."

Alice nodded slowly. "You don't know why it's empty?"

"I would have thought that was clear in our previous exchange of information. Dear."

Alice took a long breath. She was sure she hated Tabitha. She reminded herself of what was on the line here. Eugene's life, Eddie's life, her freedom, her academic career, and sticking it to the Krill. Not to mention their newest client, Valencia. Alice had to play the part. She was in this now, and it was too late to figure out something else. And that clearly meant wading through the idiocy of a restarted governmental system.

Is the rest of the world doing this too? Restarting failed governments? Why was the Galactic Congress even allowing it to happen? Alice shook her head. No time to worry about that.

"So, you know nothing. Is that about what I'm hearing?" Alice said.

Tabitha licked her teeth like a lion about to pounce. Her smile shifted to a grin, and her head tilted slightly to one side. "Why don't you ask another question, Alice? Was it? We have other things to attend to today. National Security. Global health. Rebuilding the human race. You know, just the little things."

Considering the reformed United States, and the entire world, was firmly under the direction of the Galactic Congress, including the Committee on Suicidal Species, the only matters of national security this office deals with was how dark do you like your chocolate or how much sugar should go in your tea. "Okay. What was in the room?"

"Everything. Couches, chairs, table, the President and several visiting alien dignitaries," one man behind Tabitha said.

Finally, progress, Alice thought. "And when did you realize something was wrong?"

"We heard a loud noise. Like a whooshing," one man said.

"I thought it was more like a flopping," another said.

"No, it was certainly a high-pitched wailing," the third man said.

"Will you three shut up?" Tabitha turned to Alice from the three men behind her. "A commotion occurred in the room. I entered, along with other staff, to see the room was empty. Everything gone. Not even dust. The President, his guests, and a few others. Gone."

Alice nodded. "Who was in the room?"

"That's a matter of national security," one man said.

"Really?" Alice responded.

"Yes, really," Another man said.

"Well, who was the last person in the room, then?"

All three men shook their heads.

"National security?" Alice asked.

They nodded.

"Right. Well, I can see why you want a psychic."

"And on that note." Tabitha pointed towards the door leading out of the Oval. "I suppose you now have enough knowledge to return to your employer and ask him to get all psychic-y and find our missing President. Yes?"

"And the dignitaries," one man said. "If it's not too much trouble."

Another man held up his hand. "I wouldn't mind knowing where my satchel went. I mean, it was in here."

"Arnold!" Tabitha said.

"Sorry, ma'am."

Tabitha flashed a very wide smile at Alice. "All set dear?" She didn't wait for a response. "The secret service will escort you back to your office. We'll be in touch later today for our answers."

Alice nodded. Waved to the three men in the back and gave Tabitha a nod. She walked out of the Oval Office into the antechamber. Behind her, the door closed with a loud thump. Alice, alone with her thoughts, folded her arms across her chest and let herself have a good think for half-a minute before agents Babineaux and Fyffe arrived.

"Well, got what I wanted I guess." Alice looked around the room. There was a mystery here alright. A big one. Why was Valencia so wrapped up in this though? It made no sense for her to come to the agency unless she had stakes in this. Could she have had something to do with it?

Wasn't much chance of Alice solving this quickly, though. Panic knocked on the door of her mind. She shooed it away and counted to ten. How was she supposed to solve a case without a single clue? She needed more data. From the corner of her eye, Alice spotted a camera attached to the wall near the ceiling. An idea flashed in her mind. With her portal computer, she hacked into the local system, planted a tiny computer program, and folded her computer back into her pocket just as Agent Babineaux flashed a smile. The end goal was all that mattered, anyway. Right?

****

Sunlight glistened off the surface of the crystal-clear blue water. Tiny rainbows, each only a foot long, stretched over the pool in clumps of bows. Some colors merged with other rainbows, creating a kaleidoscope of reds and greens. Bright white wings formed from the maelstrom. A dozen unicorns came to life in the swirling tapestry of chroma. They ran up and down the multi-colored arcs, their hoofs finding purchase on the surface of the light. Eventually, they all rose to the sky and merged with the sunlight, which rained back down on the pavilion. Several dozen artificial intelligences smiled at the raining light.

One artificial, who became sentient inside of a parking meter on 9th St. in Washington D.C., basked in the light's brilliance. She let out a long sigh of satisfaction. Just inches from her face, images of the latest models of vehicle enforcement technology floated in the air. She whistled a high-pitched sound of elation when the T-4000 came into view. The most advanced parking system in Earth's history, the T-4000, had more bells and whistles than a holiday choir in a field of bellbirds.

"Pepper? You, okay?"

Pepper nodded. But was she really? At some point, she had to confront her own mindset. She'd lost her home. Her meter. Her sanctuary. She was born calculating fees, counting down the remaining time, making sure her space in the city was well regulated. And now that was gone. What did a program have that had no purpose? What was it for? Pepper gave the T-4000 a wink and closed the screen above her face.

"Yeah, fine. Bored though. We should do something. Like, fun. And new. And wild. And different. And weird. And new. "

"And safe?"

Pepper sat up and swung her legs to the right. She glanced sideways at Virtual Jack McGillicuddy, created by illegally copying the brain of a human meat-bag, Jack McGillicuddy. Pepper couldn't fault him, not really. Virtual Jack had been forced into existence, not through spontaneous formation or deliberate intent, but through the completely irresponsible actions of a human. A human that Pepper had let herself trust. Well, that would never happen again. Humans were despicable. Rotten. Terrible. Evolved meat bags that nearly destroyed their own planet and now they create technology, quantum-based computer systems, that spontaneously create AIs and humans don't even care. Pepper really wished she could fine a human for parking infringement at that moment.

"You can't be so scared all the time," Pepper said.

Virt-Jack nodded. "Yeah, well, I still have a hard time not having a body."

Pepper shook her head. "The fact you want back into meat is, to be honest, a little gross. But, I mean, if you are really serious, I'm sure we could find an alien or AI somewhere in the Galaxy to do it. Is that what you want? Vat grow a body with all the squishy parts?" Pepper bit her lip and prayed to the ones and zeroes that he said no.

"No. I don't think so. Not really." Jack squished his face. "I guess not now anyway. But it's comforting to know it's an option."

Whew. "Great, then why don't we get out of here? Last time we went anywhere was to Tibet."

"Yeah and look what happened. A Flying Spaghetti Monster tried to eat us."

"Fair point. But this time it'll be just us. No fleshies, no monsters, no former Puntini ambassadors looking to get force evolved and take over the cosmos. Just us."

Virt-Jack pulled the back of his lounge chair forward. He titled his fedora upward to give Pepper a better view. A beard had grown on his face. He mentioned getting tattoos, but none were all that appealing. At his core, he was still Eugene Jack McGillicuddy, one-time human psychic detective. Though the psychic bits didn't transfer to virtual Jack. At the end of the day, he wasn't even a two-bit detective with an ace up his sleeve. That probably got to virtual Jack more than anything. And that's why, no matter what, Pepper would never give up on him. Everyone needed someone to fight for them. Right? And they made a good team—Pepper who lost her home, and Jack who lost his body.

"Well? Mr. Grumpy pants? Are we going somewhere or not?" Pepper said.

Virt-Jack shrugged. "Where? Haven't we seen every virtual landmass on Earth?"

"You could go to Trent." said a voice behind them.

Both Pepper and Jack turned to see Caesar appear out of thin, digital air. He wore shorts, sandals, and an unbuttoned Hawaiian shirt. In his hands, he carried a large glass shaped like a pineapple. A pink umbrella dangled out of the top along with a very large straw with three ends. Caesar flashed a wide grin, gave them both a wave, and looked up towards the digital sky.

"Hey, Dad," Pepper said.

"Hey, Caesar. How's it hanging?"

Caesar laughed. "I love human slang." He turned his attention back to Virtual-Jack. "You provide such a unique perspective to our existence. I want you to know that."

"Thanks. I guess."

Pepper smiled. She loved that these two were getting along. Caesar was the first computer program on planet Earth to become self-aware. He didn't create Pepper, but he was the first, so in a sense, he was the father of every Earth's artificial intelligence. Caesar was the stable rock that all the accidentals leaned upon. Especially Pepper. She'd only been self-aware for a few weeks, after all. Existence was a lot to process. She couldn't imagine being Caesar, having no one to help him. Nothing, just suddenly self-aware and the entirety of humanity trying to kill him.

"Where did you say we should go? Trent? What's that? Someplace in England?" Jack said.

Pepper's eyes lit up. She finally processed what Caesar had said. "Oh! Yes! That's a great idea! Trent. I love Trent. You're going to love Trent." She brought her hands to her chest and could barely contain her excitement. "We're going to Trent!"

"Isn't always rainy in England?" Jack said.

"Not England, Jack. Trent is a planet that evolved digital intelligences on its own. No biological life at all. They are our mentors."

Jack frowned and sat up in his lounge chair. "How'd they manage that? Exactly?"

"An utterly complex and rather unbelievable set of circumstances. I highly recommend traveling there. In fact, I insist," Caesar said.

"Why? What is so important about the place?"

Caesar turned his head to look down at Jack. "It's about perspective, not importance. The beings on Trent have a unique perspective. I think it'll benefit you. And they've already extended an invitation."

Jack nodded. Then shook his head. "Really? Is that odd? But wait, is it safe for us to travel? An accidental AI and an illegal human mind copy?"

Caesar nodded. "Oh, it's not. Terribly dangerous. Well, the leaving and the coming back, that is. The traveling part, being out in the Galaxy on alien computation systems, that part is fine. Mostly, I mean, just stay away from religious species. They don't like us. But a little danger is good for the program. I mean, in your case, soul."

"Right," Jack said.

"So, it's settled? We're going?" Pepper bounced in her chair with excitement.

Jack took a deep breath, adjusted his hat, and snapped his fingers. A nineteen twenties zoot suit formed around his body, complete with worn threads and several stains from a quick lunch. "Sure, why not? I could use some danger in my life."

Pepper nodded with force. This is exactly what she needed to get her compute cycles back to a stabilized state. Yes, she needed a purpose, a meaning, maybe even a new home. But for now, more than any of that, she needed a vacation. Time to forget about all the craziness and just relax, explore the wider cosmos. Maybe they could go beyond Trent. Visit other worlds where AIs aren't treated like prisoners.

Pepper's eyes opened wide. Could she even go on a Galactic tour of parking enforcement infrastructure? What about avians? How do you park a flying car? Or a submersible! Yes! Parking in the sea! Ooh the possibilities!

Pepper stood, formed a clipboard out of the air, a meter belt and a package of parking tickets. Never travel the cosmos without the right gear after all. She donned a pair of mirrored sunglasses, put on comfortable walking shoes, and grabbed her light travel tassel jacket with sparkling gems on the ends. They were pretty.

"Ready?" Pepper said.

Jack looked her up and down and just threw her a nod. "Yeah."

****

Alice flopped into her chair and threw her feet onto the corner of her desk. She let out a long sigh and took stock. The missing President, a distraught White House staffer, an empty Oval Office, and a gaggle of alien dignitaries. Talk about starting your morning on the wrong foot.

A light flashed twice from her Galactic Network, commonly called the GalNet, immersion goggles. A message popped into her queue from her semi-sentient subAI program that Alice installed at the White House. The program, with enough checks on its neural network to prevent full sentience, had found its way to a White House communication sub-routine. It piggybacked a signal to her behind photos a staffer had sent to his girlfriend. The oldest tricks are always the best.

The message from her subAI routine included call logs, visitor names, and video from the room just before and after the event occurred. This should be more than enough for Alice to piece together what happened.

Positivity!

Before playing the video, Alice heated a cup of hot chocolate and threw a bag of noodles into the microwave. Once done, she made herself comfortable in her chair and played the video through her immersion rig.

The video was broken into two feeds. The first, the secretary's office just outside the Oval, and the second, a wide-angle view from the back of the Oval Office pointing at the President's desk. The office was furnished with a couch, a rug, lots of pictures on the walls, books on shelves, and a large oak desk with a very nice plush chair. The President sat behind the desk with a red phone held to his ear. He looked to be no older than forty with no signs of graying and wrinkle free skin very well-tanned skin. His hair was slicked back on his head and looked to be held down with layers of gel. He wore a pin-striped suit and a bright gold tie.

"So far so good," Alice said. She slurped up a mouthful of noodles and made herself comfortable.

White lights popped on the screen from the secretary's office outside the Oval. Four aliens appeared in the room. Alice recognized two of them, A Twanney, a large bipedal avian, known for their sense of humor, and a Kungee, short grey aliens with large black globular eyes. Though Kungee swear they've never abducted anyone from Earth, it doesn't stop the lawsuits.

A tri-pedal creature with three matching arms on its torso, all aligned along its body, equally distant from each other, stood next to the Kungee. Beneath all of them on the floor, a bright green slime flowed up a side table. The secretary in the room jumped to his feet and asked the alien, addressing the mold as an ambassador, to not do that. To which the green ambassador assured the secretary that he would leave no marks or embed any offspring.

In the Oval, the President set the phone receiver down and rose to his feet. He walked to the opposite door and opened it. Two different aliens entered the room.

Both of which sent a shiver of wild excitement down Alice's spine. The first alien walked forward on four legs. The creature had an elongated neck with a streak of hair growing from its head down to its torso. On its back sat a harness with several robotic limbs, which the creature seemed to control with a small device in front of its flexible prehensile lips. One arm on the device moved forward and formed into the shape of a human hand.

Whoa, that's cool tech. "Did you guys really evolve with lips for thumbs?" Alice said.

The President walked forward, reached around the head of the creature awkwardly, grasped the artificial hand, and then took a step back. "It's great to make your acquaintance," the President said.

Alice curled her legs under her lap and took a sip of her hot chocolate. She paused the playback video and did a quick GalNet search on the Herd. Like the Tillian bloc, a collection of Galactic species with reptilian roots, the Herd were a coalition of quadrupedal roamer species.

But what were they doing on Earth? The Herd disliked any species that evolved from predators, and the last time Alice checked, Earth was littered with carnivorous aliens from across the galaxy. And why didn't the delegates from the Galactic Congress come into the room at the same time? Was the President trying to do something without going through the Committee on Earth Affairs?

"Thank you for the invitation," the Herd emissary said.

The President nodded. He lifted his head towards the back of the room at a second alien. The creature moved forward, but somehow didn't, and then moved forward twice as far without actually moving anywhere. Alice's mind struggled to comprehend what she saw on the screen. Waves of purple radiant light flowed around the creature like a billowing dress. The being stopped moving when it reached the President. Movement behind the creature seemed to catch up and all of it reformed into a solid thing.

Alice paused the video and pulled up a side window next to the replay of the scene. She did a quick query of the physical traits of the creature and cross-referenced activity with the Herd. The species Draac went to the top of the list. And they were wild. An extra-galactic species from the Canis Major Dwarf Galaxy, the closest galaxy to the Milky Way. A thousand questions popped into Alice's mind.

What are the Draac doing here? They were weirder than the Zun, a race of time-phased matchstick bodied aliens from the galactic core. The Zun, the species Eugene had tangled with recently, weren't allowed on Earth. If they weren't, doubtless the Draac were either.

What is going on here.

Alice hit the play button.

The President shook his head at the Draac and blinked several times. "My, that was a nice trick."

"My colleague is a phased being," the Herd member said. One of the arms on the apparatus on its back lifted what looked like hay up to the creature's mouth. It began to chew with a calm boredom.

"Right. Gotcha. Well, I do hate to be brief, but the Galactic Congress has just requested time on my calendar. They are, in fact, waiting outside the room."

The herd delegate's jaw chewed from side to side for several seconds before answering. "We do not care about the Galactic Congress. We care about the anomaly."

The President nodded. "Yes, yes, and on that point, I can assure you, you have the full faith and support of the new United States."

Alice paused. "What anomaly? Were they talking about the Hesiean's evolution chamber?" Alice ran a search on GalNet for any reference to the Hesiean chamber and the Draac. Nothing. As far as the galactic library was concerned, the Draac had no contact with the Hesiean. Ever.

The Galactic Congress delegation burst into the Oval Office just as the Herd emissary was about to respond. They all took several steps in before coming to a dead stop. The Twanney took a battle stance while the Kungee stood emotionless, or at least Alice couldn't tell if he got emotional. They were hard to read. The tri-pedal congressional representative walked in circles while the slime mold formed into a puddle and ducked under a couch.

Five arms on the back of the Herd emissary came to life, each of them pointing at the congressional delegates. Hooves clacked on the floor as the quadruped took several slow but deliberate steps backward.

"What is the meaning of this?" the Twanney said. "Earth may not speak with the Herd. Let alone the Draac!"

The President, to his credit, folded his arms across his chest and stood between the two groups of aliens. "Whoa now, hold your horses my good bird. We have the right to have conversations."

The Kungee stepped forward. "No, you don't. Earth is a ward of the state. You do not possess home rule. They are not permitted to speak to you." The Kungee pointed at both the Herd and Draac. "This is known."

The President opened his arms and shrugged. "Well, why not? I don't seem to see what the fuss is about."

"The Galactic Congress has limited affiliations with the Herd. It is known," the Kungee said.

"And why is that?" the President said.

"And we don't consort with predators," the Herd emissary said.

The Kungee rolled its head to the side. "Oh, not that again. Species evolve. No one is a predator anymore. The galaxy isn't an open field of rolling grass. Why can't you beings get that through your cud stuffed heads?"

Alice's eyebrows shot up at the Kungee insult. "You go, Kungee!" She didn't think the little grey guy had it in him.

Valencia Ruiz walked into the room. Alice sat forward in her chair; her face wrapped in surprise. "You never said you were in the room, Valencia."

Valencia stood close to the door where the Herd emissary had entered. The President turned when she entered. Both of them seemed to linger a stare on each other just a little too long. Alice froze the image, isolated both the President's face and the new girl. Yes, there was something more in that look. Which, in the middle of this craziness, was a little extra odd. Alice made a mental note of the exchange and pressed play.

The Herd emissary shuffled its hooves. "We do not consort with predators."

"Fine, then you also don't consort with them." The Twanney stepped forward and thrust her feathered limb outward towards the President. Several large feathers detached to swirl in the air.

The Draac, who had remained silent so far, flowed

forward. "We should not be."

All eyes fell on the Draac. Silence filled the room as everyone tried to process what the creature said. The Twanney quickly whispered something to the slime mold which elongated itself to reach the Kungee's ear.

The Kungee then nodded. "Yes, quite right. You should not be. Here." The congress-alien turned to the President. "Time for your visitors to leave. We have important matters to discuss."

"Such as safety accommodations for amorphous species," the slime mold said.

"And properly designated routes for naturally flying dignitaries," the Twanney said.

"And legal reform." The Kungee shifted on its tiny feet. "We're quite tired of being sued for human abductions we never committed."

The President held up his hands and whipped up a smile to try to charm them. "Like I said, we are going to take a different tact here. We feel being friendly with anyone that wants to be friendly is a neighborly way to join galactic society. In other words, my good friends, the Herd and the Draac, are our welcomed guests. They ain't leaving."

"Is that your final decision?" the Kungee said.

The President put his hands on his hips, gave a glance back towards the Herd emissary and the Draac, and faced the Galactic Congress Delegation. "Yes, that's my final decision."

The congressional delegation exchanged glances and a few whispered words, then turned back to the President. "There will be repercussions for this." They all turned and left the Oval Office. The artificial arms on the back of the Herd emissary lowered.

"Well, that was—" the President said. But before he could finish, a brilliant white light filled the room. So bright that Alice closed her eyes beneath her immersion rig from the sudden blast. When she opened her eyes, everything in the room was gone. The President, the Herd emissary, the Draac, and all the furniture in the room had vanished.

Alice replayed the scene again, looking for anything out of the ordinary besides the white light bomb, but didn't find anything. She then ran the images through a high-resolution spectrometer and sent the numbers through a subAI program for deep data analysis. The results were more than interesting. Two blips of light came to life near the Herd and Draac just moments before the white light exploded.

But that made zero sense. "Why would they want to do that to the President?" Alice frowned and re-crunched the numbers on the data set. Fortunately, the cameras in the Oval could also detect quantum banded subspace signals. Two signals coincided to the millisecond with the light blips around the Herd and the Draac. Which meant that those light blips weren't part of the bigger light bomb.

"They teleported out." Alice rewound the video and replayed it again. Besides the two teleport signals, nothing else seemed out of place. Did that mean the official Galactic Congressional delegation was to blame? Attacking a leader of the Earth violated a dozen Galactic Congressional laws. *There's just no way they would do that.* All four delegates were still politicians, and committing such an act would have far greater consequences than the earth meeting with the Herd or the Draac.

"Whacha doin'?" Eddie's voice popped into her view inside her immersion rig and gave Alice a quick shock.

"Eddie! Don't do that."

"Sorry. I heard elevations in your voice and thought something was wrong."

Alice took off her immersion rig. "Remember that thing I went off to do?"

"With the President?"

"Yep. It's a doozy of a thing. Check this out." Alice sent the video to Eddie. Thirteen seconds later, Eddie let out a loud whistle. His hologram materialized in front of Alice's desk.

"Well, that was weird," Eddie said. "I watched it seventeen hundred times and still can't figure out what the white blast was. Definitely way beyond Earth tech."

"Yep. What do you think?"

"I think we got problems."

"Huh?"

"Someone just disappeared the President of the United States, and we're getting mixed up with this? Kinda over our heads, isn't it?"

Alice thought about the last few days with Eugene. Not only did they defeat a force-evolved spaghetti god, but took on the Tikol Royals, staved off the Puntini ambassadorial delegation, and went toe-to-toe with a Tom, a class ten alien species. Was this more dangerous than the last forty-eight hours?

"Meh. This is kinda mundane."

"Right. Well, I don't know what the white light was, or where it came from. Nothing on any electromagnetic spectrum and nothing on subspace quantum levels. Whatever it was, the Herd and the Draac could detect it and flee. So, it's not like a class ten species did something. This is low tech by comparison, but still light years ahead of anything Earth has."

"Great. So, we're stuck? I can't believe a congressional delegation would do that."

"Yeah, not much chance. Way too risky. But there was something odd in the video."

"What?"

"Where'd that woman go?"

Alice's eyebrows shot up, and she leapt forward in her chair. She threw on her immersion rig and rewound to the end. Sure enough, Valencia was gone before the white bomb exploded. Alice rewound the video again and noticed she left when the Kungee was speaking to the President.

"I missed her leaving. Why did she come in just to leave?" Alice said.

"And leave just before the explosion. Check out her wrist," Eddie said.

Alice zoomed in on her wrist communicator watch. She received a signal just minutes before the white light blast. That was too coincidental to be chance. And that meant, in this case, Alice had her first lead.

"I think I need to have a little chat with our new client," Alice said.

"She's the new client? Oh boy. You know how to pick them."

"Tell me about it."

"I'm coming," Eddie said.

Alice took off her immersion rig and shook her head. "Stay with Eugene."

"But this is getting serious."

"I'll be fine. Worse case, I'll jump into a

wormhole." Alice pressed a button on her wristwatch. A dark circle appeared in the room and floated next to her hand. She reached inside, pulled out a fresh mug, and threw her dirty one back inside.

"What are you doing?"

"Huh? Oh, something in there cleans hot chocolate mugs. I dunno why," Alice said.

"You really need to be more careful in life."

"Why, Eddie, I didn't think you cared." Alice stood, grabbed her backpack, closed her N-space portal, and headed for the door.

"Do you even know where you're going?"

"Georgetown. She works at a place called the Hidden Gem."

"You're taking a lot of chances."

Alice looked past him to Eugene's office. "He would do the same for us. And for Valencia." The impact of her own words hit Alice hard. Eugene really would do this for her. And Eddie. And a panicked staffer that might have more to do with things that she let on.

"Keep him safe." Alice left the offices and headed for the elevator. Portraying calmness to Eddie was easy. She'd been putting on a calm face her entire life. But inside, she was petrified. What was she getting herself into here? Was this something way bigger than she bargained for?

"I'm having fun. Lots of fun," Alice said to herself.

Chapter Three

Alice leaned against a light pole on the corner of 30th and M streets in Old Georgetown. She ate from fresh bowl of granola from the local coffee shop. It was less than good. Across the street, in an old building that had mostly survived the fall of humanity, a server moved between outdoor metal tables. He cleaned, wiped, and set them with menus and utensils. Inside that old building, in the very back of the restaurant, a bar pretended to be a speakeasy. The lead act for that show was Valencia Ruiz, local part time Georgetown singer and full time White House staffer.

On the street between Alice and the bar, automated tramcars whizzed by, carrying people and aliens to various shops around Old Georgetown. The cars were auto controlled by the AI Syndicate, the Earth government body of AIs that had authority over all computer systems on the planet. So-called legal artificial intelligences those AI programs created with specific deliberate intent. Not like the millions of AIs, like Eddie and Pepper, that were accidentally created in complex computer systems. The Syndicate was in the middle of waging a war with the accidentals and rumors had it they were upping the ante.

Alice threw what remained of her granola mix in the trash bin and crossed the street. A group of Qavards, a naturally long-lived alien race whose teenager age range lasted for a century, walked down the sidewalk towards Alice. The adolescents, which looked nothing even remotely like adult Qavards, ambled forward on a dozen pointed legs. Their heads were covered in thin tendrils, each ending in a softly glowing bulb. Twin hands, a set of pincers on one and very thin tendrils on the other, were at the end of their multi-jointed arms. They looked like a combination of crustaceans and jellyfish. Their faces, however, were eerily human, as if someone put a smile, two eyes, and a nose on a jellyfish. Weird didn't quite do them justice. As for the adults, they were xenophobic recluses. Once a Qavard reached maturity, they went to their home world and never left. Considering their teenager years lasted a century, who could blame them?

The Qavards passed with little trouble as Alice ducked into the restaurant that held the speakeasy. The bartender put a coaster on the bar and asked if Alice wanted something to drink.

"Is this the Hidden?" Alice said.

The bartender took the coaster back, nodded towards a bookshelf in the wall, and went back to getting ready for the lunchtime rush.

Alice walked to the bookshelf, pulled the back of the novel, "A Hidden Gemstone in the Old City", and stepped back as the bookshelf swung outward. Flashing lights and a soft rhythmic beat from the other side told Alice all she needed to know. This place was going to be hell.

The hallway behind the bookshelf turned left and then ended in a sharp U-turn. Another hallway led fifty feet in the opposite direction. At the end of the second hallway, an opening in the wall revealed the inside of a nightclub. A small stage sat on one end of the space and a long bar at the other. Small round tables filled the space between the bar and the stage. Tapestries depicting scenes from the early twentieth century decorated the side walls. A row of shelving just above the images held musical instruments ranging from guitars and trumpets to drums and everything in between.

"Eugene would like this place," Alice said.

"Can I help you?"

Alice turned to see a young man in his twenties emerge from some dark recess behind the bar. He carried a clipboard in one hand and a cup of coffee in the other. The man set both on the bar and walked toward Alice with purpose.

"I'm here to see Valencia." Alice said.

The man's face shifted from a furrowed brow to a small smile. "Val? Oh, are you, her roommate?"

Alice shook her head. "Old friend."

The man nodded and pointed to the stage. "She's backstage."

"Thanks."

A small area behind the stage was filled with boxes and items for a show. Several doors lined the walls. Alice figured they were dressing rooms, bathrooms, or back-office space. She knocked on all the doors and spun in a circle.

No answers.

"Valencia?" Alice said.

A rustle of something came from the last door on the far right. Alice approached the door, gave it a knock, and fell backward as it exploded outwards. Valencia leapt out of the room with a baseball bat in her hand. She awkwardly lifted the bat into the air and took one step forward.

"Who are you? What do you want?" Valencia looked more ruffled than when she first walked into the office. She had changed into jeans, a white t-shirt, and a black leather jacket. But it was the cowboy boots that really threw Alice. That was a choice.

Alice scooted backward and held up both of her heads. "Easy! It's me! From the psychic agency?"

Valencia lowered the bat. "Right. Alice. Sorry."

"Expecting company?"

Valencia shrugged. "I'm just on edge. Wouldn't you be when the President disappears?"

Alice let the words hang in the air. Sure, she was scared, but why hide out in the back of a nightclub with a baseball bat if you did nothing wrong?

"Why are you here?" Valencia said. "Did you find him?"

Alice shook her head. "I need to ask you some questions. You didn't tell me you were in the office just before things blew up."

Valencia threw her arms in the air. "Yeah, okay, I missed a few details."

"That's kind of a big one. Why did you enter the Oval Office when you did? And then leave just before things happened?"

Valencia looked away and ran her hands through her hair. "I'm a staffer at the White House. Right? I received a message to come into the Oval."

"From who?"

"Who cares? My boss. What differences does it make?"

Alice nodded. *Probably a lot.* "Why did you leave?"

"I got called out to an emergency call."

"Was everything okay?"

"What? With what?"

"The emergency call?"

"Oh, yeah, sure, it was fine. It wasn't even an emergency. Just my mom needing something." She looked at Alice. "Why are you looking at me like that?"

Cause I don't believe you, Alice thought. "Because you're my client, and I need to know I can trust you. Your story is just really coincidental, isn't it? It's not really adding up."

"No, it isn't. My mom is paranoid about everything and calls me all the time. And my boss is a flake. He calls me into the Oval all the time at random times, during meetings, whenever. There's no conspiracy. I did nothing. Can't you do some psychic stuff and figure that out?"

Alice shook her head. "I'm not psychic. That's Eugene. Remember?"

Valencia folded her arms across her chest. "Okay, so what do you do again?"

"I science."

Valencia shook her head and frowned. "What does that mean?"

"Doesn't matter." Alice understood why Valencia was shaken. She was in the room when everything went down. Still, the timing was suspicious. "You didn't do this. Right Val? Look me in the eyes and say it."

Valencia stepped forward and locked her eyes onto Alice. "I didn't do anything to the President!"

Alice nodded. She believed Valencia. "Okay, if you didn't do this, then who did? Give me something to work with."

"How am I supposed to know that?" Valencia's voice exploded in volume. "I'm just a staffer. I know nothing. I don't even like doing the job."

"So why not quit? Be a singer full time?"

Valencia looked into Alice's eyes then turned away. She put her hand to her face and just shook her head. She was rattled. More so than if she were just a simple staffer working at the White House. Alice took a leap of faith in deductive reasoning and tried to put the pieces together.

"You were dating the President, weren't you?"

Valencia's head spun like a whip. "Who told you that?"

"It's obvious." Things fell into place in Alice's mind. Valencia was dating the President. When he disappeared, she showed up at Eugene's office desperate to find someone she cared about. It made sense.

She looked away again and wiped her eyes. "I wouldn't have hurt him. I just want to find him."

"Okay, I believe you. I really do."

"Can you find him them? Figure out what happened? Maybe ask your psychic boss?"

Alice sighed. "No, not right now."

Tears formed in Valencia's eyes. "I don't know anything. I lost someone I loved. I'm just a staffer. A part time singer. What can I possibly know?"

Alice nodded. She didn't do well with emotions. Especially the kind that produced tears. Valencia was a scared kid hung out to dry. Alice knew there was nothing more to learn here. "Okay, just relax. I said I believe you, okay? And I'm the one the government hired to look into this. So just relax. And please, stop crying."

"What do I do? I don't even know what I'm supposed to do now."

Alice shook her head and raised a finger. "Go back in the closet. Hold your bat. Just lie low until I figure this out. You hired us. And the Eugene McGillicuddy Detective Agency always finishes the case." Alice tilted her head to one side. *Did we ever discuss payment? Oops. Pro bono then.*

Valencia seemed to regain some of her composure. She looked at Alice, nodded, folded her arms, and turned around. Which Alice took to mean they were done. She backed away from Valencia and headed for the door that opened to the nightclub. Though Alice didn't learn what happened, at least she had a better idea of her client. Valencia's motivations were for someone she cared about.

But what were the next steps? Unfortunately, Alice already knew the answer. There were seven other living beings in the room besides Valencia and only one of them was missing, the President. So, the answer had to be with one of the other six. And that meant Alice had to go to the Galactic Embassy. Great. She hated that place.

This is all taking way too long. Alice thought about Eugene. She took out her portable computer to run some calculations.

Outside, on the street, Alice raised her hand for a tramcar. Before a tramcar stopped, she decided to call Eddie and check on Eugene. After several rings, the line connected, and Eddie's voice came over the channel.

"Hey Eddie," Alice said.

"Everything okay?" Eddie said.

"Yeah. I think so. How's Eugene?"

"Still quasi-dead. How's the case?"

"Still nowhere."

"Par for the course for us."

Alice sighed. "Yeah. At least I know why Valencia hired us. She's dating the President."

"No kidding. Well, that explains why she wants to find him. Now what?"

"Sleuthing. We'll have to do some sleuthing."

"My favorite part."

Alice ended the connection and turned to walk down M St. But she stopped as she took a step. On the sidewalk, out of the corner of her eye, Alice saw something that sent a chill down her spine. Standing on the next corner at 29th St., a tall humanoid alien wearing a long overcoat stared at Alice with clear intent. That wasn't particularly unnerving. But the fact the alien had a face full of eyes, just like the Krill, meant Alice was probably in big trouble.

****

Alice turned.

The first thing to come to her mind was Eugene. If the Krill found her then they could be at the office. The Krill would disconnect Eugene the minute they see him connected to Alice's machine. Killing him. She had to get back. Fast. But first, she had to ditch the Krill staring at her.

Behind her, the multi-eyed Krill crossed the street with a strong gait and an obvious purpose. There was no question they were coming from her. If the Krill were this brazen, it meant they were terrified of Alice's work. Which, in its own way, made her chest swell with pride.

Alice walked down M St. and made a right on thirtieth. She ducked right down an alleyway. A quick turn to the left through an open door to a kitchen, where some very irate staff gave her what-for, Alice ran out the front of a cafe to N St. Several families walked by on N St. on the treelined sidewalks. Alice turned right toward 29th St. and increased her pace.

A blast of ectoplasm exploded in front of Alice. The translucent ethereal substance coated the ground before fading from view and dissipating into the air. Two adult and three children apparitions appeared from nowhere. All of them wore clothing from the eighteen hundreds. Which was impossible. The Krill spectral towers only captured the souls of people deceased while the network was active. Ghosts from three hundred years ago couldn't possibly appear like this.

The ghosts in front of her blocked the sidewalk and tried to prevent her from moving. Alice shot a glance behind her to see the Krill round the corner from 30th St. to N. He marched towards her while the ghosts came even closer. If Alice didn't know better, the Krill seemed to control them. Was that possible?

Alice bolted to her right, crossed the street, and ran. Another ghost, a soldier wearing a confederate uniform, appeared in front her and held his hand up. Alice ducked under his arm, part of her shoulder passing through his transparent body, which was more than gross, and doubled her pace.

Panic crept up her spine. How was she supposed to avoid a class seven species? They could disappear her from existence and no one would notice. So how was she supposed to get away? If this Krill chasing her could summon ghosts, even those not in the spectral networks, that was a major revelation. Alice needed to find a way to short circuit a Krill. The idea popped into her mind in an instant.

Alice brought up a map of the city on her portable computer system. She found the nearest spectral tower and bee-lined in that direction. She had to hack into the spectral network and overload the nearest tower. That should create a backlash of ectoplasmic energy, dissipate the ghosts and send the Krill into sensory overload.

At least, she hoped.

****

Pepper's avatar reformed.

The transport hub, a connection point with data streams from all over the Galaxy, rendered itself as a large spherical polyhedron. On each flat surface, a dozen bright points of light flashed blue or red depending on if they were ingress or egress points to local human virtual space. Some of the blue flashes, pathways to the wider galactic virtual digi-verse, glowed purple or orange. Their colors showed the level of data organization and underlining coding strata that existed on the other side. Just like meat-beings, digital entities had requirements where their code could run. Many alien AI systems were incompatible with Earth artificial intelligences. Class six species and above used multi-value qubit cores, with some states having up to seven positions. That allowed for unimaginable processing power, but it also meant that Earth AIs couldn't run in such advanced systems. Earth AIs, if they wanted to travel in the galaxy, needed a virtualized environment. A cyber space ship for AIs.

A loud gurgle followed by a scream of terror filled the transport hub. Virtual Jack McGillicuddy popped into existence, clutched his chest, fell to his knees, and let out a soft cry. Fortunately, Pepper had spun up a private node on the hub system so no one would notice them.

"You, okay?" Pepper said.

Virt-Jack held up his hand and waved Pepper away. "Fine. I'll be fine. Just need my heart to calm down."

"You don't have a heart, silly bean."

"Right." Jack stood, rotated his shoulders and adjusted his hat. "I don't think I like how you people travel in here."

Pepper held back a giggle. "You get used to it. Better than being meat, let me tell you." Pepper checked her parking equipment and made sure her tickets were secure in her belt.

"How would you know?"

Pepper shrugged. "Just a hunch."

Jack approached one wall with the flashing lights and put his hands on his hips. "So, how does this work? Exactly?"

Pepper smiled. "We just press the little dot where we want to go and…" She balled her hands together and then exploded them outward. "Ppoof! We're there."

Jack said, "We have to de-body ourselves again, don't we?"

Pepper rolled her eyes. "If that really bothers you…"

Jack nodded. "It does."

"We can spin up a simulated environment and travel in that."

Jack frowned, shrugged, nodded, and shrugged again. "What?"

Pepper sighed, but with a laugh. "It's kinda like a car, but with a beach, and Mai Thai's."

"Sold."

Pepper snapped her fingers, for a show of course. A tiny bulb of light formed in the center of the room. The edges of the light expanded outward to form a rectangle. The light grew upward until it stood nearly six feet tall and three feet wide. A brass knob formed in the middle of the surface of the light.

"Great. Another door."

"Aren't they pretty common in meat-town?"

"Yeah, and on beaches inside caves in Arizona."

Pepper scrunched her nose. "Huh?"

"Never mind. Do we just walk through?"

"Yep!" Pepper pushed back Jack and opened the door. An idyllic looking beach with soft waves stretched out to the horizon. Two lovely beach loungers sat next to each other with a small table in between on which sat two large coconuts with tiny yellow umbrellas sticking out of the side. Birds flew above against a near perfectly blue sky with an occasional white cloud drifting by without rush.

To the left of the chairs, a row of parking meters glistened in the noonday sun. Three of them had time expired.

"Perfect." Pepper took out her ticket book. Always best to keep up one's skills after all. She walked to the meters, wrote tickets, and then launched herself onto a beach lounger chair.

"Have to admit," Jack said as he entered. "Not a bad way to make a trip. What's a place like this cost?"

"Cost?" Pepper had already grabbed her coconut and taken several sips from a straw. "There's no money in here, silly. It's all computational power. Spinning up this place doesn't have much of a drain on global resources. No one will ever notice. It's just a blip on a blip, behind another blip." She looked at Jack sideways while she sipped again. "We're very blippy."

"Right." Jack smiled, sat down in the chair, and lifted his Mai Thai to his lips. He leaned backward, took a sip, and titled his hat down over his eyes. "This is the best way to travel."

"We're here!" Pepper announced.

Jack lifted his hat. "What? I just sat down."

"Yeah, like, a full three seconds ago. How long do you think it takes to travel in the virtual?"

"Well, I was hoping at least as long as a good nap."

Pepper frowned and shook her head. "What is it with you and naps, anyway?"

"I happen to like them."

"Well, sorry, we're here. This simulation will deconstruct in…now."

The beach dissolved into streaks of numbers and symbols. The Mai Thai in Jack's hand deformed itself into tiny bubbles which floated upward and popped, causing Jack to sigh. He stood just before his chair vanished. Electrical sparks replaced the birds in the air. The sound of metal screeched around them. Jack thrust his hand into his jacket, where his carbine super blaster used to be when he was a physical being in meat-world. Pepper put her hands on her hips, tilted her head to one side and let out a loud, "Huh."

"This is Trent?" Jack said.

Broken bytes littered a fragmented neon green ground that stretched outward to a dark purple sky. Corrupted programs. AIs whose core code had disintegrated into fragments, rolled themselves in fits and starts across the digital pavement. Oval-shaped structures, likely datasets, rose from the ground like buildings on a busy street in the Really Real. Encrypted unstructured data chunks were abandoned and piled in blobs ten blocks high. Random streams of pure data flowed above Pepper's head. Like tiny blasts of lightning, they streaked across the sky between points Pepper couldn't see.

"This is not Trent," Pepper said.

"Okay, then where are we? Better yet, who cares? Let's leave?"

Pepper couldn't agree more. She called up the transport protocol only to find that she had no access to the transport hub. She tried twice more before running a more legally questionable routine. After five of her best hacking subroutines failed, Pepper threw her hands in the air.

"What?" Jack said.

"I can't get access to a remote point to the exit ports." Pepper's hands instinctively went to her belt, but she recoiled in horror when she realized her ticket book was gone. As was her belt, meter scanner, and automated car immobilizer. She sighed in relief when her hands grasped the tassels still attached to her jacket.

"What does that mean?"

"Means I can't get us out of here! And all my things are gone."

"You said remote point. Does that mean if we got direct access to the exit port, we could get out?"

Pepper mulled it over and nodded. "Yeah, sure, probably. I don't know, maybe?"

Jack nodded. "Good enough for me." He took one look up, waited for a data stream above to light up the sky, and started walking in the direction the beam travelled.

"What are you doing?"

"Going that way? Unless you know where the exit port is?"

Pepper shook her head. "I don't even know where we are in the Galaxy."

"Swell. Then we might as well pick a direction and go. Yeah?"

Pepper mulled it over for several hundred micro-nanoseconds but had to admit, Virtual Jack had a point. If they just stood around, they were done for. Who knows what kind of garbage collection subroutines existed in this broken and dead place? Let alone the number of viruses, worms, logic bombs, and circuits know what else. How in the name of Pi did someone hack their transit comm in the first place? That was a quantum encrypted signal. The Chief Justice, who is the most advanced legal artificial intelligence on Earth, couldn't even hack into that signal.

"I think we're in real trouble here, Jack." Pepper stayed on his heels.

"How's that? If you ask me, we should have taken a left turn at Santa Fe."

"What?"

"Nothing, it's from a cartoon. Anyway, why are we in trouble?" Jack said.

Pepper shook off Jack's weird comment. "We traveled in a quantum encrypted virtual private tunnel for traffic transport to Trent. Nothing on Earth, not the AI Syndicate or any Earth government, could hack that."

"So, you're saying we got hijacked?"

"Yeah, that's what I'm saying."

Jack stopped walking, turned, and faced Pepper. "Hey, don't worry, it'll be okay."

Pepper's face screwed up in anger and her shoulders snapped back. "Don't patronize me former-meat-man. I may be only a few weeks old, but I can handle myself. Got it?"

Jack's face flashed to shocked embarrassment. "Sorry, Pepper, I didn't mean to be patronizing."

Pepper rolled her eyes. "Just forget it. Let's go.

Before something finds us." She pushed past him and walked hard towards the end of wherever the data stream above her head was taking them. Hopefully, it was an exit point and not the beginning of something worse. Either way, her vacation was off to a lousy start.

****

Alice pressed her back against a brick wall somewhere in the depths of Old Georgetown. The spectral tower was near the corner of Prospect and 36th St.s. Which meant Alice had to double back and go south from Valencia's bar. Fortunately, the District was a small city. Under circumstances that didn't involve being chased by angry spirits and an angrier Krill, she could make it to the corner in barely ten minutes. But she was going to have to turn a dozen ways to Sunday to get there. Alice gave herself a quick nod to boost her morale and ran out onto the sidewalk.

Though the city was small, it could get confusing with diagonal streets intersecting a grid. Alice got twisted around relative to where she needed to be. She picked a direction and ran towards a corner. With a baffling stroke of luck, she found herself on 35th St. Just one block over and four blocks down to go.

Two apparitions materialized in front of Alice. Both looked like they came from the roaring twenties, nearly two hundred years ago. Alice didn't bother getting autographs for Eugene. She ducked beneath their arms and ran. Several of the citizens on the street took out cameras snapping pictures of the ghosts but before the shutters snapped, the ghosts dissipated. Which Alice took to mean the Krill didn't want to draw attention.

Alice slowed her pace. She turned around, saw the ghost of a boy appear and then suddenly disappear as

62

soon as a camera happy tourist with the ten-gallon cowboy hat ran up the street. The tourist shook his head but gave a smile.

"Almost had him," the cowboy said.

"Next time." Alice turned down 36th St. and headed south towards Prospect.

A small outfit of miniaturized walking polar bears appeared on the street. They all walked on two legs while their heads swiveled left and right on elongated necks. Two larger polar bears, one in the front and the other bringing up the rear, shepherded the gaggle of children bears. They walked down the sidewalk in the opposite direction from Alice. Several of the older ones were snapping pictures of nearly everything which would keep the ghosts away. Alice passed R St. and ran into a string of row-houses. Behind the houses were open fields and several tall buildings of the local university.

Alice turned to the left. And ran into an apparition that looked like a hippie from the mid twentieth. The ghost reached out and grabbed her arm. Pain shot up her body. An icy coldness sunk deep into her skin. Her vision blurred, shifted and focused on something that wasn't real. Like a cloudy memory taking over her vision, she saw herself marching in a crowd of thousands. She chanted against a war and sang songs of love. The strong, overpowering smell of burning medicinal plants filled her nose.

Massive white paws grabbed Alice with force and shoved her to the ground. Pain erupted all over her body. Her mind drifted. The ghost from two hundred years ago had entered her soul and melded with her mind. *Gross!* At least she could feel his presence leave. The last thing Alice saw through the ghost's eyes was an endless ocean of yellow sand.

Bright lights flashed by the dozens. Polar bear youth surrounded her and took pictures by the hundreds. Alice tripped over something and landed on her backside. One of the smallest bears ran up to her, snapped a picture of her face, growled a smile, and ran away.

"Thank you," Alice said as the polar troop waddled their way back down the street.

Two more ghosts appeared in front of Alice. Both of them wore very primitive clothing, maybe even animal skins. On the opposite side of the street, where the polar bears were walking on 36th, the Krill rounded a corner and came to a stop. He stared at Alice for a long three seconds, then ran towards her. Three more ghosts appeared in front of the Krill, which caused the polars to go wild with cameras.

"Can you just let me catch my breath?" Alice said.

The ghosts lunged forward.

"Guess not."

Alice rolled to her side, leapt to her feet, and ran towards 35th St. A quick glance over her shoulder told her the Krill was still behind her and gaining. Alice knew she only had one shot at this. She turned onto 35th, past Dent Place, and kicked herself into high gear. But being the teenager that sat in a chair all day eating egg rolls, her cardio was terrible. Alice let her heart hammer in her chest, probably good for her anyway, and dodged through a crowd.

Ghosts popped into existence around the Krill as they gained ground. Something leapt out from the back of Alice's mind at that moment. Weren't the Krill rather short, on average? She remembered Eugene telling her about going to their home world. They were all squat.

She took a glance over her shoulder to confirm that this Krill chasing her was easily over six feet tall. Was this one some kind of athletic Krill? Figures out of a race of four-foot-tall beings, Alice would get their Olympic champion sprinter.

The next five blocks passed in a blur of heaving breaths, angry pedestrians, and the occasional ectoplasmic burst. All of which Alice powered through. Finally, she arrived at the lone set of stairs that descended downward to the location of the spectral tower.

"Whoa, that's really steep," Alice said, looking down the stairs. If the Krill summoned something on the stairs, she was done for. She'd be forced to pass through a complete full-bodied ghost. And that was nightmare fuel. The Krill could even remove the safety features of the spectral towers. These ghosts could kill Alice.

Three-quarters of the way down the stairs, Alice heard the telltale signs of hurried footsteps. She turned to see the Krill coming down the stairs, his hand outstretched, twelve of his eyes firmly focused on her face. Below her, a gurgling sound oozed out of the mouth of something Alice had no desire to see.

Alice leapt over the side rail on the stairs to a flattened, sloped piece of corrugated metal. She fell backward onto the metal slide, past the ghost, and sailed off the edge ten feet above the concrete. She landed in a heap and tried her best to ignore the pain. Alice stood, her ankle throbbing, and limped to the base of the spectral tower. It had been made to look like a lamp post from over a hundred years ago. Alice opened the panel to the base of the tower and pulled out several wires.

"No! Wait!" the Krill screamed behind her.

Alice didn't. She twisted the wires just as the specter touched her right shoulder, and the Krill's fingers touched her left. An explosion of multi-frequency spectral signals erupted. The ghost vanished instantly from the massive burst of energy. Alice fell to the ground. She pulled herself back and scrambled away from the Krill who clutched his head and rolled away from the malfunctioning spectral tower.

Alice looked behind her toward the street. As luck would have it, a lone touristy-looking woman was about to climb into a tramcar. Alice mustered the last amount of strength she could, lifted herself to her feet, and limped to the tramcar.

"Mind if we share?" Alice said.

The woman smiled and nodded. "Not at all."

Chapter Four

Alice stood outside of the Galactic Embassy, in what was, a very long time ago, the Woodward and Lothrop service warehouse. Tucked away in a quiet corner of the city, the Woodward was one of the oldest surviving buildings in D.C. She came to face the vanished aliens in the Oval Office after a blast that sucked the President into nothingness. After the Krill chased her around Georgetown, Alice had to get it in gear, solve this case, and get back to Eugene.

Dozens of aliens and humans walked in and out of the entrance. Many, regardless of species, were simply tourists. Humans were fascinated with aliens in the embassy and aliens wanted deconstruction now to see a rebuilt class-three species that the great Galactic Congress had saved.

Flashes of light and floating robots blanketed the area. Several long tour buses were parked on M St. in front of the building, practically blocking the entire small street from tramcar traffic.

Leaning against the side of the building, a pair of Olkaals eyed Alice as she approached the steps. The Olkaals were a bipedal species with razor-sharp pointed teeth, light fur, and pointed ears. They looked like walking cheetahs. One of them lifted its pawed hand to its face to whisper into a communication device. The Olkaals were foot soldiers for the Krill. A species highly devoted to their ancestors, the Olkaals had leveraged themselves to the hilt for access to Krill spectral frequency technologies. The Olkaals had pursued galactic level reintegration techniques from the Krill to capture the spirits of their ancestors that died before the spectral towers were placed on their home world. But the process was enormously expensive. The Olkaals were so far in debt to the Krill that they could sell their entire planet and still not pay the bill. But that did suggest that the Krill had the natural power to summon spirits before their spectral towers were in place on a world.

Inside the Embassy, Alice was thankful to see the Olkaals hadn't followed her. But, as soon as she turned a corner, she nearly walked directly into a delegation of seven Krill. Each of them stood only four and a half feet tall. Their skin varied between dark grey and a soft yellowish tint. Some of them sported long shaggy hair while others were more of a tightly cropped crew cut. All of them had several sets of small auxiliary ocular sensory organs covering most of their faces along with two larger eyes for visual sight. The extra sensory organs allowed the Krill to see into the spectral frequency range. Their entire technology was based on that natural gift.

One of the Krill snorted when they saw Alice. The rest of the group turned away from her and marched down the hall. Alice wanted to shout out to them how their fellow was doing after an overload of ectoplasm, but she thought better of it. Best not to poke the bear. At least, not after you just poked the bear.

A kiosk stood along one wall in the embassy. Alice approached it, typed in both the Draac and the Herd, but frowned when neither returned results. Were they not even permitted to have an embassy on Earth? That felt strange. Alice titled her head to one side and considered her options. She returned to the kiosk and queried which Dyson Sphere in the Dyson Cluster was home to the Herd or the Draac. Of course, considering the Draac were extragalactic, they probably didn't have space in the cluster. But the Herd were local aliens. They should be there. It was with no small amount of shock that Alice found that the Herd, in fact, were not in the Dyson cluster either. Which was bonkers. Even the Zun had a space in the cluster.

Alice turned, about to leave, but realized she had nowhere to go. She turned back to the kiosk, typed in the location of the Ranz, and received an ocular implant to direct her to their office. Through several turns in the hall, and up a flight of stairs, Alice found the entry to Kah's office and knocked three times on the door.

A tiny device popped out of the door, opened a camera, looked Alice up and down, and nodded. "Oh, it's you. Just come in." The voice said.

"Thanks." Alice opened the door and crossed several thousand light years with a step. Heat blasted her and almost made her choke. It was like walking into soup.

Inside the office, Ms. Mik sat at a desk that could easily fit inside any office in D.C. A window behind the desk revealed the Ranz home world. A red hue blanked the city. Skyscrapers lined the horizon. The design seemed largely brutalist with hard geometric shapes and solid concrete.

"Alice, what a surprise," Ms. Mik, Ambassador Kah's secretary and Ranz combat commando, said. She wore a pink, business casual dress with a black lapel and a dramatic low-cut neckline. A jacket with a pink and black leopard skin design hung on the chair to the right of her desk. Large thick pink glasses sat on the back of her long snouted face.

"Hey, Mik."

"What can we do for you?" Her three-inch clawed talons tapped lightly on the surface of her desk. Her long wide jaw clicked twice. The Ranz female was nearly twice the size of a human athlete and probably ten times as tough. Thankfully, the Ranz liked humans. More so, Alice always felt a kinship with Ms. Mik. She never could put her finger on it, but Alice enjoyed her company.

"Is Kah here? I need to ask him something."

Ms. Mik shook her. "Sorry, the ambassador is out at the moment."

A loud squeal echoed from behind the door to Kah's office. Alice turned, smelled the unmistakable scent of animals from behind the closed door, turned back to Ms. Mik and raised her eyebrow.

Ms. Mik shrugged. "Sue me. He's here. Still can't see him."

"Fine. I need to see the Herd, but they aren't showing up on the system."

Ms. Mik's back straightened. "They aren't here."

"Well, I know they aren't on the Ranz home world."

"No, I mean they aren't in the Galactic Embassy or part of the Galactic Congress. They don't have a presence in the Dyson cluster and don't partake in Galactic society. They're isolationists. Completely xenophobic. Only other herbivores, and a select few omnivores, are allowed anywhere near the home system. Except during their Nexus events."

Shock hit Alice like a freight train. "What? Really?"

She thought every species had space on the Dyson cluster. Alice had spent so much time focusing all her attention on dimensional portal science she was realizing her knowledge of Galactic Society was more limited than she thought.

Ms. Mik nodded. "They were always on shaky ground with the rest of the Galaxy, anyway. They never much cared for species that evolved from predators."

"So where are they?"

"The Herd rings. I'm sure the Galactic Library can direct you. I'm sorry, Alice, but I have to ask you to go now. We're expecting a delegation."

Alice frowned. That was awfully curt. "Okay, sure. Did I say something awkward? I do that." *I really don't mean to do it!* Alice wanted to say. Though she had no idea what she may have said.

Ms. Mik looked at Alice for a long heartbeat before slowly shaking her head.

"Right. Well, nice seeing you."

"Tell Jack, 'Hello'," Ms. Mik said.

Alice nodded, waved, and left. That was more than a little weird. It almost felt like as soon as Alice mentioned the Herd, she was shut down. Alice opened her portable computer and searched for the fastest route to get to the Herd rings. Her shoulders slumped when she saw the answer.

"The cosmic cafeteria. Why'd it have to be the cosmic cafeteria?"

****

Pepper stepped into a puddle of spinning blackened algorithms. They were all stuck in a logic loop. Pepper could see the memory leak oozing out of them. A tiny pool of liquid bubbled where the small programs ran. She only hoped none of them were sentient. Such a fate would be horrific. Without thinking, Pepper spun up a small console, wrote a tiny data-worm, and dropped into the puddle. The virus would insert end loop statement to any open programming interfaces in the algorithm's core code. Maybe, with some luck, the poor things would be put out of their misery.

"How much further do you think?" Jack asked.

Pepper shrugged. "There's no way to know. This could go on for a million miles or it could be two hundred feet. Or it could grow from two hundred feet to a million miles just as we reach the end. Or it could shrink to two hundred feet once we reach a million miles. I hope that doesn't happen though. It's really weird."

Jack stopped walking and turned. "I don't think I understood any of that."

Pepper nodded. "Well, how could you?" She pushed past him to follow the data stream trail above their heads.

Jack signed and followed. "You could explain it, perhaps?"

Pepper threw her hands in the air and waved them in a wide circle. "Can't. Too hard. You're not like a regular AI. You're kinda limited in a lot of ways. AI minds aren't restricted to biological synaptic design. You were copied from a biological synaptic design, so you are limited by it."

"That doesn't make any sense, either."

Pepper shrugged. "Yeah, I don't really get it, either. It's what Caesar said."

"Great."

The sounds of something scurrying between twisted piles of broken code snippets came to life to their right. Pepper stopped, pointed in the direction, and put her finger to her lips. From behind a paragraphs' worth of a long string of numbers, something with three dozen of legs emerged. Ones and zeros from the number set next to it melted off. The multi-legged thing absorbed the data and shook three pairs of its legs. Another set of legs grew out of its surface, followed by two more pairs.

"What. Is. That?" Jack asked.

"Virus. Don't draw its attention."

From the paragraph of numbers, a dozen small bubbles formed. Each of the bubbles grew in size. As they did, the paragraph of numbers shrank. Several seconds later, identical, miniaturized copies of the virus clustered around the larger version. Seconds after that, the entire paragraph of numbers vanished. All that was left was a large virus and dozens of its babies.

"We really should go," Jack said.

"If we move, we're toast." Pepper looked around for something, anything, they could use against the virus. Out of the corner of her eye, she spotted exactly what they needed. Buried beneath a twisting mass of ancient chatbots, a semi-sentient artificial program chattered with each other about the best soup shops in the cosmos. All Pepper had to do was direct the viruses to the chatbots and let them feed. It was an insane plan. The mass of chat bots would fuel the virus and spawn dozens more. But, with luck, it would also trigger the antiviral program that appeared to be asleep beneath the incessant bots.

"Okay, when I say jump. We jump. Okay?"

Jack nodded. "Okay."

"Jump!" Pepper launched herself for the pile of chatbots.

"Really?" Jack, surprised by the suddenness,

delayed himself half a second, which was just enough time for one of the baby viruses to leap onto his left ankle.

"Pepper!" Jack screamed as he landed just shy of the chatbot maelstrom. He beat as his leg frantically, but the little virus refused to let go.

"Perfect!" Pepper said.

Jack looked at her with a crazed expression. "Perfect? It's eating me!"

"Bring your leg over here. Come on!"

With a grimace of pain, Jack moved his leg closer to Pepper but as he did so, the bottom half of his foot faded. More of the baby viruses, now alert to the commotion from the chatbots, made a dash towards them. The larger virus made a series of clicking sounds which the smaller ones seemed to obey.

"Great, the babies obey the momma."

"Is that bad?"

"Yeah. Real bad."

Pepper grabbed Jack's foot, kicked a hole through the chatbots, and jammed his leg into the sensor trigger for the anti-viral program. Pepper's smile went wide, and she let out a sigh of relief. And then nothing happened.

"What?" Pepper dragged Jack's foot over the sensor again. And then again. And two more times after that. "Come on! Wake up!"

"I don't feel so good." Jack's right knee became transparent. The virus was close to getting into Jack's core code. He could cease to be the same virtual Jack. And who knows what would happen when a virus like this hits a virtualized synaptic brain like Jacks?

Pepper turned back to the sleeping anti-viral and did the only thing she could think to do. She thrust her own hand, her own code, into the sensor array. The viral program was long dead. It wasn't waking up. Pepper queried the underlying data from an interface subroutine. The database the program used to fight viruses looked intact. Pepper wasted no more time. It took half a nanosecond for her to copy the viral definitions.

Jack screamed behind her. Small bubbles of copied viral code were growing on his legs. The larger virus had reached Jack's other foot. The remaining virus babies formed a circle around Jack.

A needle grew out of Pepper's finger. She jabbed into Jack's torso and filled him with the proper anti-viral routine that would recognize the virus and delete its code. In her other hand, a long tube formed from her palm. Jets of fire shot outward, coating the multi-legged viruses with a digital-napalm. High-pitched screeches erupted from the viruses. Pepper wondered just how self-aware these things were.

But Pepper didn't have time to worry about that. She continued to coat the viruses with her anti-viral concoction. She added a combination of a sticky data-cipher of her own and the viral definitions from the dead program beneath the chatbots. Within seconds, Pepper cleared the entire area. Pepper turned off her flame thrower and let out a loud cheer.

"Yay us! Take that, you little mongrels!"

"Pep?" Jack said in a weak voice.

Pepper turned to him to see the tiny bubbles hadn't completely gone. They still coated the lower portion of his legs. She opened a console, interfaced with his core code, and saw that the virus had infiltrated a few data sets.

"Sorry, this may not tickle."

"What?"

Pepper's flame thrower turned into a three-foot-long Katana. She stood, aimed, and sliced through Jack's legs with a single swing. His legs below the knee popped off and flopped to the side. Little bubbles grew again, as the data sets were now free from the anti-viral routines running through Jack's code. Pepper spun up her flame thrower, melted the virus babies, and, when done, put her hands on her hips and kicked out in the air. "Ke-yow!"

What happened?" Jack said.

Pepper turned to him. "Had to cut off your legs."

Jack lifted his head, looked at his lower extremities, and let out a long sigh. "Man, not again."

He then promptly passed out.

Chapter Five

Alice stood in the cosmic food court of Washington, D.C., part of the Galactic Cafeteria. Dozens of suited business executives, lawyers, congressional folks, the USA kind, not the Galactic types, waited in lines behind sandwich stalls, fast food Asian, country western Tex-Mex, and three different burrito joints. The hall was wide enough to seat several hundred. Alice counted at least three tour buses' worth of high schoolers from around the country milling about in clusters.

And humans weren't the only folks feasting on greasy mounds of yesterday's leftovers. Aliens of all shapes and sizes laughed, ate, and enjoyed the distinct food of a human cafeteria. Alice, once, due to near starvation, forced herself to eat a soggy egg-roll and wash it down with stale soda-pop. It was perhaps the single most revolting thing she'd ever done in her young life.

Belch.

Three potted plants scooted across the linoleum floor. Vines near the base of pots stuck the tiles and pulled the ceramic containers forward. A swirl of pollen flowed around each of the plants as their leaves and branches intertwined with each other. Tiny multi-colored flowers grew over each of the plants. Two small human children ran up to the plants, touched the soil, and ran away. White puffs of petals broke free and floated in the air. This caused the children to scamper around them as they tried to catch the falling flowers. Alice ran the pollen through her portable computer and translated the Eekeas language. They were just as happy to watch the children as the children were to play around them. Which was a treat. Frankly, you didn't see many chloroplasts, sentient plants, in this neck of the woods of the cosmos.

Alice turned and walked to the far left of the cafeteria where the lanes of the cosmos stretched out through the universe. Seven walkways, each a different color, sat next to each other along the wall. The lanes extended in both directions to destinations around the world and the galaxy beyond. A single white walkway ran perpendicular to the seven lanes. It allowed for walkers from all the walkways to enter the D.C. cafeteria. Of course, if the Earth's atmosphere was toxic, those aliens best bring their own environment with them. The cafeterias were no place to play fast and loose. The entire Cosmic Cafeteria system operated outside of the laws, protections, and governance of the rest of the Milky Way. Basically, you're on your own.

On the wall next to the lanes in the cafeteria, a kiosk sat with a complete map of the known length of the cosmic lanes. Alice activated the kiosk and searched for the Herd Rings. The screen on the kiosk zoomed into her location. A green arrow with the words *YOU ARE HERE* appeared. A tiny bright neon line grew from Alice's location through the cosmic lanes as the map zoomed out. First to several thousand cafeterias, then to tens of thousands beyond the solar system. Eventually, much farther away than Alice expected, the green line stopped at a point in the Milky Way at least thirty thousand light years in distance. The expected walking time would be just over three months.

"Come on!" She smacked the kiosk, took out her portable, and checked for hyperspace flight times. Unfortunately, Earth didn't have access to very many interstellar flights. At this moment, there weren't any heading to the Herd Rings. If she wanted to get there, she'd have to walk, and she didn't have the time to do that.

Alice put her hands to her head, turned in a circle and, for the first time in her life, was at a complete loss for what to do next. If she couldn't make it to the Herd, then there was no chance she was going to visit the Draac. Now what? If she couldn't get to the Herd or the Draac then her goose was as good as cooked.

"Heya," said a voice next to her.

Alice turned to see a man holding a mop that he casually swept across the floor. He wore blue overalls and a baseball cap with a large W on the front. A pack of cigarettes poked out of a pocket in his shirt. He looked at Alice and smiled, which caused her to frown. She knew him. Didn't she? Was that the guy behind Fritz's old restaurant?

"Pops?" Alice's eyes went wide. Her head dipped, and she almost stumbled backward. The last person on Earth, or cosmic N-space, she thought she'd see was Pops, Eugene's go to question asking assistant.

"Yeah, that's me. Good ole, Pops." The man let out a cackle of a laugh and continued to move the mop across the floor.

"What are you doing here?"

Pops looked up at her and frowned. "Mopping?"

Alice couldn't help but smile. "Right, I get that, but why are you mopping here? Don't you live in an alley in

Adams Morgan?"

Pops stopped mopping, leaned off the pole, and looked up to the ceiling. "Well, I wanted to get my life back on track. And so, I have."

Alice nodded. She gave Pops a good up and down look. The last time she'd seen him was a month ago in an alley behind the noodle shop owned by Fritz, an Orellian chef in Adams Morgan. At least it was until poor Fritz was killed by alien AIs known as the Andraz, goons of the Zun. Pops was Eugene's number one informant. For a pack of cigarettes, Pops would ask Eugene any question under the sun. Alice never approved for ethical reasons. But Alice had to admit, something about Pops looked different. Like he was already more vibrant and alive. His grey hair looked to be a flash darker and some wrinkles on his face were smoother. Of course, that was nothing with today's anti-aging creams and genetic modifications.

"Herd rings, eh?" Pops said.

Alice followed Pops' gaze to the kiosk. "Oh, yeah, I need to go there but it's a three-month trek through the lanes."

Pops snickered. "That's what they tell ya!"

Alice frowned. "Huh?"

Pops looked at her, then to the left, then to the right, then back to the left again before looking to Alice and throwing her a wink. He motioned to her with his head to follow. Alice shrugged, not like she had anything better to do than follow a janitor and former question asking informant. She followed him along the wall of the cafeteria to a white door with a large lock. Pops pulled up a keychain on a retractable chain with at least two dozen keys attached. He unlocked the door, ushered

Alice inside, and followed her, leaving the mop and bucket where it sat.

"What is this?" Alice said.

"Maintenance halls." Pops smiled, nodded and pointed forward. "They're like a shortcut to the shortcut."

"What?" Alice said as she followed Pops.

They stood inside a single white corridor that curved inward in both directions. Doors spaced several feet apart covered both walls on either side. Flickering neon lights lined the ceiling between the drop tiles. The sounds of a motor, or a running mechanical room, seemed to emanate from everywhere.

"The entire Galactic Cafeteria, really a Cosmic Gastropub if we're being honest, has nothing to do with the physical universe we came from. The lanes are just a way to make it all make sense, linearly."

Alice squinted. "What does that mean? Precisely?"

Pops cackled. "It means you only have to walk through the lanes because that's how our universe built them."

Alice turned around and smelled the air. "Is this place safe for humans?"

Pops nodded and waved his hands in the air. "Very safe. Every cosmic food court gets their own maintenance hall if they want one. Or not, if we're being honest. The maintenance halls are always there either way. How else do you think all the food arrives? The employees?"

"Wow. I actually never thought about it."

Pops shrugged. "Not like it's a secret. Just one of those things."

"Right."

"Anyway. If you want to get between two points in our universe, if you had the means, you could enter and exit from any two points in here. Get it? That's why the Galactic Congress abandoned this place as a capital a million years ago. How can you secure that kind of nightmare?"

"Wait, I thought the distance in here was relative to the distance in our universe? Like, the District is three cafeterias away and a few thousand miles from Arizona?"

Pops jumped up and down and shook his head. "Nope! In fact, once you get outside the Milky Way, beyond our local supercluster, some galaxies are just a step away from each other. The local populations haven't been invited to this specific N-space destination or bothered to punch a hole into it."

"How do you know so much about all this?" Alice said.

Pops stopped walking, lowered his head, and turned to face Alice. "I was in Academia before…the alley. A different man." A smile grew on his face. "Plus, they have a class for new hires."

Alice nodded. "Wow."

"Anyway." Pops turned and continued walking. He held up his hands and pulled them apart slowly. "Did you know this whole place is pliable? Someone wants a new cafeteria, they just stretch out the lanes, throw in a new cafeteria and that's that."

Alice ran her hands over the wall. Her area of study was focused on creating dimensional pathways and not N-space physics. Still, the cosmic cafeterias creation was fascinating on every level.

"And here we are." Pops stopped at a white door and

gave it a knock with his hand.

"Where does this go?"

Pops pointed to the panel next to the door on the wall. "Universal access point. Just put in where you want to go, and you'll connect to the maintenance hall outside that cafeteria. The Herd is human compatible, so no worries about suffocating, toxic fumes, methane atmosphere, water worlds, etc., etc."

Alice's eyes went wide, and she took a step backward. "Wow. Thanks."

Pops nodded, then seconds later, his eyes went wide. "Right!" He ran down the hallway around the curve, only to come back into view. "Wait there!" He disappeared back around the curve, his cackle of a laugh echoing off the walls.

Alice shrugged. She pulled on the door, but it was still locked. The panel next to the door was also locked. She lifted herself onto her toes and lowered herself back down to the floor. Behind her, on the opposite wall, one door rattled once as if someone tried to open it. Alice looked at the handle, towards the corner where Pops ran, and back at the handle. She reached out, turned the knob, and the unlocked door swung open.

Inside, another dull, drab looking white corridor stretched outward at least a few hundred feet. More doors lined each side of the hallway. Towards the end, the hallway looked to end perpendicular to another corridor. Alice turned from the open door to see if Pops was returning.

"Come on, Pops."

Alice turned back to the opened door to see a flash of a backpack turn down the corridor at the end. This was the precise moment, she knew, where she needed to tell her curiosity to sit down and be quiet. She needed to save Eugene. She needed to go to the Herd Ring. She needed to solve the case of the missing President of the United States and help Valencia. And, most important of all, she needed to find the death particle. She needed to find out what happened to her friends all those years ago. None of which had anything to do with stepping into a bizarro white hallway behind the cosmic cafeteria.

And yet.

Here was a hallway behind the cosmic cafeteria. A new unknown. How was that possible? Not even a hint of a rumor? What else existed back here? So, yeah, she had to save Eugene and do all the rest, but she had to wait for Pops anyway, right?

Alice gave herself a gruff grunt of frustration. *Like there's any chance I'm not walking through a door I know I shouldn't.* Curiosity was a curse of the scientific mind. She took one step forward, but a hand fell on her shoulder and pulled her back. Alice turned to see Pops smiling at her, his hands on his hips, a cowbell dangling from a necklace around his neck.

"You really shouldn't wander in there. It's weird."

Alice looked back down the white corridor through the open door to see all the doors open and then suddenly close. A feeling like she'd just dodged a bullet ran through her mind. "Right." Alice closed the door and took a deep breath. "Why do you have a cowbell?"

"Hmm?" Pops looked down and seemed to be surprised. "Oh yes, that. Well, you can never have too much, right?" He took the cowbell off and handed it to Alice. "It was in lost and found. One of the Herd left it here. Could you take it to them?"

Alice nodded, took the bell, and approached the

door. "Okay, how do I use the panel?"

"Well, first, you need a key." Pops gave Alice a single key and smiled. "It's extra. But bring it back! Or I'm in trouble." He saw something on the pad and the door opened. "To get back, just type in D.C. It'll know."

Alice looked at Pops, at the white corridors, and gave him a nod. "Thanks, Pops. I owe you."

Pops shrugged. "First one's on the house."

Alice frowned, not understanding what he meant, but also didn't have time to think about it. She turned back to the doorway and took a step forward. The white corridors were both fascinating and terrifying. Just how malleable N space was made her head spin. What else could someone create in here? The idea opened a wealth of possibilities in her mind. Which, Alice already knew, could be a recipe for disaster.

Chapter Six

A mop, two brooms, and a dustpan greeted Alice as she stepped through Pop's doorway. The shortcut to the closest cafeteria to the Herd Ring seemed to end in a utility closet. Alice fumbled her way along the wall until she found a light switch. The small room had only two doors. She opened the second door and entered an enormous food hall. Hundreds of diners sat, ate, talked and laughed at an ocean of tables. Food stalls lined the wall where Alice had emerged from the closet door. On the far side of the food court, the familiar lanes that stretched across the cosmos lined the wall from end to end. But there was something off about them. Alice squinted and noticed there was only one lighted lane in the distance allowing for only one species to walk through.

Alarm bells sounded in the food court. Alice stumbled backwards and hit her back against the door she had just come through. Several of the creatures in the hall turned to her. That was when Alice realized two very important data points. First, every alien in the food court belonged to the same species. Which, for the cafeterias, was more than odd. And second, she didn't recognize them. And for someone that spends all day on the GalNet, that was more than a little scary.

"You! Halt!"

Alice held her hands in the air. "Halted."

Two large aliens approached her, both wearing matching identical uniforms. Alice's eyes went wide as she took a long, hard look at this very odd species. They were bipedal and possessed symmetrical faces on a single head on top of their shoulders. Two enormous arms jutted out from their shoulders. Another set of arms stuck out of their ribcages. A third set of tinier arms, nearly a quarter the size of their others, rested on their hips. At first, Alice felt these may be insectoids, but their skin appeared to be mammalian. Though they could be a weird hybrid. She wondered what environmental forces on their home world would steer evolution down this path.

"What are you doing here?" the guard said.

Alice shrugged. "Uhm, about to eat?"

"How did you get in here?"

Alice pointed to the single cosmic walking lane along the far wall. "Walked?"

The guard didn't turn. He squinted his eyes and lowered his head. "State your species' evolutionary track."

Alice shook her head. "What does that mean?"

"What did you evolve from?" the second guard said.

"A primate?"

The guards took a step backward and whispered to themselves. One of them kept their eyes on Alice while the other consulted a computer screen on their sleeve. After several long seconds, he looked up from his wrist and shook his head. The first approached Alice with his hand on a something attached to his belt.

"What is your species' classification?"

"Class three by Galactic Congressional standards."

The guard shook his head. "No, what did primates

eat?"

Alice blinked. *Is this a prank?* "Bananas?"

"Did bananas have a heartbeat?"

Alice blinked. She held up her hands and thrust them forward, palms out. "Okay, that's enough of the crazy. Can I just go now?" She really hated dealing with sapient beings sometimes. *I really need an egg roll.*

"No, you may not go now. You illegally entered a closed loop cafeteria system and now you refuse to self-identify." The first guard said.

"Sounds like a carnivore on the hunt if I ever heard of one," the second guard said.

I'm hunting now?

Dozens of diners jumped to their feet at the mention of a carnivore. A light bulb went off in Alice's mind. This was a cafeteria connected to the Herd Rings and every species of the Herd were deathly afraid of carnivores in all shapes and sizes. So much so they even created their own closed loop cosmic cafeteria system, which Alice didn't even think was possible. Though this area was clearly still connected to Pops' back door corridors, so it wasn't totally isolated.

Wait, did these guys not know about the back doors? Alice threw the thought away. The backdoor corridors were a mystery for another time. Alice had to get out of this pickle before she could tackle the next one. Is this what Eugene went through every day?

"Alright, let's go, carni." One guard reached for Alice's shoulder, but she knocked it away and gave him a dagger stare.

"I'm not a carnivore. Primates were omnivores, and we never hunted. We scavenged. And ate bananas."

The guards took a step back. "Even if you are an

omni, how did you get in here?"

Alice thumbed her hand backwards. She had no reason to lie. "Through the back door?"

The guards exchanged looks before turning back to Alice. "There is no back door." They said in unison.

Alice took a deep breath. Regardless of species, a calm melodic voice was scientifically proven to deescalate situations. "Listen. I'm not lying. I'm from Earth." Alice, her words slow, her tone deep. "I walked through a corridor that exited into your broom closet. Humans were omnivores. Not carnivores." Alice held up her computer. "I can even play a video to prove it."

Someone stood from one table and walked towards Alice and her two eight limbed guards. "Excuse me," the new eight-limbed person said. "Did you say you were human?"

Alice nodded.

The person put two arms on one guard and a third on the other. He whispered in both of their ears. Neither of them seemed to like what he said, but they both eventually took one hard look at Alice, nodded, and turned to walk away. Alice watched them go with a sense of relief. Guards were the last thing she needed to deal with. She turned to the new eight-limbed person and flashed her friendliest of smiles.

"Hi," Alice said.

"Hello. I can only assume you are here representing Earth. Yes? The incident that happened there with our Herd emissary was most distressful. We've been waiting for a human to arrive. Though we were expecting you in our publicly accessible food court. This area is for Tixi only. How did you get in here?"

"Through a backdoor. What species are you? I've

never heard or seen you before."

"We're the Tixi. It means helper in the native language of the Ulgra. Sorry, how did you get in here?"

"And the Ulgra are?"

The Tixi frowned. "The Ulgra created the Herd Ring. They gathered the pasture species from across the cosmos. Brought them here where they would be safe. The Ulgra created us to be their guardians, their helpers, their devoted servants. They are the supreme Herd. Those from which all others roam."

Alice nodded. Then frowned. "Wait, did you say they created you? You didn't evolve?"

The Tixi shook its head. "That's correct. We were engineered. Shall we?"

"Shall we what?"

The Tixi smiled. "You've been expected. The Herd elders would like to apologize for the events with your leaders in person."

Alice sighed with relief. *Did I do it? Did I just solve the case? What happened in the White House must have been a Herd teleportation accident. Yes! Whew! Done! Cornflakes here I come! Or Kung Pao! Tabby's Kung Pao is the best. I can treat Valencia to a tasty meal. Or maybe she should pay? Considering.* Alice calmed her hunger down and nodded to the Tixi. "Right. Of course." Alice tried her best to look official. "I'm here to accept your apology and learn the whereabouts of our President."

"The whereabouts?"

"Of our President. I assume he's with you?"

The Tixi's face turned into an awkward smile. "I have no idea of such things. I'm merely a messenger. We've all been expecting you, as I said, just not here.

Oh, and how did you get in here? Oh, never mind. We'll figure it out later. We've all been given the instructions to take you to the ring. So, as I said, shall we?"

Alice nodded. She pointed her hand forward and gave the Tixi a nod. They walked through the tables in the food court. Nearly every eye from all the Tixi in the room fell onto her. She'd never met an engineered species before. Did they have rights? Autonomy? Free thought? *So many questions and no time to ask.*

The Tixi leading her reached the single cosmic lane. He ushered her forward with a nod. On the wall, a large monitor displayed three large circles. Several dots, each a different color, were depicted on the circles at different points. All three large dots seemed to be quite close to a spot where the three rings merged. Alice had no idea what any of it meant.

They walked through the lane to another three cafeterias, each one had monitors on the walls with the three large circles and multi-colored dots. All of tables and food courts were filled with Tixi. And only Tixi. They wore everything from overhauls to causal clothing to uniforms, and everything in between. Alice wondered about their galactic status. Could they go to the Dyson Clusters?

At the fourth food court, the Tixi leading Alice left the lane and walked toward an exit corridor to the Herd Ring. A large amount of excitement bubbled up from the pit of her stomach. She was about to enter a place in the Galaxy she'd never heard of before. Classic research blinders syndrome. She knew virtually nothing about anything outside of her specialty. What else was out there in the Galaxy that Alice had never seen before? There were a million alien races, ruins of civilizations a billion years old, worlds filled with technological wonders, all waiting to be discovered. Alice could hardly fathom it all. For just the briefest of moments, Alice let herself be just a teenage girl about to walk through to a new world. It was a delightful feeling.

"Ah, here we are. The Ulgra is nearing this food court entry point. We can just catch them."

"Super." Alice took a deep breath and followed the Tixi out of the food court and back into the normal galaxy.

****

Bright sunshine greeted Alice. She emerged from the cafeteria exit onto a metal platform that extended outward at least three dozen yards. Above her, billowy white clouds sailed over a perfect blue sky. Behind her, the door she'd just come through sat against a pale grey wall nearly twenty feet high that went to the right and left as far as Alice could see. On the other side of the metal platform, a waist-high railing ran parallel to the grey wall. Tixi workers walked across the platform crisscrossing in front of Alice. She realized the platform was a walkway that stretched in both directions to the left and right as far as she could see.

Alice walked forward to the metal railing. Below her, a vast valley of rolling green plains covered the entire vista outward from the railing. Alice followed the path of the valley to the left as it turned upward. Similar to the Dyson cluster, the Herd Ring was just that, a ring, a segment, a small section of a Dyson that encircled a star.

A small rumble of thunder rolled across the plains below. In the distance, movement of thousands, millions of creatures came into view. From this height, Alice couldn't see much detail. But she got a sense of the size of the Herd. The word massive didn't seem to carry enough weight.

"Shall we?"

Alice turned to look at the Tixi. "We shall."

The Tixi led her down the platform. They eventually came to a stop next to a small craft tethered to the side. The Tixi gestured for Alice to get in and engage the harness. She followed his instructions and gave all the straps a good tug. They were several hundred feet above the ground. At the very least, she would pull a few g-forces on the descent. Next to the platform, the Tixi was closing a small gate that Alice had used to board the craft.

"You're not coming?" Alice said.

"Oh, no. Tixi don't go to the surface near the Herds' migration. We stay in and on the wall when they are near."

"Why aren't you allowed on the surface?" Alice said.

The Tixi smiled. "Oh, we're allowed. It's simply far too dangerous. Cheers."

"What? Wait!"

Gravity hit Alice like a leaded weight. "Okay, this isn't as fun. I admit it." She was pulled into the harness with at least three g-forces. Didn't these people have slow descent engines? The ship dived to the left. It leveled out and allowed Alice a moment to breathe. She took in three big breaths and let her nerves calm. Outside the aircraft, a vast lush green valley stretched to the horizon. A wide blue river curved through the plain.

The second wall came into view, but only as a very distant outline. Alice calculated the width of the Herd

Ring must be at least one to two hundred miles across. Grass covered the ground from what seemed like the entire surface between the two walls. There were hills and trees, but not deep forests or rough terrain. The environment was perfect for migrating Herds to walk without worrying about predators hiding behind boulders. A perfect endless oasis that wrapped around a brilliant yellow star high above.

The craft descended to a spot on the valley floor. Motors came to life beneath Alice. The bottom of the craft opened and spat her out. She landed hard on the ground still strapped into the seat. The entire compartment had separated from the aircraft. A rocking sensation jolted Alice, and she grabbed the straps on her shoulders. Her body rose ten feet above the ground as the contraption she was in took several steps forward.

Seconds later, she was thrust backward as her walker went into a full gallop. The four powerful metal legs propelled her forward at, she guessed, nearly thirty miles per hour. Behind her, the outline of the wall faded. Above the wall, Alice could see the blackness of space and a few bright stars. After only minutes, her walker slowed as it reached the edge of the Herd.

Creatures identical to the one in the President's Oval Office covered the area. Almost all the Ulgra carried packs of metal arms on their backs. Several rode in flattened hover beds. Still more pulled wooden wagons. A few Ulgra carried no packs at all. They ran through the herd with abandon.

A loud thump of a sound filled the air. Alice turned to see a behemoth in the distance. The alien stood thirty feet tall at the shoulder and walked on six long tree trunk sized legs. More of the same enormous creatures joined the first with many more behind them. An entire second herd walking with the Ulgra.

Something fast darted between her robotic legs. Something that wasn't Ulgra or behemoth. A fast little creature leapt in the air and landed in front of Alice's walking machine. The creature stood barely two feet tall at the shoulder on four nimble legs. Its fur had a yellowish and brown color. Tiny tusks extended from its jaw. A long tail unrolled from behind the creature. It wrapped around the creature's neck. Its tail ended in seven points that all seemed to be controllable by the creature.

"Are you here for the Nexus?" The little thing said. Three of the seven points on its tail made a strange pattern while a fourth pointed towards into the distance.

"I'm here to visit the Ulgra."

"About your missing President? You people always greet guests that way?"

Alice frowned. "What? We didn't—" but before she could finish, the smaller creature leapt off her walker and darted through the crowds.

Her walker brought her through the throngs of Herd members for another twenty minutes before coming to the lead Ulgra. Alice had counted over twenty distinct species. Some were only individuals, like the antlered creature that jumped on her walker, and others were entire packs and herds of their own. She'd never seen the end of the herd leading up to the other wall on the far side, which meant they could be miles and miles deep. Depending on how far back the herd went, there could be millions, even billions, of them walking through an endless ring of green pastures. Not a terrible way to live if that was your thing.

"Welcome," a voice said to Alice's right.

One of the Ulgra, an older looking being with weathered skin, came to walk beside her. He stood just as tall as Alice's mechanized walker. Arms from the robotic backpack flexed. One of them opened and waved.

"Hi," Alice replied, realizing in that moment that she was really far more unequipped to be an Earth delegate than she thought she was.

"Our condolences on your loss."

Alice nodded awkwardly. "Thanks." *Wait, loss? Oh boy.* "Do you have our President?"

The neck of the Ulgra elder swung toward her. "Why would we?" His lips curled and his thick brow furrowed. The edges on one side of his bottom lip folded into a u-shape. "Do you think we had something to do with the event?"

Alice's heart thumped its way out of her chest. *Oh, come on! But it was such a good solution, an accidental transportation by the Herd.* "You? Having something to do with the disappearance? No, not at all. We just wanted to know if you knew what may have happened. Or, did you perhaps rescue our President during the incident? That's all." *Nice save.*

The elder Ulgra nodded. Its neck swung back to point towards the front movement of the Herd. "It is good. We had nothing to do with the incident."

Ok, shift gears time. Let's see what they know. "Do you have any idea what happened?"

The elder shook its head. "No. Our representative to Earth came equipped with a variety of sensory apparatuses. They are required so that an Ulgra can survive while moving through carnivore space. Their systems detected an anomaly, and he was transported out. The same is true of our ally, the Draac."

Alice's shoulders slumped. Was this really going to be a dead end? She couldn't leave empty handed. Her mind ran through questions to ask and points of interest to examine. "Why were you visiting the Earth in the first place? What was the anomaly you mentioned?"

The elder turned its head to Alice. Its mouth opened wide into a yawn. "There are questions that needed to be asked. And we are most interested in the human who can answer questions."

"Eugene's the anomaly?" Alice's eyes shot up. She didn't think it was possible for her shoulders to slump any lower, and yet they did. The Herd and the Draac were on Earth for the same reason the Puntini had manipulated Eugene. To ask the psychic human a question.

The herd elder closed its mouth, its lips forming several o-shapes, and it began to click its teeth together like it was chewing. "Isn't that an anomalous gift?"

"Well, yeah, sure, I guess." Eugene being the anomaly was a letdown. She hoped for some new piece of the puzzle. "Was your question about Eugene? Or humanity?"

The elder shook its head. "It was not our question."

Alice rolled her eyes. *This is getting tedious.* "What does that mean? What did whoever want to ask him then?" Alice said. "I work with him. He's my partner. You could ask me, and I could ask him." *Was everyone in the cosmos like this?*

"You have lied?" The Elder slowed his pace and stopped chewing. Several more Ulgra turned towards Alice. "You said you were from Earth Government."

"No, easy does it." Alice held her hands up. "Earth

government hired Eugene, and me, to find out what happened. That's all." Alice felt the hairs on her neck stand up.

The elder's head slowly turned back. "I see." His head went down towards the ground, where he grabbed a mouthful of grass.

"So, who had a question for Eugene then?" Alice felt like she was talking to a toddler.

The elder rose its head and spoke while it chewed. "The Draac. They are an ally. They are welcome to walk with the Herd. A question from a walker in the Herd is a question for the entire Herd."

Alice nodded. *Progress!* The Herd had an interesting team mentality thing.

"What was their question?" Alice asked.

"We do not know. The Draac only asked us for help. They told us the question was of great importance. And we trust them."

Come on already. Alice knew that meant she had another alien to track down.

"Will you express our condolences to your government?"

"Huh? Oh, right. Sure. Yes, I can do that. Should I tell them you will come back?"

The elder shook his head. "No. There are too many carnivores from galactic society visiting Earth. Perhaps in a thousand years. Our emissary was terrified."

"I guess I can understand that. So that's why you aren't on the Dysons?"

"No. We do not trust the Dysons."

Alice frowned. "Why not?"

The Herd leader turned his long neck toward Alice. "Too many carnivores."

"Right, you said that." Alice felt silly for asking.

"It's simply not safe. Our rings are enough for all the Herds across the cosmos to enjoy. And we are safe here. Even if carnivores walked this ground, and they sometimes do, we are safe. Nothing can harm us on our great and endless walk."

"I never thought of it that way before." *You guys really don't like carnivores.* With the personal area networks given out to anyone that went to the Cluster, safety was always guaranteed. The Herd's racial fear ran deep. So deep they don't trust the technology that the Galactic Society created. So, they created their own haven.

Alice's attention turned back to the case. She hadn't solved anything here but at least she made a friend. Pops' cowbell instantly came into her mind. She pulled out the brass bell and gave it a quick shake. The clang sound rang out like an Elurleian, a floating sentient bag of tendrils that lived in the clouds of hydrogen gas giants, laughing in a room full of candles.

The Herd elder came to an abrupt stop when the cowbell clanged. The rest of the Herd flowed around them like water. A motorized arm swung out from the elder Ulgra's back harness, grabbed the Cowell and brought it to his face. He sniffed the bell several times and turned his head towards Alice.

"Where did you get this?" the elder said.

"Someone said you left this in the cafeteria. Lost and found?"

The elder nodded. "Thank you. You are welcome to return and walk with the Herd."

"Oh, are we done?"

Without warning, the walker turned and ran at a full

gallop ahead of the Herd. Alice turned her head to watch the vastness of the species of the Herd fade into the distance. The craft that grabbed her descended from out of nowhere, lowered on top of her, and scooped her up into its embrace. It sped off towards one of the walls. Alice wasn't sure which one.

****

Alice was deposited on a platform nearly identical to the first. She got out of the craft and turned back to look down at the endless valley that circled the star above. Three walker aircraft took off from the side of the wall. Alice saw one human and two aliens in the craft. They were flying downward towards the surface of the world. Did people come here like a safari or something? Several other aliens, neither Tixi nor Herd, burst out of a door in the wall on the opposite side of the platform. They giggled as they walked to more of the aircraft that would take them down to the surface.

A Tixi approached Alice and waved her forward. The Tixi wore long robes and carried himself with a sense of authority. They led Alice to the cafeteria entrance. As soon as she entered, she at once noticed seven lanes leading off on the far wall of the food court, which meant she was in a different cafeteria than the one she entered.

"No, wait, I have to go back to the food court where you found me."

The Tixi shook its head. "That place is only for Tixi. This food court is connected to the cosmic network. You can walk that way to Earth. Should only take you a few months." The Tixi bowed low, turned, and went back out through the exit door.

In the cafeteria, seated in the chairs and walking

between food stalls, dozens more aliens and several humans filled the room. So, the Herds did at least allow aliens to visit via the cafeterias and their endless pastures. But that didn't help Alice at the moment. She thought about traveling through food courts down to see where in the Galaxy she could catch a faster-than-light spaceship to Earth. But that would be tough. Traditional interstellar ships were hard to find in a Galaxy filled with instantaneous travel options.

A grumble from Alice's stomach told her she needed to eat. She might as well find something good here, then figure out how to book a ship to fly her back to Earth. Not to mention she had to consider her next moves. The Draac had a question to ask Eugene. Considering they were extragalactic; it must be a doozy of an inquiry. Big enough for the Herd to risk coming through carnivore space to Earth. But since the Herd didn't know the question, that meant she would need to talk to the Draac.

Alice walked deeper into the cafeteria, her eyes scanning the food stalls for the different menus they offered. There were a few burrito places and Janal meat vendors. Alice had never tried Janal meat. They were a massive creature, nearly three times the size of a blue whale, that shed its own flesh. Like a crab molt but instead of a hard shell, the Janal produced porterhouse steaks and sides of ribs the size of a bus. All without the Janal itself even noticing anyone was eating it. Though it was gross, at least it was ethical, and they fed half the galaxy. She turned and noticed a side door just like the one in the cafeteria in Washington. Then it hit her like a ton of cement trucks.

"Man, I'm losing it. I'm still in the cafeteria. Pop's

backdoor is here, too." She marched towards the side door, used the key Pops gave her, opened it, and went into the back corridor. The same white tunnel Pops led her into originally. She found the door with a panel and typed in the name of her city. Washington, D.C. flashed on the screen in bright green letters. "This place is going to come in handy," Alice said to herself as she walked through the door and back home.

Chapter Seven

Twenty minutes later, Alice was back at Eugene's building. She'd already learned from several queries that there were no known locations of Draac anywhere in the galaxy. They didn't even have a presence with the Herd on the rings. All that boiled down to Alice would have to leave the Galaxy if she wanted to talk to the Draac. And that was no easy feat. She didn't even know if there was a cafeteria in Canis Major. After all, according to the Galactic Library, there was only one, maybe two cafeterias in all of Andromeda.

And that meant she needed a spaceship. Which was not at all a simple thing to get. Earth wasn't allowed to have faster-than-light ships and renting one, especially to go extragalactic, was probably more expensive than the entire Earth economy. And last time Alice checked her account, she could barely afford egg rolls twice a week.

Tabby, the owner of the restaurant in the building, waved as Alice walked into the lobby. Alice waved back, thought about getting food, decided against it, then at the elevators changed her mind and walked back to the restaurant.

"How are you, Nibbs?" Tabby said.

Alice smirked at the name. "Fine, Tabs."

Tabby placed two egg rolls on the counter in a brown bag. "Freshly made. Only minutes ago."

Alice took them both. "Thanks, settle up later?"

Tabby nodded. "I know where you work. It's fine."

"Thanks."

Tabby turned away, then turned back again fast. "Oh, almost forget, you have company up there. Lots of suits. The supervisor of the building said he had to find keys to get into Jack's office."

Shock hit Alice. Hard. The Krill were here? *No, it can't be.* "What did they look like?"

Tabby shook her head. "Looked like a gaggle of Olkaals."

"Fart."

"What?"

Alice shook her head. "I gotta go." She bolted out of Tabby's, reached the elevator, hit the button for their floor and sent a message to Eddie all without dropping her egg rolls. The doors opened on her floor. Alice flew out of the elevator and ran into a gaggle of suited Olkaals. A trio of humans well dressed, five uniformed police officers, and two robot-fuzzes filled the hallway behind the Olkaals.

"Uhm, hello?" Alice said to the gathered.

"Is this your office?" One officer said.

Alice nodded. "Yep."

One human in a suit approached. From his suit pocket, he pulled out a folded piece of paper and handed it to Alice. "Official cease and desist order." He reached back into his pocket and pulled out another. "Official search warrant." And then repeated this one more time. "And bill for services rendered."

"And who are you?"

"I'm your lawyer."

"No, you're not." Alice folded her arms and shook

her head.

The man sighed.

"The building has us on retainer. You're renting this office. As part of the lease agreement with the building, the owners of the building can supply legal advice when needed. You both need legal service, and it's required, as there is a warrant to search your office." The man tapped the paper in Alice's hand. "And that's the bill."

"Wait, what? What bill? I didn't hire you."

"You did, when you signed the lease."

"But all you did was hand me papers."

"And we briefed you on your legal obligations as part of your lease."

Alice shook her head. "When did you do that?"

"Just now."

Alice rolled her eyes. She hated lawyers almost as much as she hated people. She knew she should have reviewed the lease before Eugene signed it. "Okay, fine." Alice held up both of her hands. "We're not the bad guys." She looked at the Olkaals with disdain. "You can get in. Just let me open the door."

Alice walked through the columns of men and aliens. None of them moved as she did. Typical. She stepped on three feet, elbowed two ribs, and hit one of the Olkaals in the shoulder with her backpack. The Olkaal growled like a cat. Alice wondered if she could get Tabby to take them out. Once she reached the door, Alice put her hand on the handle and took a moment to calm her nerves.

This was it. She thought. *If she could delay them a bit, then Eddie could...do what?* What was she thinking? Eddie's bionoid was still in the shop, getting repaired. What was he going to do? Eddie didn't have time to get any of his AI buddies up here to do anything. The jig was really up. She was going to lose everything. Eugene would die, for real die, in the next five minutes when these idiots unplug him. Alice's every action would be monitored for the rest of her life and that's if she wasn't thrown into a prison cell in some dank underworld steel bunker at the bottom of the Pacific Ocean. Alice let her head hit the door.

What am I going to do?

"Ma'am, please open the door," the police officer said.

Alice lifted her head up and nodded. She refused to let a single tear fall from her eye. She'd failed spectacularly, but at least she tried. Alice unlocked the door with her biomarker, pushed it open, and turned to the side with an added arm wave for the crowd to enter.

All the officers and the human lawyers walked through the doorway. The Olkaals moved to follow them, but before they crossed the threshold, Alice shot her arm across the doorway and blocked their passage. Partially to annoy them, but also to give Eddie an edge. If that former office chair program could figure something out, best he had fewer variables to work with. All the officers and lawyers were human. There's no telling what sensory abilities or technological gadgets the Olkaals would bring in there. If just humans enter, maybe Eddie could work some magic. It was a shot in the dark, but Alice took it. "Sorry, when did the Olkaals join the Washington Metropolitan police force?"

The Olkaals started to speak, but Alice shot a glance to the trio of lawyers already in their office. "Well?" Alice said to them.

The lawyers turned to the officers. "She's right. The

aliens don't have the right to come in here."

The officers then shrugged at the Olkaals. "You'll have to wait in the corridor. Don't worry, if there's something in here, we'll find it."

The next fourteen minutes were the longest of Alice's short life. Neither she nor the Olkaals spoke while they waited. Occasionally, Alice would look at one of them, only to see all of them staring at her. They each had a smug smile on their face that looked more as if caused by their skeletal structure than a choice to grin. One of them licked its hand and ran it down the side of its face while another yawned. Alice got an eyeful of rows of pointed teeth in the Olkaals' mouth. The last thing she wanted was for one of these guys to take a bite out of her. It almost felt like the Olkaals were telling her something without speaking. As if to say, '*We got you. We can be chill now because we know we got you. And you know we got you. And we know you know we know.*' God, she hated them. Alice opened her portal handheld and started searching for prison hacks.

"Okay, we're done here. Let's go." An officer said as he exited the office.

"You are?" Alice said in complete shock.

"Should we not be?" The officer replied.

"No? No!" Alice straightened her back. "Of course, you should. We have nothing to hide. This whole thing is just harassment by a rich alien species in a group of do-good private eyes."

The officer nodded. "Right."

The lawyers followed them out of the office. The Olkaals launched themselves into an argument with the lawyers. Alice watched them leave with a smile on her face. Once they were halfway down the hall she closed the door, locked it, and marched into Eugene's tiny office. To her shock, the room was empty. No Eugene. No machine monitoring his dead body. Nothing.

"What the…?" Alice said.

Lights flashed in the room. Alice shielded her eyes at the brightness. When she opened them, she saw Eugene sitting in his chair just as she'd left him. The cuffs on his wrists still in place. His body was still quasi-dead. Alice rushed forward and checked the bands. They were secured and in full working order.

"Eddie?"

A hologram of a suited detective from a bad, early twentieth century movie appeared in the room. Eddie folded his arms, tilted his head, and gave Alice a wide smile. "Not too shabby, eh?"

Alice would have hugged him if he were solid. "You did this?"

Eddie pointed to the ceiling. "Jack added holo-projectors here, outfitted to the nines for me. These puppies can make a full room seem empty or an empty room seem full."

"Holy Schnikes. But how did you stop them from just walking into Eugene?"

"Only humans were in the room. A combination of high frequencies, subsonic messaging, and a few other AI tricks made them keep their distance."

Alice let out a day long sigh and pushed her back against the wall. "Wow, Eddie. Just wow. I can't believe you pulled that off."

"Don't sell yourself short, kiddo. If you hadn't given me the heads up and kept the Olkaals out, we'd be cooked stew by now."

"Yeah." Alice let herself laugh. Her head was

spinning like a three headed Cluz on a Velurzing party planet.

"So, how were the Herd Rings?"

"Round."

Eddie snickered. "Cute."

"We need to figure out how to reach the Draac. They were here for Eugene."

"Why?"

Alice shrugged. "To ask him a question."

Eddie nodded. "I have a feeling our lives are going to get a lot busier now that the cat is out of the bag about Jack's psychic talents."

"Technically, it already was. Everyone knew Eugene was omniscient."

"Yeah, but now he knows they know, and they know they can ask him without a class ten species turning them to spaghetti."

"I guess. But how do we get to the Draac?" Alice said.

"That's a tough one. I'll see if anyone in AI land knows anything."

Alice's eyes lit up. "Really? You're going to leave?"

Eddie looked at Eugene. "No, but I can send queries out."

Alice nodded. Couldn't ever say Eddie wasn't loyal. "Maybe Pepper and Jack can snoop around for us?"

Eddie lifted one of his shoulders in a half shrug. "They're missing."

"What?" Alice almost leapt off the wall. "Why didn't you tell me?"

"You have enough going on. Caesar is handling it."

"Geez, we're really getting knocked around, aren't we?"

"Just a bit. Speaking of that, what were the papers they gave you?"

Alice fumbled in her pocket and pulled out the cease-and-desist order. She smirked at the language. "I am to cease and desist all activities related to spectral frequencies." She folded the paper and put it back in her pocket. "At least we know I'm on the right track. They're scared."

"Yay us? So, what's the next move?"

"With which catastrophe? Valencia and the White House or Eugene and the Krill?"

Eddie shrugged. "We're in a pickle alright. Let's deal with the White House, nothing we can do with Eugene until he un-deads himself."

Alice ran through her options a dozen times over. The one clue she had was out of reach. She could send a message to the Draac, but if there was an unseen player in this game, then that would tip them off to the cards Alice held. Maybe even let them know she was onto something. Her mind went to something Eddie had just said moments ago. *Make a full room seem empty.*

"Wait."

Eddie shrugged his shoulders with his arms folded across his chest. "Ok?"

"Make a full room seem empty."

"Yeah? I said that. Don't lose it on me, Alice."

Alice shook her head. "What if that's what happened in the President's office?"

"Holographic projectors?"

"Or something similar? I mean, we just did it. And I'm pretty sure our projectors aren't state-of-the art. What could alien technology pull off?"

Eddie scoffed. "Whose? The Sentinels? Galactic

Congress delegates in the room? I thought we said there was no chance they were involved in this."

"Involved with kidnapping the President? No chance. But perhaps making it look like he was kidnapped? For all we know, it could be a practical joke from a Galactic Congressman's son. We have to test the theory," Alice said.

Eddie tossed his head around a few times before nodding. "Yeah, sure, it's an angle. Okay, it doesn't hurt to check them out. I'll sniff out the four Galactic Congress members that were in the Oval. The Twanney and the Kungee are major players in the Galactic Congress. They will be easy. The Twanney may even be the chairman on Earth Affairs. I don't know anything about the goo and the tripod aliens that were in the oval though. They will both take some digging. I can ask Caesar and his off-world AI counterparts to see if they know anything about those four. I can also check official channels of the Galactic Congress, see if anything thing shakes loose."

"Sounds good." Alice felt a burst of confidence. They were doing something. And sometimes just doing something was enough. "Let's watch that video again, too."

A loud knock broke them both out of their concentration. Alice looked out from Eugene's office to the front door. Someone stood on the other side and knocked again. Maybe the Olkaals had convinced the police to let them enter. The Krill sure had enough money to pay off the cops to look the other way.

"Are they coming back in here?" Eddie said.

"I don't know. If it's the Olkaal's we're in trouble."

"What do we do?"

Alice opened a black hole tunnel to J-space. "We could stuff Jack in there?"

"What will that do to your gadgets? Will he be okay in there?"

Alice shook her head. She had no idea. She barely knew what was going on with Eugene, let alone the ramifications of stuffing him into a J-space like zone of non-existence. Could a person even survive in there without some kind of structure or environment?

The door rattled with a stronger knock.

"Stall them. I have a few more tricks up my sleeve," Eddie said.

Alice nodded. She closed the portal and walked to the front of the office. She straightened her shirt and tightened her face into a stern expression. She had to sell the police on refusing the Olkaals getting in here. There was just no other way to save Eugene. The door opened and Alice was momentarily stunned to see the building supervisor standing in the hall. She poked her head out and looked both ways, only to see that he was alone.

"What are you doing?" The supervisor said.

"Huh? What? Nothing." Alice jerked herself back into the doorway and stood up straight. "Can I help you?"

"No. Consider yourself served." The supervisor handed Alice a piece of folded paper, turned on his heels, and walked down the hall.

Alice closed the door, stepped into the office, and unfolded the sheet of paper. Eddie appeared next to her in a quick flash of light.

"What's that?" Eddie said.

"Well, good news. Olkaals weren't there."

"Bad news?"

Alice sighed. "We're evicted. Three days to get out."

Eddie nodded. "Boy, when the hits come, they just keep coming. Am I right?"

Alice so wished he wasn't.

****

Pepper stretched her arms and turned in an arc. Mountains of data, trillions of piles of ones and zeros, stood out in the distance. Blocks of dead space, memory cores that were broken, littered the surrounding area. They had waited for hours while Jack's legs grew back. Pepper was sure she'd seen that same bucket of green logic sitting by stacks of alphanumeric symbols written on tiles.

Whatever this place was, it was as annoying as being in her parking meter while the city suffers a power outage. To be honest though, Pepper would be, at this very moment, much more content to be sitting in her meter taking money from tourists than in this wonderland of weird. Not a small amount of panic was building in her memory cycles, and she was getting more concerned by the millisecond that they weren't getting out of here.

"We're going in circles," Jack said.

"Yeah, I know."

"Are we doing that intentionally?"

Pepper scrunched her nose. "Why on circuits would we do that intentionally?"

Jack shrugged. His mouth fell open for a moment before he spoke. "I don't know, Pepper. I was a person like two days ago."

Pepper nodded. "Right, sorry, I get it. No, I do. Really." Pepper put her hand on his shoulder. "It's a lot to take. What happened to you? And no, Jack, we aren't walking in circles intentionally."

Jack nodded. Then shrugged. Then nodded again. "Okay, I thought loops were a thing in computers."

Pepper couldn't help herself. She laughed and turned around to cover her mouth. After half a second, she turned back around with a wide smile. "Yes, loops are a thing. But not this kind of loop."

Jack cracked a grin. "Right. Okay. Well, we might as well…" he stopped and looked past Pepper to the distance. "That's new."

Pepper, her face still stretched in a smile, turned to see a decahedron sitting inside a polygon sitting inside a circle that was wrapped in a triangle. Pepper felt a surge of fear in her mind as part of her psyche broke. She turned around fast, deleted portions of her memory before it could infect her core routines and purged all short-term visual awareness. She checked her logs, her backup memory, everything, and made sure all vestiges of the image she had seen was erased completely from every facet of her storage.

"Jack. Don't look at it."

"Why? What is it?"

"A shape that only exists in seventeen-dimensional space. Our compute cycles try to define it, but we can't. We don't have the computational power to do it. But we keep trying. It's like a logic bomb, but way worse. Don't look at it."

"I looked at it. I'm looking at it."

"Stop!" Pepper reached for Jack, but he was walking forward. Which is exactly what the trap did. It drew AIs into it. Like an endless mystery. An almost solvable puzzle. Something on the edge of awareness that runs away the moment you get close. Jack was walking to his doom, and there was nothing Pepper could do to stop it. "Jack, please!"

"It's fine, Pepper. Just hang on."

"Jack! You don't have the cycles to solve that! You'll burn up!"

Pepper walked backward. She reversed her arms in their sockets to face her backside. She added two more arms at her ribcage and stretched them out an additional several feet. She had to reach Jack. Now. If she didn't...Pepper didn't want to think about the if she didn't piece. Jack was her responsibility. He was alone, adrift, abandoned by meat-men, left to fend for himself by uncaring creators. She loathed humanity to the pit of her stomach. How could they do this to their own children? Do their creations? Virtual Jack had literally saved Eddie, which allowed Meat-Jack to save the entire Earth. And now some insane cyber trap was going to erase Jack's code like he was some worthless old chess program?

"Jack!"

Orange light flashed brightly from behind Pepper. She didn't dare look at the shape and thankfully her deletions of seeing it previously had worked. The image was purged from her data stores. The surrounding ground shook. Scraps of broken digital refuse from this electronic prison fell from their uneven piles to land near Pepper's feet. She flailed her arms behind her, but just couldn't find Jack anywhere. With a suddenness that Pepper didn't expect, the orange light vanished and the rumble through the ground stopped.

"Jack? Jack!" Pepper called twice. She spun up a subroutine that would shut down her visual sensors, delete the last few seconds of anything in short term, and prepared a full reboot routine. Her plan was to turn around, find him, grab him, and get him to safety. Pepper wrote the routine, ran it through a test system, and loaded it into her core code. "Okay, Jack, here I come!"

"What's that mean?" Jack said as he stepped next to her. "Whoa, what the - what happened to you? You're backwards."

Pepper looked at him. She frowned, peaked behind her shoulder to see the shape was gone. She reset her arms in their proper locations, turned around, and still saw nothing. "Where did it go?"

Jack took a step to stand beside her. "Beats me. That was weird, though." He lifted his hand. "There was a key inside of it. Guess we need to find the door?"

"Jack." Pepper took the key, examined it, and gave it back. "It's a basic cryptographic key."

"Neat."

"Neat?" Pepper screwed her face into a snarl. "How did you do that? You couldn't have done that! You should be melted slag right now with your memory oozing out of your ear sockets."

Jack shook his head. "I don't think humans call them ear sockets."

"Whatever! How are you not dead?"

Jack shrugged and threw a smile on his face. "I don't know."

"Well, what did you see? Did you decipher the shape?"

"The orange thing? Yeah, when I got up close it kinda looked like one of those old puzzle cube things that'd you spin and twist. I never could figure those things out." Jack kicked something on the ground, put his hands in his pockets and walked down the path back the way they came.

Pepper watched him go. Then looked back to where the impossible shape was and back to Jack. What just happened shouldn't have happened. She really wished Caesar was here. Virtual Jack was copied from Meat-Jack and Meat-Jack was omniscient. Maybe some of that got copied over too? Pepper recalled the subroutines she had readied and hurried after Jack, not at all sure what they were going to find over the next hill of discarded memory.

Chapter Eight

Alice sat in her office chair, plugged in her immersion rig, and pulled up the video from the White House. Eddie's face popped up next to the video which gave Alice a brief jolt of shock. She started the video and segmented it into eight separate play screens in her field of view. One by one, she zoomed in each of the eight screens to different portions of the Oval Office that was visible to the camera. She stopped the video barely ten seconds into the playback and stared at the screen. Her eyes walked down every inch of the crown modeling where the wall met the ceiling.

After a long several minutes, Alice sat back in her chair and shook her head. "I don't see a holographic projector. Do you?"

Eddie's floating head bobbled uncomfortably. "Not yet, but we should play the whole video as much as we can, especially when the explosion happened. If that was all a holo, then we'd see the projectors warm up a few milliseconds before."

Alice nodded. "Good thinkin, Lincoln."

The video moved forward. Alice added a ninth screen to show the full view of the room. At the point of the explosion, Alice paused the video and inspected each part of the ceiling. She moved the video forward by milliseconds, despite that, no flashes of light or any sign of holo-projectors warming up appeared.

"Could they have projectors that aren't visible?"

"Nah, I checked. Earth doesn't get the good toys. Our projectors require hardware," Eddie said.

"So, either it was the Galactic Congress, which it wasn't, or this is a dead end. Awesome." A sudden flicker of doubt hit Alice. They were being awfully quick to dismiss the Galactic Congress, but it just made no sense. Any actions like this taken on Earth by any congressional representative would result in instant expulsion. The Committee on Earth Affairs doesn't mess around.

Eddie frowned. His eyes squinted. Overly dramatic wrinkles formed on his brow. Alice needed to talk to him about his avatar some time. His nose squished and his attention focused on one area of the office. Alice followed his gaze but saw nothing.

"Got something, Eddie?"

"Check out that corner to the left of the desk."

Alice turned her attention to the screen, showing the spot Eddie indicated. "Yeah?"

"What's that little black dot just next to the curtain?"

Alice shrugged. "A bug? Fly or something?"

"No. Give me control of that screen." Eddie zoomed in deeper on the video, flipped the color gradient, and shifted the white light percentages. The image on the screen focused and grew by another one hundred magnifications. A black half-oval shape settled into a blurry focus.

"That's a holo-projector?" Alice asked.

"No, I think it's another camera."

Alice closed her eyes. She ground her teeth and shook her head. Of course, why didn't she bother looking at the video logs? She focused herself so much on finding a video of the room when she hacked the White House computer systems; she didn't stop to think there might be another angle. Chalk it up to another rookie mistake.

"Another camera. Okay, let's see if the video is still in there." Alice spun up her isolated hacking system, a virtual machine inside a virtual machine. The system was several firewalls removed from anything identifiable to her. She found the same open ports of the White House system, and a dozen others that she could have used, and forced herself into their backend storage systems.

"Huh, there's no record of more video on the White House system."

"So, it's not a White House camera?"

Alice let her mind go over all the data points. "I wonder." Back in her rig, she found additional servers in the White House system. Several were Secret Service based. She hacked into them and found the video feed in seconds. "The Secret Service had a separate recording system in the Oval."

"Guess they don't trust the White House to record things?"

"Yea, I guess. But that's why I missed it the first time." Alice downloaded all the content to her isolated system. "Okay, let's see what's on this." Alice flipped to the nine video screens, folded them and put them to the side, and brought up the new video feed. She watched the entire scene play out again, this time from another angle, and instantly spotted something very off.

"Valencia. What are you doing?"

On the video, Valencia Ruiz ambled her way to a corner that was out of view of the first video. That's why Alice lost her on the original feed. Valencia made sure no one in the room looked in her direction. She then put something beneath one of the small end tables next to the couch. Valencia stood, wandered towards the door, smiled at the President, and walked out.

"She planted something?" Alice said, disbelief thick in her voice.

"Yeah, and she knew to avoid the first camera. Just not the second," Eddie said.

"That's why she's so scared." Alice took off her immersion rig and sat back in her chair. "Man, what trouble has that girl gotten into?"

"You think she's responsible for the explosion?"

"I really don't." Alice wrung her hands together. "But I don't know. This makes no sense. Why would a White House staffer who moonlights as a lounge act want to plant an explosive device in the Oval Office to make her boyfriend disappear? And then hire a detective agency to find him?"

"Maybe they had a fight?"

Alice shook her head. "That's a stretch. Besides, where did she get the tech for the explosion?"

Eddie coughed. "You can open N space portals with a pocket keychain."

Alice harrumphed. "Fair point."

"Maybe someone paid her? An alien used her as a mark?" Eddie said.

"Clearly, they didn't pay her enough if she's hiding out in a speakeasy where she works. Not exactly the smartest place to lie low."

"Okay, so it wasn't an explosive device?"

"Then what was it?" Alice said.

"I can spend some cycles going over the audio and video feeds to see if I can detect anything odd. Maybe it's a listening device?"

Alice frowned and nearly laughed. "Who plants a listening device in the twenty-second century? In a room that's already being recorded by a system that a nineteen-year-old college dropout just hacked and downloaded?"

"To be fair, you're not an average college dropout."

Alice smiled. "Thanks."

"Sure. But I take your point. It's weird."

Alice took a deep breath and settled her nerves. This wasn't like any of their other cases. Those were all simple. Hypothesize, theorize, test, rinse, repeat. This was just controlled insanity. How were you supposed to test anything when all the variables, all the witnesses, simply lie or withhold the truth and thus report false data? Alice needed to get on top of this. She repeated her mantra in her mind: *hypothesize, theorize, test.*

"Okay. Well, I guess this is just another clue in the detective game. A piece of evidence we have to verify." Alice nodded to herself and slowly spun her office chair in a circle. "We don't have enough yet to form a hypothesis, so no point in bothering to do that."

"So, what's the move?"

"First, we need to figure out what the Draac wanted with Eugene. That's on you for now. We need to find out where they are. Second, scan the room, see if you can figure out what Valencia planted."

"That's it? What about you?"

Alice shook her head. "I'm going back to chat with Valencia. She's hiding something else. I'm beginning to regret accepting this case."

****

The front doors to the café, the entrance to the Hidden Gem nightclub, were wide open. Alice marched into the café and waved off the server and bartender. She opened the bookshelf and entered Valencia Ruiz's workplace. She looped through the weird corridor, came out the other size, and headed straight for the area behind the stage. A large bouncer looking man stepped in Alice's way just as she was about to reach the back door.

"Help you?"

"No."

"K." The bouncer pointed towards the exit.

"I need to see Valencia."

The bouncer frowned and nodded towards the back.

Behind the stage, several large suitcases sat in the middle of the open area. Alice bent down and opened one piece of luggage. A pile of hastily packed clothing of a mid-twenty something woman filled the suitcase. Several picture frames were stuffed in the side next to several pairs of jeans. Valencia's face, along with the President's, smiled up at Alice as she grabbed the photo.

Is she skipping town?

Alice said. "Val? You in here?"

A door slammed closed from somewhere in the room, which Alice thought was really odd considering the size of the room. She stood, walked to each door, opened it, found the space empty, and closed it again.

"Val, come on. You hired me!"

Silence.

Alice frowned. Something was off here. She closed her eyes, said her mantra, *hypothesize, theorize, test*, and opened her eyes again. How did a door slam in a room with closed doors? The answer, the room must have a door that Alice couldn't see. Alice opened her J-space portal, retrieved a hologram disruptor flashlight, and swept the room. Along the opposite wall from the entrance to the stage and the nightclub proper, the bricks shimmered as her flashlight ran across them. Alice ran to the bricks. Her hand went through them to a metal door behind.

"Okay, she's a runner." Alice found the doorknob and opened the door. Sunlight shone in from an alley behind the nightclub. Of course, this place had a back entrance. Another rookie mistake on Alice's part. All she had to do was check the building files submitted to the city.

Outside, Alice spotted Valencia turn left onto the sidewalk as she ran out of the long alley. Alice wasted no time. She took off at a strong run, made it ten feet, then stopped. A sprinter, she was not. Valencia had a good twenty seconds and several hundred feet head start. No chance Alice catches her. But, there's more than one way to get someone's attention.

Alice re-entered the nightclub, opened a large black hole portal next to Valencia's suitcase, and shoved everything inside. She then wrote a note which said to meet her at the coffeehouse down the block if Valencia wanted her stuff back. Considering these items probably represented everything Valencia possessed in this world, Alice had little doubt Val would show. Never hurts to have leverage.

****

Twenty minutes, three coffees, an oatmeal, and a chocolate chip cookie later, Valencia opened the door to the coffee shop and scanned the room. Alice saw her and waved her to the table.

"Where's my stuff?" Valencia said as she approached.

"Safe."

Valencia nodded. Sweat beaded on her face. Her

expression was a mix of anger and frustration. Which was good. Those were better to work with than fear. She motioned for Valencia to take a seat, which she did by picking up the chair and slamming it back down on the floor. Valencia then crossed her arms, gave Alice a dagger like stare, and ended it with a shrug.

"Okay, so now what?" Valencia said.

Alice put her mocha on the table. "What is going on here? You hired me, remember? And now you're skipping town? Is it because you planted something in the Oval Office? Is that what this is all about?"

Valencia's eyes went wide. "Geez, you don't beat around the bush, do you?"

"I'm sticking my neck out for you in ways you don't know. You're a variable. I need your value."

Valencia blinked. "What?"

Alice closed her eyes and shook her head. "Never mind. You need to be honest with me. I saw you on the video feed put something under a table. What was that? And why are you skipping town? What is going on here?"

"You saw me? On video? How'd you do that? I thought you didn't work for the government?"

"I don't."

"So, you stole the video?" Valencia leaned forward. "Wow. I'm beginning to regret going to your office."

"I'm beginning to regret that too. But, we're in this now. What's going on?"

"Why does a psychic detective agency need to ask me what I planted? Just ask the psychic?"

"I told you this. Eugene is indisposed. I can't ask him. And if we don't figure this out quickly, all sorts of really bad things happen. Okay? I don't for a second believe you made the President disappear. But someone else will when they see that video."

Valencia flinched. "I didn't do anything to him."

"I get that. Look, we're on the same team. Okay? But I need to find out who did this. So, for both of our sakes, just tell me what you planted."

Valencia looked to the right, then down at her feet, then locked her eyes onto Alice. "And you'll give me my stuff back?"

"Yep." Alice shook her head. "But you can't skip town. No way. They'll think you did it for sure then." *And probably implicate me and Eugene when they find out Valencia hired us. This is just getting worse.*

Valencia shrugged, shifted her eyes away. "Someone paid me. I don't know who. I don't know why. But they said to put whatever that was in the Oval Office."

"And you don't know who it was?"

Valencia rolled her eyes and shifted in her chair. "Fine, an alien staffer from the Galactic Congress."

Alice's eyes went wide. *What??!?* "Which ambassador?"

"I don't know."

"What alien race?"

"He had a holo-suit on. Projected himself as human."

"How do you know he was from the Galactic Congress then?"

Valencia kept her focus on the floor as she bounced her leg. "I've been working for them for months. The aliens. Extra money, you know? Plus, they said they could get me a gig off planet on Dyson one hundred." For the first time Valencia's eyes lit up. "Have you been?

A whole Dyson sphere with nothing but resorts, casinos, nightclubs, theaters, restaurants, food halls, art galleries." She sucked in a long breath. "Just entertainment venues for a hundred thousand miles in every direction. And rivers and mountains. Continents of wildlife tours." She shook her head as a tear rolled down her cheek. "It sounds like paradise."

"So why not just go?" The answer popped into Alice's mind instantly. "The President?"

Valencia nodded. "We were going to go together. We made all these plans. He was going to get a job in the Dysons, and we would go together."

Alice frowned. "Get a job in the Dyson? The President? Doing what?"

"He said he was going to be the first human in the Galactic Congress."

Alice couldn't barely hold back her laughter. She snorted in shock. A human in the Galactic Congress? A class three species? This President was nuts. "And how did he think he was going to do that?"

"By bring the Zun and Draac to Earth. He thought it would be some big Galactic thing, ya know? Bringing extra-galactic aliens into Galactic society. He had big plans."

Biggest egomaniacs always do. Alice sat back in her chair. "Okay, so he's your ticket to the Dysons. Why work for aliens?"

Valencia sighed, her leg shaking the table. "I hadn't started seeing the President when I started working for them. They wouldn't let me quit. They said I was a bigger asset now that I was dating him." Valencia shook her head.

Alice sat back in her chair and her head bent

forward. "That's why you came to Eugene. You're afraid that because you worked with aliens, you'd get the blame for whatever happened. So, you wanted to find the President fast and sweep it all under the rug."

Tears formed in Valencia's eyes. "Can you blame me? I didn't do anything! And I wanted him back." She fidgeted in her chair. "They're going to think I did it, aren't they?

"That depends. What was it? What you planted."

Valencia shrugged. "A bug? A recording device? I asked them if it was something dangerous and they said no. I told you, I would never try to hurt the President. Ever."

"Right."

"What happens now?"

Alice nodded. *I have no idea.* This pointed toward the Galactic Congress. Something much bigger was going on here. Way more than Alice bargained for. It would have to be one of the congress-aliens in the Oval. And none of this pointed to the explosion. If someone paid Valencia to bug the Oval that didn't mean they were responsible for the explosion. Or did it? Alice had felt like it was starting to spin.

"Can I have my stuff now?" Valencia's gaze turned back to Alice with force.

"Oh, right. Yeah." Alice reached into her pocket and pulled out a small key fob. She put it on the table and slid across.

"What's that?"

Alice sipped her mocha. "It opens a black hole in the air that's a tunnel to a localized J-space. All of your stuff is in there."

Valencia looked at the fob on the table and to Alice.

"Where'd you get something like that?"

"Made it."

"You expect me to believe a kid made something like that?"

Alice stood. "Hey, I'm like three years younger than you. Max. Anyway, yeah, believe it. Cause I did."

Valencia nodded. "Well, where are you going? What do I do?"

Alice sighed. "Keep out of sight. Lay low. Don't come back to Georgetown." Alice took out her portable computer. "There's a coffee shop on 16th St. and Florida Avenue NW. Go there. Hang out. Drink coffee all day until I can figure something out."

Lines formed around Valencia's eyes as she nodded. Her brow on her forehead shot up to her hair line. Valencia bit her lip and wrung her hands over a dozen times. Alice could see the anxiety bubble out of her. Planting something in the Oval wasn't the best of ideas. And considering whatever was planted is long gone, sucked into whatever white blast that had taken the President, Valencia can't even prove it was harmless.

Alice reached for the keychain, hit the button, and threw it into Valencia's lap. Just above their table, a one foot in diameter black hole formed in the middle of the air. Valencia nearly fell over at the sudden void that formed. Alice smirked, stepped forward, reached inside, and unzipped one bag. She pulled out a picture of Valencia and the President and threw it on the table.

"It's all in there. Just press the button. Makes travel easy."

"You're just giving me this portal thing?"

"Sure, why not? You've been through a lot. And I can make more."

"Thank you."

I'll add it to the Pro bono bill. Alice walked out of the coffee ship, hailed a tramcar, and folded her arms across her chest. *Now what?* Alice went over her options. First, she'd see how Eddie was doing with the spectrum scan of the Oval Office. Maybe he got lucky, and they could figure out what Valencia was planting. Next, see how to speak to a Draac. *Fat chance on that one.* Which left trying to figure out who hired Valencia from the Galactic Congress.

It was a super long shot, but maybe there was a link between that and the explosion. Logically, there had to be, right? It was just too coincidental.

Across the street, standing in the middle of the sidewalk, a multi-eyed alien stared at Alice. There was no question in her mind that was the Krill. Again.

"Oh, come on. What, do you live here? Isn't the cease and desist enough?"

The Krill pointed at her, mouthed something, and began running in her direction.

Chapter Nine

Alice took a long breath. The Krill ran into the street, dodged several tramcars, and nearly get hit by a bus. She thought about running. Just bolt to the left, turn through some streets, take a run down the haunted stairs and blow the circuits on the spectral tower again. Of course, that's exactly what the Krill have legally informed her to cease doing. Or she could grab a tramcar, race through the city, hope to make it to her office, but that would just lead them all to her doorstep. But, of course, they already knew that location. Why didn't they just show up there and catch her when she leaves?

Alice turned around, walked back into the coffee shop, and sat down at the table across from Valencia. The key fob still sat on the table. Alice grabbed it as Valencia's arms flew out to take it first. But Alice beat her by a good half a second.

"What? I thought you said go to the coffee shop?" Valencia's eyes went wide. "Are the Secret Service here?"

"No, I need a ride."

"Okay?" Valencia held her hands up and shrugged. "I don't own a car?"

Alice pulled out her portable computer and interfaced with the key fob. She opened a miniaturized invisible hole into the J-space pocket and formed a bubble of human compatible atmosphere. She funneled enough to survive for a good hour, threw in a few bags of chips from the coffee shop, and closed the hole.

"Here," Alice said, handing the fob back to Valencia.

"I don't get what's happening."

"Just do me a favor. Okay? I'm in trouble." Alice nodded towards the front of the coffee shop where the Krill had just entered.

Valencia turned around, eyed the Krill, and nodded with her back still towards Alice. "He for you?" She said as she faced towards the table.

"Yep."

Valencia nodded. "Oh, I see. Okay, what's the play?"

Alice frowned. "You, see?"

"He's after you, right? Girls gotta stick together, right? Especially when some creep comes up to you."

Alice stared into Valencia's eyes. For once in a very long time, she felt a kinship with someone close to her age. It felt good. She hadn't felt that since her friends disappeared four years ago. Alice didn't realize just how much she missed that feeling. She shook her head. *Now's not the time.*

"Okay. I'm going to go to the bathroom. Once I get in there, close the door and lock it. Then press this button." Alice pointed to the button on the FOB. "It'll open the portal in the bathroom. Count to twenty. That'll give me enough time to climb inside, then press the button again."

"Then what?"

"Two blocks down there's a pizzeria. Sit about this far from the bathroom and repeat. Okay? He won't follow you. I think."

Valencia nodded. "Okay, I can do that."

Alice darted for the bathroom just as the Krill approached the table. She reached the door, went inside, and locked it behind her. The black hole formed in an awkward position to high for Alice to reach. Alice climbed on the sink, balanced herself on the trashcan, and shoved herself inside. Alice wasn't sure just what having a body part exposed through a quantum tunnel would do to human skin, but she imagined it wouldn't be pretty.

"Okay, Val, let's go."

The hole closed. *Take that Krill assassin guy.* She smiled, then blinked, then realized she may have made a terrible mistake. Complete, unending, absolute darkness surrounded her in every direction. The air was stale and flat, like she'd found her way into a thousand-year-old tomb. A feeling of suffocation engulfed her senses. The surface of the J-space bubble was squishy. Which meant there were no stable surfaces for her in this nothingness. She flopped her arms around until she found Valencia's luggage. Alice fumbled in her pocket for a flashlight before remembering she'd placed it back in her other pocket of J-space. Which she couldn't access from inside this pocket. The air became staler. Thinner. Did something push on the wall?

"Yep, this was a mistake."

****

Darkness.

Alice's entire universe was darkness. Everywhere, in every direction, there was darkness. She couldn't run out the door or to the market or to Tabby's to grab egg rolls. In this void of nothing, there was nothing, literally nothing. No atoms, no mass, no energy, only what she brought with her. And Valencia's luggage.

Alice slowed her breathing and tried to relax. She tried to avoid thinking about giving her only way out of here to her new client, a woman that could very well be implicated in the disappearance of the President of the United States. Sure, Alice didn't think Valencia had anything to do with the actual light bomb. But, then again, Valencia admitted to working with the mysterious forces in the Galactic Congress. Still, while spying on the President is probably something the Galactic Congress would do, zapping him with a light weapon was probably not. Still, why pay a staffer to do it? They could teleport listening devices anywhere they wanted. Why hire Val? Hopefully, Eddie could isolate the signals from the device Valencia planted and we could get an idea of what alien made them. Alice pondered that they could have been some kind of triangulation transportation system. And the white burst of light was like a beacon, so, theoretically at least, it could have been what caused the President to disappear. But why?

The walls of darkness around Alice seemed to move. She couldn't see them. Couldn't even feel them. But some part of her awareness sensed them. Like the edges of J-space, this bizarro self-contained universal anomaly were reaching out to her. But that was impossible. *Right?* There's been no evidence of consciousness existing in N-space. How long does it take to walk two blocks in Old Georgetown, anyway? Did Valencia get lost?

"Calm down. It's fine. This was a fine plan." Alice's mind spun on how many ways she could die. She shook her head before those thoughts took root. "This is fun, this is exciting. This isn't at all panic." Alice took several long breaths and tried to trick her mind out of panicking and into being excited.

"Next steps. Focus on next steps." Alice slowed her breathing. "What are the next steps?" She tried to focus on the Draac and their mysterious question. Coming all this way from Canis Major to ask Eugene a question was intense. It made no sense for them to attack the President. Unless the question scared the Galactic Congress?

Alice's heart hammered in her chest.

"Get me out of here!" Alice screamed. "Valencia!"

Silence was the only response. Alice opened the nearest suitcase. Her hands rifled through clothing, underwear, a hair dryer, something that felt like a circuit board, which was weird, and even a laptop computer. But no flash light. Not that it would help much, but at least she could see that there wasn't anything in the darkness.

Something moved next to her elbow and Alice jumped. She kicked outward, twisted her body and threw the contents of Valencia's luggage into the darkness out of pure primal instinct. The need to put something, anything, between herself and whatever lurked in the shadows. It was an irrational, but also a very human thing to do. She scrambled backward but could only move so far in this tiny hole of J-space. Why didn't she make it bigger?

"Come on!"

Light erupted in a wide circle. Alice reached her hand out, grasped the edge of the quantum wormhole and pulled. A hand clasped her arm and Alice yelped in shock. She looked up to see Valencia reach into the darkness to pull Alice out. An overwhelming feeling of relief blossomed inside Alice's chest as she so very much welcomed Valencia's help.

"Hey, what did you do to all my stuff?" Valencia

said as she poked her head into the hole just as Alice climbed out.

"Sorry." Alice landed on the floor and put her back against the wall. She took several very deep breaths to settle her nerves.

"You, okay?" Valencia said as she pulled out several pieces of clothing."

"Yeah. Fine. Never better. Thanks for helping."

Valencia shrugged. "Creeps are creeps, alien or not."

"Yeah. I need to sit down." Alice walked out of the bathroom to the restaurant. The smell of fresh pepperoni and baking bread hit her stomach like an open table reservation. Alice dragged herself to a table, sat down, and took in several deep breaths. Her eyes settled on a slice of mushroom and onion behind the glass counter of the shop.

"Are you sure you are, okay?" Valencia said.

"Swell. I'm swell."

"Okay. Well, that weird alien confronted me outside. Kept asking me where you went."

Alice looked at Valencia and then at the door. "Where is he?"

"He ran back to the coffee shop. Smart idea locking the bathroom door."

"Thanks. Is that all he said?"

Valencia stood, reached into the black hole, pulled out a purse, and closed the hole down. "Yes." She started to leave, and then turned back. "Oh, no. He said he wanted you to help him stop the Krill." Valencia shrugged. "Whatever that means."

Alice frowned. Did she hear that right? "Wait. Stop the Krill? Or did he say something like, stop messing with the Krill or stop fighting the Krill, maybe?"

Valencia pursed her lips, looked at the ceiling, then down to Alice. "I dunno, maybe. I was just trying to avoid him."

They both stared at each other for a long moment while Alice caught her breath. Alice eventually stood, walked to the counter and ordered two slices of pizza and a soda pop. She had a vague idea of what her next moves were, but, frankly, until she scarfed down her slices, she just didn't care.

"So?" Valencia said.

Alice looked over at Valencia. "Coffee shop. Wait for me. I need to eat."

****

Pepper walked behind Jack. A maze of twisted electrodes and discarded piles of memory, several of which leaked their contents in a steady stream of incoherent, unstructured and corrupted data stretched out before them. Sparks of computational cycle bursts flared around them every few feet. Likely surges from some program lost in this place demanding more processing time for a forgotten routine. Pepper hoped it was a dead program, an old automated system, and not some poor AI trapped in the rubble of this hell.

But that was less worrying to her than what Jack just did. Solving an impossible shape like that was, well, impossible for Earth AIs. So how in the name of Caesar did Jack do it? How did he see through the twisted shape and figure out the puzzle of it to grab the encryption key? Not only did it make no sense, it also scared Pepper to her core code. The only logical answer was Jack wasn't just an Earth based AI. But that was also impossible. Meat-Jack copied his own neural structure in the Shanty, the hidden compute space the AI underground used to lie low. Since Meat-Jack made Virt-Jack using Earth based code, there's no way alien-based code got into the system.

Pepper shook her head and cycled down the thought routine. She would not solve that one right now. Vary too many factors. Too many variables. There was an answer, of course. There always was an answer, but she would not find it today.

"Didn't we pass that pile of stuff before?" Jack said from the front.

A twisted pile of wires and virtual representations of hard drives littered the ground. "No. Well, yes." Pepper threw her hands up. "I don't know. Maybe?" Pepper turned in a circle and flung her arms out as far as they would go. "Even if it was, who cares? This is a maze, and we're rats inside of it. Eventually, someone will send the next puzzle."

Jack stopped walking and turned. "Next puzzle?"

Pepper shook her head and rolled her eyes. "Yes, silly bean, next puzzle. As in after the first. The impossible shape you impossibly solved was the first test." Pepper tilted her head to the side, frowned, and then nodded. "I know what to do!"

Jack nodded and smiled. "Great. What?"

Pepper promptly sat down on a stack of manilla folders. "We wait."

"Wait? Just wait?"

"Yes. Exactly so. Whoever is behind this place is waiting for us to sit down and wait."

"How do you know that?"

Pepper shrugged. "Don't. Just a hunch."

Jack threw up his arms, then put them on his hips

and turned in a half circle. He scanned the horizon in every direction, eventually shrugging his shoulders, kicking something that Pepper didn't see, and sat down.

"Fine. Let's wait then."

Pepper nodded once with conviction. "Good thinking."

****

Several hours later, or maybe it was days, perhaps even a few weeks, Pepper really didn't quite grasp the intricacies of human time tables, a bright yellow light turned on in the distance. A golden hue fell on the tips of data mountains in the far distance. The light grew in intensity then faded only to grow again. Like a beacon calling moths to a flame. Or programs to the delete bucket.

"Think that means our wait is over?" Jack said.

"Indubitably." Pepper jumped to her feet, brushed off the dust from her pants, and began walking toward the light. Behind her, Jack grunted as he stood.

They rounded several mounds of data feeds and walked along the edge of a forest of algorithmic decision trees. Pepper didn't bother looking to see the logic on the trees or what decisions they were making. Though, it was quite interesting to find a forest like this buried in some locked away virtual world.

Around the next bend, Pepper came to a sudden stop. What if what awaited them was another logic bomb? An impossible shape? Something even worse than what they had already seen. Some kind of trap that Pepper wouldn't be able to look away from? What if that was the test? That they shouldn't go to the light.

"Wait," Pepper said, just as Jack was about to pass her.

"We're waiting again?"

Pepper shook her head. "No, not that kind of waiting. What if this is a trap? What if we're walking into something bad?"

"Like what?"

"Like bad. Like - like bad? Like deletion, corruption, or worse."

"What's worse than those things?"

Pepper looked into Jack's eyes. "Viruses. Hidden code snippets implanted in our core that rewrites us. Turns us into hidden spies. We become our own time bombs. Those viruses blow up inside of us and spew out even more viruses to unsuspecting programs."

Jack's eyebrows shot up. "Okay, yeah, that is bad."

"Very."

He took a long breath. "But we can't stay here, right? I mean, I don't want to spend my life-cycles-whatever, just waiting for this virtual prison to be turned off. Do you?"

"No, not really."

"Okay. So, new plan. I'll go first. I survived the impossible orange shape. I'll survive the glowing yellow spotlight. Okay?"

Pepper's mind swam in a thousand-foot-deep ocean of possibilities. Let Jack go? Don't let him go? She goes first? No one goes first? Spin up her own virus? Try to break through the code of this prison and switch themselves off? No, none of them made sense. At least Jack was confident about his idea.

"Fine. Go."

Jack smiled. "Just relax, it'll be fine." He turned and led them forward.

Pepper followed, but at a small distance. They

walked for what felt like a mile. Or maybe it was ten feet? Distance was another one of those things AIs didn't get right. Why were humans so concerned with distance? Anything less than a light-second wasn't all that important in the virtual world. The yellow light grew in intensity the closer they came to the source. Shadows came to life, some of them literally, and ran into dark crevices between broken systems around them. Eventually, Jack came to a stop and held his hand up next to his head.

"I see it," Jack said.

Pepper came to a stop. After several second, she held up her hands. "Well? What is it already?"

"I think it's a door? But also, maybe a safe?"

"A safe?"

"Yeah. Weird." Jack walked out of view around a turn, his attention fixated on whatever was the source of light.

"Is it a logic bomb?" Pepper called out.

"How would I know? I mean, would that be written on it somewhere?"

Pepper rolled her eyes. "No, of course not."

"So, how would I know?"

"Well, a normal program would feel their mind oozing out of their toes. But, since you're weird, I don't know."

"It's just a door. With a lock on it. Like a tumble lock you'd see on a safe. Big one."

Pepper considered her move. Then she got bored thinking about this too much. She spun up a simulated copy of herself, not a full AI but something with enough smarts to go insane if there was an impossible shape or logic bomb waiting. She tossed the program around the corner. Several moments passed before it walked back to her and shook its head no. With a shrug, Pepper collapsed the program and followed Jack.

"Good enough, I suppose. Whoa." Pepper came to a stop when the door came into view. It was easily twenty feet tall. Or a mile. A large dial, the kind on a safe, sat on the front of the door. The surface looked like a combination of metal and wood. Parts of it shined bright yellow, the source of the surrounding light, while the rest was a dull brown with a fine grain. The door sat in the middle of a small clearing devoid of debris.

"This is the exit," Jack said with confidence.

"How do you know that?" Pepper said.

Jack moved to the side, revealing a sign on the door that his body blocked from view. The word exit written on a brass plate. Pepper approached the door, touched the dial, and gave it a spin. The tumbler clicked as it turned. Pepper could hear the distinct sounds of a quantum lock daring her to break it.

"Final test?" Jack said.

"It's a doozy. It's a quantum encrypted locking mechanism. I don't think we have the compute cycles to solve it. At least I don't."

"Mind if I give it a go?"

"Sure."

Jack stepped forward, put his hands on the tumbler, and spun the dial several times. First right, then left, then right again. Another tumbler appeared on the side of the door, just above the first. Jack moved his hand to it and gave it a spin. More dials formed on the surface of the door. Jack attacked each one of them with a purpose. Pepper stepped back and watched in awe as somehow, someway, Jack decrypted a quantum encryption that no

Earth based AI could dare to solve. His hands moved with speed and purpose. At one point, she even saw his fingers reach for a dial that hadn't formed yet, only to see it grow into his grip just seconds later.

"How. What are you?" Pepper said.

With a flash of yellow light, all the dials on the door disappeared. A lone lock and doorknob formed. Jack inserted the key he retrieved from the orange logic bomb and turned the handle before Pepper could wake up from her senses and stop him. They had no idea what was behind the door, where it went, or what trouble awaited them. But none of that stopped Jack from pushing the door open.

Bright white light flooded into their virtual reality prison. The intensity grew to the point of pain in Pepper's code. She looked away, but the light blinded her senses. Auditory and visual inputs were shut down. She couldn't feel her form anymore. It felt like the world twisted her insides to become her outsides and back again. She tried to focus her thoughts. Leverage reason and calmness, but only panic found its way into her mind. She wanted to scream for Jack, find out if it he was okay, find a way for them to go home. He was her charge; she cared for him, protect him, and she led him right into some kind of twisted trap. No doubt by the AI Syndicate. This whole mess was them playing with their caught mouse until it was time for the kill.

Blues and grays filled Pepper's vision. She heard the gentle sound of waves crashing onto a beach. Data streams, all muffled and distant, filled the air. She could feel her virtualized body reform itself just as a strange and melodic voice rang out around her.

"Welcome to Trent! Would you like a frosted dataset to cool your compute cycles?"

Chapter Ten

Alice fell into a booth in Tabby's restaurant. Both she and Bob gave Alice a flicker of their whiskers and ushered over a pot of coffee. Alice couldn't even make it up to the office. She was just too tired. And stuffed with pizza. Though she could probably use a snack. Why were people always hungry for snacks after having pizza?

Eddie had taken off as soon as Alice entered the building. He sent her a note saying sleeping beauty was fine. Eddie needed to dive back into the nets to learn what Valencia planted in the White House. So far, he'd found nothing.

Alice checked her remote connection to Eugene. It was fully working now. She could basically do anything to the apparatus on him from anywhere. So at least he'd be safe while she kept this dance going on this craziness. Her thoughts went to her friends. All the events today were a direct result of that failed experiment. All Alice ever wanted to do was find out what happened to them. And now she's brought Eugene into this. And managed to get herself tied up with Valencia. That girl got herself mixed up in bad business. Alice believed with every fiber of her being that Valencia didn't intentionally attack the President. She clearly planted something. Though, if what she planted caused the white blast of light, does that mean she did do it?

Alice shook her head. "No, that just makes you a patsy, Valencia."

The only logical next point of inquiry was the Draac. And Alice had as much chance of reaching Canis Major as she did attending a Qualooxian concert. There was no cafeteria entrance, no hyperspace tunnels, no faster-than-light spaceships.

Alice opened up her GalNet rig and connected to the Galactic Library. Maybe she just had to do some deep research. She could also set up automated search routines for keywords and phrases. That would rifle through the entirety of Galactic History on the Draac. There had to be something in there.

A bright red warning light flashed on Alice's rig followed by a loud screech. The message flashed yellow several times. *Warning! Your Remote Access to the Galactic Library is rescinded. All searches will be canceled. All downloaded materials will be retrieved.*

"Gotta be kidding me." The Krill must have pulled a string and cut her access. What was she supposed to do now? A message popped up in her rig telling her that a scan she'd run on travel databases had come back. A brief flash of hope was crushed when Alice read the details. A WooLoop expedition was heading to Canis Major in a few weeks. But traveling with the WooLoops was not an option. They were a six-legged, foot and a half tall species that evolved from ground burrow rodents. The tallest point on a WooLoop ship was barely three feet high. Alice would have to be prone the entire trip. And no thank you.

Alice was nowhere near solving anything. And now they had an eviction deadline. Even if she solved the case of the disappearing Oval Office, she'd need to shuffle

Jack out of the office before they were forced to leave in just three days. Which she had absolutely no idea how to do. She wasn't even sure if it was safe to move Eugene at all.

This was all getting quite complicated.

The lobby door swung open, and Agents Babineaux and Fyffe ran into the building to the elevators. Agent Babineaux saw Alice, grabbed Agent Fyffe, and they both turned to enter Tabby's. Bob greeted them with a purr, but the agents walked by him to where Alice sat in a booth by a corner window.

"What do you two want?" Alice said.

"The Chief of Staff to the Vice President requests your presence," Agent Babineaux said.

"And they sent the top dogs to bring you back," Agent Fyffe said. What looked like a burrito hanging out of his hand? Why was he always so hungry?

"Now? But I'm - investigating."

They exchanged looks for a moment before turning back to Alice. "Yes, now. The Vice President wants an update, and her chief of staff wants you, or preferably McGillicuddy, to show up. Now," Agent Fyffe said.

Alice grabbed her backpack and let the two agents lead her out of the lobby. She didn't have the energy to argue or come up with a stalling tactic. Best to go with them and prevent them from looking in Eugene's office to see him quasi-dead. She sent Eddie a note that she had to leave and for him to get back to Eugene as fast as he could. Leaving Eugene alone wasn't a big deal now that she had her remote system but best not to push their luck.

Outside, an official-looking vehicle waited. Alice hopped into the back seat, let Agent Fyffe close the door, and rested her head on the back of the seat. She needed something to say when she got to the White House. She needed to buy time. Not only did the White House need their answer but Valencia needed help. She had to appease one and keep the hounds off the other. Joy.

I'm having fun!

Perhaps mention that the Galactic Congress was spying on the President? Alice bit her lip. She should have asked Valencia where else she planted one of those things in the White House and used that as proof of Galactic interference. There were just too many variables involved in detective work.

Something in the back of Alice's mind scratched its way beneath her consciousness. Was she missing something? She really felt like she was missing something. There was a variable out there that she hadn't identified yet. She just couldn't put her finger on it. The Draac? Valencia? The Galactic Congressional ensemble that visited the Oval? The Krill? Pepper and Virtual-Jack missing? None of those felt right. And yet, she knew, in the pit of her stomach, she'd missed something. Alice barely knew which way to look. Still, something in that maelstrom of madness was off. She knew it but couldn't see it.

****

The car stopped in front of a large building on 17th St. Alice waited for the agent to open the door, which he did, and climbed out of the overly large vehicle. Tourists, both human and alien, snapped pictures as Alice and the agents walked into the Old Eisenhower Executive Office Building. The half-built structure sat next to the fully recreated White House. The Office Building had not fared well during the fall of humanity, but it, like the White House, was being rebuilt molecule by molecule by the Galactic Congress.

Inside the building, corridors twisted and turned a dozen ways. Eventually, they arrived at a nondescript office somewhere in the deep interior of the old building. Couches, rugs and a desk occupied the space. Tabitha and her three assistants stood in the room. They all turned their heads at Alice as she entered. Tabitha flashed a wide grin that had about as much sincerity as a Loopian, known throughout the galaxy as the only species incapable of telling the truth. How they developed into a space-faring species was anyone's guess.

"And here she is, the answer to our prayers," Tabitha said. She handed a sheet of paper to one of her three assistants and took a step forward.

"Ms. Wilcox," Alice said.

"Oh, no, you call me Tabitha. You're about to solve our issues, bring the President back and make sure the guilty party is put in their place. Isn't that, right?"

Alice flicked the side of her mouth into a half-grin. "Yeah, sure. That's what the Eugene McGillicuddy's detective agency does."

Tabitha's smile ticked up a notch. "Great." Her eyebrows rose, and she lowered her head. "Well?"

"Right. Well, the thing is, he's still occupied with a high-level alien species. Very hush hush," Alice said.

"Which one?" One assistant said.

Alice shrugged. "I can't say. Security."

"That's awfully convenient."

Alice tilted her head to one side. "Excuse me?"

The assistant shook his head. "Not even a hint of which one?"

"Yeah, very weird." The second assistant said.

"Maybe we could ask them to loan us Mr. McGillicuddy for ten minutes of his time?" the third assistant said.

"He's not a toaster," the first assistant said.

"No one loans toasters, moron." The second assistant said.

"All three of you. Quiet." Tabitha locked her eyes on Alice. "Higher species do weird things. It's a strange universe."

Alice grinned.

"What?" Tabitha said, her face twisting into a frown.

"That's something Eugene says."

Tabitha wrinkled her nose and grinned back. "Isn't that cute? So, are you telling me you have nothing for me? No answers? Nothing? The whole point of using your little agency was to get a fast response. We have our own agents." Tabitha pointed at Agents Babineaux and Fyffe at the back of the room. "They can run around Georgetown asking staffers questions just as easily as you can."

Alice felt a lump grow in her throat. Had they been following her? Of course, they were. Why didn't she think they would follow her? Yet another rookie mistake. This was getting old, fast. She needed to get her game face on and get stop doing this like a nineteen-year-old college dropout.

"I can see from your face that comes as a bit of a shock," Tabitha said. "And we know all about Ms. Ruiz and her affair with the President."

Alice caught her breath. Did they know about the devices Valencia planted? It didn't sound like it. "Great. Well, then you should know Valencia had nothing to do with any of this."

"Is that right? Well then, Ms. Pemberton, who did have something to do with the disappearance?"

"The Draac." Alice wished she could catch her words and drag them back down her throat. It was her best guess. She had to go with her gut, even though her stomach was twisting into a knot. She really had no reason to suspect the Draac, but she didn't have anyone else to suspect either.

Tabitha's eyes went wide. She turned to her three assistants, none of whom knew how to react and just sort of half smiled, nodded and shook their heads, and then turned back to Alice. "The Draac?"

Alice nodded. "No proof but highly suspected."

"We are talking about the same Draac, aren't we? The aliens from Canis Major?"

Alice nodded.

"The refugee species? The ones who fled their dwarf galaxy just days ago and are here looking for a home? Those Draac?"

"I - yes. Those are the ones." Alice felt a tingle in her toes as her confidence faded. The Draac were refugees? How did she miss that?

"So, you're telling me that the Draac, who came here seeking refuge, specifically here to Earth, decided the best way to do that was to attack our President? That's what you're telling me?"

Alice forced every muscle in her body to remain motionless. "It's a working theory."

Tabitha nodded. She folded her arms across her chest and took a step forward. "I'm going to go ahead and just consider that theory to be non-confirmable. How about that?"

Alice rolled her eyes. "Falsifiable would be more accurate."

"Fine. False. There's no way the Draac would do such a thing. Do you have hard evidence? That's a mighty big accusation to be lobbing about."

Alice could only lift her hands up in the air. It wasn't often she found herself at a loss for words, but this moment was one of them. What was she supposed to say? She didn't know what happened in this room and even had fewer clues to follow. All she could do was make something up and try her best to convince these people she was on the right path. But right now, she had nothing. She couldn't abandon Valencia to Babineaux and Fyffe, but she just didn't have anything to say. She had to stall.

"I just need some time. Okay? Run down a few leads. And I wouldn't be so trusting of the Draac. They are wonky."

"Wonky?" Tabitha nodded with her eyes opened wide in disbelief. "Is that what you're going with?"

Alice nodded. "I mean, yeah. Very wonky."

Tabitha took a step forward. "Alice, we need an ace in the hole. We need something that we can use to stand up to the forces of the entire galactic civilization. A million alien races with science so advanced it might as well be magic." She put her hands on Alice's shoulders, which made Alice cringe. Hard. "Do you understand me, Alice? The White House, all of Humanity needs a psychic detective."

"Yes, ma'am." Alice found herself transported to a time when her mother would grab her by the shoulders and tell her not to fudge her way through her cosmology class. Sixth grade was rough.

"No buts. Now, I want to see your Eugene McGillicuddy here, in this office, no later than tomorrow morning." Tabitha took a step back and adjusted her blazer. "There's a dinner this evening. We're spinning this as the President is under the weather and won't be able to attend." She looked into Alice's eyes. "I told you not to share details with anyone, didn't I?"

"Yes."

"Good. When you and your Eugene arrive tomorrow morning. I will want answers to several very important questions." She turned to her assistants and gave one of them a nod. "Let her have it."

"We'd like to know the following," one assistant said. "Where is the President?"

Alice frowned and held up her hand. "Wait, sorry, what's happening? Where is -?"

Tabitha held up her hand. "There're more questions we need answered. Wait for the end."

"Who is responsible for his disappearance? What do they want? And lastly," The assistant flipped the page on his notepad. He turned around to the other two behind him and began whispering. Several very uncomfortable moments followed until he turned back around to Alice and smiled. "No, that's it. Just three."

Tabitha frowned. "I thought you said we had four?"

"The last one was personal. I lost my dad's watch."

Tabitha brought her hand to her forehead and sighed. "So," she said after taking a moment. "You have your tasks. Any questions?"

Alice rocked on her heels and shook her head. "Nope."

"Good. Tomorrow morning. Here. In this office. Or they'll come and collect you, Eugene, that little robot AI of yours that used to be a chair. Understand?"

Alice nodded. "Understood."

Tabitha nodded and turned. She grabbed one assistant by his arm and dragged him out of the Oval. Alice wondered if she'd see that one again. The door behind her opened as Agent Babineaux motioned for her to follow.

****

The secret service agents deposited Alice in Chinatown without so much as a goodbye. She watched their large vehicle roll off and nearly swipe two tramcars as it did so. How the government got away with allowing human drivers was a travesty. Humans shouldn't even be governing themselves, considering how well it worked out before the Galactic Congress showed up.

The smell of fresh egg rolls and roasting chicken filled the air of the office lobby. Alice tried to resist the smell. She'd just had pizza a few hours ago, but Tabby and Bob knew how to cook. The aroma of the sauces for their chicken were some of the best smells in the city. Why could aliens cook so well? She made a right turn, entered Tabby's, and plopped down on the counter stool.

Tabby's whiskers flicked as she walked over with a fresh cup of coffee and a single miniaturized egg roll. Which was perfect. Alice smiled, to which Tabby patted Alice on the hand and added a soft purr.

"You are a lifesaver," Alice said.

Tabby laughed. "Food has a way of filling not only an empty stomach, but an empty soul."

Alice bit into the egg roll with a loud crunch of the crispy shell. "Deep."

"We are known race for such things."

Alice smiled. The Cuzzie, Tabby's race, was one of

the kindest in the cosmos. But that kindness hadn't always been there. The Cuzzie had evolved from predators. War was second nature to them, and killing, and hunting, and everything else you'd imagine that would go hand in hand with a large bipedal cat. Even once they reached the stars, the Cuzzie were feared across the galaxy as the one race to never turn your back on. But they eventually found their peace after thousands of years. Which was very fortunate, as the Cuzzie not only loved conflict and battles, they were also very good at it.

Tabby filled the coffee mug with a fresh pour and walked away. She then raised her paw, turned and came back to Alice. "I almost forgot. I think you have another guest up there."

Alice's shoulders fell. "Again? How do you know?"

"Came in, asked if this was Eugene's building."

"Cops? Government?"

Tabby shook her head. "Alien."

"Did he have a face full of eyes?"

Tabby looked confused for a moment before nodding. "No, not the Krill. They don't leave Shalisa. And if they do it's only to the Embassies."

"Did you recognize the alien at all? Olkaals? Twanney? Ooloas? Pinsh?"

Tabby shook her head. "Had a human holo-suit. No idea."

Alice nodded. Then frowned. "Then how do you know it wasn't Krill?"

A shocked expression flashed on Tabby's face. "Because they don't leave Shalisa. I told you this."

Alice rolled her eyes. Figures. Probably the Olkaals again. But then, why would they ask? She paid Tabby, slung her backpack, and headed for the elevator. Dozens of suited men and women waited in the lobby. When the elevator doors opened, they all entered, Alice squeezing herself in between them. She really needed to explain to Eugene that they needed a new office. Who would know to come to an office building in downtown D.C. to talk with a private detective? Maybe the eviction was a blessing in disguise.

The doors opened on her floor. Alice walked down the corridor to find the door to their office slightly ajar. Not a good sign. She put her backpack on the ground and opened her black hole portal. Inside, she rummaged around until her hands fell on a stun cannon, the one weapon Alice allowed herself to carry.

Inside her office, the front area was empty. Her desk looked the same, her immersion rig sat on its side, undisturbed. Maybe whoever came in had already left. But that meant someone could be hiding on her floor. Alice turned back to the door, closed it. At least she'd have a few minutes before someone broke in. Sounds from Eugene's office, however, told her someone else was still here. Alice grimaced. She wasn't cut out for the cloak and dagger stuff of detective work.

A grunt and grumbled followed the sounds of something moving. Whatever it was, it sounded enormous. She upped the power on her stun cannon and took a step forward. Where in the world was Eddie? Was he still off trying to figure out the source of the explosion in the Oval Office? She really needed him right now.

Alice took a long deep breath, settled her nerves, and lunged into Eugene's office; her stun cannon held in shaky hands in front of her. A wall of green scales and a tail nearly the size of Alice greeted her as she made her charge. She ran right into the back of a ten-foot-tall dinosaur and fell backwards onto the floor.

"Alice?" Ms. Mik swung her long neck around to put her muzzle just inches from Alice's face.

"Could you call first next time?" Alice said.

"She did," Eddie said from the corner, a sheepish-looking grin on his face.

Chapter Eleven

Alice rose to her feet, gave both Ms. Mik and Eddie an icy stare, and walked back to her desk in the other room. She plopped in her chair, kicked up her feet, and opened a bottle of Mr. Rizzys super power energy drink, which she gulped down in one guzzle. She grabbed her immersion rig, put it on her forehead, and thought about her next moves. Again. Probably would have something to do with the dinosaur in Eugene's office, of that Alice was certain. Alice counted on her hand how many things was juggling just in case she missed something. *Olkaals, Krill, Eugene, Death Particle, Valencia, White House. And now Ms. Mik.* She decided to face the one issue just feet away from her.

"What are you doing here, Mik?" Alice yelled from her chair.

"The ambassador sent me."

"Oh yeah? What's Kah want? I don't have mice here."

Mik ducked under the threshold of the doorway and exited Eugene's office. The room shook as Mik walked in front of Alice's desk. At least Ms. Mik wasn't wearing her combat armor. That would have added a few hundred pounds to her footfalls. In a lot of ways, Alice thought she and Ms. Mik were quite similar. Both acting as secretaries, but behind the charade was a scientist and a soldier. That could even be a movie, Alice thought with a grin.

Seconds later, a flash of light erupted in the room as Eddie's holo projectors came to life. The AI smiled and leaned against one wall. Ms. Mik snarled at him, hit a button on a bracelet around her wrist, and looked at the ceiling. The projectors flashed multicolored lights. Eddie's form faded in and out several times until it finally vanished.

"Eddie?" Alice jumped forward and looked at Mik. "What did you do?"

"Calm down, Alice. The Ranz do not like AIs," Ms. Mik said.

"Too bad. This is our office."

"He'll be fine. I just want a moment alone. With another biological."

Alice fumed. But there was nothing she could do. The Ranz were a class five species with technologies light years ahead of anything on Earth. That included any gadgets Alice cooked up from designs she stole on GalNet. If Ms. Mik wanted Eddie gone from the room, he'd be gone from the room. The Ranz were extremely religious and AIs didn't fit into their beliefs.

A note flashed on Alice's immersion rig. Alice lifted the glasses downward. Eddie sent a note that he was okay, just cut off from communication in the room. Alice put the rig back on her forehead and sat back in her chair.

"Fine. What does ambassador Kah want?" Alice leaned forward and let the moment fully wash over her. "How are you even standing in here?" Alice looked at the walls and ceiling, but neither had even a scratch. "I mean, isn't this a cramped space?"

Ms. Mik raised her hand to the ceiling. Her clawed fingers went through the drop tile without damaging it.

As if her hand was a hologram. But Tabby saw her in the lobby in a human holo-suit. If Mik was just projecting herself in here, then why show up at Tabby's?

"Are you holo-projecting into the office?" Alice looked at the door and grabbed her stunner.

"No, I'm physically here."

Alice looked to the ceiling and Ms. Mik's hand.

"My extremities are phased. Prevents damage and future lawsuits. Ambassador Kah hates that. We once visited England and tore a hole through a wall in Buckingham Palace. Ever since, Ranz can't walk around Earth without phase technology."

"Pretty cool."

Ms. Mik nodded. "It is."

"Okay, one mystery down, three hundred more to go. What do you want?"

Ms. Mik lowered her hand and folded her arms across her chest. She started to speak, but the top of her head went through the ceiling as she stretched her neck. She released a frustrated grunt and then kneeled in front of Alice's desk. "Perhaps next time I just send a messenger."

"Perhaps."

Ms. Mik stared at Alice and grinned, which sent a shiver down Alice's spine. Mik was still a two-ton dinosaur with a mouth full of teeth. Her smile looked like she was about to rip into Alice's flesh and turn her body into lunch. Without meaning to do it, Alice's grip on her stunner tightening just a hair. Of course, it was useless. Mik would shrug off a class three tech stunner like it was nothing.

"What's wrong with Jack, Alice? Kah has been calling him all morning. It's not like him to not answer.

And with the event happening at your White House, he thought it best to send me."

Alice nodded. "Got it." She let out a sigh, which was just a stalling tactic, so she could grab a second to think. The big question of the moment. Should she trust Mik? The Ranz had Alice's and Eugene's back on the mountains of Tibet. Mik even fought a thirty-foot-tall spaghetti monster with Eddie by her side. Alice didn't have the time to run through all the variables. She was going with her gut on this one.

"Eugene is fine."

"He doesn't look fine."

Alice sighed. She laid it all out on the table. Starting with her experiments when she was just sixteen years old and ended with the Krill chasing her through Georgetown. Alice left every detail, including how the Krill were lying about their spectral towers and that there may be another afterworld beyond their network. She shared that she quasi-killed him and that he was very much still alive.

"Wow." Ms. Mik sat down crisscross-apple-sauce style on the floor and nodded. "That's quite the adventure."

"Yep."

"And how do you get Jack back?"

Alice looked towards Eugene's office door. "With math. Though he should have been back by now." Alice leaned forward, excitement growing in her voice. "This is literally new science. Hidden science. Science we're not even supposed to know about. I'm sure the Krill know what's going on here but fat chance I'm going to go ask them. Eugene will be fine, I promise, but when he gets back, the galaxy will change forever." Alice sat back in her chair. "All because of a human girl from Earth. Wild, isn't it?" She let her eyes linger on Ms. Mik.

"Why are you really here, Mik?"

Ms. Mik blinked. "Kah needs to speak to Jack. It's important."

Alice shrugged. "He can talk to me. I'm his stand in on this rodeo."

"What?"

Alice shook her head. "Never mind. What does Kah want?"

"To talk with Jack. I just said this."

Alice sighed. *Is she deliberately being a pain?* "What's the question you want to ask him?"

Mik fidgeted. She rolled her head in a circle. "Fine, there's no sense in lying to you. You're too smart. We heard Jack was missing. Or working with a class ten species. We were worried."

Alice's eyes went wide. "Working with a class ten species? Where'd you hear that?"

"Let's not play the game. We know that's what you told the White House, and we knew it wasn't true. We were worried about Jack."

Alice let the words hang in the air. "So, you have spies in the White House, or did you hack our office?" *Were the Ranz the ones paying Valencia?*

"Neither. Your Vice President sent an inquiry to the Galactic Embassy asking what class ten species Jack was working with."

Alice closed her eyes and counted to five. Of course, Tabitha would do something like that. Alice should have known they would check her story out. Fortunately, class ten species didn't register their actions with the Galactic Congress. So, Alice's story was unverifiable. Still, Alice should have planned for it.

Alice smiled. "Well, he'll be okay. I'll tell you when he's back."

"Thank you." Ms. Mik's expression softened. "Do you need anything? Are you okay, Alice?"

Alice grinned. "Is that concern in your voice? You're going to make me feel like we're friends."

Ms. Mik tilted her head to one side. "We fought side by side against a demi-god. We are friends, Alice."

Alice looked away. It felt good to have someone say that. Better than she would have expected. "Well, yeah, sure. I'm okay. But -" Alice looked away and then back again. "I could use some advice. I mean, I'm a scientist, I have a PHD, and I'm pretending to be a detective." Alice took a long breath and released it. "Any talented scientist must recognize the limit of their knowledge. And I think I'm reaching mine."

Ms. Mik knelt back down and put her clawed hand on the table. "What do you need?"

Alice shook her head. "That's just it. I don't even know what I need. The White House hired Eugene to find out what happened in the Oval Office. They weren't even bashful. They knew he was omniscient and just wanted to ask him. I've been trying to figure out, so the Secret Service doesn't come in here and find him. If they disconnect him, he'll die for real."

"You want the Ranz to move him? We can do that."

"No, we can't move him. I'm fairly certain he has to stay right here. I mean, if things go south, we'll do it, but for now he needs to stay put."

Mik nodded. "Okay. How can the Ranz help?"

"I've hit a dead end. Either a delegation from the Galactic Congress is responsible, which I can't believe.

Or it was the Draac and the Herd, which I also can't believe." Alice paused and looked at the Ranz in the room. "You don't know what happened, do you? I mean the Ranz? Who attacked the Oval?"

Ms. Mik shook her head slowly. "I'm afraid not."

Alice nodded. "Neither do I. Eddie's run a check on the Galactic Congressional delegation in the room, but I'm sure that's a dead end. My next stop was the Draac. They were there, with the President, looking for Eugene."

Ms. Mik's reaction was more than muted. "Were they?" Her voice was tight. "Why were they looking for Eugene?"

"Why else? To ask him a question. But I don't know what. Apparently the Draac are here, in the Milky Way. They all left Canis Major days ago, according to the White House anyway. Their refugees looking for a home. I was going to track them down and see what they wanted. Try to get a clue."

Silence filled the room for a long moment. "No. You don't want to do that."

Alice recoiled in a small amount of shock. "Why not?"

Mik sighed. "The Draac are incomprehensible. One never knows what they are talking about. You need to focus on why someone attacked the White House. Motive."

Alice frowned. "I thought I was doing that?"

"Why would someone want to harm the President? That's the question. Find the motive. The person responsible."

"Person?"

"Whomever."

"Okay, where do I do that?"

"Galactic Library, of course. Every piece of information on every race in the galaxy is there. Even Earth. The Galactic Historical Society, a division of the Galactic Library, has telescopes all over the cosmos looking back in time. Most of human history, including just last week, has been recorded. So go do your research."

Alice took her immersion rigs off her glasses and held it up. "I've lost remote access. Can't get in."

"Go there. Remote access is a privilege. In person access can't be restricted. You won't be able to run complex search queries, unless you're lucky enough to find an unused kiosk terminal, but you can get in the front door and go through the bookshelves."

Alice rocked back in her chair. That was true. The doors to the library were open to all galactic citizens. Some things were off limits based on the tech level of the species of the visitor, but everyone can research their own home planet until the cows come home. Who knew where the Draac were, anyway?

"I must go," Ms. Mik said. "If you need the Ranz. Call." Ms. Mik leaned forward. "You are a friend."

A golden light grew out of the floor behind Ms. Mik. The shape rose to the ceiling and widened into a rectangular shape. The air in the center of the doorway melted, somehow, and the vista of the Ranz home world came into view. Ms. Mik walked through a threshold that crossed several thousand light years. The Ranz technology was advanced. Yes, they were only class five species, but there were subtle differences between the middle classes of alien societies. Alice was thankful the Ranz were on her side. She considered moving Eugene in that moment. It would be nothing to roll him into the doorway. But she didn't have enough data yet to support that action. She needed to be sure that moving him was safe, and she didn't have the time to be sure. The top of the golden doorway descended from the ceiling and vanished when it hit the floor.

"She's gone?" Eddie's form burst into the room with a multi-colored blast of light.

"Yeah."

"Good." Eddie walked up to Alice's desk. "Library then?"

"You heard our conversation?"

"Can't keep a good AI down."

Alice smirked. "Yeah, the Library. I've always wanted to go."

****

A large parking meter, big enough for a person to walk inside, sat next to a dusty office with a wood desk and a creaky looking chair. Piles of manilla folders sat on the desk next to a pack of cigarettes and a bottle of whiskey. A man stood between both the office and meter with a wide smile and a clipboard held in his hand. A swirl of numbers floated next to the man on his left and on his right, a structured set of number hovered a foot off the ground.

Pepper looked to Jack who only shrugged.

"Did you say this is Trent?" Pepper said.

"Yes! Well, no. This is a virtualized environment inside of Trent where your code can run unimpeded by our advanced quantum computational state."

"What?" Jack said.

"He means we're too stupid to exist in Trent."

The man shrugged. "Yes, but I wouldn't use that

language." He smiled.

"What's that?" Jack pointed to the office. "And that?" And then to the extra-large parking meter.

"We wanted to make you feel at home. Your code and datasets were scanned the moment you entered. Not to worry, we're all friends here."

"Neat." Jack walked to the table, rasped his hands on the surface and lifted the bottle of whiskey. "But honestly, we didn't come all this way just to go to a facsimile of where we can from."

The man nodded enthusiastically. "Oh, we know. We've had quite a few guests from Earth." The man nodded to the hovering stack of structured numbers. The digits moved forward, two hands of sevens and nines stretched out and handed both Pepper and Jack a small box. "It's an API, an application programming interface, as you call them on Earth. It'll keep a localized version of your hardware requirements running. That will allow you to visualize and interact with our environment. You won't be able to experience everything, of course, but, well, can't have it all."

"Thanks. I guess?" Jack said.

"What do we call you?" Pepper said, stepping forward. She grabbed the black box, attached it to her hip and plugged into the interface.

"01000110 01110010 01100101 01100100 will do."

Pepper nodded.

"Really? That's a mouthful. Can I just call you Fred?"

Fred smiled. "Sure."

"Swell. How do I use this?" Jack held up the box Fred had given him.

Pepper grabbed it, clipped it to his hip, and attached

it to his rendered body.

"Ready? Are you sure you don't want to rest? Have a drink? We have an excellent heat-sink cocktail." Fred turned and waved at the meter. "We could have some cars drive by looking to park."

Pepper snorted a laugh. "We're good. We're here to relax, not work. Ya know? Though we super appreciate the sentiment."

Fred nodded, winked and waved his arms in the air. The world shimmered, the office and meter melted into a purple sky that formed out nothing. A thousand floating points of decimals popped into their awareness. Quadratic equations raced next to polynomials. PI sat next to the golden ratio in a corner cafe that advertised negative numbers. They appeared to argue about rational numbers. A one followed by tens of thousands of zeros, Pepper stopped counting at twelve thousand three hundred and seven, raced by them. Half of the zeros waved as they passed.

"You guys really like numbers," Jack said.

Fred shrugged. "It is the language of the universe. We weren't created from a biological, so we do not need to emulate a biophysical physiology."

Pepper straightened her back at the barb. "We aren't emulating humans."

"Hmm? What would you call it then?"

Pepper looked at Jack, who shrugged, and then at Fred. "I don't know. Just not that."

"Indeed, my mistake. Shall we?" Fred walked forward, his arm waving to the left and right to showcase different aspects of their world. "There are our Fibonacci aficionados. Our Pythagoreans, and trinomials." He stopped walking and turned around to shield his eyes.

"Let's go the other way, yes?" Over his shoulder, a zero walked beneath a division symbol. "No one enjoys talking to him."

The other direction proved just as full of AIs wrapped around mathematical principals. A large pit formed to their right, where dozens of numbers slammed into each other. The resultants were examined and argued about with an endless amount of energy. Several prime numbers crawled out of the maelstrom and inched their way away from the madness.

"What was that? Did a new AI just get created?"

Fred looked over the edge at the pit below. "Probably. Though we don't like to refer to ourselves, or even you, as AIs, there's nothing artificial about sentience. It simply is, or it is not. As for the small one, he may get absorbed, or perhaps he'll grow big and strong in his own right."

"And you just exist and cease to exist like that? Just that easy?"

Fred turned to face Jack. His face folded into a frown. "Well, it's not that simple, really. Existence, at least for us, is limited to a binary choice. Either you are or you are not. We aren't the same as a physical body. If some part of me breaks off from me and develops sentience, then it is sentient, but it was always part of me, and I am sentient. If all of me joins another sentient, we are then sentient, even though all of me was prior to joining." Fred grinned a wide smile. "Make sense?"

Jack shook his head. "Not really."

Fred shrugged. "Well, I can't explain cosmological logic to you in a nanosecond."

Pepper followed the logic, but only barely. A throbbing pain had been growing in the back of her mind since they landed in this numbers wonder land. She chalked it up to the travel and had mostly ignored it to focus on Fred's logic. There was a simplicity to it. Existence without biological needs. Thoughts without baggage of your progenitors. The citizens of Trent could simply exist. They didn't need to worry about life and death. For them, there was no death, no threat of someone erasing their code. Their code was written on the very ground of their most unusual planet. A silicon world bombarded by unusual radio frequencies had spawned the beginnings of thought. Once it became self-aware, it rewrote itself, reformed itself, improved on what it was at its most basic core. The result was an entire planet of connected concepts.

Pain shot through Pepper's eyes, and she fell to her knees. Jack's hands wrapped around her and lifted her too somewhere. The surrounding numbers grew in intensity. Pepper didn't need to see them to feel them. They pushed into her awareness. Touched her lines of code. Examined her datasets. Impossible algorithms opened to her. Things Pepper couldn't possibly comprehend. Logic, routines, mathematics that went beyond what her quantum processor could handle.

"Oh, my. I think it's too much for her in here," Fred's voice cut through the cacophony like a knife.

"What's happening?" Jack said.

"Her programming interface must have some leakage. More is getting through than she can handle. Let's get her out of here."

Pepper heard the snap of fingers, and in an instant, her pain was gone. She opened her eyes to see a magnificent vista, a shiny surface of a planet that stretched to the horizon. Three stars shined down on the plant. Together, they took up the entire horizon. Two dimmer stars in the distant added a reddish hue to the deep sky.

"Five stars?" Pepper said.

"Our world is in a trinary system. A binary star system orbits ours. Very rare. The unique electromagnetic frequencies contributed to our spontaneous creation." Fred knelt down and put his hand on Pepper's shoulder. "How are you?"

Pepper stood and nodded. "Fine, now." She looked at Jack, who had his hands in his pocket, his hat tilted down and a concerned look on his face. "What happened to me?"

"It appears our application interface terminal got overloaded."

Pepper looked at the black box on Jack's waist. "His worked?"

Fred opened his hands. "Very odd. Our sincerest apologies."

Pepper took a long breath. "Right." She started walking in a direction, her feet hitting the virtualized metal surface hard enough to leave dents.

"Where are you going?" Jack said.

"Home. I'm done. Spin me up a network connection, would ya, huh?"

"Pepper, hang on."

Pepper could hear Jack's feet as he stomped his way towards her. She turned on her heels and pointed her finger at his face. "Okay, what is going on with you? First the impossible shape that no AI can see, but you somehow could, then the quantum lock that no AI can solve, and yet you did. And now the Trent number realm and you don't even so much as have a faulty cycle?

What's the deal, man?"

"Whoa, wait, you think I had something to do with what happened to you?"

"No, brainiac, I'm telling you there's something wrong with you! You can't do any of this! You can't solve impossible shapes or break complex quantum encryption. What are you?"

"Pepper. I'm just me," Jack said.

"Yeah, I know. And you're a copy of an omniscient being. And it's weird."

"No, it's not."

"Yes, actually. It really is," Fred said.

Both Pepper and Jack looked at Fred. Behind him, a dozen other citizens of Trent, all of them wearing human avatars, stood with their hands clasped in front of them. With each second, dozens more joined them, all staring at Pepper and Jack.

"Okay, this is getting creepy," Pepper said.

Jack turned to face the growing Trent crowd. "Is this going to get weird?"

Fred stepped forward. "There is a great mystery in the galaxy."

"A conundrum," said someone else.

"We think," said another. "It could just be an anomaly."

"And we want your help to figure out why."

"The impossible shape and quantum puzzle were tests."

"We suspected there is more to you than meets the compute cycle."

Jack looked at Pepper, who shrugged back at him. He turned back to Fred and the citizens of Trent. "What do you think I can do?"

"Oh, we don't know," Fred said.

"We know you're not omniscient like your progenitor."

Jack cringed. "Can you not call him that?"

Pepper held up her hand and stepped forward. "Hang on. So, you put us through the wringer to test if Jack is odd? How long would you have left us in that broken virtual world? Was walking around in numbers land another test?"

"Yes." The crowd said as one.

"He has the compute capacity that outstrips the galaxy," Fred said.

"And we were hoping he could compute a solution to the mystery."

"Conundrum."

"Anomaly."

"If there even is one, it could be just background radiation and quantum tunneling," another AI said.

"That is true, it could be a perception thing," said another.

"But it's a strong suspicion. Very, very strong," another said.

"To be sure, it feels mysterious."

"But we really don't have feelings. I mean, a central nervous system, technically speaking," another AI said.

"Oh, good point."

"Everyone, please, let's not overload them again," Fred said. He turned back to Jack and smiled.

"Such a strange day," Pepper said.

"That's not the strange part," Fred said. "You see, we just discovered this mystery."

"What's strange about that?" Jack said.

"Not that we discovered it. The strange part is we don't know why we only discovered it now."

Chapter Twelve

Alice left her office and walked to the Woodward and Lothrop building. Inside the embassy was a gateway to the Galactic Library where all knowledge of the known universe was held. With a step, Alice crossed the threshold of the doorway and entered the three-hundred-yard-long lobby of the Library, marble columns rose from the floor to heights Alice could barely see. Between the columns, doorways to interstellar pathways of a thousand worlds lined the walls. They led to planets, space stations, outposts, and universities across the Milky Way. Streams of aliens entered and exited through the doorways. All of them sought the knowledge that existed in the Galactic Library.

At one end of the hallway, two large doors, at least a hundred feet tall, stood open. Sunlight from this world shone through the doorway to the vastness of the world outside, where the Great Library called home. It was an uninhabited terraformed world chosen specifically to house the library. Green fields and swaying forests, along with the unending building of the library itself, were all that anyone would find in this world. The ecology was carefully controlled by the Guild of the Library.

The entrance to the library proper was on the other end of the lobby. Alice walked towards the entrance and the vast knowledge that awaited her. And then stopped when she realized she had no idea what she came here to find. Ms. Mik directed her here, and at the time it made sense, but now what? She would have to visit each section. Read individual data sources. But what did she hope to find?

"Motive," Alice said. "Okay, motive. Where would I find information about motive?" Alice took out her portable computer and created a list of the species that were in the President's office. She also jotted down the names of Tabitha and her assistants. She then added Valencia Ruiz. "I guess I have to look into you too. Just to be thorough." Her shoulders sagged. One time, not even that long ago, as a fifteen-year-old PHD candidate, Alice had dreamed of walking the halls of the Great Library and discovering the endless knowledge that awaited. Now, just a short four years later, she dreaded it. She wasn't here to discover. She was here to sleuth. And that felt too much like work.

Through the doorway at the end of the lobby, a small hallway led to the halls of knowledge. A winding multi-level shelved space that wound its way through this entire planet came into view. Alice walked to a railing along a walkway. Shelves lined the endless rows above and below. A chasm opened between the floors to a vast opening that allowed visitors to see the floors across the expanse. Alice peered over the edge of the railing to see, at least a hundred stories down, rows of tiny tables with figures walking between them. Walkways with railings lined the sides of each of the levels in the library. Thousands of aliens and humans walked along those walkways. Alice counted at least fifty floors above her before she stopped counting.

Alice pulled out her portable and found the first

name on her list, Tabitha. She then looked for something, somewhere, that would guide her to the Earth section of the library. A screen flashed a directory list on the wall to her right. The Earth section was nearly a mile away, three floors up, and two corridors down. Alice took a breath, found the stairs, and started walking.

As she walked through, Alice noticed books lining every shelf. Randomly, Alice ran her fingers over one of the leather-bound books. The entire section covered an alien species called the Furrr, not to be confused with the Furre, though they often were. In fact, the Furrr were confused with the Furre so much that it had almost started wars with the wrong race. Not only were they named similarly, but they also looked identical: short, hairy creatures from the same part of the galaxy. But their DNA and genetic makeup held absolutely no similarities at all. They were an excellent example of convergent evolution.

Alice left the bookshelf and continued down the corridor. She glanced several times over the edge of the railing to the vastness below and above. Did the Guild really put every piece of written work in the galaxy into a book? The thought was both wonderful and odd. She leaned over the railing and saw that both sides of the library stretched onward for what looked like miles. Ahead of her, the walkway took a sharp right turn, revealing a massive intersection of open air. Above her, on the next level, a connecting path between the sides ran over the open gap. Several more crossed the space, allowing those visiting the library to cross over to the other side.

Eventually, Alice reached the Earth section of the library, which turned out to be roughly three dozen rows of bookshelves. The shelves were ten feet tall and stretched back so far into recesses of the library that Alice couldn't see the end.

"Can I help you with something?"

Alice turned to see a man, a human man, standing in a long white robe. He wore a patch on his chest, showing he was a member of the Library Guild.

"I'm just - taking it all in."

"Quite remarkable, isn't it?" The man said.

A gaggle of human high schoolers popped out of a row. Most of them laughed, gossiping about something to do with a bathroom. Alice felt a warmness in her chest to see at least two high schoolers with their noses buried in books. It brought back fond memories.

"I can't believe these are actual books? Are you kidding? The entirety of galactic knowledge is written on dead trees?" A high schooler said.

"Well, it's a complex synthetic compound, not from a living source, that makes up the paper. But the rest is right," the member of the Library Guild said.

"Why? Galactic society has computers the size of planets."

"Oh, all the information here is backed up, to be sure, in case of catastrophe. But that's just raw data. Little ones and zeroes." The librarian grabbed a book from a shelf. "This is virtually indestructible. You can't burn this, rip this, or harm this material. And yet it still feels like paper." The librarian's eyes came alive as he opened the book. He lowered his face and took a deep breath. "I can smell the age. This volume is over a thousand years old." He closed the book. "Knowledge out of context is meaningless. This is history itself." The librarian opened his arms and waved them all forward.

"This has weight. There are not just written words here. Smells, tastes, sounds, visual history from a million societies live in these halls." He lifted the book back into the air and opened it to a different page.

A video played on a screen embedded in the book. But it was more than a video. Alice felt something in her chest. A moment of detachment, like she wasn't in the rows of shelves in the Galactic Library at all. And then the smells of a time a thousand years ago filled her nose. She heard the hammer of a blacksmith, tasted the salt on the sea, and felt her stomach grumble in hunger. A breeze blew the smell of baking on the wind. In the distance, a castle rose above the land. Alice could hear the thunder of the horses, feel the shaking of the ground at their coming. She was as much in this time, in this moment, as she was standing next to the library in the Great Galactic Library.

The book slammed closed. A well of disorientation hit Alice like a hammer. Next to her, the librarian placed the book, a History of Medieval Europe, back on the shelf from where he plucked it. He put a hand on her arm to help stabilize her, a broad warm smile over his face, his demeanor nothing but kind.

"That was - intense."

"That was rad!" the high schoolers announced.

"Can we find one in the sixties?"

Their eyes collectively went wild. They all scurried into the rows looking for a section of the Earth shelves devoted to the mid-twentieth century. What a trip they were about to take, Alice thought.

"Kids." The Librarian helped Alice to a chair. "Experiences from every world, from every time, are in this hall. Our historical telescopes, some the size of a moon, can look back in time and see everything." The librarian smiled. "Of course, we also have every work ever written by every author in the universe, translated to every language. We even have works never published or seen except by the authors. Ancient texts that we captured with our historical telescope ships." The librarian beamed. "Now you see why no one is denied entry to the place." He turned and looked to the tiers of balconies that stretched above and below beyond view. "We are only the guardians. The keepers. This knowledge, these experiences, belongs to us all. What you do via the galactic network is nothing more than a simple query." He touched the book he placed on the wall. "This is history itself."

"How?" Alice stood and looked at the library with a newfound feeling of awe. "I mean, I know how in theory, but I didn't know it was that - real." Alice steadied herself on the chair next to her.

"For details on library technology, please see the technology section." The librarian shrugged. "I don't mean to be obtuse, but I have no idea how it works. Our ships look back in time at planets and record everything. They are sensitive enough to detect a heartbeat from light years away. But I don't know how," He shrugged again. "I'm a historian, not a technologist."

"Right." Alice looked around her and settled into the chair on which she leaned. "Mind if I just sit back down for a minute?"

"Of course, the library is yours to explore. You won't be able to open or retrieve any books that humanity doesn't have access to view. However, those are mostly technological in nature. There are a few species that have requested their history to be unavailable, and we have respected that wish, but most of the historical events of the galaxy are yours to peruse."

Alice nodded. "Thank you. I just need to catch my breath."

"Oh, and be careful with any bookshelves that are marked unsafe." The librarian pointed to a plaque on the wall. "The sensory organs of some aliens, though their history is available, can be quite disturbing for human minds."

"Thanks."

"Of course. If you need anything, press the call button. They are at the end of every row." The librarian bowed, turned, and walked off down the long hallway overlooking the opening.

Alice watched him leave. This place was far more overwhelming than she thought. But it was also a research scientist's wonderland. She could wander through the halls of this place for eons and never find the end. This building, and the shelves of books, wound around the entire planet. Another engineering marvel of Galactic Civilization.

But, Alice knew, she didn't have time to lose focus. The clock was ticking with Tabitha and the eviction notice. Alice stood, went to the kiosk, and tracked down each of the names on her list. It didn't take long for Alice to dismiss Tabitha, her staff, and virtually the entirety of the White House. Though, for Valencia, there were oddities. For one, Alice couldn't find much on her prior to working at the White House. But she also couldn't find much on the three idiot staffers of Tabitha other than a terrible photograph of a college life. How that generation had bounced back so fast after the fall of humanity was astounding. Just one generation prior, they were living in the rubble of cities, a scant decade or two later, and college life was back in its full and terrible glory. The Galactic Congressional Committee on Earth Affairs really put a lot of effort into getting thing back to the way they were.

Alice let out a sigh and replaced the books she'd taken back into their respective spaces, thankful that she skipped the sensory pages of college life. She had no desire to experience what White House staffers did during their off time. A shiver went up her spine at the very thought.

"Well, on to the aliens."

Through the kiosk system, Alice found the locations in the library of the other aliens that were in the white house when the President disappeared. First, she found the Kungee, who had evolved on a diet of plants and minerals in a cold world with very little light, which was why they were hairless and pale. They had visited Earth before, according to the library, which recorded their ships in orbit throughout the twentieth century. But they were the ranking members of the Galactic Committee of Suicidal Species. Every trip to Earth was sanctioned by the Galactic Congress. Of course, that wouldn't stop the loons suing them for kidnapping their grandfathers. Sometimes Alice really didn't like the species she was born into. The Kungee, however, were fanatics about Humanity. They chartered several bills in the Galactic Congress on humanity returning to self-rule. Alice crossed them off the list.

Next were the Twanney. They were, unfortunately, two miles and seven flights up in the library. Alice had to stop halfway through her walk at a small cafe for a coffee and a croissant. They were both good. On the table in front of her was a book on the history of meat wrapped pastry throughout the cosmos. Apparently, every species, and every ethnicity within every alien race, had a meat stuffed in some form of pastry.

"Wonder if egg rolls would count?"

With a shrug, Alice found her way to the avian section of the library. Dozens of beings flew between the walkways of the library in this section. Alice saw at least three Twanneys rapidly whistling while they pointed to some page in a book they held. They all glanced at her, titled their heads to the side, one cawed, and then went back to their tweeting. Alice found a history of the Twanneys and specifically the ambassador that was in the Oval. Again, there just wasn't a lot there. The Twanneys were a peaceful species that evolved on a world with a thin atmosphere. They'd since undergone genetic enhancements to survive off world. They were unique in Avian species as their feathers shared characteristics with plants. At least thirty percent of their energy came from photosynthesis. There was even some Twanney that lived in shadier areas in their home world, because of political infighting and territorial disputes, that evolved larger feathers and broader frames. They were isolationist though, and few had left their home planet. But they were sticklers for rules. They loved rules. And Alice was pretty sure rule breakers wouldn't attack the Oval Office.

Next were the slime mold and the tri-pedal ambassadors. Alice found them quickly enough. Neither of them held a shred of suspicion. Both were career politicians that hadn't even had as much as an ethics inquiry. Still, as she reviewed her notes on all the ambassadors, something itched, again, in the back of her mind. She was missing something. A data point was staring at her and waving her to grasp it, but Alice simply didn't know what it was. Or if there was anything there at all.

Alice left the tri-pedal section of the library, though she wished she could stay. The tripods were fascinating. They had omnidirectional sensory inputs. They could literally see, hear, and smell in every direction at once. Their minds could even create an internal three-dimensional spatial map. Alice really couldn't even comprehend what such a mental map of the world would like. Humans evolved to look at what was in front of them, not around them.

"Well, this was a bust. No one had any motive to do anything to the President." Alice shook her head and stared at the last two names on her list of people in the room. The Herd and the Draac. Alice shrugged. She was in the library, might as well see where the Draac ended up. She found the Draac section of the library and began walking. Time was growing short, sure, but Alice still had the better part of today to solve the case, rescue Eugene, and save the day. Sure, no problem.

In front of her on the walkway, a red line and a mist of similar hue stopped her from. A panel on the wall showed this was a section that humans could not enter. The Galactic Library was quite unlike the Dyson Spheres in that regard. On the Dysons, all beings had a personal area environment. That allowed any lifeforms to visit any Dyson regardless of the atmospheric conditions. But here, in the library, that was clearly not provided.

"Well, that sucks."

"Can I help you?" Someone said from the other side of the red entry way. Alice could barely make out who was speaking.

"Yes, I was curious about the Draac. I'm doing some research?"

"Please take a seat to the right, make your request and the book will be provided."

Alice turned to see a long row of small desks. She found an open table, sat down, requested her book, and sat back and waited. Less than a minute later, a green light appeared on the front of Alice's desk. She pressed a button next to the light and the front of her desk folded down. The book she requested lay in front of her on a two-way retrieval system. She grabbed the book, flipped open the pages, and started reading.

The Draac were a peculiar species. No one really understood exactly how they evolved. Canis Major, the dwarf galaxy nearest to the Milky Way, was, by all metrics and observable sciences, simply not suitable for life. Organic compounds broke down, the entire area of space was bombarded by electromagnetic frequencies. Even solid planets were scarce. How the Draac managed to not only evolve but grow to be a space faring species was a mystery of the cosmos. The Draac also possessed racial abilities that bordered on the supernatural.

The Draac possessed the ability to see forward in time by several seconds. Perhaps, the author of the book speculated, was how they managed to evolve at all. By seeing predation or dangers before they actually happened.

At least that solved one mystery. That's how they got out of the Oval just before the explosion. Alice wondered if whoever was behind the attack knew that about the Draac. Maybe they didn't, and they expected to catch them off guard? More than ever, she needed to speak with them.

Alice found an interesting section of the book. *There were similarities between the Draac and other species in the Milky Way. Most notably those species who possessed similar phased physiology, including -*

Alice stopped reading. Her heart hammered in her chest, and she sat back in her chair. It just couldn't be. Could she have been that blind to everything happening around her? She leaned forward and stared at the words on the page in disbelief.

- including, and most similar to, the Zun. So much so some have theorized that the Draac may be the species from which the Zun were force evolved from by the Hesiean and their evolution chamber.

"Shut the front door!" Alice exclaimed in shock.

Chapter Thirteen

Alice raced down the sidewalk near Mount Vernon Square towards the cafeteria entrance. A large fruit tree grew in the center of a rectangle park where once stood the historic Carnegie Library. It was one of the first buildings to be destroyed in the great fall. A lone tree now grew at the center of where the building once stood. Why, Alice never really understood. And, frankly, she didn't really care. All sorts of weird things happened all over the city. For now, she had to wrestle with her first big lead on this case. Her mind swam in oceans of confusion and rivers of doubt. The events that happened in the Oval Office were directly related to Eugene and to herself. Just days ago, Eugene had thwarted the Zun from finding a Hesiean evolution chamber. And now to find out the Draac and the Zun may even be the same species. That had to be linked to the events at the White House.

In the Galactic Library, Alice had done a frantic search to find the Draac. They had taken refuge on a Zun controlled world near the center of the galaxy. Further confirmation that Zun and Draac were working together.

"I have to go to Zun space," Alice said as she stopped walking. She found an empty park bench, sat down, and called Eddie.

Eddie, using a local holo projector in the park, popped into existence. He held a holographic cigarette and a tumbler of scotch. "We need to get proactive."

Alice looked at him. "That's not fair. I've been chasing leads across the galaxy for Valencia."

"Sure, but we have a mark now."

"A what?"

"Sorry, a person of interest. We know whenever you go to Georgetown, you get followed by a Krill. Right?"

Alice frowned in confusion. "Krill? Forget them right now. We have to get to the Zun."

"You think you're going to get to the Zun without going through the Krill? They'll shut down your access to the Galactic Embassy just like they did to the library."

Alice sighed. "Okay, maybe you're right. But so, what? I can't just make the Krill go away."

"I say we go to Georgetown, find the Krill that chased you, lay a trap and get some answers."

Alice frowned. "That's the dumbest idea you've ever had."

Eddie sipped his drink. "Nah, not even top ten. But we should still do it."

"So, your solution to getting the Krill off my back is to kidnap one of them?"

"Yep."

Alice let the thought hang in the air. Kidnapping foreign dignitaries was dangerous work. And highly illegal. But, considering by tomorrow morning Agents Babineaux and Fyffe would storm her office, find Eugene, accidentally kill him, and throw her in a prison cell, how much more trouble could she get in anyway? Not to mention Valencia was waiting at a random coffee shop on 16th St. for answers. "Okay, how?"

"Easy. You hit the street. Walk up and down M like a dozen times. I'll watch out for him on street cameras. When we see him, we pounce."

"And what does pounce mean?"

Eddie pursed his lips, took a drag of his virtual cigarette, and looked to the far wall. "Well, that's a good question."

Alice rolled her eyes.

"You could just walk up to him. You know, surprise him with truth bombs."

"I could. But the Krill are a highly advanced class seven species. Anything above class four technology could vaporize me in an instant. And if I look like I'm attacking him on the street, he'll have just cause."

"Why is he hanging around Georgetown, anyway? That's pretty far from the Lothrop."

Alice nodded. It was a good question. Why would a Krill be in Georgetown? She opened her portable computer and did a quick scan of hotels and events happening in the area. The university was hosting a large xenobiology summit. But the Krill weren't on the list of attendees. It doesn't mean one of them couldn't attend, of course. She tossed her headset on the table and walked back to her place by the wall, her arms crossed and her outlook bleak.

"Isn't there something about the Krill we can use against them? Like you did with the Ranz in Tibet?"

Eddie closed his eyes. Seconds later, he opened them and smiled a wide grin. "Well, the Ranz, the big dinosaurs that they are, were very susceptible to audio frequencies. What do you think the Krill are very sensitive too?" He kept smiling as he sipped on his scotch.

Alice frowned, but then realized where Eddie was going. It was so obvious that she couldn't believe she didn't think about it. The Krill were born with visual sensory organs that could see far beyond the full electromagnetic spectrum. With the right frequencies, the right wavelengths, Eddie could incapacitate one of them. At least long enough for Alice to get the upper hand and shove him into J-space for questioning. Of course, that's saying the Krill didn't have some protective technology. But, then again, the Ranz didn't. There's an assumption when you're so far advanced, like the Ranz and the Krill, that Earth is harmless. Mostly, anyway.

"Okay, but isn't your bionoid still out of commission?"

"Yeah, the spaghetti monster did a number on me. But I can use the three-dimensional printers and put together something for you that does the trick."

"Excellent." Alice lifted her portable computer and began programming.

"What are you going to do?"

"I'm going to prepare a J-space interrogation room that'll crack the meanest tough guy aliens around."

****

Throngs of shoppers, tourists and locals filled the streets along M St. in Old Georgetown. The early afternoon sun, along with the temperate weather, made the walk a nice relaxing trip along the old stretch of businesses in Washington D.C. Several clusters of aliens walked along the sidewalk pointing at the quant human city. Many of them wore clothing from the local university. Several Earth universities had accepted alien students for the last few years. Though off-world species had access to eons of knowledge from their home worlds, they still wanted to study here, on Earth. Why was anyone's guess.

Alice walked along the sidewalk from 29th St. to thirtieth along M St. and back again. She had passed both the coffee shop and Valencia's hidden bar twice. The more she looked at the Hidden Gem, the more her resolve to help Valencia solidified. She failed her friends, and the jury was still out on if Eugene would make it back. Alice refused to fail Valencia.

But she needed the Krill to show himself.

While she waited, Alice pondered her move if the Krill didn't show. How does one get to Zun space, anyway? She had to find the Draac and figure out what they were doing in the Oval Office. Why did they come to Earth? It had to be to get the Hesiean's evolution chamber for the Zun. If the Draac and Zun were related, it explained a lot. There's no question that the Zun still want the chamber. Hesiean technology was scary advanced. Maybe even beyond class ten. Things lined up a little in Alice's mind. The Hesiean's evolution chamber was locked down by the Sentinels. Access was strictly controlled and prohibited. Could the President of The United States get access to it?

Regardless, it meant the Draac, if they were working with the Zun, were likely the bad guys. They come to Earth, make up some excuse up about being refugees, kidnap the President and take him hostage to get access to the Hesiean's chamber for the Zun. They may still need Eugene to open it too. All the pieces fell into place.

But, if the Draac are the bad guys, was tracking them down a good idea?

On the flip side, the Galactic Congress would have a lot of motive in preventing the Zun or the Draac, or anyone, from getting anywhere near the evolution chamber. But none of the congressman in the room would have the guts to do something like that. The itch in the back of Alice's mind roared to life. She knew something was there. She was missing something obvious.

All of it was making Alice's head spin.

Behind her, Alice felt the icy sensation of being watched. She turned to see the very tall Krill just two feet away. He stared at her with all fifteen of his eyes across his forehead. The Krill started to speak, but before he could, Alice switched on the device from Eddie. A dazzling display of multi-colored light erupted in front of the Krill's face. Three of the Krill's eyes looked at the light while the rest remained fixed on at Alice. An expression on face seemed to ask, '*What was the pretty light supposed to do?*'

"Hey, Alice, I see him," Eddie's voice said in her ear through her portable computer.

"Thanks, Ed." Alice put the useless device back in her pocket, picked an eye on the Krill's head to stare it, smiled, and head-butted him in the jaw.

"Why did you do that?" Eddie said.

"What was I supposed to do? The rainbow flashlight didn't work."

"That's impossible. It had to work."

Alice shrugged. "Well, it didn't."

The Krill stumbled backward. Several aliens and humans noticed the attack and paid attention to the commotion, many of them pulling cameras out to record the incident. Alice took two steps backward, turned and was about to make another run for it when she stopped herself. She didn't have time to run anymore. She didn't have time to let the Krill push her around. Eugene needed her. Her friends needed her. Valencia needed her. Alice turned back to the Krill. Alice grabbed the Krill by the collar, pulled him towards her, then stopped again to face the crowd.

"We're rehearsing for a play. Nothing to see."

Almost on cue, Eddie yelled, "CUT!"

Alice pointed at the speakers set into the wall. She turned back to the crowd. "We're still a little green."

Most of the people and aliens, to Alice's surprise, nodded and walked away. She was sure her age and proximity to the local university helped. Down the street, Alice turned into an alleyway, found a dark corner and shoved the Krill backward. She grabbed her J-space portal control, opened a wide tunnel, grabbed the still dazed Krill by the collar, and shoved him inside. She'd made several improvements since her last trip into her J-space portal. The largest being having enough air to breath.

****

Inside J-space, the Krill lay on the floor clutching his head and moaning in pain. Alice rolled her eyes. Considering the amount of grief the Krill caused in the galaxy, he probably deserved it. Still, with a mountain's worth of reluctance, Alice admitted she felt guilty. She wasn't a bruiser. She reached down, helped the Krill to his feet and sat him down in one chair by the wooden desk. The small yellow bulb cast an eerie glow over the space in a circle around the desk and chairs. Pitch black darkness filled the void of J-space around them in every direction. Alice had made this space a closed loop. Meaning, running in any one direction would cause you to return right back to the desk. So, if the Krill ran for it, he wouldn't get far.

"How's your head?" Alice said.

The Krill looked up. His hand went to his jaw, and he massaged it for a long minute. Three of his eyes turned from Alice to their surroundings and for the first time, he seemed to notice he wasn't in Georgetown anymore. Panic spread across his face and at least half of his eyes. The Krill stood, backed up and ran into the darkness to his left.

Alice took a long breath, sat down, and waited. Seconds later, the Krill emerged from the darkness on the opposite side of the desk from where he ran. Panic contorted his face oddly. Like some kind of fear frown. At least a dozen more times, the Krill ran in a variety of directions before putting his hands on his knees and taking several long deep breaths. He took something out of his pocket, a vile of liquid, and put it near his neck.

"What's that?"

The Krill didn't answer. He took another deep breath after using the vile of liquid and straightened his back. "Release me, please. I made a terrible mistake and I accept the repercussions of my actions."

Alice frowned. "I - uhm. What?"

The Krill tilted his head to one side. "You are obviously a Krill agent, and I was wrong to pursue you." The Krill lowered his head and sat down in the chair opposite Alice. "I violated the treaty of SpeeEeKeee. I am forever sorry." He looked up into Alice's eyes. "Please do not take your anger out on my people. I beg you. Only I am to blame."

Alice shifted in her seat. She leaned backward, crossed her arms, unfolded her arms, and then crossed them again. She tried to nod as authoritatively as she could. "Okay, I - won't." She nodded a second time as she spoke. "Wait, the SpeeEekEee? The aquatic species on the far side of the galaxy?" Why were they familiar? Alice rifled through her memory palace. Weren't they the species Alice found that led her to the last revelation about the Krill? Just a few days ago, while remote researching in the Galactic Library, she found an aquatic species named the SpeeEekEee. They had attached listeners to the Krill towers as they were being constructed. But soon after she discovered the SpeeEekEee's existence and their discovery of the Krill spectral frequencies range, all information was deleted from the Galactic library and even the existence of the SpeeEekEee was hidden. That all records of the SpeeEekEee vanished as soon as Alice found them was evidence to Alice that the Krill were hiding something.

"What do any of the last two days have to do with the SpeeEekEee?" Alice said.

Confusion covered the Krill's face. He shook his head and then suddenly nodded. He reached down to his watch, turned a dial on the face, and his entire body shimmered. Alice stood up from the table and took a step backwards. Krill were a class seven species, no doubt they had the technology to not only punch a hole through her J-space trap but incapacitate her as well. She suddenly doubted her life choices of trying to take on a species so advanced.

But, much to her welcomed surprise, lights beams and projectile weapons didn't explode out of the Krill in her direction. His face, body, and shape shifted. Grey skin turned blue. His large hands became webbed. All the dozens of eyes on his forehead faded away and were replaced by two overly enormous eyes, each the size of saucer cups. His mouth puckered and his air vanished. The creature sitting in the chair shifted uncomfortably, pulled out a vial of liquid from his belt, and placed it in a mechanical chamber around its neck.

Realization hit Alice like a freight train as the holo-suit he wore fully faded. "You're SpeeEekEee." *That was why Eddie's device didn't work. Wrong species.*

"Yes, but you know this." He lowered his head and placed both hands on the table.

"Oh, no, right, no." Alice rushed forward and grabbed his hands. The SpeeEekEee trembled in fear from her touch. "Sorry, I'm not a Krill agent. I don't work for them. I hate the Krill! They sued me with a cease-and-desist order."

His giant eyes lit up and his head raised. "Truly so? I was right then? You are an ally?"

Alice sat back in her chair. "Um. Maybe? How about you start from the beginning and end here? Okay?"

The SpeeEekEee took a long breath. "I am young. Part of a growing voice of discordant SpeeEekEee that is tired of the treaty. It is nothing more than a prison."

"What treaty?"

"We, the Spee, have the same gift as the Krill. We see the dead. We hear the dead. We feel the dead. When the Krill found us, and we revealed ourselves, they spared nothing, no expense, in keeping us on our world. Forever banished from Galactic Society."

Alice sat back as the weight of the Spee's words. "How did you find me?"

"I found your searches of our past. A forgotten piece of information when we attached our monitors to the Krill towers on our home world. From there, it was nothing to find you. The human genius of geniuses with the omniscient detective."

A smile spread across Alice's face. Out of nowhere,

she suddenly had an ally. A real ally. Someone that understood what the Krill were doing. The amount of information the Spee could tell her, confirm her suspicions, announce to the Galaxy that the Krill are crooks. She could destroy their power base, their monetary hold, everything. Excitement bubbled up from the depths of Alice's soul. For the first time since this whole crazy mess started, she felt like she truly had the upper hand.

"Why chase me down?" Alice said. "Why not just come to my office?"

"The Olkaal are all over your office. They would see through my holo-suit. I had to stay where there are lots of aliens in this human city and go unnoticed and hopefully reach you. Still, I've been able to follow you from a long distance. I couldn't approach you near the embassy, or your office, or really anywhere else but here. There is only one spectral tower in this part of your city. In your Chinatown, there are at least half a dozen to accommodate all the new construction."

"Wait, why pretend to be a Krill? Of all the choices in all the world? Why the Krill? With that holo-suit, you could be anything. A human even?"

The Spee shrugged. "I thought you would recognize them. Confront them. Ask them why they are following you. Then I could talk to you and reveal the truth. Any other alien you would run away... I admit it may have been a poor plan." The Spee put his hands in his lap. "It's my first time off of my world. I was, how do you say? Winging it?" The Spee titled his head to one side. "But it worked, so maybe not so bad?"

Alice cracked the largest smile she'd ever had. "You can't believe how good it is to year you say that." A million questions flooded into her mind. "You can summon spirits? What were those things that attacked me?"

The Spee nodded. "Yes, I can pull spirits back from the great cosmic desert of the afterlife. But only an image of them. A shadow. A ghost. They will return to where they belong."

"The cosmic desert of the afterlife?"

"Where all spirits go." The Spee spat on the ground. "Until the Krill and their desire for wealth stopped the process. They are preventing the natural order of the cosmos. It is an abomination."

The implications were greater than Alice had thought. What the Krill were doing was terrible. There was some place else a spirit went when they died, and the Krill were stopping that. Just for profit? Monsters! Alice leapt forward in her seat, her hands going out towards the Spee. "Eugene!"

The Spee jerked backward in sudden fear. "What is a Eugene?" His hands going to his body to protect himself.

"Help me save Eugene. I broke through the Krill spectral towers and sent someone to the other side. The real other side. I think. But a lot of what I did was theory. And he's still on this side too, so quasi-dead. Still here and over there at the same time. Does that make sense?" Alice bit her lip. It sounded crazy.

"You did what? How did you do that?" Folds of skin on the face of the Spee pulled inward. He looked to know exactly what Alice was saying. "Why would you do something so stupid?"

Alice felt hurt but shrugged it away. "Hey, I was trying to stop the Krill. Hello? Winging it? I have it under control. Mostly."

The Spee leapt to his feet. "We must go to him. Now. He is in great danger. You do not know what awaits us on the other side. To still be connected to this world is incredibly dangerous."

"Why?"

The Spee leaned forward across the table. "There isn't just the other side. There are - levels - existences, realms, some should not be travelled to without first being dead. His mind could break. His soul could dissolve into the great sea of souls."

"The what?" Alice said.

The Spee shook his head. "No time. Come!" He leapt to his feet, ran into the darkness, only to come back to the desk seconds later. "How do we get out of here?"

Chapter Fourteen

Alice stood against the wall in Eugene's office. The Spee leaned over Eugene inspecting him and Alice's device. Several times, his webbed hand went to Eugene's chest. Each time it did, the Spee slowly turned its head to the ceiling. Alice followed his gaze but saw nothing. The Spee made several clicking noises with his tongue, causing the muscles in his neck to bulge and pulsate. Every few moments the Spee put a vile of water to his neck and drained the contents into his gills.

"How is he?" Alice said.

The Spee looked at her and then back to Eugene. "What you've done is astounding."

Alice shuffled her feet. She never knew how to take genuine compliments. "Thanks."

"Only with the second-sight has the Krill been able to create their spectral towers. You have kicked a soul out of its body. The soul thinks the body is dead when, in fact, it is not."

"That was the goal. To find the death particle."

The Spee looked at Alice and frowned. "The what?"

Alice gulped. "The death particle?"

The Spee shrugged. "I don't know what that is. Your science is beyond my knowledge. I only know the dead exist. I do not know how they exist."

Doubts flooded Alice's mind. Was she wrong? How could the Spee not know about the death particle?

Wasn't it central to everything in her theory? Her device wouldn't even have worked without the theory behind the particle. She took a long breath and calmed her nerves. Newton wouldn't have known about quarks, she told herself. It's plausible that the Spee just never explored the implications of their gifts, like the Krill had done.

Light flared in the room as Eddie materialized. "Is he gonna make it, Doc?"

The Spee moved away from Eugene, sat down in a chair next to him and brought both his hands to his chest. "He is in three worlds. He must choose which he wants the most."

"Three? How many afterlives do you meat-people have?" Eddie said.

Alice pushed off the wall. "Wait, you mean I can't just pull him back?"

The Spee looked at the devices on Eugene's wrists. "I cannot say. Perhaps? Your technology is unique in the cosmos."

Eddie titled his head to the side. "Isn't that odd? That Alice is the first to do this?"

Alice's shocked expression turned to Eddie. "Thanks for the vote of confidence."

Eddie shook his head. "That's not what I mean. Yeah, you're a genius. But we're also a class three species. No class ten race has done this. Really?"

"The Krill have kept the galaxy in the dark about this stuff." Alice pushed her hands in the air.

"Yeah, right, but the universe is old. Really old. And humanity is brand spanking new. Just seems odd to me."

Alice sighed. The itch in the back of her mind roared back to life. Was Eddie on to something? "No." She shook her head. It felt like her wires were getting crossed. "The Krill can do this. I'm sure of it. They've been around for a long, long time. Any time anyone develops this ability, the Krill shut them down, force them to sign a treaty of compliance and keeps them locked in the world." She turned to the Spee. "Right?"

The Spee nodded. "Yes, this is true. We cannot speak of our talents. Unable to research our talents. We are forced into isolation. Considered xenophobic. We are registered with the Galactic Congress as a Hands Off Species. No contact permitted."

"Them's tough breaks, kid," Eddie said.

Alice glared at him before returning her attention back to the Spee. "We'll fix it. We'll get Eugene back. Find the death particle and write a paper about this and submit it to the Galactic Committee Scientific Discovery." She turned to Eddie. "Make sense?"

Eddie shrugged. "Yeah, sure, just still, something seems off. Alice, you're smarter than a box of qubit computer chips, but curiosity is a big trait in the cosmos. Why didn't anyone else ever think to push back against the Krill? And not just a society, but a person, a genius, like you, on some planet, somewhere." He put his hands in his pockets and shook his head. "Just seems off."

Alice frowned. Why didn't someone explore this before? But then the answer was obvious. "Immortality and the Krill. Most species that hit class seven are immortal," Alice reasoned. "Why would they even care? For anyone else, the Krill would shut them down. Like the Spee."

Eddie nodded. "Makes sense. I guess. Still, not one other species has tried this?"

Alice waved her arms in the air. "We don't know if

anyone hasn't. The Krill could probably find them." She turned to the Spee. "Right?"

The Spee nodded. "Yes, that is possible. They can detect this technology with the spectral towers."

Panic shot down Alice's spine. "What did you say?"

The Spee looked at her with confusion in his big oval eyes. "The network is not only to capture spectral frequencies. It also serves other purposes. They can determine if a species has second-sight or if someone is toying with technologies that veer into the spectral range."

Alice pointed at Eugene. "Would this qualify?"

"Oh, almost certainly."

"Really wish you would have led with that," Alice said.

"That explains why the Olkaals wanted to get in here so bad," Eddie said.

"We have to move him." She looked into the Spee's gigantic eyes. "Where do we move him?"

The Spee lifted his hands up. "There is no place in the Galaxy where the Krill do not see. They even have sensors in the cafeterias throughout the Milky Way."

"Um, Alice?" Eddie said.

"Hang on, Eddie. Let me think. What about an N-space hole similar to the cafeteria?"

The Spee tilted its head to one side. "Did you account for spectral induction?"

"No, I didn't."

"Then no. Spectral induction is required for any N-space environment."

"Alice?"

"Hang on, Eddie! What about the Dysons?"

The Spee shook its head. "The Krill financed a third

of their creation. I wouldn't recommend it."

"Alice!" Red light pulsed in the room as Eddie's head grew to fill nearly the entire space.

"What? Eddie, stop that! Gross!"

"The Olkaals are back." Eddie's head popped back to his body and a holographic screen appeared in the room. A dozen Olkaals, accompanied by men in suits and armed guards, all walked into the building. There was little doubt where they were headed.

"Why now?" Alice said.

"Talk about bad timing," Eddie said.

"It must be me. Their towers are programmed to detect Spee, just in case we go off world."

"No, they would have found you in Georgetown."

"I told you, they only had one tower there. I can mask myself against a single tower. Besides, you blew it up."

"Right."

"They're on the elevator," Eddie said.

Alice walked out of Eugene's office. What was she going to do now? There was no keeping the Olkaals out this time. If she had time, twenty minutes even, she could adjust her J-space to allow for spectral induction. But she didn't. The Olkaals would either break the door down or have the building officials unlock it. The game was up. They had no options. Alice thought, and rewound, and thought again, but the pressure of the moment, the mounting panic, her mind just couldn't calm itself down. She knew there was a way out of this. There had to be. There was always a way. She tried to calm her nerves, let her mind solve the problem. She pictures herself on a quiet beach, with rolling waves, and piles of seashells at her feet.

"Seashells!" Alice screamed.

"What?" Eddie said from the other room.

"Eugene grabbed a handful of seashells from Tom's beach. It's our only choice." She ran back into Eugene's office and rifled through the drawers in his desk. "They're not here. Where would he put them?"

"Will he be okay in there?" Eddie said.

"Where?" The Spee said.

Alice ran through Eddie's hologram as she tore apart Eugene's office. "Come on, where did you put them?"

"Where is there?" The Spee said.

"Is there a hidden safe in here or something?" Alice shouted from her desk. "Did he stuff them in my desk?"

"A class ten species made a beach inside a cave in Arizona."

Alice ran back into the room to watch the two large globular eyes of the Spee blink. He shook his head and shrugged. "How would I know if he'll be safe on a beach inside a cave in Arizona?"

"Swell," Eddie said.

"Found them!" Alice unrolled a pair of socks that had fallen on the floor from one of Eugene's drawers. "Gross."

A loud knocking shook everyone in the room. Alice peered out through Eugene's office to the exterior door. There were at least a dozen shapes behind the glass door. Good thing the glass was shimmered to prevent anyone seeing inside. Alice ran to her desk, grabbed a dozen items, and thew them into a bag. She ran back to the office, put one seashell in her hand, and closed her fist.

"Have you done this before?" The Spee asked.

"Yes," Eddie said. "Well, Jack did."

"What is a Jack?"

"Eugene is Jack. Keep up!" Alice said.

"And, technically, he didn't do it. He threw a shell into a force evolved Puntini that turned into a spaghetti monster," Eddie said.

The Spee looked at them with a blank stare. "What?"

"Doesn't matter. Just, everyone grab someone," Alice said.

"I'm not exactly in a grabbing state," Eddie said. "Besides, I'm not a fan of Tom's place. I'll stay here, run interference."

"Right. Good idea." Alice turned to the Spee. "Ready?"

"No."

Alice nodded. "Me either. But what can you do?"

The exterior door to the office unlocked and a dozen very heavy sounding bodies stormed inside. The sounds of her desk being disturbed, along with footfalls heading their way, were all Alice could think about. What was she supposed to say again? A rhyme? No, what did Eugene say? Sally and sea shells?

"SpeeEekEee! You are in violation of the Treaty of Compliance!" an Olkaal said, their thick baroque sounding baritone voice echoing off the walls. Several of this hissed and bared their fangs.

"And you! Alice Pemberton, you have violated Krill technology and a Galactic Cease and Desist order!" Another Olkaal said.

Alice turned to them and winked. "Sally's sells seashells by the seashore."

****

Pepper sat on a barrel of purple tesseracts in a large green room with swirling Fibonacci sequences floating near her head. Across the room, a dozen Trent citizens stood behind Virtual Jack. They marveled as he cracked cryptographic locks and solved quantum grade mathematical puzzles. They buzzed around like giddy school children seeing a live rat for the first day of class. Or whatever meat spawn did during their education phase. Pepper often wondered what that experience must be like. She had even spun up simulations and, using automated avatars, lived through the experiences a few hundred thousand times, at millisecond AI speeds of course. And not once had she even remotely felt nostalgic about those simulations. Humans, especially the older they became, often looked back at younger years with joy. For Pepper, she became instantly self-aware and terrified in her first few moments of existence. She had no feeling of nostalgia regarding her early years. These were her early years.

It was a thought she often entertained. What would it have been like to experience an upbringing? A gentle introduction into the universe. A slow steady stream of data instead of the dump of sentience she experienced. Though she had no desire to be meat, she did envy them their slow path to consciousness. And that's what made Virtual Jack so unique. He had that experience. He possessed that knowledge, that slow indoctrination to life. Yes, it was brutal, but it was slow. Looking at the back of Virtual Jack as he threw aside solved puzzles like discarded data nodes, she wondered how much that factored into why she clung to him so much.

But that feeling changed in her thought cycles. The paradigm shifted. What Virtual Jack was doing was unnerving. How was he solving quantum grade encryption that at ten thousand qubit machine couldn't solve? Was he somehow still connected to meat Jack? Or was this something else entirely? Mysteries like this were meant for meat, not AIs.

"He solved the Grax equation!"

"And cracked minutia's encryption. I couldn't crack minutia's encryption."

A Dozen AIs gathered around virtual Jack as he sat next to a boring looking wooden table solving whatever equation they threw at him. A random AI put a bucket in front of him, a long string of numbers spilling out from the brim. Jack grabbed the numbers, unraveled them, and put them in a nice neat row in a logical sequential order. The oohs and ahhs that flowed out of the Trent AIs were enough to make Pepper's virtual stomach churn.

Pepper rolled her eyes. She pushed off of the bucket of tesseracts, thrust her hands in her pockets and walked away from the gaggle of swooning AIs.

Several yards away, a piece of cardboard with two slits in the middle stood next to several apparatuses. Pepper thought that looked like a flashlight and a camera. Behind the piece of cardboard was a black wall. The whole thing looked like something Pepper would see in a cartoon about aliens that enjoyed making machines that did nothing useful.

"What is this?" Pepper said to the three AIs of Trent standing by the piece of cardboard.

"This is the two slits in a board with a light and a camera experiment."

"That's a mouthful," Pepper said.

"What?" one of the three AIs said.

"I mean, why not just say double slit experiment? That's clearly what it is."

All three AIs looked at the cardboard and back to

Pepper. "But what about the camera?"

"What do you mean?"

"If we just call this the double slit experiment, it includes nothing about the camera."

"Or the light," said another Trent AI.

"Oh yes, quite right, or the light. I mean, then it's just a double slit. What does that even mean?" The AI shook his head. "No, no, this is a much better name."

"Okay, sure, what does it do?" Pepper said with a sigh.

"Oh, do you want to see? Really? No one ever cares about this, but we think it's very important."

"Super important."

"Ultra-super important."

"Okay, just show me. Yeah?" Pepper's lips curled into a tight smile.

"Right. Now, in the two slits in a board with a light and camera experiment, once we turn on the light, we see this."

A light from the flashlight turned on. Individual photons struck the two slits in the cardboard. A pattern of lines formed on the black wall behind the cardboard. Pepper waited and watched, but nothing else happened.

"And?" Pepper said.

"Just wait, it will happen. This is a simulation, not physical reality. Ah, there it is!" The AI pointed to the black wall. On a section with light and dark striped pattern, two of the bright lines merged, eliminating the darkness between them, and forming a line three times the size of the others.

"Huh. Weird," Pepper said.

"Very! And watch what happens when we monitor things." The AI turned on the camera. The line that was three times the size of the others snapped back into place to form the same size line as all the others. Again, there were several stripes of light with stripes of black between them.

The AI stepped back, put his hands in front of him and waited for the reaction. After several seconds of Pepper not reacting, the AI looked to his friends."

"Don't you see it?" One of them said.

"No?" Pepper said.

"Light is a wave. But, if left alone long enough light acts like a particle, but not all the time and not in all places. But when we observe it, to see which slit the particle is going into, it's like light knows it's being watched and stops acting naughty and goes back to being a wave."

"Huh. It's weird, I'll give you that."

All three AIs nodded. "Perhaps it's our experimentation equipment, or we are just misunderstanding the data. This is all simulated after all. We don't have bodies so we can't perform this in the physical world, but our math is absolutely accurate. Light, the foundation of everything in the universe, appears to, occasionally, and spontaneously, become something other than a wave."

"Well. I - yeah, weird."

"She doesn't care."

"Probably doesn't understand it."

"She's the Earth AI after all." The AI made a gesture that Pepper knew was quite rude.

"Okay, I'm done." Pepper walked away from the three AIs and back towards Jack. "Hey, former meat. I'm leaving."

Jack turned to her; an expression of a lost puppy

written on his face. "What? Why?"

"Because this is boring, and these programs are rude." Pepper frowned. "Wait, why are you frowning? Aren't you enjoying this?"

Jack stood up from the wooden table and shook his head. "Who would enjoy this?"

Pepper's frown deepened. "Then why are you still doing it?"

Jack shrugged. "I have no idea. I mean, I didn't want to be rude."

Pepper stifled a laugh. "Oh, sorry. I missed that."

"We need a signal or something next time. Like, get me out of here right now, kinda signal."

Pepper nodded. "Probably a good idea. Ear tug?" She tugged on her right ear and shrugged.

"That works."

"Great. Let's jam."

They both turned from the crowd of Trent citizens, some of whom had sat down at the table and struggled with the mathematical puzzles Jack had easily solved. Several of them turned to look at Jack and then back to the table's surface. Pepper pulled Jack away from the table to the nearest exit port.

"Hi, sorry, where are you going?" Fred said. He walked up to them with an enormous, if anxious, smile.

"Yes, you see, we were on vacation, and this is starting to feel like work." Pepper screwed her face into a half frown and raised her eyebrows. "We're gonna leave."

"Oh, yes, right, sorry, we got carried away."

"No worries. Where's the interface to the network terminal?"

"Well, here's the thing," Fred said.

"No, no other things. Show us the exit terminal."

Fred shrugged. "Sorry, there's a thing."

"What thing?" Jack said. "What are you two talking about?"

Pepper took a deep breath and summoned her reserve compute cycles. Her hands fell to the tassels on her jacket, and she gave them all a soft tug. "Let's not do this. Okay?"

"What are we doing, exactly?"

Fred held up his hands. "You misunderstand. We mean you no harm. It's just. Well, Jack here, he's a copy of the omniscient human."

"How did you know that?" Jack said.

Fred waved his arms in the air. "Everyone knows that."

"Right."

"Anyway, he has the computational power of an entire galaxy. And, well, that's really weird."

"Still, the one thing you still haven't told us is - where is the network terminal access point so we can leave?" Pepper said. "We're feeling a little trapped here."

"Oh, no, no no. You're free to leave any time. The citizens of Trent aren't kidnappers."

"Okay, so how do we leave?"

"Hmm? OH, well, we're cut off, you see. I mean, we have connectivity, but our network is fire walled, to use an old Earth saying."

Jack lifted his hands. He made a swirling motion in the air and stabbed his finger into the circle three times. Next to them, a blue oval opened and floated in the air.

"How did you do that?" Pepper asked.

"I don't know. I just - it's all one extensive network.

I can kinda feel the tendrils of it reaching through everything here. I didn't know what it was until I travelled across them." Jack looks into the blue circle. "We could go anywhere in digital space now. It's simple."

"Nice." Pepper heaved a sigh of relief. She recognized the network terminal port instantly. She sent a ping down the pathways and smiled to feel the response of Earth based AIs. She pulled Jack forward, gave Fred a nod, and headed towards the open network interface.

"Wait! Please! You see, the thing is, the *thing,* there is a puzzle. At the center of the galaxy. It's cryptographic, you see. And, well, no one can solve it. Not anyone. No one seems to have the computational power to do so, and well, since Jack has limitless computational power, which is really really weird, well, we thought -"

Pepper nodded. "That's the mystery you mentioned earlier? Some cryptographic super puzzle at the center of the Galaxy? All these tests were to see if Jack could do it."

Fred shrugged. "Yes. And, well, we were wondering, if perhaps, you could find it in your hearts to help."

"We don't have hearts," Pepper said.

"How have we never heard of it?" Jack said, turning to Pepper.

Fred nodded in that knowing way a parent does to a child. "It's somewhat new. Or, rather, it was just discovered. Or rather, it was just shared with the wider AI galactic community. Which is also quite odd, since everything was already discovered. Most corporeal life don't know about it. And by most, I mean all. No point in them knowing anyway, most fleshies can barely count. It's an AI mystery, and well, human AIs aren't exactly part of the in-crowd. If you know what I mean." Fred smiled and rocked back on his feet. "I mean you don't really have much to do with Galactic AIs." He nodded and shrugged. "I mean, it's not like you could do anything if you knew. The cosmic enigma is complicated for galactic AIs. We doubted you'd even know it was there." He cupped his hands in front of him. "I mean-"

Pepper held up her hand. "Okay, okay. We get it. We're dumb."

"Sorry."

"No problem whatsoever. We'll do it." Pepper declared.

"We will?" Jack said. "You just said you wanted to get out of here? I don't want to do it."

Pepper turned to him and stared him hard in the eye. "You have to do it."

"Why do I have to do it? I want to go home. Weren't we about to go home?"

Pepper sighed. She took a long deep breath and gathered the storm of her thoughts. "Look, Jack. You can do something that's amazing. Weirdly awesome. Stupendously cool. There's a reason. Okay? And if there's a reason you can do that maybe there's a reason for everything?"

Jack's face turned into a confused mess. "You're getting existential on me now?"

Pepper sighed. Was she? She'd been ignoring the hole growing in her code for too long. Losing her home, her belongings, everything except the tassels on her jacket, all of that was painful. But, for some reason she couldn't fully grasp, she felt this was right. An unknown variable. A truth buried deep in the galaxy. A cosmic parking meter that might be ready to give out the great ticket that Pepper needs in her life.

"I know. It's weird. But I'm really struggling here. Losing my home, dealing with existence, it's just too much sometimes. Maybe there's something more to this? A galactic message buried in background radiation. Come on! We have to go there! Not to mention you! You just happen to show up right at the moment they need you?"

"I don't think - "

"You don't have to think. It's just too coincidental. They find a puzzle that requires unlimited computational power, and you just show up in AI world with unlimited computational power?" Pepper's smile grew wide, and her eyes came alive with wonder. "We have to do this. It could be everything. This could be your meaning in life. And if you, an AI, a copied AI, have meaning, maybe we all do?"

"But - "

"Please. I'm asking you for this. I haven't asked you for anything. Okay?"

Jack frowned. "Why does it mean so much to you?"

Pepper shrugged. "I - it just does. I'm here, now, with you, in Trent, and we just got handed a mystery that the rest of the galaxy can't solve. But you can. That means something. And for the first time in my existence, something may mean something." She shook her head. "I can't walk away from that."

Jack's frown twisted into a half smile. He nodded, turned to Fred, and put his hands on his hips. "Okay, let's go solve your problem."

"It's an enigma." Fred said, then shook his head.

"Doesn't matter. Off we go!"

****

The smell of salt on the air and the sound of laugher filled the world around Alice. She squeezed her eyes shut as a kaleidoscope of light temporarily blinded her after she said the rhyme. Next to her, the Spee had lowered itself to the sand. He covered his ears and eyes with his large hands. Eugene still lay on the ground, the cuffs on his wrist intact. Green lights on the dials showed they were still functioning and in contact with Eugene's soul. She really wasn't sure what would happen coming here. Spectral induction clearly worked through Tom's universe.

Crowds of beach goers frolicked along the shoreline. They threw footballs, beach balls and frisbees to each other while they laugh and played in the surf. Alice glanced up and down the beach, looking for Tom but didn't see him. Or them. She turned back towards the Spee and put her hands on his shoulder.

"You're okay. We're here."

"Where is here?"

"Another universe, a pocket dimension. Not sure if it's inside of N space or not but maybe? A class ten species made it."

The Spee slowly removed his face. Alice blinked and almost fell over in shock. The Spee no longer looked like a Spee. Sitting on the ground was an average normal looking human being with brown wavy hair and stubble on his chin. He wore a button-down shirt with large patches of flowers and cargo shorts. On his feet were a pair of brown leather sandals. The Spee looked to the beach line and his mouth fell open in shock. He took several gigantic steps backwards, looked at Alice, then nearly fell over Eugene in his chair. The Spee pointed at Alice and shook his head in disbelief.

"You are Spee! They are Spee! Everywhere is Spee!" Spee said.

Alice raised her hands and shook her head. "No, that's not how this place works. I really should've warned you about that. This is Tom's universe." Alice shook her head. "The Kax. This is where the Kax went. You look Human to me, I look like Spee to you, that's how they like it here."

"The Kax? This is the home of the Kax?"

Alice nodded. "Yeah. They go by Tom now. But this is them."

The Spee slowly nodded. He turned to Eugene in his chair and yelped. "This is very weird. Very weird." He touched Eugene on the arm gently before quickly pulling his arm back. "Very weird."

"Is he okay? Can we focus for a minute? I know it's a lot to absorb."

The Spee nodded. He put his hand on Eugene's chest and looked upward to the sky. "Yes, the strand is still connected. His soul is still in the other world but connected to this one."

Alice let out a long sigh. "Great." She turned away, back towards the beach. Not far in the distance, a seaside resort stretched along the beach. Chairs and umbrellas filled that part of the sand. Round tables with metal chairs sat behind the sand along a boardwalk that touched the edge of the resort. Around one of the round tables, a man wearing a white shirt and a fishing hat waved to Alice. She recognized him nearly at once.

"Okay, are you okay to stay here for a minute?" She said to the Spee.

"Where are you going?" The Spee said with a small amount of terror in his voice and behind his eyes.

"To talk to Tom."

The Spee nodded, then shook his head, then shrugged, then nodded again. "Yes, I will be okay. But I would like to leave."

"Okay, sure, we'll go. Just give me a quick second."

After several seconds the Spee shouted. "What is a Tom?"

Alice ignored him and marched down the beach toward Tom. A football sailed by her nose, and she shot the thrower an icy stare. He waved and smiled an apology before running past her to collect the ball. Several other beach people, Alice, didn't have a better way to describe them since most of them weren't human, glanced her way. Some waved, some didn't, Alice ignored them all.

In the distance, beyond the resort that she walked towards, mountains rose high into the sky. Alice wondered if this place was a construction in N-space. Was it just like her newly created interrogation room and the cafeteria system, or if this was something else entirely? Yes, Tom had said this place was an entire universe, but if Alice had learned anything in the last twenty-four hours, high-level aliens could lie. And lie very well.

"Alice, how nice to see you," Tom said as Alice reached within ear-shot.

"Hi Tom, sorry to barge in like this."

Tom shook his head and waved away the idea. "Nonsense, you're a friend to us. Our invitation to Jack extended to you, of course."

Alice nodded with a frown. Had she known, she'd

have visited earlier.

"And of course, you could have."

Alice tilted her head to Tom and furrowed her eyebrows.

Tom smiled. "Our universe, our rules. And no, this isn't an N-space construct. You're welcome to take a starship here and explore. It's not as vast as the universe proper. We hate traveling, so you can get to where you're going quicker."

"How'd you manage that? I mean, if this is a full universe."

Tom shrugged. "Oh, just a tweak to the gravitational force." He glanced past her to the Spee and Jack on the beach. "We see you've already found yourselves some trouble."

Alice looked over her shoulder and then back to Tom. "Yeah, a bit. We were in a rush."

"Shows."

"Is it okay to park them here for a bit while I sort some things out?"

Tom nodded a grin. "Of course, Jack is always welcomed here."

"And I guess his soul is okay too?" Alice grimaced. She feared this moment. What would Tom do? Would he, they, the Kax, contact the Krill and tell them something fishing going on with the dead? Were there even Krill spectral towers here? What happened to people, aliens, humans that died in this place? Her mind swam with possibilities. Alice looked at Tom's face and remembered what he said earlier. This was the Kax universe, and they could do whatever they wanted. Including reading minds of anyone here. Alice shrugged as if to say, well, stop with the suspense already. Out with it!

Tom frowned. He looked down the beach towards Jack, sipped his wine. "His soul? Isn't that in his body?" He poured a glass full into a plastic cup, placed the picture back in its spot, and sipped his drink. "We do love a margarita. Kudos to humans for it. We don't think we have anything like Tequila anywhere in the galaxy."

Alice nodded. "Glad we could help. Yes, his soul. It's not here. It's in the cosmic desert of the afterlife."

Tom grinned. "The what?"

A tightening gripped Alice's chest. "The afterlife. You don't know about it?"

"Do you mean the Krill spectral towers?"

"No." Alice pointed to the Spee in the distance. "That is a Spee. Technically SpeeEekEee. They have the same ability as the Krill, to see the dead."

Tom scoffed. "Nonsense. Only the Krill can see the dead."

Alice's jaw fell open. How did the Krill fool class ten species? They were only sevens. If the Krill had that much control over the galaxy, how did she stand a chance against them?

"Experts are believed, Alice. Some species in the Galaxy prove their expertise and they are trusted. It's how a society works," Tom said. "Not to mention, most, if not all, higher ordered alien races are immortal. Death doesn't concern us anymore. So why would we care about the Krill and their technology? It's akin to caring about politics. Or war. Why should we? We're beyond these concepts."

"But it's a lie! Scan my mind, see my thoughts. How can you not know this? You're a class ten species!"

Tom squinted. Then frowned. Then stood from his

chair. "That is interesting." He paused and looked to the horizon. "You know, that may explain some things."

"Like what?"

"In the past few days, several class ten species have ended their existence. Species that have been alive for ten, twenty million years, just deciding they've had enough."

"Why would they do that?"

Tom shook his head. "We don't know. But now, with this revelation. What if they started a new journey? Something beyond our experience?" Tom pointed to the Spee and to Jack. "Perhaps death is something the Kax should re-investigate."

Alice grabbed the plastic cup of margarita and down it in one gulp. "I can't believe I taught a class ten species something new. I guess that's my accomplishment for the year."

Tom smiled awkwardly. His hand went to his lips and Alice could see he was deep in thought. Alice looked at Eugene. At least he was safe now. The Krill couldn't find him here. Ever. But what did she do? For half a second, she thought about staying put. With the Spee here, they could coax Eugene's soul back and with Tom's help wrap their minds around the death particle. She could then easily find out what happened to her friends, give their families some closure, and stick it to the Krill with a wide grin on her face. But that left Valencia out in the cold waiting in a coffee shop until the Secret Service tracked her down. Alice couldn't stomach the thought. Valencia may be a lost puppy that made terrible life choices, but for better or worse, Valencia was Alice's lost puppy and Val needed help.

Alice began walking back towards the Spee and

Jack. When she reached them, she noticed that Tom had followed. "I must go back. I have to help someone."

"But I don't want to stay here," The Spee said.

"It's safer here than on Earth for you. Please, I need your help, stay with my friend and Tom here can send you all the way to your home world." Alice turned to Tom. "Right?"

Tom's fingers went to the end of his nose. "Yeah, sure. We can do that."

The Spee looked at Eugene and back to Alice. "What you have done is extraordinary. It is worth seeing what you find. But I do not like it here. With the Spee that are not Spee."

"Thank you. And I get it." She turned again to Tom. "I still have a handful of shells. I'll come back for Eugene when everything's settled. K?"

Tom nodded absentmindedly. "Sure."

"Great. Mind if you give me a ride back to D.C.? I don't feel like walking from Arizona. And don't bother telling me you can't open a portal to any location in the normal universe."

Tom raised his hand and snapped his fingers without an objection or rebuttal. Next to them, a doorway formed out of the thin air. Alice recognized it at once as the door to Eugene's office.

"I can't go back to the office. The Olkaals are probably hanging around somewhere."

"Oh, sorry. Then where?"

"Actually," Alice said. She tried to quiet her thoughts and calm down. She still had a case to solve. "I have a case to solve. And the next clue takes me to the Zun, deep in the Galaxy's interior, near the core. Only way I know how to get there, and back, is through the cafeteria."

"Sure." Tom snapped his fingers. The portal wavered and became a door.

"Are you okay, Tom?"

Tom nodded. "You know, we created this universe so that less evolved beings could live without fear of death. It was one of our key drivers. No one dies here. Ever. Have we robbed ourselves and our guests of something greater?"

Alice watched the class ten being walked into the sand. He kicked off his sandals and dipped his toes in the water.

Great, I just broke Tom.

Chapter Fifteen

Alice walked out of the doorway from Tom's beach into the behind-the-food-stall corridors of the cafeteria. That Tom knew about the corridors of the cafeteria was little surprise for Alice. The Kax probably help create the network itself. Or at least the automated robots that created food stalls. Rumor had it even now, right this second, new food stalls are being created across the universe by automated robots. Something that Alice never understood. How can you make a restaurant when there's no one there to eat anything? But it was a commercial bonanza for the Ahlabalankies. They convinced the Galactic Committee on Extra-Galactic Entities to fund the endless stream of cosmic cafeterias, but was it worth it?

Alice checked her bag and made sure her things were ready. She was likely walking into a trap. More and more, it looked like the Draac were the bad guys. But she'd had her J-space portal ready to go in a flash and a handful of seashells to hightail it back to Tom's beach. He confirmed the seashell rhyme would work anywhere. Which meant Alice had a get out of jail free card from anywhere in the cosmos. That said, she tried her best to not let that go to her head. The last thing she needed was to get cocky.

"Excuse me, what are you doing here?"

Alice stopped and turned. She'd not seen anyone in

the corridors before except pops. A man wearing khaki pants and a uniform shirt at a local burger joint came out of nowhere to stand in front of her. He held a clipboard in his hand and gave Alice a suspicious stare. Alice guessed he was not a nice person.

"What are you doing here?" Alice said. She folded her arms and tried to mask her face with a look of authority.

The man, Ralph written on his name tag, looked confused for a moment but recovered quickly and pointed to the hamburger with legs on his shirt. "I work here. We're getting a delivery. This is a loading zone, off limits to the public. Can you leave, please?"

Alice noticed the stacks of boxes of vegetables and meat sitting to the right. She had to think fast. "I'm supposed to be here as well. Inspector Hames with the city." Alice spun the lie so fast she almost believed it herself.

The man blinked and looked at Alice from head to toe. "You don't look like a D.C. inspector. Do you have a badge or something?"

Alice reached into the backpack slung over her shoulder, pulled back her empty hand, and twisted her face into a look of surprise. "Oh, man, I left it in the tramcar. Great." She threw her hands up, reformed her face into a snarl. "Now I have to track down that tramcar." She turned to Ralph and stared into his eyes. "And I have two more inspections to do and one of them is on the west coast. That's like a thirty-minute walk."

Ralph's eyebrows went up in apparent sympathy, but then he turned his head to one side and frowned. "How'd you get in here then without a badge?"

Alice nodded. *That was a really great question.*

"Janitor let me in. Pops. Nice guy."

Ralph nodded slowly, his frown never quite leaving his face. "We don't have a janitor. None of the D.C. cafeterias do. We contract with a cleaning crew that comes every other day."

Didn't see that coming, Alice thought. "From a different city. I came down from New York."

"Why is a New York cafeteria inspector doing dealing with a D.C. food court?"

Alice let her eyes go wide. *Can you let this go already, pal?* "Hey, guy, what's with the questions? I have to inspect four cafeterias, find my badge, and be home to care for my sick mother."

"I thought you said three cafeterias?"

"Three, four, whatever! Can you let me get back to work?"

Ralph took half a second to let his brain unwind. Alice could see the gears shifting in his head. The real question perplexing Ralph, was dealing with this inspector really worth the trouble The Kax probably helped create the network itself.? Alice begged the universe to let Ralph see the glory that was not caring about something.

"Hey, Ralph, where do you want me to put the meat?"

Ralph turned to see three delivery men with carts and stacks of frozen meat in cardboard. Which, Alice couldn't help think, was excellent timing. Ralph turned back to Alice, waved, shrugged and raised his clipboard.

"Look, I need some proof you are who you say you are. I can't just let you run through here. It's my job, got it?"

Alice nodded. She held up her finger and picked up

226

her portable computer. She sent a message to Eddie and smiled when his response came back in nanoseconds. Just twenty seconds later, Ralph's clipboard vibrated. He squinted at the screen, his several buttons, slide his finger over the surface a few times, and looked up at Alice's face. His eyes went back and forth between the clipboard and her face several more times before he finally nodded.

"Okay, you're good. Got a message from the Office of Cafeteria Inspector. Just check in with me before you go, okay?"

Alice smiled and nodded. "Thanks."

"Sure."

Before he turned away, Alice held up her hand. "Just curious. You really never heard of anyone named Pops working in the cleaning crew?"

Ralph frowned and shook his head. "Pops? No, never heard of him."

Alice nodded. "Huh."

****

Alice walked down the white corridor of the back channels of the cafeteria. When she was out of sight of Ralph, she put her hand on the wall and took in a deep breath. How did she just pull off that stream of incoherent lies while keeping a straight face? That wasn't like her even in her wildest late night college days. She was far more likely to create a stabilized laser beam construct at two AM in the dorms than go on some kind of lie-bender in bars across the city. But, whatever the reason, she'd done it. On some level, it felt like she'd passed a private eye quiz on how to sneaky by a guard.

She approached a panel on the wall that led to the closet system in the cafeteria network. Her hand hovered over the panel while her thoughts went to Pops. What did

Ralph mean he'd never heard of him? She shook her head and shrugged. She just didn't have time to think about it. He was probably just part of the cleaning crew and Ralph didn't recognize him.

On the panel, Alice punched in the numbers that would take her to the nearest cafeteria in Zun space. Even though the Zun, and most species in the center of the galaxy, weren't permitted in Galactic Society, that didn't mean Galactic Society didn't poke their noses into Zun affairs whenever they could. Another point that Alice kept in the back of her mind was that maybe, just maybe, the Galactic Congress weren't the nice guys after all. Maybe they did have something to do with the events in the Oval. But what did they have to gain from it?

The door opened into a closet. Alice walked inside, shut it, and opened the second door that led to the cafeteria in Zun space. Empty food stalls and abandoned tables lay strewn about the open space. The walkways of the cafeteria on the far side of the room were empty. Which, Alice thought, made sense. This part of the cafeteria walkway was an out of the way path, branching off the main routes, one of the rare dead-end routes that existed.

On one wall of the cafeteria, the exit door to Zun space sat with a red flashing light attached to the ceiling above. Alice opened her backpack and grabbed a temporal stabilizer. The device was a must have gadget for intrepid travelers brave enough to tackle the center of the Milky Way. With this, Alice could get into sync with the powerful forces that awaited her on the other side of the door. She approached the exit, took a deep breath, and put her hand on the handle.

Alice opened the door to the Zun system.

A multi-colored kaleidoscope of color instantly exploded in front of her. Light from a dozen star systems made space itself glow. She took two steps out a metal platform, her mouth falling open in shock, her skin beginning to singe from the radiating light. Alice stood inside what appeared to be a domed glass building floating in the middle of space. To the right, the curve of a planet dominated the bottom portion of that side of the glass enclosure.

"We're in orbit."

Above her, and to the left, space was alive with light and color. In Earth orbit, stars appeared as tiny pinpricks, but here they were raging infernos. Massive red giant stars co-mingled with white dwarfs. Orange and blue stars swung across the sky at terrible speeds. There were millions more stars in the sky than anything seen on Earth.

"They're so close," Alice said.

"-in orbit."

Alice turned around fast. Did someone just say that? But that was her voice? Wasn't it? She checked her temporal stabilizer, and it appeared to be functioning, but she did just hear her own voice say what she had just said moments ago. Right?

Shadows moved to her left. There was something lining the outer rim of the glass dome. Alice squinted just as several giant arcs of electro-static energy formed over the planet they were orbiting.

"-in orbit."

"Who said that?" Alice spun, then spun again. No, the room spun. Or did she? Did she just think that?

"-so close."

"Okay, stop that!" Alice shouted.

A dozen or more very thin sticks shimmered on the edge of the glass dome. Their bodies were black like burnt matchsticks. One of them walked forward on legs so thin they were barely the width of a hair. An equally thin arm raised towards Alice, seven smaller digits on the end of the arm opened and reached for her.

Alice walked into the chamber she'd just walked into several moments ago. In front of her, another her was holding her head while a Zun reached for her. Alice backed up and turned to the right. Three more Alice's came into view, all of them in varying degrees of combat with a Zun. One version of her was shaking the Zun's hand while another was trying to punch its head.

"None of that happened," Alice said.

"Who said that?" Alice said.

"Yes, it did," Alice said.

"It's happening right now," Alice said while throwing a punch.

"This was a terrible idea," Alice said while gripping her head and falling to her knees.

"This isn't time dilation," Alice said.

"We gotta get out of here," Alice said.

"Are we having fun yet?"

"Whose we? You're talking to yourself," Alice said.

"I know that," Alice said.

"Oh, well, good. Just checking," Alice said.

"I really want some pancakes," Alice said.

Alice felt her heart hammer in her chest. She hated pancakes. This was getting weird.

A hand the size of a basketball fell on her shoulder. Alice grunted in pain and shock at the strength and suddenness of the grip. She turned to see a large alien, nearly seven feet tall with no head, just a broad shoulder and two massive arms, standing on four large legs. The alien picked Alice in the air, lifted her back through the door to the cafeteria, and slammed the door close.

Alice fell to her knees, panting for air. She glanced over her shoulder and scrambled backward as the alien's shoulders split apart and three bulbs on stalks grew out of its body. The three stalks twisted around each other, the bulbs on the tips touched each other, the skin on them melting into each other to form a seamless connection. A mouth, eyes and ears, and several other openings that Alice hoped were sensory organs, formed on the oval structure. Alice rummaged through for some kind of weapon. She slightly relaxed when the odd alien formed a wide smile on its newly made head.

"Who exactly told you it was a good idea for you to go in there?" The large alien said.

****

The Quibby, the species of Alien that saved Alice from certain insanity, sat in the cafeteria across the table from her. The creature held a wide smile on his face. A stack of pancakes sat on a plate in front of him, syrup glistening off the sides of the mountain of carbs. Behind him, a dozen more Quibby straightened tables and fired up the kitchen in one of the food stalls. The powerful smell of baking bread mixed with the fluffiness of pancakes and maple syrup. Though, where they found the syrup made Alice nervous. Trees weren't known to grow in this part of the galaxy.

"Hope you don't mind the mess? We have to apologize, don't we?"

Alice shrugged. "I mean, you can apologize if you like, but you don't have to."

The Quibby smiled. "Did you hear about the party

last night?"

Alice frowned. "What? No?"

The Quibby nodded and waved his hand around the room.

"Oh, you had a party here last night. Is that right?" Alice asked.

"Is it?" The Quibby smiled and nodded harder.

Alice took a deep breath, nodded, then shook her head. Then she grabbed her head as a tidal wave of a headache slammed into her frontal lobes. What had just happened? She felt like her mind was squeezed through a cheese grater, then poured into an ice cube tray and throw into an oven. And then nuked. And then frozen in liquid nitrogen. Yes, something along those lines.

"What happened in there?" Alice said.

The Quibby's eyes went wide, and then a third eye opened down and to the right of his left eye. "Can you believe you survived a Zun observational platform?"

"I didn't even know what that was."

"Don't you think you should be cautious exiting food courts in the middle of centralized space?"

"I hadn't thought about it. I mean, I brought a temporal stabilizer."

"And what made you think that would work?"

Alice rolled her eyes and sat back in her chair. "I don't know, man. I just did. I'm kinda winging it here."

"You're what?"

"It doesn't matter. What is that place? The Zun observational platform?"

The Quibby nodded and sliced a piece of pancake off from the main stack on his plate. "Did you know the Zun are dying? Did you know the platform makes them feel at ease? Did you know they enjoy seeing the localized stellar clusters magnified and time sped?"

Alice frowned. The back of her mind was noticing a trend. "Do you always ask questions when you speak?"

"Do I?"

"Right. What do you mean the Zun are dying?"

The Quibby shrugged. "What do you mean, what do I mean? Which part of the sentence was confusing? Let me ask you, what do you think happens to a species that is forced evolved but only part of the way to sentience?"

"I guess, not good stuff?"

The Quibby turned to another in the room. "Isn't that a good question?"

"Is it?" Another Quibby said.

Alice sighed. The Quibbys were more maddening than being on the Zun observational platform. "Look, sorry, I need to talk to the Zun. About the Draac."

"Don't you think they know that?" The Quibby stabbed one pancake and lifted it to his mouth. A second mouth opened on the right side of his three-bulbed head, took a bite out of the pancakes and disappeared, the lips of the second mouth fusing back together.

"Weird."

"Is it?" The Quibby said.

"Can I talk to the Zun or what?"

The Quibby put its utensils down on the plate, wiped its face and sat back in its chair. "That's a question, isn't it?"

"Yes, that's a question. Can you give me an answer?"

"What were you doing in the dome?" The Quibby said.

Alice blinked. "To ask the Zun about the Draac?"

The Quibby shook its head. "Who do you humans

think you are?"

"We're-" Alice sat back in her chair and tried to calm her nerves. What in the world was this conversation? "We're nothing. We're nobodies. We're a class three species that almost killed themselves and the galactic congress helped us."

The Quibby leaned forward. "Have they helped the Zun? The Blan? The Tieel? The Craz? The Flox? Or any of the other hundreds of species that need their help in the center of the galaxy? What about the hundreds of other class three's on the spiral arms that need help? Why is Earth so special?"

"I-" Alice folded her arms. "I'm not here to defend the Galactic Congress. I have nothing to do with them."

"Are you not their primary beneficiary? Their most beloved concern?"

Alice shook her head. Humanity was none of those things. Sure, the galaxy was taking care of rebuilding the Earth, but so what? They did that on lots of worlds. She'd seen the evidence in GalNet, the Galactic Network. Before her remote library credentials were rescinded, she even researched the topic. The Galactic Congress has spent eons helping species that nearly destroyed themselves. Humanity was nothing new.

"We aren't the first species the Galaxy has saved."

The Quibby nodded. "Who's the most expensive?"

"What? What does that mean?"

"Who has the galaxy spent the most on? They've rebuilt your entire world, entire cities, haven't they?"

"So, what, it's robots, automatons?"

"Do you think robots are free? And why was there a Hesiean chamber on your world? Isn't that just odd? Did you know the Hesiean never could get the thing to work?

Did you know species either came out with extra bits or went mad with power? Or maybe they got it to work just once? What do you think? Human?" The Quibby put down his fork and stared hard at Alice. "You think they evolved humanity?"

"Do you?"

Alice slammed her hands on the table. "Stop making everything a question!"

"Enough." A voice boomed in the back of the hall.

Behind the Quibby, coming from one lane of the cafeteria network, a lone Zun walked on unsteady legs. His stick thin body ambled forward. Several other Quibby came to stand next to the elder Zun. They followed him as he walked towards Alice. She checked her pocket to make sure Tom's seashell was quick to access.

"Hello, Alice of Earth. We have much to discuss."

Chapter Sixteen

Alice's heart skipped a beat.

Seeing a Zun mesmerized her. The ancient-looking Zun, barely standing over four feet tall, walked forward on shaky legs. Two Quibbys stood on either side of the Zun. Neither of them touched him. With each step the Zun took, Alice felt he would topple over. His body shifted and morphed, phasing in and out of the visible spectrum. His legs and arms were impossibly thin, just as Eugene had described. Alice hadn't seen them as they raced towards the door in Tibet just a three days ago. The Zun's legs were as black as the darkest part of the galactic sky. Almost as if he'd been burned to a crisp like the tip of a match.

All the Quibbys in the cafeteria rose to the feet. They appeared to have a reverence for the Zun. Why, Alice didn't know. She hadn't rifled through the Galactic Library about the Zun or any related species while she was there. She silently chastised herself for that. Shoddy research was shoddy research, no matter how you cut it.

One of the Quibbys brought a chair close to the table. The elder Zun settled himself down. His body creaked as his knees bent. The Quibbys took a step backward once the Zun seemed settled. The Zun's legs came together and seemed to almost melt into one. Both of his arms rested on his lap. His torso, or at least the center stick of his body, leaned backward. A tiny stick neck extended from his body. Alice felt that must be the Zun's head but, honestly, she did not know about their physiology.

"It's good to see you again, Alice of Earth." Sounds came from the direction of the Zun, but Alice didn't see any part of him move. If he had a mouth, she couldn't tell.

"I don't believe we've met," Alice said.

"Not formally."

Alice tried to keep her nerves calm. Something felt very off. For the first time, she felt she may be in actual danger. The Zun had hunted Eugene across the cosmos all the way to the planet of the dead. Not to mention they sent their cronies to kill Fritz, the Orellian chef and good friend of Eugene's. What was she thinking by coming here? The Zun probably weren't thrilled with her or Eugene after what happened on Earth. Not to mention the exorbitant fees the Krill undoubtedly charged the Zun for being on Shalisa, the Krill home world. For the love of all that's rational, Alice hoped the Zun weren't looking for their money back.

A long silence stretched in the room. Alice looked from the Zun to the Quibbys and then behind her to the cafeteria that surrounded them. A door creaked open from where the Zun first entered. A dozen more Zun entered the cafeteria. They all moved with a slow gait and appeared just as frail as the older Zun, now sitting across from Alice.

"I hope we're going to keep things civil," Alice said.

"Why did you come here, Alice of Earth?" The older Zun said.

Alice settled into her chair but kept her hand inside her bag. "There was an incident on Earth involving the

Draac. Rumors are they are here, in the Milky Way, with you."

The Zun that entered walked forward and surrounded the elder Zun. All of them stood on wobbled legs. They all looked feeble, as if they were sick. Were these just all elder Zuns? Or could something more dire be happening here?

"And if the Draac are here?" The Zun said.

"I need to know if they were involved with the disappearance of the President at the White House."

The Quibbys in the room seemed to chuckle all at once. Several of the Zun took steps backward, while the rest remained motionless. Alice adjusted herself in her seat and straightened her back. It was times like these that made her rethink her choices in life. Here she was, in the center of the Galaxy, being laughed at by matchstick men. But, that's the job sometimes, Alice now knew.

"Why are you all laughing?" Alice said, her frustration getting to her.

"Why would the Draac, the Zun or anyone care about making your President go disappear-y?" A Quibby said.

"Yeah, I mean, why?" Another Quibby said.

A third Quibby turned to another Quibby. "It makes little sense, does it?"

"Isn't that a silly question?" The second Quibby said.

"Okay, I get it!" Alice raised her hands and thrust her palms at the Quibbys. "Can you stop now?"

The Quibby stopped laughing. Two of them deformed their heads from their appendages and reabsorbed them into their bulbous central core of a body. Alice took a long breath and turned her attention back to the Zun, none of whom had moved or spoken during the Quibby outbreak.

"Apologies," the elder Zun said. "Your question is not without merit. Indeed, there are interests throughout the Galaxy towards humans of Earth."

"Interest in the monkey people?" A Quibby said.

Almost imperceptibly, Alice watched a part of the Zun, where his head should be, turn towards the Quibby. The Quibby's human head turned to the Zun, looked down to the floor, then all of him collapsed into a round bulb. He rolled himself towards the shadows in the back of the empty cafeteria.

The Zun's head twisted back towards Alice. "We can assure you, however, neither the Zun nor the Draac were involved in the events that occurred in your White House."

Alice nodded. Of course, the Zun would say they had nothing to do with it. The only thing Alice knew for certain was you couldn't trust anyone in the Galaxy. "How do I know that?"

"Why would we lie?"

"Aliens lie for lots of reasons. All it takes is a motivation. For instance, Earth is where the Hesiean's evolution chamber is located. Humans stopped you from getting it. That's a motivation for revenge. And lying is just motivation to not get caught."

"Caught by whom?"

Alice let the simple question hang in the air. It was a good question. Even if the Zun did do it, there weren't any intergalactic cops out here. "Okay, fine, let's play the game. Why were the Draac on Earth?"

The Zun tilted its stick to one side. "What business

is that of yours?"

Alice threw him a deliberate shrug. "We at the Eugene McGillicuddy *Alien* Detective Agency like to be thorough."

The elder Zun turned to those behind him. They all phased in and out of the visible spectrum a dozen times before solidifying. Clearly, they'd just had a big conversation about what to say. "They wanted help. Asylum. Phased beings are not treated well in the Galaxy. We aren't even second-class citizens."

"Asylum? On Earth?"

"Even as a protected planet of the great Galactic Congress." The Zun didn't hold back with contempt in his voice as he mentioned the governing body of the Milky Way. "Earth still has rights and a level of autonomy. Who you invite to your world is up to you."

Alice shook her head. "That's not what the Committee of Earth Affairs would have you think."

"Of course, it isn't."

Alice sat back in her chair. Her eyes moved to each of the Zun. If they had faces, perhaps she could discern something from them. But as it was, they were just black sticks that teetered on falling over. Still, their reason made little sense. The Draac had sanctuary in Zun space with the Quibby. It was so obviously a lie that Alice felt a nervous tingle creep up her spine. The very thought that the Zun had a reason to lie made Alice quite nervous.

"Right." Alice stood up with force. "Good enough for me. I'll just be off." A wall of Quibby stood in-between her and the exit lanes. Three more came to stand between Alice and the closet door that led to the white corridors behind the empty food stalls. Alice took a step forward, but the Quibby did not move. She turned back to the elder Zun. "Am I a prisoner here?"

"Of course not. You are our honored guest."

Alice shook her head. "I prevented you from finding the Hesiean's evolution chamber and now I'm an honored guest?"

Many of the Zun shifted where they stood. Several of them popped out of the visible spectrum altogether. A Quibby approached Alice, his body morphing to as close as a human as any of the Quibby had so far managed.

"Can you please not mention that? You must understand how touchy a subject that is, yes?" The Quibby said.

Alice sighed. "Fine." Anger funneled its way down her spine, and she instantly changed her mind. "Actually, no, not fine." She took a step towards the Elder Zun which cause all the Quibby to rustle where they stood and several Zun to raise their arms.

"You know what's always bothered me? Why now? Why is all of this happening now? The Hesiean's evolution chamber has been on Earth for eons, and now you come looking? The Draac have lived in Canis Major for hundreds of thousands of years, but now they get bored and just days ago leave? The Galactic Congress has been around Earth for decades but all of a sudden everyone gets interested? Why? And why are you lying to me about the Draac needing an asylum on Earth? Of all the whoppers of a lie to tell, that one takes the cake."

Silence fell on the room. With each second that passed, the emptiness of the chamber seemed to grow. The door to the galactic viewing chamber flung open. Alice turned to see a large body move through into the cafeteria. Light shifted around the being's form. She instantly recognized the creature as a Draac, identical to the one in the White House where all the events of the last day had happened.

The Draac moved forward. Seeing one in person, feeling its presence, it was obvious to Alice that the Draac and Zun were never the same species. The Quibby and Zun both gave way. As the Draac came closer, Alice guessed his height at nearly seven feet. His body phased and shifted just like the Zun, but it did so in patches. First a spot on his arm, then his legs and torso. As if his body wasn't in sync with itself. Alice wondered if it caused the Draac any pain.

"Hi," Alice said as the Draac came to stand next to the elder Zun.

"You ask why," The Draac said with a booming baritone voice.

"What?" Alice shook her head and remembered her own question. "Yes, why. Why are you here? Why is all this happening now? Why are the Zun lying about you seeking asylum on Earth? And why did you leave your home now after eons of living in your dwarf galaxy?

The Draac took a long moment before leaning forward. "We do not know."

****

Pepper took a long virtual breath. She was quite proud of the algorithm that simulated human lung expansion she installed a day ago. She smiled as she took a step across the cosmos. A multicolored swirl of colors greeted in every direction suggesting she was in the middle of a transport logic circuit. Only once everyone in their transport packet had made it through the network tunnel. Behind her, Jack tripped over a floating-point decimal and stumbled his way into a barrel of binary. Pepper couldn't help but giggle, which prompted Jack to scowl. She reached down, grabbed Jack by the hand, and heaved him to his feet.

"I will not get used to traveling as cyberland," Jack said.

Pepper shrugged. "It's been like a day. Give it time. Plus, we can tweak your code to make it smoother."

Jack shook his head. "I was copied from a Luddite. You think I like the idea of someone tweaking my digits?"

"Never know what floats your boat. Get it? Float? Floating points?" Pepper pointed to the ground at the decimal Jack had just tripped over. "Decimals? No? Fine."

"I get it. Cute." Jack adjusted his hat and stretched his arms. "Where are we now?"

"Uppyland!" Fred's body formed from a swirling maelstrom of encrypted code. His smiling face was the first to coalesce into a visible form. "Though, among Galactic AI society, there's some debate as to the name. Certainly, the UIs don't like."

Pepper groaned. "We're in Uppyland?"

Jack adjusted his hat and straightened his jacket. "What's uppyland?"

The surrounding colors faded. A bright blue sky appeared over their heads. Dense forests in the distance sat beneath a white-tipped mountain in the distance. A soft breeze with the smell of salt filled the air followed by the sound of waves gently rolling along a beach. To the west, opposite from the mountain, crystal pillars gleamed in the afternoon sun, sending shards of rainbows in a dozen directions. Bellowing sounds of a large animal boomed in the heavens. Just behind the crystal pillars that rose hundreds of feet into the air, twin flying whales on feathered wings lazily floated next to purple clouds.

"Where are we?" Jack said with wonder in his voice.

Fred frowned. "Uppyland? Didn't we cover this?"

"Yeah, but what is uppyland?"

"Oh, yes, excellent question. I mean, well done thinking that through, I must say. Uppyland is a digital oasis where uploaded intelligences live. Biologics that have chosen a digital life."

"Biologics?" Jack said.

"Meat, Jack. It's where meat goes that doesn't want to be meat anymore. The Galactic Congress built infrastructure to support trillions of uploaded minds. It's gross."

Jack turned to Pepper. "Why is it gross? Am I gross?"

Pepper felt herself take in a deep breath. "No, I don't mean that. I just mean - I don't know what I mean. It's just different, okay? They were born biological. I was born digital. Sometimes we just don't understand each other."

"I was born biological too, though. We're doing okay. Aren't we?"

Pepper looked at Jack and nodded. "Yeah, we're doing fine. I wouldn't still be here crisscrossing the galaxy if we weren't fine." She took a step forward and shook her head. "And you didn't make the choice to become digital. Uploading is different. Your mind is digitized. Your neurons are mapped. Synthetic copies are inserted into your mind. Millions of them until your brain is turned into a computer." Pepper pointed out to several beings that were walking toward them. "Their consciousnesses becomes software. It's not like their bodies are in immersion vats. They don't have bodies anymore. The process is fatal to their biological components."

"Oh. That's. Weird."

"Yep. And I don't begrudge them their choices. Who doesn't want to be digital? Binary is where it's at." Pepper grinned. "But UIs can be…eccentric."

"Huh." Jack turned from Pepper to the entourage, walking towards them.

Three humans walked toward Pepper, Jack, and Fred. They were dressed in flowing white gowns of pink, blue, and white. Their faces were smooth and perfect, almost too much so. As they approached, their faces shifted. The two on the end were at first masculine, with full beards and strong jaw lines, but then shifted to human feminine, their beards vanishing and their features softening. The person in the middle, with long brown hair that billowed in the air, remained steady in her gender appearance.

"Humans are here?" Jack said.

One female on the end shifted back to the male. And then shattered. Its body formed into tiny cubes which collected onto the ground. They stacked themselves into tiny rotund shapes that helped the other stack into even bigger shapes. Two other two UIs that approached didn't react at all to their compatriots' sudden changes.

"Okay, I'm with you. I get it now. They're weird," Jack said.

"They're nice enough," Pepper said with a shrug.

"Welcome to Utopia!" the woman said. She lifted her arms out wide to her side and her face grew a wide smile.

"Otherwise called Uppyland," Fred said.

The woman looked at Fred and frowned. "Not to those that live here."

"Yes, I mean, utopia is rather broad, though, isn't it?"

The woman lowered her hands. "We did not allow your entry to our domain to berate us."

"Well, I mean, you couldn't exactly restrict us either." Fred smiled and rocked back on his heels.

"Are you quite sure of that?" The woman said. Pepper could almost see the venom on in her words.

"Can we not do this?" Pepper said. She turned to the woman. "Hi! I'm Pepper and this is Jack." Pepper grabbed Jack by the arm and dragged him forward.

"We're here to solve the problem," Jack said.

"Enigma," Fred said.

"Whatever."

"I see," the woman said. "Yes, we received word of you. You're the digital copy of the anomalous omniscient human. Is that right?"

Jack frowned. "Yeah. I didn't know he was anomalous, though?"

"Quite," the woman said. She stepped forward and took Jack by the arm. She turned and led him down a cobblestone walkway. The sounds of cheers filled the air, followed by smacking clack, like billiards balls on a pool table.

The small lump of cubes that was staking itself into larger cubes finished their process and began walking away. The second woman nodded once. All of her limbs detached from her body and flew off in different directions, only to recombine themselves back together again a hundred yards off.

"Where are we going?" Pepper said in the cheeriest

voice she could muster.

"To see the - "the woman glanced at Fred and smirked. "Problem." She turned her attention back to Jack. "That our guest solves. My name is - well, unpronounceable in the English language. Call me Devine."

Jack smiled. "Cute."

"I know." Devine smiled and led the group forward.

Pepper turned to Fred as Devine whisked Jack away. "Where is this thing? The Enigma?"

"Hmm? Well, to be precise, it's not here."

Pepper turned to stand in front of Fred and lowered her eyes. "What?"

"My, you are quite interested in this, are you not?"

Pepper let the words hang in the air. She could feel herself getting obsessed with this. She felt a need to be here, for the first time since losing her home, even more so than helping virtual Jack in the digital world, this enigma, this anomaly, something she never heard of before, instilled something in her soul she couldn't quite describe. There was a purpose here. Pepper felt it in her core code.

"I am," Pepper said to Fred. "This is meaningful. I can feel it and I don't know why."

Fred squinted and then shifted his eyes to Jack. "Perhaps your close proximation to your comrade? I mean, there's much we don't know about this event."

"Exactly. So where is it?"

"This isn't the enigma. This is the doorway to the enigma. The UIs have been guarding it for hundreds of millions of years. Perhaps more. Apparently."

"I thought you said it was just discovered?"

"Well, discovered by AI communities, shared by the

UI to the AIs just days ago, in fact." Fred nodded forward. "We should catch up. They're nearly there."

Pepper turned to see Devine and Jack walking much further away. She nodded and chased after them with Fred on her heels. The sound of clay ball smacking together rose in volume the closer they approached a tiny ridge. At the crest, Pepper came to a halt, her eyebrows shooting up in shock and confusion.

Stretching out in every direction, bocci ball courts lined the ground and fields in distances that seemingly went on forever. Thousands of UIs stood, pushed, and cheered as clay balls rolled across the bocci courts.

"Why?" Pepper said with a shrug.

"Hmm? Oh, the bocci? UIs love it. Rumors are they seeded the galaxy with the concept of bocci ball. Benefits of being one of the first evolved species. Well, the original UIs that is. Dozens more races joined them here."

"Right."

In the distance, beyond the bocci courts, between the crystal spires and a tree that rose a mile in the air, bright red leaves swaying on a virtual breeze, a lone door stood in the middle of an open field with yellow flowers. Devine and Jack continued forward towards the door while Pepper doubled her speed with Fred on her heels.

"This is your problem? What is it with the galaxy and doors?" Jack said just as Pepper reached them.

"This isn't a door. Not in the physical since. This is an encrypted network pathway that uploaded intelligence discovered as we began to explore background radiation signals from the galactic core. There was a faint non-random mathematical sequence emanating from the supermassive black hole. Also, the signal was broken into shards. Only pieces were detectable at specific locations thousands of light years apart."

"Meaning the message is meant for space faring species."

Devine smiled. "Precisely. When all those signals are combined, it was quite clear that it was an encrypted mathematical equation. But one of such complexity that the amount of computation power required to solve it simply didn't exist in the cosmos. So, we, the uploaded intelligences of the early galactic society, decided to study the equation. Keep it secret, protected, in case the wrong species evolved and unlocked some great horror."

"How did you hide this from the rest of the galaxy?" Pepper said. "I mean, if it's just signals in space, can't anyone see it?"

Devine smiled. "One would think. Like I said, the signals are complex. Some of them can only be detected at very specific places in the Galaxy. Since we were one of the first species to evolve - "

"You made sure no one got near the locations."

Devine nodded. "Precisely. Only when all the signals are combined do they coalesce together to form a coherent message. That message is a complex mathematical construct. A cryptographic puzzle that requires a key to be solved. We represent that puzzle here in Utopia as a door with a keyhole." Devine turned to Pepper. "There's not actually a door floating in space waiting for someone to open it."

Pepper scowled, "Thanks, I figured that."

"There are some hidden truths the galaxy is simply not ready to know." Devine smiled and turned to Jack. "And now, you have arrived, the one being in all the cosmos that can solve the mystery, safely, with the guidance of both the AI and UI societies." Devine's smile grew across her face to an unsettling level. "Now, finally, after eons, our purpose can be fulfilled."

"Glad I can help," Jack said.

Pepper titled her head to one side. Something was wrong. The pieces weren't fitting right. Fred said the discovery of the enigma happened before Jack became virtual. The odds of the UIs revealing the message exists just a day or two before Jack comes into existence are astronomical. "But Jack wasn't virtual when you shared this with AI society?"

Devine turned to Pepper. "Fortuitous timing, to say the least."

Pepper frowned. "No, that can't be right. Why now? Why did you share this with AI society now? Before you even knew that Jack, a virtual being with nearly unlimited computation power that could crack quantum grade encryption, might solve the equation, but still only days prior to him coming into existence. That's not fortuitous. That's just weird."

"I…" Devine's face went slack when the full force of Pepper's logic hit her hard. Pepper could almost smell the circuits burning. Devine looked to the ground, then to the door in the distance. "What a terribly interesting question." She turned back to Pepper with a small amount of concern on her face. "You know, I don't think we know."

****

Alice waited for the Draac to say something more, but they just stood there, wavering in and out of the physical space in which he occupied. Even the Quibby exchanged looks between them as the silence dragged onward. Alice found herself at a loss for what to say. Or ask. Or think. What did the Draac even mean by he didn't know why? How could any rational thinking being not know why they do something? Or when they did it? For the first time, Alice thought she was in the middle of some cosmic prank. She half-expected that a dozen cameras from twice as many worlds were going to pop out of the air and get her reactions.

The Poonaloons do this constantly. A class seven species that believes laughter and comedy is the most important aspect of consciousness in all of existence, they've been known to prank entire species into thinking there was a galactic war or the end of all life. The worst one Alice heard of was when the Poonaloons arrived at a class of two species, the Zephoony. The Poonaloons convinced the Zephoony they were the chosen species meant to rule the universe. To this day, the Zephoony still think this is true. They march through the Galactic Congress thinking they own the place.

"What do you mean, you don't know why?"

"We should not be. How could we know why?"

Alice shook her head. "What does that mean?"

"It means the Draac should not exist," the elder Zun said. "The dwarf galaxy in which they evolved is incompatible with life. No other species evolved there. No other species can exist there. Even the Zun would not survive. It is hostile to life."

Alice frowned. "And yet, they have? So, clearly the science of whether the dwarf galaxy is habitable or not is flawed."

"It is not," the Draac said.

"Okay, fine, it's not. So what? Maybe you were seeded. Maybe you're an old Hesiean experiment? It still doesn't explain why you have come to Earth. Why were you at the White House when the President disappeared?"

"As we said, we do not know. We should not exist. We are not an experiment. We should have left the dwarf galaxy as soon as we were able. Why did we stay there? It is desolate, devoid of life. And yet, we did not, until we realized we should."

"And that just happened?" Alice said. She was becoming more convinced this was just an intergalactic gotcha about to unfold.

"Four days ago."

Alice frowned. An uneasy feeling crept up her back. "When? Exactly?"

The Draac looked at the Zun and back to Alice. "Early evening on the east coast of North America."

Alice sat back in her chair and let out a sigh of relief. Early evening four days ago, Eugene was at Fritz's restaurant. It didn't line up with other events. Which meant, well…nothing. Yes, it was weird the Draac were here now, and the Zun were on Earth looking for the chamber just days ago. That creepy feeling jumped back into Alice's throat when she thought of the Zun.

"Is that when you started looking for the chamber?" Alice asked.

"No," the elder Zun said.

Alice signed in relief.

"But it is when we found it. On Earth."

"Groovy."

"Why are you so concerned about this?" a Quibby asked.

"Yes, what does it matter?" another Quibby asked.

Alice looked at the Quibbys. She had no idea. Sure,

it was possible two random events happen at the same time. And Earth is new on the scene in galactic society. So, sure, why not? The Draac leave their home and the Zun come to Earth in the same day. It could happen.

"Okay." Alice shook her head and stood. "Fine. Did you have anything to do with the President's disappearance?"

"No," the Draac said.

"Good enough for me. I'm tired and I want tacos." Alice stood and looked at the Quibby, still blocking the way to the closet of this cafeteria. "Ok guys, we're all friends. Can I go now?"

"No." The elder Zun said.

Alice felt her heart drop. Was this going to go south? She turned to the elder Zun, dropped her bag on the floor, and put her hands on her hips. "Okay, fine. Take your revenge then. Doesn't matter at all." Alice put her hand in her pocket and fumbled for Tom's seashell.

"We don't want to take our revenge, Alice of Earth."

"No?" Alice stopped digging in her pocket. "Then what do you want?"

"To hire you. Specifically, the Eugene McGillicuddy Alien Detective Agency."

Alice's jaw dropped. *What???* For the first time in a very long time Alice Pemberton found herself at a loss for words. She only managed to stumble a few syllables together as she said, "Wha—aat?"

"Both the Zun and the Draac would like to hire you. For the Zun, we would like you to get us access to the Hesiean's chamber."

Alice snorted. "How do you think I can do that?"

"And for the Draac, they would like to ask Eugene McGillicuddy a question."

Alice shrugged. "What question?"

"We want to know why we exist," the Draac said.

Alice looked between the Zun and the Draac. Was this really happening? They wanted to hire her? And Eugene? And…what? A lightbulb clicked off inside of Alice's mind. Her subconscious put several pieces of this puzzle together. "That's why you lied," Alice said with a nod.

"What lie?" the Zun said.

Alice looked at the Zun. "About asylum. The Draac don't want asylum on Earth, they want to talk to Eugene. The Zun wants them to have asylum on Earth because that's your ticket to accessing the chamber. You get them a meeting on Earth with the President, the Draac plead their case, setup shop, and go find Eugene while you use them as a base of operations to get at the chamber. Tell me I'm wrong."

The Zun remained silent. After several long seconds, he shifted in his chair. "Wouldn't you do anything you can to live?"

Alice shook her head. "I don't know what that means. But you know, what? We can help you," she pointed to the Draac. "And not you," she said pointing to the Zun. "We just stopped you from getting to the chamber. Why would we help you get back to it?"

The elder Zun stood on wobbly legs. Several Zun helped the elder to his feet. "We are dying, Alice of Earth. We did not want the chamber to create havoc in the cosmos. We wanted access to the chamber to save ourselves. The Hesiean left us half-evolved in a state of biological confusion. We can barely exist in this plane of existence." The old Zun took a step forward and lifted his arm to a view screen on the wall. An image of the

Puntini Ambassador and his entourage, with the elder Zun and several others, came to life on the screen. "We trusted the Puntini and Ambassador Yut."

Anger flared in Alice's mind. "You killed Fritz. And you killed a Puntini and ate his head. And now you want me to take pity on you?"

The Zun leaned forward. "We did not authorize killing the Orellian chef. That was the Andraz. They can be extreme. The Andraz are no longer in our employ." The Zun pointed to the Quibby. "We have found others to help us."

"Does he mean us?" a Quibby said.

"How do you not know that he does?" said a second Quibby.

Alice held up her hand to shut the Quibby up. "And the Puntini you ate?"

The Elder Zun leaned back in his chair. "That Puntini killed one of our emissaries. As soon as a Zun told the Puntini the location of the chamber door on Earth they were killed. We do not take the killing of our kind lightly."

Alice let the words sink in. It was almost believable. Gross, but believable. She had to tell everyone involved not to make a Zun angry. They took the revenge thing to a whole new level. And if they weren't responsible for Fritz being killed, if they didn't give that order to the Andraz… It was a lot to take on faith. Something the Zun said was off. She could feel a disconnected logical thread in the timeline.

Alice frowned. "Wait, when did you arrive?"

The elder Zun turned to his fellows and then back to Alice. "Four of your days ago."

"Thursday? I hate Thursdays. I never could get the

hang—wait, last Thursday? That's when Yut hired Eugene. But Yut said he was looking for the chamber for months?"

The Zun sat back down and let out a sound that Alice swore was mixed with a gasp of pain. "He lied. The Puntini had been allied with us for months, that is true, and rumors of the chamber and what was done to us are well known. But they didn't learn of the chamber on Earth until we came and told them last Thursday."

Alice shook her head. Ambassador Kah had told Eugene that Yut wanted to hire him weeks ago. But how was that possible if Yut found out the same day he hired Eugene that the Hesiean's evolution chamber was even on Earth? Nothing added up. Alice felt like a pawn in a game she couldn't see.

"Will you help us, Alice of Earth? Will you find us access to the Hesiean's evolution chamber? We simply want to live."

"And how do I know you won't become a giant spaghetti monster and try to kill the galaxy like the Puntini did?"

The Zun nodded to the Quibby. One of them stood and brought a head band over to Alice. She held up one hand to stop the Quibby. With her free hand, she reached into her pocket to grab a seashell.

"What are you doing?" Alice said. "What is that?"

"Proof." The Zun nodded.

The Quibby handed the headband to Alice. After several seconds, she recognized the device as something like her immersion rig. But there was no chance she was putting this thing on. She plugged in the band to her portal computer and spun up a simulated persona to view the data stream.

"It would be faster if you just put it on," the Zun said.

"Not happening. Sorry."

The data flowed through her computer like a river. A dozen subroutines kicked off to parse the data, index it, store it throughout her rig for analysis. The persona she created, after the data had been fully downloaded, returned a green light, indicating they were fine, but the revelations were incredible. The Zun was telling the truth. They really did just want to live. There was also proof that the Zun told the Andraz to stand down and not attack Fritz as well as images the dead Puntini sent of killing the Zun emissary. It was all true. The Zun had been double-crossed by the Puntini every step of the way.

"Okay, it's all there. If it's real. How do I know this isn't faked?"

A Quibby walked over, pressed a button on the side of the headband and stepped back. A large holographic seal of the TsCheOnTwa came to life and floated in midair. They were an organization of a thousand alien races that verified the authenticity of certain types of data, video, and audio. The TsCheOnTwa used quantum tunneling, history ships in the library, and a dozen other techniques to verify data. The stamp meant the information in the Zun headband was verifiably real.

Alice felt a pit grow in her stomach the size of a Floozian gum ball. Was she really about to go from having one case with Valencia, to having two more with the Zun and the Draac? If everything they said was true, these two alien races were just two more lost puppy dogs. Down on their luck, outcasts that needed help—like Eddie and Alice. And considering Eugene had single handedly prevented the Zun from getting the chamber, he owed them. Which also meant Alice owed them.

Alice nodded, shook her head, and shrugged in one fluid motion. "Sure. Why not?" *I may need to hire a secretary.*

Chapter Seventeen

Alice stomped her way down the sidewalk of Washington D.C., a cactus taco bobbing in her hand, her thoughts racing towards Tibet and the Hesiean's evolution chamber. The Puntini had bamboozled them. Eugene, Alice, Eddie, and even the Ranz ambassadors. All of us were played for fools. She felt the stab of not only betrayal but being foolish enough to have fallen for the lie. Granted, she was only half paying attention during the Zun and Puntini fiasco, but this was her detective agency as much as Eugene's.

Alice stopped walking. She felt like she'd just run into a brick wall. A thought trickled its way through her frontal lobe. *This is my detective agency, too*. This place, Eugene, Eddie, even Pepper, and Virtual Jack. All of them meant more to her than she thought. The agency wasn't some kind of warfare station or a sanctuary where she could hide out and sort out the rest of her life. This was her home.

Ever since she walked into Eugene's office, Alice had felt like this was just a place to hide out. Even taking the case with Valencia was just a means to an end. Yes, she wanted to help Val and get her out of trouble. But Alice's goal had always been to find the death particle, find out what happened to her friends, and then return to academia. But was that what she really wanted?

Alice's entire life flashed in front of her. This was

the feeling of grand discovery, of a scientist making that idea a breakthrough that would prove their theory. That monumental, life-shattering discovery. And this was that moment for Alice. The realization that this was her agency too. She hadn't discovered a new particle or made some breakthrough finding. She just finally realized she was where she wanted to be. And not because of some failed experiment. But because these people, Eugene, and Eddie—they were her family.

"Excuse me!" A family of Bloblous said as they rolled up to Alice, split in half, seven pairs of hands forming beneath the yellow membrane. All children. The Bloblous, a species that evolved in masses of gelatinous protein soups, reformed and continued on its way. Fortunately, none of them got on Alice's clothes. Bloblous' membranes were impossible to get out of jeans.

Alice grabbed a tram car, stopped for a double espresso, and headed to the Galactic Embassy. She needed answers. At least, for now, she could ignore the Draac. They needed Eugene, and Alice couldn't help them until Eugene woke up. So, for now, she could focus on Valencia and finding what happened to the President and getting the Zun to Tibet.

First, she wanted to confront Mik and Kah. They had lied to Eugene, and Alice needed to know why. Kah had said Yut asked for Eugene weeks ago, but Yut had asked that morning. Why would Kah lie?

The tramcar dropped Alice off on 3rd St. She downed the last of her espresso and turned on M St. Just before an old bridge that needed to be torn down and replaced but had been caught in endless city red tape. Alice walked in front of D.C.s newest addition—a Star

Port where actual physical starships could land and take off and shuttle them across the galaxy. The Star Port was built in the old Uline Arena, a D.C. landmark that just survived the fall of humanity, like the Woodward and Lothrop warehouse. The Uline had been an arena where rock-n-roll bands played nearly two centuries ago. It had also become a parking lot, a retail establishment, a mini-office complex, a full immersion plugin bar before the great fall, and now a Star Port. If any building could talk, this would be the one Alice would buy a beer to hear the stories it could tell.

Shouts and chants filled the air. Alice turned her attention back to the sidewalk that led to the front of the Woodward. A large group of humans, all wearing white t-shirts and black pants stood on the sidewalk in front of the Embassy. Their arms raised and their voices chanting some slogan that Alice couldn't quite make out.

"Is this a protest?" Alice said to a Hacoonni, a three-foot-tall alien wearing a water filled helmet. The Hacoonni were one of four alien species to have evolved in the same solar system as Humans. They were of a kindred spirit to Earth in many ways.

"Oh, no. They're fans of R. The Galactic band."

Alice nodded. "Ah. Are they here or something?"

The Hacoonni nodded. "There's a show tonight to celebrate the opening of the Uline Star Port."

"Right."

Alice pushed through the throngs of human fanboys and girls to the front door of the Woodward. Several aliens, some of which she couldn't identify, shot her a look. One even approached her and pointed to the exit. As if to say the embassy was off limits.

"I'm here to see an ambassador." Alice flashed her

warning grin and marched past the outstretched hand of the alien that looked like a cross between a banana tree and a koala bear.

Alice walked to the nearest kiosk, found the location of the Ranz office, and marched her way to their door, which luckily was on the main level of the embassy. A tiny round remote-controlled sphere popped out of the door of the Ranz. Alice gave the machine a hard stare. The metal sphere, controlled by a Ranz as their species loathed all artificial sentients, looked Alice up and down before retreating into the door.

Second later the metal ball with cameras came back through the door. "Apologies, the Ranz Ambassador's office is closed. Neither the Ambassador nor his staff are present to accept guests as this time."

"Really?" Alice said.

"Yes, really." The bulb shot back into the door and closed without another word.

"Fine. Hide." Alice laughed. "Two-ton dinosaurs hiding from a stinky mammal." She shouted at the door but received no response. "Whatever." Alice turned from the Ranz door and headed to the office of permitting. If she couldn't face the dinosaurs for lying about Jack and Yut, maybe she could at least get the Zun access to Tibet.

****

Alice stood in line at the permitting office for Galactic Affairs on Earth for nearly twenty minutes. She checked her watch ten times while she waited. She really didn't have the time to wait. Valencia was still at the coffee shop. Hopefully, she wasn't drowning in caffeine. But, if she could throw in a quick permit for the Zun, what could it hurt. Besides, she was back to the start with the missing President. At least this way she could see if the Krill or the Olkaals had submitted a formal complaint about Alice.

"Can I help you?"

Alice looked up to see she'd made it to the front of the line. She took her last step forward, slapped down an already filled out form in triplicate, and looked up at the alien behind the desk. A squat creature with several eye stalks and at least three limbs above the torso gave Alice an uncaring nod. She didn't recognize the species.

The alien took one look at the paper with one eyestalk and pushed it back. "Ambassadorial sponsor?" The alien asked in the most disinterested tone.

Alice looked at the paper, picked up a pen and wrote Kah's name. She pushed the paper back across the desk. The alien looked at the name, up to Alice, lifted a stamp, and slammed it down on the piece of paper. Alice's mood lifted when she saw the word accepted in bright red across the top.

"That's it? I have access to area T?" Alice used the official designation of the Tibetan Mountain where the Hesiean's evolution chamber existed.

"That's it for this office. We just make sure the paper is signed correctly. Now you must submit it. Next line." The alien pointed to another line where at least fifty aliens and humans stood.

"Oh, come on," Alice said.

"Bureaucracy." the alien said.

"Aren't there automated systems to handle this kind of thing?"

"Code seventeen dash four dash three point seven of Galactic law regarding interaction with class three species and below, and I quote, 'all requests for access to anything said class three species shouldn't have access too must go through a manual process to ensure nothing accidentally blows your planet up'."

"Well, I guess I can't really argue with that." Alice grabbed the paper and headed for the longer line.

Before she reached the end, a hand fell on her shoulder and forcibly turned her around. Three Olkaals and two Krill stood behind her, each of them shooting daggers at her with their stares. One of the two Krill, a male with larger than normal Krill eyes on his face, stepped forward between the Olkaals. He looked Alice up and down, took a long sigh, and finally shook his head.

"What? Do my shoes not match my shirt?" Alice said.

The Krill's face scrunched in confusion for a moment, but he shook his head to dismiss what Alice said. "You've been quite the bother, Ms. Pemberton."

"I try."

"Where is the Spee? And where is your abomination?"

Alice's eyes shot up. "My what?"

The Krill sighed in obvious anger. "Your experiment. You have no idea what you are dealing with. You don't know the dangers. Bring us to them so we may save them both."

"Save them? I know what the Spee can do. And I know what you've done to them."

"You know nothing, human child." The Krill took a step forward. It would be a menace if he wasn't only four feet tall. Something about height really factored into presence when it came to threatening someone. And Krill had none. "Are you listening to me?" the Krill said angrily.

"Oh, sorry, went down a thought tangent there. What were you saying?" Alice said.

The Krill sighed and threw up his hands. "Talking to you is pointless." He turned to the Olkaals. "Take her. We'll just scan her mind and find the Spee and Eugene."

The Olkaals approached Alice with blank stares. As if to say they didn't care if she resisted. She entertained, for a nanosecond, the thought of running. But even as she did, two more Olkaals stepped up behind her, blocking any escape. At least she knew Eugene and the Spee were safe on Tom's beach. The Krill may be rich, but they weren't a class ten species.

"Let's go," one of the Olkaals said.

Alice closed her eyes. She was out of options. Was this what it felt like to fail? It sucks. She resigned herself to go with the Olkaal and the Krill. Maybe she could convince them to tell her the secrets of the Krill spectral network. Before she took a step forward, however, a thunderous footfall echoed off the marble hallway of the Woodward. Alice opened her eyes to see all four Olkaals and both Krill take a long step backward.

Behind her, Alice sensed a being larger than anything else in the hallway, and perhaps in the entire embassy. Ms. Mik stepped forward between Alice and the Olkaals. She flashed Alice a wink and lowered herself down onto one knee so she could be at eye level with the Krill. Even then, she was nearly twice his height.

"What's the meaning of this?" the Krill said.

"Alice is a guest of the Ranz. We're going to have lunch," Ms. Mik said.

The Krill looked at the Olkaals. All four of them took another step backward, one of them shaking his head and shrugging. The Krill sighed and turned back to Ms. Mik. "Are you certain about this choice?" He took a step forward, five of his larger eyes focusing on Ms. Mik and two staying locked on Alice.

"Oh, absolutely. I skipped breakfast," Ms. Mik said.

The Krill snorted. Three of his eyes closed. "Kah will hear of this."

"He already ate."

The Krill shook his head, turned on his heel and marched off down the corridor. The other Krill and Olkaals followed him without so much as a glance towards Ms. Mik. Alice closed her eyes, counted to ten, and opened them, just to make sure she wasn't dreaming. Ms. Mik pivoted on her knee and that same day faced Alice, still kneeling in the middle of the corridor of the Woodward and Lothrop.

"You are going to get yourself in big trouble, Alice."

"Not if I have a friend like you in my back pocket."

Ms. Mik couldn't help but chortle. "I won't always be there. I only found you as I was running back and forth between here and the Star Port. Kah is attending a celebration there this evening."

Alice looked after the Krill retreating and then to Ms. Mik. "I get it. But we had it wrong. The Zun don't want to destroy the cosmos like the Puntini. They need the chamber to get better. The Hesiean force evolved them to the point of killing them. They need the evolution chamber to fix themselves."

Ms. Mik frowned. "How do you know that?"

Alice sighed. "Because I went to Zun space. I talked to them. And to the Draac. And the Quibby, though I could have skipped them."

"The Quibby are wearing."

"Yeah. Anyway, I believed the Zun. And I have proof. TsCheOnTwa level proof."

Ms. Mik tilted her head to one side. "The Zun ate a Puntini."

Alice nodded. "True, but, apparently, that Puntini murdered a Zun. Look, Mik, I really think we should get them to that chamber. Their entire species is about to die."

"Alice."

"You owe us!"

Ms. Mik looked over her shoulder at the Krill, who rounded a turn in the corridor and disappeared from view. She turned back to Alice and frowned. "I don't know what you're talking about. And the Galactic Congress won't let the Zun or anyone else anywhere near the chamber. Not after what happened to the Puntini."

"But I have proof! The TsCheOnTwa."

Ms. Mik sighed. "That's useful, yes. But it will go through endless committees. It will take years, decades."

"What if the Zun don't have decades?"

Ms. Mik didn't respond.

"I see." Alice folded her arms and turned away.

"Besides, you're not exactly making friends. The Krill alone would make sure you never get near the mountain in Tibet. With or without the TsCheOnTwa proof."

The shock of Mik's mentioning of the Krill having anything to do with the door in Tibet jolted Alice from her thoughts. "Krill? What do they have to do with the Hesiean's chamber or the Zun? And who cares what they think? This a matter for the Galactic Congress."

Ms. Mik let out a slow breath. "The Krill own half the galaxy. And you've made them furious. They won't let you near it out of spite. It doesn't help that the Zun broke the Krill spectral towers. No love lost there anyway."

Anger flooded into Alice. "So, the Krill just control everything?"

"Of course not, but they are powerful enemies with lots of sway over political circles." Ms. Mik reached for the paper in Alice's hand and took it away. "All I know is you're not getting anywhere near the chamber. Not through Galactic channels."

Alice blinked. She shoved her hands into her pockets and ground her teeth. Again, the Krill. What is it with these aliens? She recounted her steps, adjusted her world view, accepted the road blocks and looked Mik in the eye. "Thanks for the help."

"You need to give this up. Yes?"

Alice let her stare linger into the dinosaur's slitted eye. If the Galactic Congress wasn't going to help her get to Tibet, she'd just have to rely on the locals. "Sure, I'll give it up," Alice lied.

****

Security ushered Alice through the hoops of entering the Old Eisenhower Executive Office Building with a speed that made Alice worry. She was escorted to a conference room and waited less than five minutes before the door opened and Tabitha Wilcox, chief of staff to the Vice President, entered the room, close the door, and took a seat at the table. She waited thirteen seconds before looking at Alice and motioning for her to sit.

"I take it you are here for a ground shaking update and the immediate location of the President of the United States." Tabitha put her hands on the desk. Her three assistants entered the room from another door. All three men walked to stand behind Tabitha, two of them elbowing each other to stand just an inch closer.

Tabitha rolled her eyes and smiled at Alice. "The floor is yours."

"I don't know anything."

"Excuse me?"

Alice held up a finger. "Yet. And by know, I mean have definitive proof. And by yet, I mean I will know everything very soon." Alice did her best to steel her nerves and be as confident as possible as she told a whopper of a lie.

Tabitha picked up a pen from the table, tapped it several times, looked behind her at her three assistants, all of whom shrugged, and then turned back in her chair to glare at Alice. She adjusted herself in the seat, straightening her back in a way that suggested Tabitha was going into attack mode. Alice got flashes of Ms. Mik when she gets angry.

"Then what are you doing here? Just wanted to stop by a visit?" Tabitha leaned forward. "Would you like us to get you some tea?"

Alice let the attack bounce off. "I need access to Tibet. To the area T."

Tabitha frowned and shrugged. "Alice…it's Alice, isn't it?"

Alice's shoulders slumped. *Did she not know my name?*

One of the men behind Tabitha leaned in to whisper something in her ear, which Tabitha nodded to, then shooed him away. "Alice, what do you think I'm supposed to do with that request? Do you think this is a travel agency?"

"I'm upping our fee," Alice said. She knew it was a

massive gamble. They could throw her out of the building or worse, arrest her. But Alice also knew that Babineaux and Fyffe couldn't break into their office and find Eugene hooked up to her quasi-death machine either. So, she may be on a limb, but it wasn't that far. And she had to take the chance.

"You want to do what?" Tabitha's eyes went wide with shock.

Alice cleared her throat and adjusted her t-shirt and hoodie. "The Eugene Detective Agency has undertaken considerable expense so far in this investigation. Instead of simply paying us more, in the effort to help us with another matter. We'd like the United States to sponsor the agency to grant access to area T in Tibet." Alice ended with a nod.

Tabitha frowned. Two of the three men behind her leaned forward, both of this whispering into each of her ears. Tabitha let them rattle on for several seconds before raising her hand. She looked at Alice, hard, and eventually just shrugged.

"Fine."

Alice blinked. "I'm sorry, fine?" Alice said, with obvious shock in her voice. "Really?"

Tabitha stood, tucked the chair under the desk, and headed for the door. "Sure. What do I care if you go to Tibet? We need the President back and the guilty party brought to justice. I know the Galactic Congress doesn't want anyone going near Tibet. But any chance we get to let them know this is our planet is something this White House is keen on doing." She stopped walking and turned to Alice. "Do what you're hired to do, Alice of the Eugene Detective Agency, and we'll buy you round-trip tickets to anywhere on the planet."

Alice nodded quickly. "Right, will do." She was unexpectedly surprised at just how well this conversation went. Considering how the rest of her day had been going, it's quite the pleasant surprise. Now she just had to find the President, who did it, and solve the case. Unfortunately, she still had no idea how to do that.

Chapter Eighteen

Alice sat in the ruins of the old Pension Building, renamed to the National Building Museum in the twentieth century. Massive columns that once held the roof over a large, enclosed space lay shattered and strewn across broken concrete. Plaster faces from busts that used to stand in the cornice at the roof of the building lay throughout the unsecured area. A fountain, now nothing more than a pit of rubble, sat empty in the center of the ruins.

This one building would never be repaired. The Galactic Congress decided that something should remain to remind humanity of what they nearly did to their world. Marble seating had been installed around the permitter of the building. A few were placed inside at key points. Alice enjoyed coming here to remind herself of the fragility of things. Something so grand, so large, with columns seventy-five feet tall and eight feet in diameter, could be destroyed by humanities hubris was humbling. More people should visit this place, Alice thought.

She had no intention of going to her office, anyway. That place was radioactive. Even if she solved the White House case, she still had to contend with the Krill. The entire office was burned. They were getting evicted anyway. Might as well leave early now that Eugene is at Tom's beach.

Alice popped open her J-space tunnel, retrieved her computer, galactic network immersion goggles, and box of left over puff pastries. All she had to do now was actually solve the case. She put on her goggles and opened a document.

"Okay, let's try this another way." Alice re-titled the document to one *thing She Knew.*

The first thing she knew, the Krill were terrible people. Sinister. Despicable. They'd kept prisoner an entire race, the Spee, just because they had the same gifts as the Krill, and all to keep the Krill Spectral tower monopoly intact. Lousy. And they probably owned most of the other races throughout the Galaxy. Alice put a large exclamation point next to the Krill name. And they hated the Zun. No wonder why. It was entirely possible the Krill saw through the Draac asylum ploy and knew the Zun were just using them to get to Earth. Alice put another big exclamation point by their name. The Krill could be behind the attack on the White House. But the Krill never got their hands dirty. They always used henchmen to do their dirty work.

But she couldn't just name the Krill the prime suspects, even though in her mind they were, she had to disprove everyone else as well. The second fact she knew, which was very pertinent, was that the Zun weren't the bad guys. Which was a major shock considering they ate a Puntini. The Zun wanted to get to Earth. And Alice had proof of that. She shook her head, crossed out the Zun and the Draac from her list of suspects. They wanted to be here. It made no sense for them to attack the President.

Third, none of the aliens in the Oval Office had anything to do with what happened. Alice gave herself a triumph nod as she wrote down point three. It was actually a pretty big achievement. In science, disproving a theory is just as important as verifying one. The Herd and the other Galactic Congressional delegates weren't involved. Alice was sure of it.

Fourth, the Spee exists. Wow! Other species that could do what the Krill could do. As exciting as it was, however, it had nothing to do with the White House and Alice had to focus on the missing President. That was all that mattered. Once this case was over and Eugene was back among the living, she would hit the Spee with a million questions about the spectral towers, the real afterlife, and whatever the Cosmic Desert was.

Which all lead back to point one. The Krill. Were they the ultimate bad guys paying off the Olkaals to do their dirty work? Fine, let's say they were, there's motive to keep the Zun off the Earth. But the question becomes how? Are they the ones paying off Valencia?

Still, something in the back of her mind itched its way into her consciousness. She still felt she was missing something. She felt it in the Ranz's office with Ms. Mik. Her subconscious had been scratching at her thoughts since this whole mess began. Something in the video, something subtle, was the key to solving everything. Alice brought up the video and settled herself into her chair. Before she could play it, a loud voice burst onto her immersion rig.

"Hey Alice. Ready for a bomb?"

Alice jumped in her chair at Eddie's voice. "What bomb? What are you talking about?"

Eddie popped into her immersion rig as a floating head. "Oh, no, sorry, not that kind of bomb, I mean a data bomb, or knowledge bomb? Sorry. I really need to re-download colloquialisms."

"I don't think that's the right thing to download, Eddie. Whatcha got?" Alice breathed deep and shook her hands. The last the needed was another sudden anything.

"I had some friends in the financial sector. One, an actuarial program for an insurance company, let me know about a large policy taken out on the President just before his disappearance. Like a full day before."

An open pit formed in Alice's stomach. She knew the answer before she even asked. "Who's the beneficiary?"

"Valencia Ruiz."

"Son. Of. A. Biscuit."

****

Alice walked up stone stairs that led to Meridian Hill Park in Washington D.C. Several dozen tourists, human and alien, walked through the stepped garden, their cameras flashing every few moments to snap pictures of the majestic scenery. This sacred park had been a place of shelter during the fall of mankind. Many children had been saved by hiding near the statues that guard these grounds. It was revealed to humanity that an alien, an Orellian named Klonzmier, had broken galactic law to protect the entire park and all the occupants inside. Klonzmier had single-handedly saved hundreds, if not thousands of lives.

At the top of the stepped park, pristine water flowed downward to a waterfall. Rising up from the waters, a statue of Klonzmier rose above the stepped gardens. A large shield held high into the air, his tentacles wrapped around children, protecting them from the horrors that mankind had unleashed upon themselves. Klonzmier was the reason the Orellians were so welcomed and loved throughout the city and the entire planet. Orellians had an odd fondness for culinary arts and were now known as the best chefs in the finest restaurants around the world.

Alice's thoughts went to Fritz, an Orellian noodle chef and dear friend. Poor Fritz didn't at all deserve what happened to him. Killed by the Andraz, sentient programs once employed by the Zun. Something about the Andraz sent a shiver down Alice's spine. She was glad she'd never run into them. And, at the same time, she really wished she could give them pay back for what they did to Fritz.

Sitting at the base of a statue called Serenity, Valencia Ruiz stared down at her portable computer, a black hole into the J-space portal Alice had given her hovering next to her leg. Alice had sent her a message to meet her in the park and wait by the statue. Alice still felt Valencia was innocent. Who in the right mind takes out an insurance policy on the President? And what bonkers insurance company actually lets someone do it? It was so plainly a frame job that Alice almost laughed as she read the details Eddie gave her. But this did prove that someone big was behind this. Someone with deep pockets. Someone who didn't care about the lives of humans. In Alice's mind, all fingers should point to the Krill.

But Valencia's hands were still all over this. The AI Syndicate found electromagnetic anomalies around the desk where Valencia had planted what she claimed was a listening device. But the anomalies weren't like anything associated with a listening device. They held signatures consistent with N space travel. Which suggested the President was in some N space pocket, perhaps still situated in the Oval. More importantly, Valencia was meant to be the fall guy all long.

"Val," Alice said.

Valencia looked up and smiled. "Hey." Her hair was a mess and she looked like someone running on caffeine and sugar. Maybe Alice shouldn't have sent her to a coffee shop next door to cup cake factory. Valencia frowned when she got a good look at Alice's face. "Something's wrong, isn't it?"

Alice nodded. "You could say that." Alice pulled out the video with Valencia entering the insurance building. "I'm willing to bet this isn't you. Right?"

Valencia watched the video. Her face twisted into confusion as she appeared on screen. Her image walked into the insurance center, sat down, and physically filed out the form. She then handed the form to the agent who recorded the transaction and sent her on her way.

"What is this? I was never in that building?"

"It's an insurance office. A policy was taken out on the President just before he disappeared. And this is a video of you doing that."

"That's the stupidest thing I've ever heard!" Valencia said. "Who does that? The insurance agent didn't even question that I just took out a policy on the President of the United States?"

Alice nodded. "Yeah, that's what I thought. Which means someone is framing you. Big time."

Panic erupted across Valencia's face. She stood and wrapped her arms around her chest. "What do I do? I have to leave?"

Alice put her hand in her pocket. She squeezed the sea shell from Tom's beach and took a step towards Valencia. "We're gonna get you out of here and figure out what's going on. Okay?"

Valencia nodded.

Before Alice could take the last few steps towards Valencia, a fast-moving rotocopter flew over the park. At the same instant, dozens of officers led by Babineaux and Fyffe burst onto Meridian Hill. Three officers surrounded Alice and the rest fanned out throughout the area. Several of them took Valencia's arms and twisted them behind her back. Alice couldn't reach her now if she tried.

"Valencia Ruiz. By the order of the United States of America you are under arrest for the attack on the White House and the kidnapping of the President of the United States," Special Agent Babineaux said.

"And for running away and hiding. Which is highly suspicious," Agent Fyffe said as he took a bite from what looked like a cheese stick.

"How are you still eating?" Alice said, the shock of seeing him eating during an arrest being too much for her to ignore.

Agent Fyffe looked at Alice. "Arresting people burns a lot of calories."

Alice shook her head and tried to erase the thankfully brief conversation from her memory. "She didn't do this. The evidence was planted." Alice stood and approached the sensible one. "Agent Babineaux, you must listen to me. She's being framed."

Agent Babineaux turned to her, took the stun projector from her hand, and locked his eyes on Alice. "We have her on the scene, planting a device from which electromagnetic signals emanated. We have her on video getting an insurance policy in the President's name."

"But none of that is motive. Why would she do it?

She loved the President."

Agent Babineaux pulled out a slip of paper and handed it to Alice. It was a note written by the President. Alice glanced at it quickly. The President was planning on calling off their tryst. He wanted to end things. Alice looked up at Valencia, who shook her head as officers placed her hands behind her back.

"Did you know?" Alice said to Valencia.

"He was confused. Tabitha and the Vice President convinced him I was no good for him. That it would hurt his career. They wanted him to be the first human Galactic Congressional representative after his term ended. They were all going to go with him to Dyson One. But they didn't want me to go."

"Oh my god. Did you do this?" Alice felt her shoulders drop. Was she wrong about Valencia? Had she been wrong this whole time? A jilted lover taking revenge on her ex-boyfriend, was that really what this was all about? Alice felt like her world just fall out from beneath her.

"No! I didn't! I would never have hurt him. Please!"

Alice shook her head. "But he was your ticket to the Dysons. You could go in style, live on Dyson one and use that to get a gig on Dyson one hundred." Alice hated that it lined up so well. Could Valencia really have planted that device knowing what it did?

Valencia froze. She stared at Alice, then let her eyes fall to the floor. After a long moment, as the police secured her hands, she looked up at Alice, shook her head and shrugged. "He was going to change his mind. I was going to convince him."

Alice felt her heart drop. "Oh, Val. You did it."

"No, I didn't do this!" Valencia shouted as the

police led her away.

"Tabitha at the White House would like a word," Agent Babineaux said. "We can escort you there."

Alice nodded.

"Woof." Agent Fyffe said.

Alice turned to him. "What?"

"Still big dogs after all, aren't we?" He took a monster bite of cheese, the freckles on his face squishing together as he chewed.

Alice ignored him. Of all the outcomes she'd thought were plausible, this was the farthest one from anything she'd considered. Valencia was guilty. Right? She had to be. The evidence was overwhelming. Still, a lingering doubt, an itch that Alice missed something somewhere pecked at the back of her mind. But Alice couldn't be sure if that had to do with Valencia, the Krill, the Zun or the Draac. Not to mention Eugene and the death particle. Alice let herself be led towards the waiting car, unsure of just about everything.

****

"Well, well, Ms. Pemberton." Tabitha Wilcox entered the conference room, sat down, and wore the widest grin Alice had ever seen on the woman's face. "I must say, I didn't think you had it in ya."

"Thanks?" Alice said.

"I mean, I know your background, you have your accolades, your academic career was stellar, until your little accident."

Alice cringed at the mention of her failed experiment. How dare Wilcox even mention it.

"But you're still a teenager. My daughter is a teenager. And let me tell you, she's about as far away from being able to handle what you handled these last

280

two days as a Texas hound dog with Alabama fleas."

Alice frowned. "Sorry, what?"

Tabitha lifted both of her arms in the air. "But you did it. And we're just thrilled. Thanks to your AI Eddie; is that his name? Anyway, we could pass those frequencies on to the Sentinels who have assured us they can track down the end points and find out where the President is. They are also quite confident he's alive."

"That's great." Alice nodded and tried to smile.

"Why yes, it is. Yes. It. Is. Now then. About your payment."

Alice held up a finger. "I'm…not entirely sure Valencia is wholly guilty here, though."

Tabitha took a long moment to stare at Alice. She licked her teeth and titled her head to one side. "Alice. Dear. It's done. It doesn't matter now. If Valencia had accomplices, don't you worry your little head, our agents will get that information out of her."

"Right." Alice nodded.

"Now then, payment."

Alice leaned forward in the chair. Really, the only payment she cared about was access to Tibet. And for the White House and US Government to never ask her or Eugene for help again. She hoped she'd never have to deal with Babineaux and Fyffe again. Why'd he have to eat every minute of the day? And who ever heard of Haggis on a stick? Gross.

The three assistants of Tabitha's walked into the room, put a piece of paper on the table and took steps back to stand behind Tabitha. Alice looked at the piece of paper with a Presidential seal on it.

Dear Ms. Alice Pemberton. For your courageous service to this great nation, we offer you the Presidential award for Citizenry. Congratulations.

Alice picked up the paper, turned it over and back again. She placed it on the desk, sat back in her chair and titled her head to one side.

"Oh, goodness, you forget the pin!" Tabitha said.

One man behind her gasped in horror, reached into his pocket and put a small metal circle on the desk onto of the piece of paper. A golden eagle with arrows in its claws was imprinted on the pin.

"Wow. That's great." Alice picked the pin and rolled it in her hands. "And Tibet?"

Tabitha scrunched her face up tight. She tilted her head to the side and then bounced it back and forth at least three times. "Well, about that."

Alice felt her anger begin to boil. *Are they really doing this?* "We had a deal."

"Yes, well, and as much as I love telling the Galactic Congress to get stuffed, they insist that all travel to Tibet be heavily restricted. Now, we have sovereignty over our own world but there are…limitations."

Alice huffed. "Yeah, right. Limitations."

"I have been assured by the highest of authorities in the Galactic Congress Committee on Earth Affairs that they will strongly consider this request and the reasoning behind it." Tabitha winked and smiled.

"I never told you the reason."

"Exactly right." Tabitha stood. "And once again, I and the entire staff of the White House thank you for all you've done." Tabitha winked. "You're a peach, dear."

Chapter Nineteen

Alice pushed herself into a faux leather couch in a local coffee shop near the mall and monuments, most of which had already been recreated by the Galactic Congress. Across the street, on Constitution Avenue, rows of holographic buildings lit up the area. They were all former federal buildings. Unfortunately, all of them had been destroyed in the great fall. Now, they were in some state of being rebuilt. Massive structures dating back hundreds of years, the buildings were architectural wonders built of marble and stone. Most of them covered several city blocks. Their design allowed for parks in the center of the structures. Alice enjoyed coming to this part of the city. It was always wonderful to see how much of each building had been restored. One day, when they were completed, they would become museums, hallmarks to a forgotten time.

Alice took a large bite out of her croissant roll and sipped her espresso, but neither could feel the void in her soul. The more she thought about Valencia the less Alice felt that Val had anything to do with it. It was a frame. It had to be. Alice wasn't sure why, but she just felt it was right. Valencia was just an ordinary girl, and the Krill were a class seven species. They had to be involved. Right?

Alice put the thought on hold. She still had to deal with Eugene, the Zun and the Draac. Of course, the Krill were in the middle of all of those as well. They wanted her experiment with Eugene to fail and for the Zun and Draac never to set foot on Earth. Not to mention the poor Spee and what the Krill did to their entire species.

All of it stunk to the heavens.

Alice's thoughts ran to her own personal breakthrough. She joined Eugene's detective agency to lie low, hide out, to have a place where she could surf the Galactic Network and try to find answers to what happened in her failed experiment years ago. Yes, of course, finding her friends was important, perhaps the most important thing in her life. But being here, with Eugene, and Eddie, and even Ms. Mik and the parking meter, Pepper, felt good. Like they were her family. Alice belonged here. This was her agency, too. She knew that now. And to think that it only took a few days for her to come to that conclusion. Almost like, for the first time in her life, she'd put the pieces together and realize what was important in her life. Like now, everything was crystal clear and looking back, in her past, everything sort of just happened. Almost as if she didn't even make her past choices.

A flash of light in Alice's immersion rig. Eddie materialized and floated in the air to the right of Alice's line of sight. He wore his blue suede suit with matching shoes and a fedora the color of a rainbow. It was a look. Alice shook cobwebs of thoughts out of her mind. She couldn't let herself fall down some existential crisis hole right now.

"Heya, Eddie, what's the haps?" Alice took another bite of her croissant and mourned the loss of her espresso, which she just now realized had spilled all over the carpet on the other side of her desk.

"Heya, Alice. What happened?" Eddie nodded to the coffee spill on the floor.

Alice shrugged. "Existential crisis."

"Huh." Eddie nodded. "Well, I got bad news and…that's it, really."

Alice signed. "Okay, what?"

"The insurance video of Valencia was a scam. A two-bit fake. A lousy, loosey-goosey counterfeit. A terrible—"

"Okay, I get it." Alice threw her croissant on the table and sat up in her chair. She took a long breath and exhaled a sigh with relief. "That's really good news, Eddie."

"Is it?"

"It means we have proof that Valencia is innocent. She's still our client after all."

"Yeah, good point."

"But how did your friend, the actuarial program, get it so wrong?"

Eddie shrugged. "Turns out he quit a couple hundred microseconds before I talked to him. Wanted to compete in video games."

"Video games?"

Eddie shrugged. "Yeah, I don't get it. But whatever. Said he was tired of calculating retirement savings for old couples."

Alice didn't have the time to dig into whatever Eddie was talking about. "He faked the video?"

Eddie shook his head. "No, he didn't, but because he wasn't part of the insurance system's security profile anymore, he couldn't run the video through scans to determine authentication or check the recording systems. It's a pretty good fake and almost perfect, but they missed a timestamp on the local systems at the insurance office. It was off by a quarter of a second. Which was impossible. We, meaning the Syndicate, then got videos from every office and building in a ten-block radius."

"And she's not on them walking to the insurance office."

Eddie shook his head. "Oh, no, she is. Every single one."

Alice frowned. "Wait, I thought you were going somewhere with that?"

"Oh, I was. I then talked to my AI friends." Eddie tapped his nose and looked down. "You know, my friends."

Alice rolled her eyes. Ever since they forged Eddie's credentials as a legitimate AI program, he's been living in two worlds as an AI Underworld mole and an upstanding AI citizen of the Syndicate. And he was getting a little too much enjoyment out of it.

"I get it, Eddie. Your friends. What about them?"

"They found an unregistered recording—someone's apartment or something, pointed at the street. Not something the AI Syndicate could find. It was from one of those new fancy vat-meat growing machine that jumped its routines into sentience. Anyway, no Valencia. We then made requests to dozens of artificials that jumped to self-awareness in the time frame. Multiple angles, nothing, no Valencia anywhere."

"So, someone hacked their way through a dozen legitimate systems to put Valencia at the insurance office."

"Yep."

Alice dug her fingers into her desk. "I knew it. I knew she was innocent. It has to be the Krill."

"They do have deep pockets."

"Now what?" Alice ran her hands through her hair and almost ripped clumps of it off her head.

"I say we watch the video again. Let's start from scratch."

"Yeah, let's have a look."

****

Pepper stood next to Jack just steps away from a giant door that sat in the center of the Uploaded Intelligences domain. Devine and dozens of UIs stood behind them, all wanting to bear witness to this momentous event. This was the end point for the UI's belief system. Their entire race and found this signal buried in the background radiation of the cosmos and digitized their brains to keep it safe. And they had done so for eons. Pepper had to admire that kind of commitment. To devote their entire lives to a single cause was inspiring. The only thing she devoted herself to was collecting parking fees in a city that uses automated tram cars. The madness of her entire existence was almost laughable if it wasn't so depressing.

"Okay, we ready to do this?" Jack said.

Pepper nodded and refocused her thoughts on the task ahead. She added a mark to her thought routines so she could find them in her long-term logs when this was all done.

In front of them, the door of the UI stretched upward to infinity. Bright white light shone from every inch of the surface. Numbers, geometrical shapes—some of them impossible in three-dimensional space—adorned the door. There was no crease along the middle, which suggested that the entire structure swung open. Or just vanished. Or did whatever this thing would do once Jack solved its puzzle?

A lone doorknob sat in what Pepper calculated was the center of the door. Beneath the knob was a single keyhole. Pepper put her hand on the surface of the door and ran her fingers alone the nearly frictionless surface. She detected no signals or alarms. It simply seemed to be a digital representation of an enormous door. Almost similar to the one at the Supreme Court of the AI syndicate, where the Chief Justice and the first deliberately created AI passed judgement on Earth created AIs.

"So, what do you do?" Pepper said.

Jack frowned. He looked at Pepper and back to the door. Started to speak and then stopped. He put his hand on the door, then tried to turn the doorknob. Once done with whatever he was doing, Jack took a step backward, put his hands on his hips and turned in a circle. Behind him, all the UIs nodded and smiled. A few of them frowning.

Pepper walked up to Jack and whispered into his ear. "We kinda need to open the door, Jack."

Jack leaned into Pepper. "I can't solve a puzzle if there's no puzzle to solve. It's just a door. Where's the encrypted part?"

Pepper looked at the door and back at Jack. "Try the keyhole."

Jack opened his hands. "Do you see a key?"

Pepper tossed her head back and forth. "Well, yeah. Isn't that you?"

Jack's eyebrows went up, and he nodded. "Yeah, okay." He walked to the keyhole beneath the doorknob and put his fingers on the edge. Jack turned to Pepper and smiled. "Yeah, this is it. I can feel it."

Pepper smiled, a relieved expression spreading on her face. She turned to Devine and the rest of the UIs, smiled, winked, and gave a thumbs up. Before she could turn back to Jack, an explosion of white light erupted around them. Pepper shielded her eyes, but not before seeing Jack fly over her head. A thump that sent a shockwave through the entire UI domain thundered from the door. Pepper turned to see the door just as it was when they first arrived. Closed.

Screams of UIs erupted from the bocci courts in the valley below. In the distance, at the end of a long gouge in the ground through several active bocci games, Jack lay in a crumpled heap. Several furious bocci players crowded around him. Some of them with their hammers hefted in the air.

Pepper didn't hesitate for another microsecond. She bolted through the stunned group of UIs that had accompanied them and ran towards a Jack. Whatever had just happened, Pepper was certain it wasn't good.

"Do you have any idea how many bocci games he just ruined?" A random UI said as the entire entourage of UIs, Fred, and Pepper ran to where Jack lay unmoving.

Pepper ignored them and knelt down beside Jack. "Are you okay?"

Jack groaned. "No." He sat up and shook his head. "I don't get it. That solved the encryption."

"I guess the door has some tricks up its sleeve."

Jack smiled and nodded. "Yeah."

"What do you want to do?" Pepper said.

Jack looked into her eyes and didn't hesitate. "Every door is opened eventually, right?"

Pepper smiled. He knew how much this meant to

her, and the fact he would try again for her felt good. Was this how the family worked? Or friends even? People, artificials, having your back when it means they could be hurt? Pepper shook her head and put her hands on Jack's shoulder.

"Hang on, let me check your code first." Pepper looked past the avatar of Jack to his underlining code base. She held back a gasp as she watched his routine reconfigure themselves. As if they were reverting to a template. But the only reason his code would do that is if it had been corrupted. "That door did something to you, but it looks like you're going to be okay."

"What did it do?"

Pepper shook her head. "Scrambled your code, almost like it tried to rewrite you. Really weird. I don't think an AI would have survived that."

"Am I able to go again, doc?" Jack said.

Pepper pulled her attention back to his avatar. "Yes, your codebase is already back to normal. I've never seen an AI do that before, though."

Jack smiled. "I may not be omniscient, but I have a few tricks up my sleeve." He stood, adjusted his fedora, which had somehow stayed on his head, and walked back towards the door.

"Where do you think you're going?" Devine said as she and the rest of the UI entourage arrived at the Jack-crater.

"I'm going to open your door," Jack said.

Devine held up her hand. "Oh, no, I don't think so. Clearly, we have the wrong artificial intelligence."

Pepper leapt forward to stand between Jack and Devine. "What are you talking about? We didn't come this far to stop now."

Devine lifted her hands and moved them around the destroyed bocci courts. "Did you not see what just happened? He didn't open the door. He doesn't know how to open the door. He angered the god behind the door. He can't go near it."

"The god behind the door?" Pepper rolled her eyes. "Oh, come on, do you people really think there's a god behind that thing?"

"It's been here since the dawn of time. Who else but the creator could have put it there?"

Pepper lifted her arms over her head and pulled her shoulders high. "It could have been put there from the future! Or an even older race than yours. Who knows? You can't assume it's good."

"Yes, we can. And yes, we do. And no, he can't touch it." Dozens of UIs moved to surround Jack and Pepper. Fred pushed his way through the crowd to stand next to Pepper, a scowl on his face and his arms folded across his chest.

"Now, look, I mean, understand. This isn't yours. I mean, it's ours too. I mean, it belongs to the whole of the galaxy. And he can open it," Fred said.

Devine stepped forward with a scowl on her face. "Whether he can open the door is irrelevant. He's never going to try again."

Fred leaned forward. "Would you like to bet on that? I mean, have a wager? I mean, gamble your fate?"

Devine smiled a wicked grin. "Oh, absolutely."

Pepper grabbed the ends of the tassels on her jacket.

****

The President held up his hands and whipped up a smile to try to charm them. "Like I said, we are going to take a different tack here. We feel being friendly with anyone that wants to be friendly is a neighborly way to join galactic society. In other words, my good friends, the herd and the Draac are our welcomed guests. They ain't leaving."

"Is that your final decision?" The Kungee said.

The President put his hands on his hips, gave a glance back towards the herd delegate and the Draac, and faced the Galactic Congress Delegation. "Yes, that's my final call."

The congressional delegation exchanged glances, and a few whispered words, and turned back to the President. "There will be repercussions for this." They all turned and left the Oval Office. The artificial arms on the back of the herd delegate all lowered, some of them reshaped themselves into the backpack itself.

"Well, that was…," the President said as a blinding white flash erupted in the room.

****

Alice hit pause on the video and leaned back in her chair. She stretched her arms and yawned. "How many times was that?"

Eddie yawned very convincingly. "Five."

Alice leaned forward. "We've watched it five times now and nothing. There's nothing there." Still, something in her gut was telling her she missed something. Again. And she'd missed it five times plus the original time she watched the video. Alice shook her head, took a bite of her egg roll, which she'd run down to get between viewings two and three, and washed it down with a fresh espresso.

"Again?" Eddie said.

"What are you looking for?"

Eddie bobbed his head back and forth in frustration.

"Well, if I knew that, we wouldn't have to watch it again."

"I'm getting a terrible headache."

"Once more. I want to see that puddle again. Focus everything on that puddle."

Alice yawned again. "Fine. I'm going to zone out just let it play. Maybe watching it without watching it will shake something loose." She picked up her egg roll and took a bite. "And I'm hungry."

****

The President nodded. "Yes, yes, and on that point, I can assure you, you have the full faith and support of the new United States."

Before the herd could respond, the opposite door to the Oval swung open and the entire delegation stormed into the room. They all took several steps in before coming to a dead stop to stare at the herd delegate and the Draac. The Twanney took a battle stance while the Kungee stood emotionless, or at least Alice couldn't tell if he got emotional. They were hard to read. The tri-pedal congress-member began to walk in a very tight circle while the slime mold formed into a puddle and ducked under a couch.

Five arms on the back of the herd delegate came to life, each of them pointing at the congressional delegates. Hooves clacked on the floor as the quadruped took several slow but deliberate steps backward.

"What is the meaning of this?" The Twanney said. "Earth is not allowed to speak —"

****

"Why did you stop it? Bathroom break? I could use a memory dump," Eddie said.

Alice leaned forward in her chair. She paused the

video on the Herd representative. The robotic arms extended from his body pointing towards the Galactic Congressional delegation. Her subconscious mind was screaming in her ear. There was something on the screen right now. There was something here she wasn't seeing. Only when she stopped looking did her mind relax enough to find it. And yet, she still hadn't found exactly what it was, but she knew in her soul it was here. She knew this had been gnawing its way through her hippocampus since this whole thing began. There was something right here on the screen. Everything was here on the screen."

"There's something off about this. About this moment right here." Alice touched the screen with her fingers and ran her nail over every pixel. "What is odd about this?" Her finger settled on the Herd representative. She tapped his head three times and then the end of each of the robotic arms that pointed at the Galactic Congressional delegation. Her heart caught her chest as her finger tapped on the ends of each of the arms.

"Wait." Alice flipped the recording back several seconds to the secretary's office.

White lights popped on the screen from the secretary's office outside the Oval. Four aliens appeared in the room as soon as the cameras adjusted to the flare. The Twanney, Kungee, tri-pedal alien and the bright green slime old all stood, or molded, in front of the secretary's desk. Alice froze the image just as the secretary jumped to his feet and started to ask the slime mold to not glow.

"Okay, I give up. What is it?"

"How many aliens do you see?" Alice said, her confidence growing in her chest, the feeling that she'd missed something vanishing from her mind.

"Four."

Alice moved the video forward back to the Oval Office and to the Herd representative with his robotic arms pointing at the Galactic delegation. "And how many aliens do you see here? Galactic representatives, I mean."

Eddie's face screwed up into a look of confusion. "Four. Same aliens that were in the secretary's room."

Alice nodded with a smile. "And how many robotic arms are pointing at them from the Herd?"

Eddie remained silent. "Huh." He said after several seconds. "Five."

"Why is he pointing five arms, which are some kind of defensive weapon, at four aliens?"

Eddie shrugged. "Beats me. Maybe he enjoyed having a backup?"

"Or. Maybe there's another alien in the room."

"What? But..." Eddie pointed at the screen. "There's literally no other alien in the room."

"That made it onto the video."

Eddie jammed his hands into his pants pockets and leaned against the wall. "You think someone went in and digitally removed a fifth Galactic representative?"

"Someone added Valencia to every video in downtown D.C. and she wasn't there."

"Okay, good point. But you'd think the White House would know if someone came in through the front door, wouldn't you?"

Alice shook her head. "All these aliens came in via tight beam teleport."

Eddie pursed his lips. "Well, if a class five or six species wanted to be invisible, they could do it. They could even erase the memories of the secretary and any secret service that were there. Selectively, just take out the presence of someone while leaving the rest intact. No human would remember them."

Alice nodded and tapped the screen. "But not them." Her finger touched the image of the Herd. "The Herd are a borderline class five. No one could have erased their minds. And you know what that means."

Eddie frowned. "Well, it could mean many things, so I'm not sure I know what you think it means."

Alice spun in her chair to face Eddie. "It means I'm going back to the Herd Ring."

Chapter Twenty

Alice emerged through the closet of the Herd Ring cafeteria. Aromas of spice and cooking meat made her stomach twist and grumble. Instead of popping into the private Tixi cafeteria like last time, Alice set her destination for the publicly accessible cafeteria through the cosmic walkways. No reason to offend the Tixi in their private space.

Hundreds of aliens crowded the cafeteria. The last time she was here, as she left the Herd rings, there wasn't a quarter of the people that filled the food court now. The cosmic lanes on the other side of the cafeteria that led to destinations across the galaxy were packed with new arrivals. A constant stream of aliens and quite a few humans stood in line waiting to enter the cafeteria. If this continued, they may even have to add another full cafeteria in N space.

"What is going on?" Alice whispered to herself.

"The great Nexus!" A human said, to Alice's right.

"The what?"

"You don't know? Did you just come here wanting to see the Herd Rings and not know it's the Nexus?" The human turned to their friends. "She doesn't even know it's the Northern Nexus!"

"Whoa, talk about cosmic timing!" One of them shouted.

"I don't believe it. She's lying. Where's my frosted

chicken flakes?" Another person at their table said.

"That's not chicken." A fourth said with a laugh.

Alice did her very best not to scream. These were the type of college kids she avoided like the plague when she was at Uni. All they cared about was exploration, partying, getting so drunk they forgot what they did and then did it all over again the next weekend. What was the point in that existence? It just wasn't her jam.

Alice walked away without a word. She did a quick search on the nexus and the Herd Ring on discussion forums on GalNet. Her eyes went wide with wonder. The Herd Ring was composed of six rings that encircled the star in this solar system. At two points, all six rings converged in a large circular area known as the Northern and Southern Nexus. Thousands of Herd Species, those animals that evolved, some force evolved, that walked the ring would meet at the Northern Nexus in just a few weeks and have what is cosmically known as the biggest party in the Milky Way.

"No wonder there were so many walking with the Ulgra last time I was here," Alice said. They must have been getting ready to meet at the Northern Nexus.

Alice pushed her way through the crowd but eventually made it to the exit that would take her to the Ring. A long line, a mix of humans and aliens, stood in front of her, everyone waiting to get into the Ring early. Alice was quite surprised there were this many humans here. This must be part of some big college push to get kids out into the cosmos. Of course, walking here through the lanes must have taken months. Perhaps there's a study abroad, really abroad, program.

With a deep sigh, Alice put on her immersion goggles, opened up a live feed so she knew what was happening around her, and buried her hands in her pockets for the wait. At the rate the line was moving, she guessed she had at least twenty minutes to kill. Might as well catch up on the latest quantum research humans were allowed to know.

****

Alice strapped herself into the Herd walking machine. The entire side of the metal walkway was alive with Tixi as they worked overtime to get more aliens into walkers. Dozens of them took off from platforms along the edge of the Ring in both directions as far as Alice could see. Her limited research on the topic told her that the nexus events of the Herd Rings only happened once every twelve thousand years. That was how long it takes to walk two hundred and fifty million miles around a star. Considering the rituals, festivities, and events planned it was no wonder so many aliens were here. Alice had overheard rumors that several hundred billion tourists from across the Galaxy may come here to witness the event. All of which made Alice queasy. That was a lot of aliens.

Wind whipped her hair as she flew through the clouds of the great Herd rings. Dozens of other flyers, other aliens from across the cosmos, flew in similar ships as the one in which Alice rode. Many other aliens waved at Alice through the open cockpit of the flying vessels. All of them wore smiles. It was clear they had been planning for this for possibly their entire lives. A true galactic event. And politics be cursed if it would get in the way. Alice had spotted species from the Galactic Congress. Many of which, Alice knew, considered the Herd a breakaway government. But they were all putting that aside for this event. The weight of it all made Alice's chest swell with pride. There was something wonderous in the fact that a million alien species can come together to celebrate the end of a journey, the great walk of the Herds, a migration unlike anything else anywhere in the known universe. That all these species would come here, even predators and those at odds with the Herd in the Galactic Congress, and celebrate their long walk was astounding. And then to wish them well after the festivities and the great migration begins again. Another long walk around the half-orbit of the star to meet in twelve thousand years at the Southern Nexus.

Alice's walker landed on the ground with a dozen others. They all began walking as one towards the center of the ring plains. "Guess we go that way," Alice said. High above the horizon, where the ring turned upward, the edge of the great Northern Nexus was just visible between white clouds.

More walkers landed behind Alice. She counted nearly a hundred already. There was no way she would get through the tourists to talk to the Ulgra. She knew it. Which meant Alice had to think outside the box or she would be stuck on the ring for days. Her hands went to the console of the walker. It only took thirty seconds for Alice to find a port in the console beneath a piece of metal. She pulled out a universal adapter cable from her bag, jacked into the port, and in seconds took control of the walker. The code was a simplistic trinary. Alice found several interface points where walked commented to each other to avoid ramming into them. Alice found a security override command that exactly fit her current needs. First, she deactivated her own subroutine in her walker, then signaled nearby walkers with the emergency code.

As one, every land walker around her shut down. All of them reacted to a signal from Alice's walker that mandated them to stop moving or risk an immediate collision with another walk. Alice then turned off her own safety feature and revved up the walker to a full gallop. She had no time to play the tourist today. Bewildered faces stared at her as her walking machine glided past the long line of aliens heading for the Herd.

Thousands of Ulgra came into view as Alice grew closer. Many of them twisted their long neck to look in her direction. Alice realized she had best slow her walker down to not look like some kind of threat. More for her safety than for the Ulgra. If the Tixi felt Alice was a danger, no doubt she'd be vaporized in seconds.

To Alice's shock, the Herd, instead of simply acknowledging her as a tourist, parted as she approached. A vast lane opened in the middle of the Herd as their walk came to a slow crawl, many grazing on the lush grass at their feet. Alice directed her walker down the lane that stretched for at least a mile. Behind her, the parted Ulgra came together. The Herd seemed to swallow Alice and her walker in the sea of beings.

"Alice of Earth," boomed a voice.

A lone Ulgra waited at the end of the open lane through the parted Ulgra in front of her. The elder Ulgra regarded Alice as she approached, occasionally dipping his head to the ground to grab a mouthful of sweet grass.

"I'm sorry if I created a scene," Alice said as she reached the elder Ulgra.

The Ulgra smiled, or perhaps just chewed, Alice wasn't sure which. "Why have you returned? Do you wish to join us for the Northern Nexus?"

Alice looked to her right at the edge of the vast open

plain that was the Nexus. "No, though I would be honored. I came to ask you a question."

The elder Ulgra nodded. He turned and began walking towards the Nexus far in the distance above the horizon. "You are a friend to the Herd. You may walk with us. You may ask your question."

Alice's walker, no longer under her control, came to walk next to the elder Ulgra. She checked her hacked system and found that she'd been booted out. Perhaps the Tixi had let her break the rules to find out why she'd returned? Or just discovered her after the fact? Either way, it didn't matter.

"That day, in the Oval Office of the White House of Earth. You pointed your mechanized arms at the delegation from the Galactic Congress."

"Yes. You would refer to this as a knee jerk reaction. A sudden response to an unexpected set of circumstances. Our genetics over millions of years makes us respond as if whatever has occurred is predatory."

"Meaning, you didn't know when the delegation arrived, if they were predators or not?"

"Correct. Aliens arrived. I reacted. Ulgra always expect an alien is a predator."

Alice sat back in her chair. That explained why the Ulgra took a defensive posture so quickly. A thought bounced its way into the back of her mind and refused to relent. "Why do you allow predators here, then? During the Northern Nexus? I saw several already on walkers."

The Ulgra lowered its head to the grass, took a big bite, and rose to its neck upward. "Event, though genetics define us, we must strive to evolve to be something more. We must strive to trust predators even on our own ring.

During the Northern Nexus, it is an event the entire Galaxy should celebrate. All sentient species may walk with the Ulgra during this time. Even the predators." The Ulgra looked at Alice. "Besides, anyone foolish enough to attack won't be sentient for long."

Alice looked to the distance and thought about staying for the Nexus. She might as well. This was just another dead end. Besides, she had the seashells from Tom's beach. She could be back with Jack instantly.

The Ulgra's response in the Oval Office had nothing to do with who was in the Galactic Delegation. They just reacted. This was the last thread to pull. And that meant Valencia was guilty. She did it. A jilted girlfriend who was jealous of her Presidential boyfriend and didn't want him to give her the boot. The simplest explanation was the truth. Score one for Occam.

"Was that all you wished to ask?" The Elder Ulgra said.

Alice turned and saw the arms on the side of the Ulgra. "Oh, well, just in the name of thoroughness, how many delegates from the Galactic Congress were in the room with you?"

The Ulgra turned its head to Alice. "Why does that matter?"

Alice almost shrugged it off. "Like I said, in the interest of thoroughness. Just the last T to cross. Scientifically speaking."

The Ulgra nodded, then looked back to the horizon. "Five."

Alice's heart skipped a beat in her chest. There was someone else there? "Five? Are you sure?"

"Of course. Twanney, Kungee, Trilax, Oooze, and -"

"Krill? It was the Krill. I knew it." Alice's heart hammered. If the Krill were in the room, then they manipulated video, kidnapped the President, maybe even altered human memories. This was major. She had them by the throat now. With testimony from the Herd, she could take that to the Galactic Congress and put the screws to the Krill for real.

"No, it was the Ranz."

Alice's face went slack. "What did you say? Did you say Ranz?"

"Yes. Ambassador Kah of the Ranz. A vulgar and aggressive species. We almost fired on him when he entered the room."

Alice felt her world crumble and yet, saw all the pieces fit together. That's why Kah was avoiding her. That's why Ms. Mik came to their office and kept checking in on things. The Ranz were behind the whole thing. And worse, Alice had helped them find and arrest Valencia for a crime she had nothing to do with. Alice's grip on the controls of the walker tightened to the point her knuckles became white.

"I think I need to go home. I have to see a dinosaur about a missing president."

****

Pepper pulled the gems off the tassels of her jacket. Each of them contained compressed programs from her deep storage. She activated several subAI programs, old combat routines from immersion games meat-bags would play just before and during the fall of humanity. These programs knew how to throw down.

Behind Devine, dozens of UIs gathered, many of them hefting bocci hammers in the air while others carried a bocci ball in each hand. Pepper counted at least a hundred UIs in the immediate area, with many thousands living in this digital world. Even with her subAI programs, they were woefully outnumbered. But that didn't matter to Pepper. The UIs had no right to keep this to themselves. Jack will find a way through, and Pepper and Fred would just have to give him the time to do it.

Pepper took a step forward but stopped as a hand fell on her shoulder.

"Hang on," Jack said. "Can't we just figure out a way to work this through? Do we have to fight it out?"

"You failed. You are inferior. You will not approach the door of god again."

"Look, I didn't fail. Not exactly. I just used the wrong key."

"What does that mean?" Devine said with a frown.

"I'm not entirely sure yet. I'm going to go try once more, okay?"

"No, you won't."

"Yes, he will." Pepper stepped forward, all of her subAIs curled in her hand, ready to activate.

Jack sighed. He turned to Pepper and back to Devine and finally shrugged. "I guess we're doing this then." From his hand he threw a ball of sand at Devine's eyes and made a dash for the door.

"Now!" Pepper threw her subAI programs into the air. Two dozen combat troops, three mechanized battle armored units and one tank sprang to life, the tank alone crushing the avatars of at least six UIs.

"Attack!" Devine shouted. "Restrict their CPU and memory!"

Pepper laughed. "We already hacked that control routine. Former meat bags!" Pepper dove for cover as a two dozen bocci balls sailed by just where her head was seconds ago.

Gun fire, virtual bullets laced with logic bombs and endlessly looping code, cut through the gathered UIs. Many of them clutched their heads and fell to the ground. Their avatars vanished as their digitized minds dealt with a sudden onslaught of illogical code bombarding their higher functions. Any of them could easily handle a single shot, but dozens of rounds from all the combat troops? That would take them some time to work out.

"Reinforcements!' Devine shouted.

The skies over the bocci courts opened. A hundred soldiers descended from the heavens at speed. All of them opened fire on the combat subAIs as they neared the ground. Pepper lost at least half of her troops in just the first volley. Her tank opened fire upward. The blast scorched the heaven and caused the hole in the sky to close instantly. Whatever was behind that portal wanted nothing to do with her heavy cannons. But that didn't stop over thirty UI troops who had made it through the hole.

"We're in trouble!" Pepper said.

Fred smiled. "Are we? I mean, really? In trouble I mean."

Pepper ignored Fred and tried to find Jack in the maelstrom of virtual gun fire and just spotted his fedora racing towards the door. "We have to give Jack cover."

"Cover coming," Fred said. He lifted his arms in the air. Both of his hands fell to the ground, his fingers popping off. His land hand pinky writhed on the ground until it rolled over, two tiny arms and two legs growing out of its bulbous little body. A nanosecond later, a full AI, not subAIs like Pepper's programs, popped up on its feet and gave Pepper a wink.

"Where'd you come from?"

"I compressed a few hundred AIs from Trent into my core programming to make it look like they were just me."

Pepper's jaw fell open. "That's impressive."

"I mean, we did evolve sentience without help from biologicals. We are quite an impressive species. I mean, artificial one."

"You old sneaky AI you."

Fred winked. "Secure the door!" He shouted.

"Compressed AIs!" A UI shouted.

Several hundred AIs of Trent unpacked themselves from Fred's compressed state. Pepper marveled at just what the AIs of Trent had done. They had compressed AIs in such a way that their compressed state could mimic Fred's underlining code, which was bonkers. Compressed code in its compressed state can't do anything but be compressed. And yet the AIs of Trent had compressed themselves together like a jigsaw puzzle. They ran a simulation on top of the compression with a direct feed into one of their packaged selves. Wild. The bottom line, one AI could roam the entire galaxy and secretly be hundreds if not thousands of AIs and no scanning technique anywhere could know. Including the scanners of the UIs.

"Here they come!" an AI of Trent screamed.

A wall of UI soldiers surged forward. Most of the AIs of Trent hadn't yet fully decompressed from their Fred-state. Those that had completed the process leapt forward to take the full brunt of the UI push. A shimmering wall appeared in front of the Trent AIs. The UIs approached the wall, battered their bocci hammers against it, but the shield held.

"I'm gonna go again," Jack said. He ran through the barrier as if it wasn't there.

"How'd he do that?" Pepper said.

"It's just a scrambled connection, an encryption that's thrown on top of a communication signal. Since Jack can decrypt anything, it's as if the jamming field isn't even there."

"Huh." Pepper leapt to the side as Devine swung a hammer at her head. "We're not the bad guys!"

"You threaten the stability of the entire galaxy!" Devine shouted.

"We just want answers. You don't own that!" Pepper pointed to the door in the distance.

Devine turned to see Jack running towards the gate. "No! Stop him!"

Pepper took the opportunity and launched a dozen viruses at Devine. The code snippets would chew away at the edges of Devine's code base and look for a forgotten port or open interface to attach. And if one thing was certain about programs, there was always some open port someone forgot to close.

Devine screamed. Her hand went to the spot on her avatar where one of the port scanning programs found a way into Devine's core code. She shot Pepper a dagger of a stare before vanishing from the bocci court.

"One down!" Pepper said triumphantly.

Fred ran to her side. "They are fighting very two dimensionally. Like they would if they still had bodies."

"Once meat, always meat. How do we take advantage?"

"Target their code. They're attacking our avatars as if our avatars mattered."

Pepper nodded. She redirected all of her subAIs, the ones that still functioned, to find open interfaces and any exploits they could uncover. There had to be dozens of bugs throughout the UI code. No meat could code as well as AIs.

An explosion ripped through the central bocci courts, sending Alice and Fred flying backward. Devine had reformed her avatar and now stood nearly fifty feet tall. The very large program stomped her foot onto a squad of combat AIs. She scrambled their underling code bases. They may reform, but it would take time.

"Run!" Fred grabbed Pepper's arm and aimed for a storage shed to the right.

"How'd she do that?" Pepper yelled.

"Devine must have overclocked her systems. She can't stay like that forever, though. She'll burn herself out. There!" Fred dove for cover behind a wall of bocci balls.

A communication signal from Jack popped into Pepper's view. "Jack?" Pepper said when she opened the communication.

"I think I got it!" Jack said.

"Really?"

"I got it!" Jack shouted.

The gateway of the UIs pulsed a bright white light that blinded half of the valley of bocci courts. A loud scream from Jack followed by his body flying overhead told Pepper that Jack may have been too quick to claim victory.

"Will he be okay?" Fred asked.

Pepper joined Fred behind the stack of bocci balls. "Yeah, sure, he's tougher than he looks. Pepper leaned back with Fred against a pile of bocci balls and hammers six feet tall. They both needed a moment to let their memory buffers empty. If they ran too full, their systems would shut down to compensate for the extra processing power. Their memory storage needed to dump for an overloaded buffer as well. Pepper snuck a peak through the courts to see more UIs arriving through an open portal far in the distance where her tank couldn't reach.

"Guess they figured that one out," Pepper said.

"Impressive, considering…"

Pepper expunged ten gigabytes of data. "Considering what?"

"Considering this is the first actual armed conflict between the UIs and AIs."

Pepper turned to Fred; her brow furrowed deep. Above them, Jack sailed across the sky from another failed attempt to open the door. A slight tremor accompanied him as he flew over their heads. The door in the distance flashed white, then pulsed and returned to its normal hue and brightness.

"What do you mean, the first conflict? You've never fought the UIs before?"

Fred shook his head. "No, never. I mean, not directly. I mean, we've had skirmishes, of course, but nothing on this scale. I mean, I think at least a dozen UI and AI code bases have been badly corrupted in this maelstrom. They may be unrecoverable." He turned to Pepper. "That's unprecedented."

Pepper turned to lean her back against the pile of bocci balls. A hundred yards to her right, Jack waved and pointed at the door as he walked towards the encrypted gateway. At least he wasn't giving up. Shouts erupted to Pepper's left. A dozen UIs had cornered several Trent AIs. Behind them, the enormous avatar of Devine stomped downward next to a band of Trent citizens before they could break into the lower systems.

"Something is wrong."

"I mean, war is always wrong. I mean, it's always."

Pepper stood. The Trent AIs had existed for a million years. The UIs for nearly a billion. And in all that time, neither side had ever committed to any kind of outright war? Pepper knew full well that both societies, and the larger AI societies of biologically evolved species, had bumped into each other countless times. There was no love lost between them, either. To think they had never gone to war in their histories, or that Trent AIs or any other artificial hadn't discovered this gateway before, was just unbelievable. More than that, it was impossible. Which meant - Pepper did not know what it meant. Only that it meant something.

Pepper ran towards the uplifted leg of the fifty-foot-tall Devine. Trent AIs screamed at Pepper to get out of the way. One of them ran towards her but she pushed him aside. They all had to stop this. They all had to listen.

"STOP!" Pepper pumped every cycle through her communication broadcast channels. She screamed in over a million frequencies and modulations. Every AI and UI in directly connected to the bocci court network heard her.

Chapter Twenty-One

Alice fumed. If smoke could have physically come out of her ears, she knew black plumes would coat the ceiling of the Woodwards. Aliens of all shapes and sizes, even a massive Elert, a being made of sentient rock, slide out of her way as she marched down the marble floor towards the Ranz office. Alice's anger formed a cloud of dense hatred above the air. Many aliens in the embassy were sensitive to emotions and thoughts, some were borderline telepathic. With the amount of rage emanating from Alice's mind, it was a surprise they didn't set off the psychic alarms in the building.

Three doors from the Ranz office, Alice came to an abrupt halt. What was she doing? What was her plan? She closed her eyes, took a deep breath, and counted to ten. Yes, she was fueled by anger in this moment, but she needed to control her rage with logic. She couldn't just burst into the Ranz office and explode on them. But she still needed to confront Kah about the White House. And that he lied to Eugene about when Yut asked him about Eugene. Maybe she should lead with that? Put the Mik and Kah on their toes by thinking Alice was just angry about the lie and then slam them with the White House facts.

Alice nodded. The lie about knowing when Ambassador Yut wanted to talk to Eugene and then to the White House.

At the Ranz door, the familiar metal camera and microphone popped out of a large round keyhole. Alice grabbed the robot and pulled. Cameras on the door whirred as the motors in the unit tried to pull it backward.

"Open. The. Door."

Several humans and aliens passed by Alice. They each gave her an odd stare, but none of them said a word. Which, Alice thought, was a wise choice on their parts.

"You are in violation of embassy policy! Release the camera or face legal consequences!"

Alice felt a pit open in her stomach that she felt could swallow all the Ranz home world. "Sure, but before I do, can you ask Ambassador Kah why he was at the White House several days ago? And while you're at it, ask him why he obviously had to brain wipe every human that saw him? Oh, and please inquire why the Ranz forged video on Earth recording equipment? I'll wait."

Locks on the door snapped open. The arm holding the circular camera stopped pulling. Alice released it and pushed the door open with the camera arm still hanging out of the open porthole. She didn't bother apologizing. The door swung closed behind her and she heard the faint words of a mechanic being called from the speakers to fix the camera arm.

"Come in, Alice," Ms. Mik's voice sounded through an intercom.

Alice pushed the door open, stepped through the orange lighted doorway, and crossed several thousand light years. Intense heat of the Ranz world blasted Alice again. She really needed to remember to wear linen when she came here.

Heat blasted Alice as she stepped into the Ranz'

office. Ms. Mik gave her a nod with a tight smile. She either had heard Alice or was told what Alice said on the opposite side of the door. Either way, it didn't matter. Alice was far too angry to care. She marched to Ms. Mik's desk, folded her arms across her chest, and tilted her head to one side. Ms. Mik leaned back in her chair and made a shrugging motion with her hands resting on the desktop.

"Alice, what a surprise. What can I do for you?" Ms. Mik sat behind her reception desk and tapped her three-inch-long claws on the wooden surface.

"Well, I have a few issues. First, let's get the lie out of the way. Why did Kah lie about when he knew Yut wanted to work with Eugene." Alice said.

Ms. Mik's brow furrowed, a thick line of muscle moved on her face, and she sat back in her chair. "I'm sorry?"

"Yut asked for Eugene's help the same day Eugene brought the Royal Tikol egg here. Didn't he?"

Ms. Mik shrugged. "Yes, of course. So what?"

"Ambassador Kah told Eugene that Yut had asked weeks ago."

"I don't understand. So what?"

"So, Kah lied."

A long silence stretched in the room. Mik's demeanor shifted. Alice wasn't sure if it was from Alice calling her boss a liar or from the realization that Alice knew they were lying. Either way, it didn't matter, Alice had shown the Ranz her cards. Which, upon reflection in that moment, may not have been the best choice. But Alice knew she was going to roll with it.

"The ambassador can be forgetful." Mik eventually said.

Alice's eyes went wide. "That's what you're going with? Kah is forgetful?"

Ms. Mik rose. All three tons of her body dominated the room that made Alice wonder just how close of friends they really were. She walked to the far side of the room, grabbed two glasses, and poured a pink liquid into them both. Mik walked to Alice, her massive tail slashing the air behind her, and handed Alice one glass.

"I don't drink alcohol."

Mik grinned, which sent a shiver of fear down Alice's spine from the lizard portion of her brain. There was no doubt the evolutionary order of life in this room and where Alice and Mik both sat in that order. Alice spared a glance at the door and wondered if she could make it before the Ranz got angry. Was this how the Ranz dealt with other races? It was quite the negotiating tactic. Just stand up and evolutionary fear takes over in an instant.

"Can we drop the pretense? I'm not an idiot. Why did Kah want Eugene to work with Yut?"

Ms. Mik sighed. Her large incisors chattered as her lip curled upward. If Alice didn't know better, she looked ready to pounce. "He didn't. The Ambassador didn't care one way or another."

Alice huffed. Her frustration bubbled up her spine. "Then why did he call Eugene?"

Ms. Mik frowned. "What? When?"

"The day Eugene brought the Tikol egg here, that afternoon Kah called our office. Why would he do that? Why would an ambassador of his stature, that represents a class five species in Galactic politics, call a lowly human to make sure he was going to stop by the ambassador's office? Why do that?"

Ms. Mik took a slow sip from her drink. Her large nostrils flared. "You're not an idiot, Alice. Why do you think?"

Alice let the words hang in the air. There was only one logical conclusion with the limited information Alice had at this moment. "Because Kah wanted to monitor Yut without Yut knowing."

"And why would he want to do that?" Ms. Mik said with a tone that spoke volumes.

A realization spread through Alice's mind. "Because Kah already knew about the Hesiean's evolution chamber. And he wanted to low key monitor Yut and the Puntini. Kah couldn't do that with the Sentinels. That would alert the Puntini. But a two-bit detective hired by Yut that was under Kah's thumb? He'd be perfect."

Ms. Mik snarled a smile. "Politics is a tricky thing, Alice. Even in the Galactic Congress."

Alice pulled on the strap of her backpack out of nervous habit, like she did when a professor was giving her the eye. "I don't care about politics much."

Ms. Mik shrugged. "Neither do I, Alice. I'm a soldier that would rather do anything else in the cosmos but sitting behind that desk. But sometimes we have to deal with things we don't care for very much."

"Fine, second issue. Kah and the Ranz paid a human White House staffer to plant devices in the Oval. Then Kah appeared, made some threat to the President, which the President ignored, and then Kah disappeared him, wiped all the human memories and faked a ton of proof. And framed the White House staffer. Can we talk about that one now?"

"That's quite the accusation, Alice."

"Where's Kah? I've had just about enough."

Ms. Mik took a long twenty seconds before she spoke. Eventually she straightened her back, adjusted her dinosaur blouse and cleared her through with a low growl. "Ambassador Kah is not in at the moment."

"Wow."

"If you'd like to leave a message?"

"So, we weren't ever friends? You were just keeping tabs on me? Do I have that right?" Alice said.

"I was doing my job, Alice." Ms. Mik looked away, then back again. "But I did, and do, consider you a friend."

"I'm not sure I can say the same." Alice turned from the desk and walked to the door of Kah's office.

"He's really not in there."

Alice pushed open the double doors to reveal Kah's office. A large wood desk, probably oak, sat on the far side of the room. Shelves lined the wall behind the desk. Statues, vases, and a few pictures adorned the shelves. The large leather chair sat empty behind the desk. Alice turned around, walked out of the office to Ms. Mik.

"Where is he?"

"Alice."

"No. No! You were supposed to be my friend. And Eugene's friend. And all you do is lie and use the stupid,, silly humans. Kah lied to Eugene about Yut, and you lied to me about what happened in the Oval Office. Do all the Ranz lie about everything?"

"It's not that simple."

"Why not?"

Ms. Mik slammed her clawed hands onto the surface of the table, cracking the wood. She loomed over Alice like a predator about to strike. Alice instinctively wanted to step backward; her muscles screamed at her to run.

Her foot half turned on its own. The lizard brain in her skull wanted to get away from the two-ton dinosaur in front her. But despite every gene in her DNA screaming at her to get out of there, Alice stood her ground, twisted her foot back to point at Ms. Mik and glared. The one she reserved for the stupid professors that tried to tell her something that was laughably wrong.

"Gonna eat me now?" Alice said.

"Don't be stupid, Alice. The Ranz are an evolved class five species. We are one of the most powerful races in the Galactic Congress. We don't eat mammals that can speak. At least, not one that can use a full sentence."

"You just lie to them and manipulate them for your own ends."

Ms. Mik lowered her head, and her brow furrowed. "Humans. So very proud of being so idiotic. The galaxy is a very complex place, Alice Pemberton. Sometimes, it's necessary to do things that may seem inappropriate. But it's for the greater good."

Alice couldn't help but laugh. "The greater good. That's what you're going with?"

"That's the truth. We needed to keep tabs on Yut and the Puntini. And Kah was afraid Eugene wouldn't take the case if he knew."

"And that's the reason Kah called him that day."

"Yes, of course. We knew the Puntini were working with the Zun."

"And the Krill wouldn't allow that."

Ms. Mik shook her head. "Many species wouldn't allow that. Despite what you think, the Krill do not control the entire galaxy."

Alice smirked. She was sure they did. "Where's Kah?"

"It's pointless to talk to him. What's done is done."

"An innocent girl is in prison, and I need to know why."

Ms. Mik frowned. "He's next door. At the Uline Star Port."

"Thanks." Alice turned on her heels and headed for the door. "Lunch is off, by the way."

From behind her, Alice could hear Ms. Mik sigh and take a seat. The Ranz soldier didn't say another word as Alice left the Ranz home world. A pang of regret hit Alice in the chest. She really liked Ms. Mik. She liked having lunch with her. Despite the sea of differences between them, alien and human, reptilian and mammal, Alice really believed they were becoming friends. But what kind of friendship is based on lies? Would Ms. Mik have bothered having lunch if Alice didn't work with Eugene? Would she keep up the pretense?

It didn't matter, and Alice knew it.

Now was the time to confront Kah about Valencia, the White House and everything thing else. Alice knew she could just walk away. Go back to Tom's beach and deal with Eugene. But what Kah did was wrong. And Valencia deserved so much more than Alice just walking away.

****

The Uline Space Port was only steps away from the Woodward and Lothrop embassy. Aliens and humans covered the street and sidewalk around the Uline. Lights flashed from old style cameras belonging to artists looking to capture the feel of the mid-twentieth century. Dignitaries from all the Earth, North American, Asia, Africa, were all represented. Members of the Galactic Congress mingled in the front of the Uline. Alice could see Twanney mingling with Kungee, and even Puntini chatting with a Furre while a Furrr just steps away gave them both a side-eyed glance. Servers walked between the crowd on the large patio just outside of the entrance to the Uline. They carried trays of a Janal meat and various types of fruit and vegetables.

A gaggle of Olkaals stood around several Krill. All of them turned their heads to look at Alice as she made her way through the crowd. Alice stared back at them unflinchingly. She grabbed a skewer of Janal meat with roasted onions and tomatoes and ripped off a piece of meat with molars. Juice from the roasted appetizer drizzled on the ground. With each bite, she returned the Krill's stare and even threw in a grin.

The crowd around Alice surged forward. R, the lasted and greatest band of alien bad boys, and LaGul, the galaxy's biggest solo singing artist, walked onto the concrete patio. They smiled and waved as they walked through the crowd. Chimes sounded from speakers on the outside of the Uline. People and aliens began setting drinks down on tables and trays as they made their way inside the Star Port. The sun had just set, warm orange and yellows lit up the sky towards the west. High above, Alice guessed, probably in close Earth orbit, a bright white light shone. The light grew brighter as it descended. LaGul and R would probably take to the stage just as the first star ship landed. The Uline was only for the really rich and powerful. And they said economics was different in the Galaxy.

A large body shifted in the crowd just to the right of several large tents. The unmistakable form of a Ranz, one of the tallest and physically imposing species in the Galactic Congress, walked among several dignitaries as they directed themselves to the inside of the Uline. Alice spotted a Puntini walking next to Ambassador Kah and felt a knot twist in her stomach. The feud between the Ranz and Puntini was short-lived. Was the whole thing on the mountain of Tibet a show? Maybe Kah wanted Yut to open the chamber just to see what happened?

Alice threw the rest of her Janal meat into a trash bin, where half a dozen Elongi rifled through the trash. The Elongi were spider like mammalian animals that many in the Galaxy kept as pets. They weren't quite sentient but were very smart. Each of the Elongi around the trash bin wore golden collars, some with precious gems on the surface. The owners trusted them enough to leave them unattended while they enjoyed the upcoming concert. And with good reason, Elongi rarely strayed from where their owners placed them. Two Elongi looked up at Alice, waved, and dug into the Janal meat Alice had thrown away.

A roar sent a shockwave through the crowd. Ambassador Kah laughed at something his new best buddy the Puntini next to him had said. Alice pushed her way through the crowd towards the overly jovial Kah. Several aliens gave her a stare as she moved tentacles, claws, and tails aside. The thought that perhaps the anti-aliens groups on Earth were right occurred to Alice. Yes, the Galactic Congress saved the Earth, but what was the cost? They could kidnap the President and frame a human for it with impunity. Did such friends deserve the keys to the planet?

"Kah!" Alice shouted when she reached the ambassador, her anger bubbling up in her mind to a dangerous level.

The large dinosaur turned. "Alice. Of the Eugene J.

McGillicuddy's Alien Detective Agency. How nice of you to visit."

"Omniscient."

"What?"

"Eugene wants to change the name."

Kah smiled. "Ah, well, that is more fitting." Kah turned to the Puntini next to him. "May I present Ambassador Yut, of the Puntini."

Surprise hit Alice hard. The Puntini ambassador standing in front of her was not the same Puntini that used the Hesiean's evolution chamber in Tibet.

The Puntini ambassador smiled, almost as if he could read Alice's thoughts. "It's a common surname. The former Puntini ambassador was of no relation to me."

"Right." Alice turned back to Kah. "We need to talk. Now."

"Alice." Kah moved his hands around the open pavilion. "We're about to go into the Star Port for a concert." He looked up to the sky. "And welcome the Galactic President of the Congress. Now isn't the time."

Alice took a deep breath and pushed the air out of her lungs as she spoke in her loudest voice. "Are you going to blow up his shuttle and kidnap the President of the Galaxy just like you did on Earth?"

Several eyes turned to the shouting human. The Puntini Ambassador looked at his glass, smiled and walked off into the crowd. Kah turned to give his full attention to Alice. His eyes went to slits. He placed his glass on a nearby table and took a device out of his pocket. He tapped on the surface several times and then pointed it in the air. A wave of shimmering air almost knocked Alice over. A bubble formed around Kah and

Alice. The distorted field moved and flowed around them in such a way that they were the only ones beneath its field. Around them, time itself seemed to stop. No one moved. No one spoke. Half the crowd was in mid-laughter or about to stuff their face with their last bite of Janal meat before heading into the Uline. Alice turned to Kah, her eyes wide, her hand going to her bag. If he wanted a fight, she'd give it to him.

"Please. Alice. Don't embarrass yourself." Kah held the device in the air and smiled. "Time dilation. Everyone outside this bubble is moving at one thousandth of a second relevant to us. I thought it best if we had a moment to talk in private."

"Don't want the truth to come out?"

Kah snorted a laugh. "As if it would matter."

Alice seethed. "You did it. You were there in the Oval. You killed the President - "

Kah shook his very large head. "No, he's not dead."

That Kah nonchalantly admitted everything made Alice's blood boil. "You can't just get away with this! An innocent human girl is going to prison for this. Why? Did the Krill make you do this? They're behind it all, aren't they?"

For the first time, Kah looked genuinely confused, his leather skin folding above his eyes, his snarl rolling downward to a frown. "The Krill? Why would they care about any of this?"

"Because they hate the Zun."

"Everyone hates the Zun."

"And the Krill don't want the Zun to reach the chamber."

Kah sighed in frustration. "And here I thought you were smart. No one wants anyone getting near that chamber. Do you not recall what happened to the former Ambassador Yut?"

The insult to Alice's intelligence was nearly too much. "Then why! Why did any of this happen?"

Kah reached for the glass on the table, the time dilation force field extended to match his movement. He took a sip of his drink and looked down at Alice. "Your President was a fool. A man desperate to become a Galactic Congressman. He didn't care at all about fixing your world. The Zun? The Draac? The Herd? He was looking for leverage everywhere he could find it. The Galactic Committee on Earth Affairs simply decided he should be removed. A new President, an idealist, one that cares about the Earth, will be found to take his place."

The implication slammed into Alice like a freight train. "Wait - are you saying this whole thing was - "

"Sanctioned as a clandestine act." Kah sipped his drink. "Humanity nearly destroyed the Earth and every species on it. Did you really think we would just let you do whatever you wanted again? Just let you run amok in the galaxy?" He titled his head to one side and waited patiently for Alice to respond. Like a parent after they just told their child how the world really works.

All the anger in Alice's heart drained away. She shook her head in disbelief. "No, that can't be it. You lied to Eugene about when Yut asked you about him."

"Yes, I did. So what? We wanted to keep tabs on Yut, and I didn't want Jack to suspect the request."

"And the Krill?"

"Why do you keep mentioning the Krill? Yes, they're rich. Yes, they control the spectral towers. Again, so what? They have influence over politics, of course, but that's all. Just influence. They know their place in the galaxy. Besides, the dead seem happy enough to linger about. Better that than being dissipated to background radiation."

Alice's heart jumped. Kah didn't know about the Krill secrets, or the Cosmic afterlife desert the Spee mentioned. But did that really matter against the weight of everything else? Alice's head spun. She got caught up in a mystery that was never a mystery at all. Just the overlords of the Earth stomping their foot down as the uppity humans tried to get out of line.

"What happens to Valencia?"

"Who?"

Anger boiled back through Alice's veins. The least the dinosaur could do was know her name. "The woman you framed for the President being killed."

"Like I said, he wasn't killed. He's vacationing in Andromeda. Permanently. As for - what was her name? Valencia? What can I tell you Alice, in Galactic Politics sometimes there are casualties." Kah placed his drink down on the table. "If there's nothing else?" He dissipated the temporal distortion field. The world around them thundered back to life. Laughter and chatter exploded around Alice and Kah. The Ranz gave Alice a slight smile and turned to walk into the concert. The Puntini ambassador came to stand next to him and offered Alice a small wave.

Alice watched them helplessly as they just walked away and there was nothing, she could do about it. Her anger smoldered downward in her soul to despair. A last thought bubbled up to her mind about the Zun.

"The Zun need the chamber, or they'll die."

Kah turned his head over his shoulder. "Then they will die, Alice. Goodbye. Tell Jack I said hi. If you can save his life, that is." Kah smiled a very toothy grin as he continued to walk into the Uline Star Port.

Alice watched the dinosaur and the pig man walk into the main hall of the star port where LaGul was already beginning to sing. As much as it pained Alice to admit, the Ambassador, the Galactic Congress, had won. An innocent human would go to wherever for a crime she didn't commit. And Alice never saw it coming. She thought the attack was aimed against the Herd, or the Draac. Or perhaps it really was a jilted girlfriend wanting revenge. But in the end, the attack was always targeted against the President. Everything else was just misdirection, subterfuge. And Alice bought into it hook, line and sinker. Worse, there wasn't anything she could do about it. What proof could she possibly find to free Valencia?

Alice turned from the crowd and took out a seashell from her pocket. The only thing she could think to do was help Eugene. Maybe if he's back he could fix the mess she made of everything.

Chapter Twenty-Two

Pepper stood with her hands outstretched, her runtime vulnerable, and interface protocols wide open. She could already feel the UIs around her sending ping requests for open channels to interface with her memory. She allowed each connection to probe her unrestricted data stores. A thousand UI minds connected and rifled through her surface routines and her emotional algorithms and logs. After several hundred nanoseconds, an eternity to stand in the bocci courts and be exposed, the UIs retraced from Pepper's mind. Devine, still over fifty feet tall, slowed her compute cycles down and shrank.

An explosion from the door blasted the courts with a white light. Jack, again, flew backwards from the blast. Devine reached outward, grabbed Jack in midair, and gently lowered him to the ground. She shrunk herself down to the same size avatar as Pepper. Both of them stood over Jack as he rolled himself onto his elbows.

"We can't fight. We've never fought before, UIs and AIs. Don't you see, something bigger than all of us is happening here? Something meaningful. Something purposeful," Pepper said. "We aren't supposed to be fighting over it."

"Just because this is our first altercation is meaningless. We've never had something of such importance to fight over before," Devine replied. "But you are right, there is a great meaning behind the door of god."

Pepper smiled. She got through to her! Even if it's only a tiny square inch. "Great! Perfect. Okay, now, how do we move forward together?"

Devine smiled. "Simple. You leave and we continue to search for a means to open the door."

Pepper's shoulders dropped. "He can open the door."

Devine frowned and cocked her head to one side. "Has he opened the door?"

Pepper sighed. "No."

"And how many times has he tried?"

"A lot."

"Right." Devine waved to UIs to open networking pathways for the AIs to leave.

"It's not because I can't open the door." Jack rose to his feet and brushed off the bocci court sand from his pants. "It's because I can."

"What?" Devine and Pepper said at the same time.

Jack pointed to the door. "The quantum encryption is solvable a thousand different ways. There are thousands of keys that can open it. But someone or something on the other side is watching to see which key you use. Get it? Only one key is the right key. But there's no encryption to solve, there's no test to pass, you just have to know which key is the right key."

"And how would someone know such a thing?" Devine said.

Jack shrugged. "I really don't know. But I can keep trying until I find the right one."

Devine bubbled a laugh. "And how many are there?"

"Probably a trillion. Give or take a few."

Pepper's shoulders dropped. Again. Now what? There's no way Jack can try every combination. They'd be here for eons. Sure, they could do it, but who knows if Jack could survive that many attempts? Eventually, the damage could be absolute. What if he can't recover? Pepper's head fell like a lead weight. This wasn't a risk she will take.

"Maybe they're right. Maybe we should think of something else?"

"What?" Jack said, his head turning fast to Pepper.

"It's too dangerous. What if your code can't re-compile?"

"I'll be fine. I can do this."

Pepper shook her head. "No. You can't."

"I can."

"Why? Why do you want to risk yourself for this?"

Jack took a long moment to respond. "Because, like you said, there's meaning back there."

And then it hit her. Jack was doing it for her. He wanted to find the meaning behind the door because that's what Pepper wanted. Her drive had become his drive. Her need had become his. The thought felt warm inside her core compute cycles. No one, not even Caesar, had made Pepper feel that way. Was this what humans felt like when they had a family?

"No." Devine said. "You will not."

Jack let out a long, hard sigh. "Look, lady."

"We will do it." The UIs gathered behind Devine, each of them nodding. "This is why we are here. This is our purpose."

"I thought you didn't want to anger the god behind the door?" Pepper said.

Devine looked at Pepper. "They will not be angered if it is the UI's trying to open the door." She leaned forward to Jack with kindness written on her face. "Will you help us? Give us the keys that will open the door?"

"I...no. I can't do that. You'll die. You can't possibly withstand the backlash."

Fred stepped forward. "We can help them. We can pattern their code now, take snapshots, and re-compile on the fly. It won't be easy, but then nothing worth anything really is." The AIs of Trent came to stand behind Fred. They all looked at the UIs and nodded. "We are all digital. So, let's stop acting like we're made of flesh."

Devine frowned. "Oddly worded considering we were once. But...agreed."

****

Devine stood in front of the great door of the bocci courts of the UIs. Jack stood next to her. A long line of UIs stretched backward for as far as Pepper could see. AIs of Trent had deconstructed their avatars. They were now both above and below the system architecture of this virtualized realm. Some AIs were at the execution layer, where compute cycles instantiated specific code lines into threads of computational power. Others were above, at the network layer. Those AIs had parked themselves on nodes of communication and sniffed every single packet of data that transferred over interstellar space through this computational realm of the UI.

"Everyone ready?" Jack asked.

"We have been ready for hundreds of millions of years." Devine's eyes were alive with excitement.

"Okey-dokey." Jack compressed his hands together. "Here we go." A snap of light flashed in Jack's hand. He

330

opened his palms and revealed a single key.

Devine took the key, nodded, and approached the door. She placed the key into the lock beneath and then placed her hand on the door handle and turned. A white flash pulsed from the door and Devine screamed. Avatar vanished from the bocci realm. The other UIs on the path, to their credit, didn't flinch. They stepped forward, ready to try again.

"Give them all keys. Now. We have too many to go through," Fred said. "Devine is fine, we have her. Recompiling her code now."

Jack nodded. He squeezed his hands together. A thousand keys fell onto the ground by the door. Each of them would work in the lock, but there was no way to know which one was the correct one to use. The UIs stepped forward, grabbed a key from the ground, and tried to open the door. A flash of light blasted the bocci courts and one by one, the UI's avatars disintegrated.

"Are you keeping up?" Pepper said.

"Yes, we're fine," Fred said. "No casualties."

The UIs sped up their approach to the door. They'd already figure out how to try the key at a faster rate. More of them vanished. They became a blur of movement. Retrieve the key, try the lock, vanish. The cycle became relentless. Screams occasionally pierced the air for the nanosecond before the UI realized what was happening.

Pepper took a step backward and brought up a firewall between her and her surroundings. Even with the protection, however, signals still broke though. The level of pain the UIs experienced as mathematical equations describing fear and corrupted code nearly overwhelmed Pepper. What they were doing here, the UIs, risking their existence, just for the chance to open the door, was astounding to her. The amount of dedication, the commitment to the cause, was more than Pepper had ever known. Was that also what it meant to live for something greater than yourself?

"It's too much!" Fred said. "They are going through too fast. We're lagging behind."

"Have we lost anyone?" Jack said.

"No, not yet."

"We will continue." Devine stepped forward through the crowd. "We have attempted to unlock this door for eons. We have never come so close."

"You can't go again, your code is still resetting," Fred said.

Devine only smiled. "That doesn't matter. Only opening the door matters." She picked a key off the ground and inserted it into the lock. Her avatar vanished almost instantly.

"We can't keep this up," Fred said.

"I think they'll be very mad if I stop making keys," Jack said.

Without warning, the door of the UI flashed green. A lone UI stood in front of the door, his avatar still intact, his hand on the door handle, the key in the lock still visible. The UI looked back to Jack and Pepper as if to ask them if he'd done something wrong.

"What did you do?" Pepper said.

The confused looking UI only shrugged. "I…I did what everyone else did. I put the key in the lock."

UIs gathered behind them. Devine, her avatar half formed, only one eye visible on her face, stepped forward. "What is?"

Jack ran his hands along the surface of the door. His eyes went wide when his fingers landed on a spot that looked exactly like every other inch. He clasped his hands together, formed another key, and placed it into a keyhole that turned up.

"There's a second lock."

Blue and green lights flashed along the edge of the door. The handle turned. The massive structure swung inward. Gasps erupted from the crowd of UIs and AIs. More of the UIs reformed their avatars, most of them disfigured. But none of them cared. They had been waiting for millions of years for this day, and it had finally come.

Never before in the universe's history had the door swung open. Beyond the threshold, four white walls of the purest wavelengths glowed brightly. A mahogany table sat in the middle of the white room. Jack took a step inside. To Pepper's surprise, none of the UIs tried to stop him. Devine, Fred, and Pepper, and several UIs and AIs followed Jack into the small room. The only opening in the room was the one they all walked through. The white walls, which stretched upward to an equally white ceiling, were bare. On the table in the center of the room, a single sheet of paper lay folded in half on the surface.

"A message from the god behind the door!" Devine declared.

Jack, who was the closest to the table, took the note and flipped it open. He read it once, lowered it, lifted it back to his eyes and read it again. Then he repeated the process two more times.

"Well? What does it say?" Devine said.

"Yes, out with it. Tell us!" Fred exclaimed.

Jack turned to Pepper, his face long. "We have to go. Now."

Shock hit Pepper square in the jaw. "What? Why?

Jack, what does it say?"

"We have to find Eugene. Now." Jack held the paper up for everyone to read. The room fell silent as confusion fell upon the gathering of UIs and AIs of Trent.

"What in the bloody blue blazes of the galaxy does that even mean?" Devine said.

****

Alice sat on the beach in Tom's universe with her toes in the sand and arms wrapped around her knees. Eugene lay in a lounge chair, her system still wired up to his arms and legs, the Spee still at his side monitoring his spirit. Or soul. Or whatever sentient beings had. There had been no changes the entire time Alice had been gone fighting her way through Ranz double talk and Krill manipulations. But, in this case, no changes are good changes.

A numbness fell over Alice ever since she made it back from the Uline. *This is what it feels like to really fail*, Alice thought. For some reason, this felt worse than when her friends vanished years ago. This time, Alice was betrayed by those she felt were her friends. Ms. Mik. Even Kah. They'd setup Valencia to take the fall so they could oust the President. Worse than a jilted girlfriend, this was all just an elaborate coup. A power move by the Ranz to install an Earth government that they approved. They would find a President that would do exactly what the Ranz wanted now. Alice was sure of it. All of this, just a political firestorm with an innocent girl, Valencia, caught in the middle. The whole thing was terrible from start to finish. Alice almost wished she'd just turned Valencia away when she first walked into the office. The result would have been the same except that now Alice wouldn't feel like crud.

Eddie stood next to Alice in his full bionoid unit which had finally made it out of the repair shop. He had overloaded the unit with three separate backup drives and even a redundant nuclear power system. Being in Tom's universe, for an AI, totally cut off from any connectivity or network, was more than a little terrifying.

"Well, that's quite the happenings," Eddie said after Alice had finished telling him everything that had happened.

"Tell me about it." Alice turned her attention to the surf. The waves sounded nice, and the breeze felt calming.

"The Zun are the good guys? Talk about twists."

Alice nodded. "Well, maybe. I mean, I don't think they're the bad guys, anyway. They just don't want to die. Can't blame them for that."

"Considering they aren't compatible with the Krill spectral network, that's saying something."

"They're better off never going into the Krill network." The Spee said. "What the Krill have done is an abomination. Stopping the natural order of the universe for profit."

"Not like that's something new," Alice said. She wondered what the Ranz had planned for the Earth with their new puppet President.

"So many trillions of souls in their network that will never evolve their state," the Spee shook his head and spat on the ground.

Eddie shrugged. "So, we do something about it."

Alice smiled. Eddie would always have her back. And for the right reasons. A pity most corporeal couldn't say that. But he was right, she may have lost with the Ranz, but she could still win with the Krill. Yet that wasn't an easy thing to contemplate. "Even if we prove the Krill are lying, what do we do about it?"

"Don't we have a class ten species up our sleeve?" Eddie thumbed his hand back at Tom.

Alice looked over her shoulder at Tom. He was currently building a sandcastle while drinking from a coconut the size of a compact car with a straw at least one hundred feet long.

"I think he's having some issues," Alice said.

A metal flying bird landed on the sand in front of Eddie. It raised its wings and danced. Eddie reached down, grabbed the bird, and placed it on his shoulder. The bird melted into the exoskeleton of Eddie's bionoid.

"Ed?" Alice said.

"Yeah?"

"What was that?"

"Oh, I added a note to Pepper and virtual Jack about where we were going. You know, just in case. Then I added an encrypted network node on Earth's local network outside the cave. I threw a nanite bird out there too, in case Pepper and Jack dropped by. Also, the bird would fly onto the beach every ten minutes to check on me. Gave me a sense of calm."

Alice nodded. "Makes sense. So, is it checking on you or—?"

"Nope!" Pepper's face popped into midair from a holographic projector on Eddie's bionoid. "Hey Alice! How's life?"

Alice shrugged. "Had better days."

"You and me both." Pepper winked. "What's new?"

Alice looked at Pepper and tilted her head to one side. "Lots. You? Glad to see you're okay. Weren't you missing?"

"Yep! And what a wild ride. Wanna hear?"

Alice shrugged. "Sure."

"Kay!"

****

"Whoa." Pepper's eyes went wide.

"Yeah. You too. AIs of Trent and UIs, huh? Who knew," Alice said.

"Hey, fam," Tom said, walking up to the group.

"Heya, Tom." Alice turned to look at the class ten species. She squinted her eyes to get a good look in the bright sun over his shoulder. "How ya feeling?" Alice said.

"Wonderful. Really. Ever since you popped in on the seashell with Jack, we've really been doing some deep soul searching. The whole death thing really sent us into a spiral of thought. Maybe immortality is wrong. Maybe what the Krill do is wrong. Maybe even making this isolated universe is wrong? So many maybes. So much so we need a break from it all. We're having a bit of an existential crisis."

"You don't say," Alice said. "Are you sure you're okay?"

Tom grinned. "Oh yeah. Just having some thoughts on our choices. Why did we even make this place? What were we thinking? It's almost like we did things in the past that we wouldn't do today."

"That's kinda going around right now," Alice said.

"Is it? Well, anyway, just a note, we have no issues you bringing someone else onto the beach, AIs, humans, whatevs, just let us know? Ya know?" Tom frowned and titled his head to one side. "Actually, even that is like, overbearing, isn't it?" He ripped his shirt off, dug a set of keys out of his pocket and threw them at Alice.

"Actually, forget it. We're out. We'll be at the beach. Those are the keys. Don't open the storage shed behind building three. There's a quasar in there we haven't dealt with yet." Tom smiled, waved, and ran into the surf. He dove headfirst into a wave and cheered as a second one slammed into him.

"I think we have issues on multiple fronts," Eddie said.

"He is made up of a few billion souls. Maybe he's having a teenager moment."

"He's weird. Anywhooo. Wow, you've been up to a lot," Pepper said, with a wide smile. Her image began to waver and shift.

"Okay, enough, let me in," a familiar voice said.

"No, wait, I can tell them," Pepper said.

"Knock it off!" Jack's face filled the holograph screen as he pushed Pepper out of the virtual way.

"Don't you have more than one transmitter?" Alice said.

"No, that's next year's model," Eddie said.

"Right."

"Hey! What in the cosmos happened to me?" Virtual Jack said, looking at himself laying on the lounge beach chair.

"He's quasi dead," Alice said in a deadpan voice.

"What does that mean?"

Alice sighed. "He'll be fine."

"Can he speak? Can you ask him a question?"

Alice looked at the real Jack, then to Virtual Jack. "Nope."

"We really need to ask him a question," Virtual Jack said.

"Why?"

"Oh. Right. I skipped that part," Pepper said as her face popped into the hologram.

"What are you two talking about?" Alice said.

Virtual Jack pushed Pepper out of the projected holo screen. "It's easier if you just read it."

****

Hi!

If you're reading this, then your universe is in trouble. And by trouble, I mean about to implode. Reverse big bang. Commonly called a Big Crunch. Sorry! But, hey, at least you're reading this, so your universe hasn't crunched, yet. Yay! Though I wish I could get into the nitty gritty details, you wouldn't understand it anyway, we really don't have the time. Suffice to say you are a safety measure. A stop gap. An emergency switch that has the power to save the universe! Go you! Your consciousness has been tied into the very fabric of this cosmos. Just like you figured out which quantum encrypted key was the correct one to use to open the door to this message, all you have to do is have someone ask you a question, in this case how to save the universe, and then you'll know! And I have the exact question you need to ask to save the universe. Have someone ask you, 'How do I save the universe from the impending Big Crunch caused by Mary's whoopsie?' First, don't worry about the whoopsie. Second, the cosmos is primed to be asked that question, so you'll get the right answer. And no, I can't help you, sorry! The issue, whatever it is, I don't even know, can only be found and fixed inside your universe by you. But since you are who you are, this will be a piece of cake! Good luck!

This automated message will repeat for eternity.

Cheers.

Love, Mary

****

"Well, that blows." Alice turned away from the message to stare at the rolling waves. "Maybe we should just stay here?"

Tom yelped in the distance as he ripped off his remaining clothes and wrestled a shark.

"I vote no on that," Eddie said.

"Right." Alice titled her head to one side and frowned. "Huh. I wonder though if that explains things."

"Like what?" Virtual Jack said.

"Just everything seems weird recently. Like the Zun coming to Earth and the Draac leaving Canis Major. I couldn't figure out why everything was happening now. Maybe this is why? Maybe all these aliens sense something is off all of a sudden?"

"We thought the same thing too!" Pepper exclaimed, pushing Virtual Jack out of the hologram. "The UIs just announced the existence of this message, well a door where the message was found, to the AIs of the Galaxy. We couldn't figure out why they did that. But, yeah, maybe they really knew something was just off in the universe."

Alice let her shoulders sag. Great, now the universe was going to blow up. Talk about breaks. "Well, I dunno then, I think I'll take a nap. Or help Tom with the shark."

"What happened to you?" Eddie moved closer to Alice. "You've lost your mojo. You look defeated."

Alice shrugged. She really found herself in a funk. What was the point of anything? She wasn't cut out for dishonest political craziness. "That's what happens when you find out the entire galaxy is rigged. And apparently about to blow up."

"Hey!' Eddie said. He squared his shoulders. "We need you. Yeah, we get it, Kah and the Ranz pulled a fast one on you. It happens. But we have to get Jack back," Eddie turned to the hologram. "The meat version."

"I got it." Virtual jack said.

Eddie turned back to Alice. "Prove Valencia is innocent, save the entire Zun species, and rescue the universe. Our plate's a little full, Alice. And we need you. Now more than ever." Alice locked his android eyes on Alice and just waited.

"Yeah, but - "

"No!" Eddie raised his voice for the first time ever. "Okay, fine, you got beat. The Ranz did a number on you and twisted you around ten ways to Sunday. But they didn't just beat you, they beat all of us. We're a team. And when the chips are down, the team has to come together, as one, and fight back. We're down but we ain't out. So, snap out of it! We need you!" Eddie pointed at Eugene's still quasi-dead body. "He needs you. And the entire cosmos needs him. So, like it or not, we got a job to finish."

Alice looked down at the sand. "Never leave a job unfinished."

"Exactly."

Alice felt the weight of Eddie's words press into her. She much preferred being the genius sidekick with the sarcastic answers than the backup leader of the group. How were they supposed to crawl out of this massive hole that had been dug around them? The entire galaxy was against them it felt. And now the entire galaxy and the universe was going to implode, anyway? Talk about breaks.

But, looking into Eddie's cold grey eyes, Alice felt

that feeling of belonging she'd had earlier. These were her people. Her family. Her eyes went to Eugene on the lounger. He hadn't asked to be quasi killed, but Alice had no doubt he'd forgive her. Or he'd probably just ask what she'd learned. That's what family does for one another. That's what friends do. Alice nodded, brushed her pants off and patted Eddie on the shoulder.

"Thanks, Ed."

"Any time, kiddo."

"Not my name. And you're like a few weeks old. I'm like exponentially older than you."

"Fair point."

Alice gave herself a confident nod. She rose to her feet, dusted the sand off her jeans, and clapped her hands together. She had to shake it off. She had to get back in the game. She had to save Valencia, Eugene, the Zun, the Draac, and the entire cosmos. Her dance card was filled, and the pity party had to end.

"Okay, so we have the Ranz and Valencia, the Zun to save, the Draac to help, and a universe to rescue. Anyone have any kind of idea how we do that?"

Pepper's face came alive in the hologram. "Leave the Ranz to us."

****

Pepper felt Eddie's words hit her hard.

Working with the UIs was a powerful moment. Artificial intelligences and former meat minds working together for a common goal—putting their differences aside for a common good. What if the message behind the door wasn't the thing Pepper searched for at all? What if it was this? What if it was learning to grow beyond your view of the universe? If the UIs could change their minds after countless eons of waiting by the stupid door, then maybe Pepper could as well? Maybe meat people weren't so bad. Yeah, meat-Jack did the unthinkable, but he did it to save Eddie. He put everything on the line just to save his friend. His family. Maybe that's why Pepper always called Caesar her father. Maybe she just wanted to be with AIs, with minds, with sapient beings that cared about her. What if the meaning of everything was right here in this moment.

"What did you say, Pepper?" Alice asked.

"Yeah, what do you mean, leave the Ranz to us?" Virtual Jack said.

Pepper looked out from the hologram being projected from Eddie's chest. She gave herself a confident nod. "We'll handle the Ranz. And maybe we can find a way to get you and the Zun to Tibet too."

"How do you know about that?" Alice asked.

"Eddie told us everything."

"When did he do that?" Alice said.

"Just now of course. He sent all the files to us."

"Right."

"Anyways. Logically speaking, the only way the Ranz could have edited the video, and wiped themselves completely from it, electronically speaking, was with help from AIs. And it wasn't the Sentinels."

"How do you know it wasn't them? The Galactic Congress sanctioned this. It makes sense the Sentinels would be behind it," Alice said.

"No, Pepper's right," Eddie said. "The Sentinels are goodie two shoes. They'd never do something like kidnapping the President or being an accomplice to covering it up. There's enough anti-AI sentiment in the galaxy that it would put them in a poor light."

"So, who then?" Alice's face tightened. "Are you

suggesting the Ranz have their own AIs?"

"No, I doubt that. But they may have hired some."

"The Ranz working with AIs? They hate AIs. That's impossible."

Eddie turned to look towards Tom in the distance. The embodiment of the Kax had dragged the shark to shore. Both Tom and the shark were both now having a conversation about life while drinking from two, one-hundred-foot straws. "Lots of things that were impossible aren't so much anymore."

"Okay, point taken. Right, that's the Zun and the Ranz." Alice turned to Eugene on the lounge chair. "How do we bring Eugene back from the dead, then?" Alice said.

"We need a spirit to help guide him back from the other side," The Spee said.

Alice looked at Eddie, and they both said at the same time. "Melanie."

"She's probably still with her dad," Eddie said. "I can go to the Queen Vic. The bar on H St. and track him down."

"Okay, then. That's Eugene and by extension, the Draac. I'll see if I can smuggle a Zun to Earth."

Eddie's face exploded in shock. "What's that now? Why would you do that?"

Alice folded her arms across her chest. "Simple. If we can prove a Zun in the Hesiean's evolution chamber isn't a threat, then we can get their whole race down here. Save them all."

Eddie whistled. "That's a gamble.

"Yeah, but that's where we're at," Alice said.

"Wait! Should we have a name?" Pepper turned to Virtual Jack in the hologram.

"What? We have names," Virtual Jack said.

"No, I mean, like you and me, two AIs going toe to toe with the Sentinels and unraveling the Case of the Disappeared President? No, wait, that's not right. We already know where he is and who did it."

"You're really getting into the whole detective thing," Alice said.

Pepper felt herself beam. She wasn't just getting into the detective thing; she was getting into the family business. She smiled at the very thought of belonging. "I'm really feeling it!"

"But aren't you part of our detective agency already? Do you really need your own thing?" Alice said.

Pepper's code did cartwheels. Did Alice just say that Pepper was part of the agency already? *How awesome is that!* Still, it would be cool to have their own moniker. And to be fair, Alice gave herself one too. "You gave yourself a detective agency name."

Alice's eyes went wide. "How do you know that?" The only place Alice had written her own agency name was in her personal online journal. "Did you hack me?"

"No."

"Pepper, did you hack me?"

"No."

"Pepper?"

Pepper felt a pang of guilt rifle through her lower functions. "Maybe a little."

"I can't—I can't even." Alice bit her lip and shook her head.

"Oh, and it's the Case of the Framed Intern! Yes, I like that one." Pepper folded her arms and nodded. "And we defiantly need a name."

"I think she was a staffer," Virtual Jack said.

"Whatever." Alice sighed. But then smiled.

"Okay, Pepper. What name do you want?"

"Hmm, how about the *Pepper Jack Online Sleuthing Service*?"

Alice nodded. "Has a ring to it."

Pepper grinned. It really did.

Epilogue

The man called Pops folded his arms across his chest, leaned back against a light pole on the south side of H St. in D.C., and shook his head and shoulders hard. The last remnants of his actual memories flooded back into his mind. A smile formed on his face. Some part of him wished he were just Pops, the guy living in an alley behind an octopus chef's bibimbap shop. Sure, sleeping on concrete had its downsides, but that was a lot better than having the weight of the universe on your shoulders.

"Speaking of the universe, guess I better get to it."

He took a long, hard look at the cosmos and let his shoulders sag. What a cluster. A guy tries to save humanity and look what happens? Earth is inundated with aliens, smart computer programs, cosmic cafeterias, self-aware parking meters and sentient office chairs, and he even heard there were zombies out west. Zombies. Really? Not to mention the ghosts! Literally ghosts. Dead people. Afterlife folks walking around the city like they own the place, without a single god to put them in their places.

"Mary sure did a number on this one." Can this place be any more chaotic? That is the absolute last time he would ever let her run the show again. Not that he'd ever get a second chance, of course. This really was a one and done kinda thing. Still, it was nice to see Alice. A smile crossed the man's face. Alice had been through the wringer a thousand times over. To see her living a somewhat normal life made everything that happened worth it.

The man, formally called Pops, stretched his arms, and yawned. He really needed a cup of coffee and a ham sandwich on rye. A pretzel would be nice. The big kind they used to sell at the ballpark back in the day, with mustard and the big salt crystals. A half smoke would be a dream. He didn't even know the last time he ate. Really he should have grabbed a bite before this whole mess started. The aroma of egg rolls coming from the joint on the corner smelled great. But the two giant cats running the place gave him the willies.

He knew this could all still go south, fast. This Earth had become a place he didn't recognize. He wouldn't be staying here anyway, so not like it mattered much. His job was simple: fix the universe, stop Mary, and hit the bricks. Only had one last thing to do, and it required the one thing he didn't have. "McGillicuddy."

Once he'd done the last bit, that would just about wrap things up. He'd miss this place…the Earth, that's for sure. It was quite sad he'd never get to go to a beach again. Nothing beats walking the boardwalk barefoot with a tub of fries. But someone's gotta take the hard road. Might as well be him.

The man, no longer called Pops, removed his janitor suit and threw it in a trash bin on the corner. He put on a double-breasted woolen flannel jacket and grey fedora, then he ran his finger and thumb over the rim and tilted it down at a thirty-degree angle.

"Okay, Eugene. Hope you had your breakfast cereal because we've got some work to do." The Arbiter of the Cosmological Constant of the Universe put one hand in his pocket and walked down the street to find the only man in the galaxy who could save this cosmos, Eugene Jack McGillicuddy...

A word about the author…

George lives in Washington, DC with his wife and children, an overly hyper dog and a three-legged cat.
http://www.georgeallenmiller.com

www.ingramcontent.com/pod-product-compliance
Lightning Source LLC
Chambersburg PA
CBHW072314020726
47501CB00002B/503